THE OTHER SIDE OF THE SUN

is a historical novel of family strife in an aristocratic setting along the coast of South Carolina. Although set at the beginning of the twentieth century, the long shadow of the Civil War still dominates the characters in this drama of pent-up emotions within a polite society that finally erupts into a full conflict filled with racial hatred and spiritual strife.

Also by Madeleine L'Engle
Published by Ballantine Books:

THE LOVE LETTERS

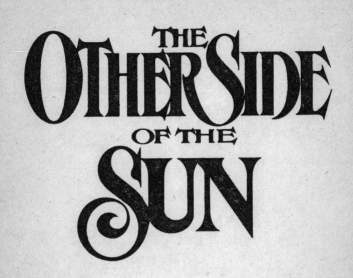

THE OTHER SIDE OF THE SUN

MADELEINE L'ENGLE

BALLANTINE BOOKS • NEW YORK

Library of Congress Catalog Card Number: 73-122824

ISBN 0-345-30616-3

This edition published by arrangement with Farrar, Straus & Giroux

Printed in Canada

First Ballantine Books Edition: September 1983
Second Printing: March 1984

For Madeleine L'Engle

1830–1917

ONE

I

THE ancient Rolls-Royce moved majestically and incongruously along the beach at the ocean's edge. The wheezing and clattering of the archaic air-conditioner almost muffled the sound of the approaching storm, but did serve to keep the young man at the wheel, and the old lady beside him, tolerably cool. In the sulphurous light outside, sandpipers stalked close to the waves, plucking at shells, paying attention neither to the rising wind nor to the car. Gulls rose screaming into the air. A pelican, brooding on a broken and barnacled piling, flopped clumsily into the water and was slapped by an incoming wave.

Stella Renier laughed, leaning towards the window so that she could watch the pelican as it recovered from clumsiness and broke up into the sky in a graceful arc. "I have a passion for pelicans," she said lightly. "They're really rather like planes, cumbersome and waddly on the ground, and incredibly beautiful in the air."

The young man took one hand from the steering wheel and patted her. "I'm glad you're here, Grandmother. And I'm glad we're going to Illyria, even if the rest of the clan is furious with us."

"I hope you made it clear that coming directly to the beach was entirely my idea?"

He sighed. "Dear Grandmother, they're very cross with me for letting you have your own way. There really are hurricane warnings."

"I don't need the weather bureau to tell me that. I've known this beach for a long time."

"You've been away for a long time, too. And you must be exhausted."

She relaxed comfortably against the worn upholstery. "Only moderately. For once, the plane came in right on time instead of circling for hours. I made my connection without any trou-

3

ble—I didn't keep you waiting more than five minutes, did I? It was all quite simple."

He smiled. "And I was supposed to drive you right into town—"

"—where the entire clan is gathered over funeral baked meats? A hurricane is a great deal less tiring." Affectionately she studied her grandson who stared through the thick lenses of his glasses at the wide road of beach stretching for miles ahead of them. "Dear Theron. You do understand, don't you, why I have to come to Illyria, storm or no storm?"

"Yes, Grandmother. I wouldn't be driving you there if I didn't. I'm glad you've come home. The world may be coming to an end, but you always bring a sense of proportion."

A gust of wind buffeted the old Rolls-Royce. The roar of waves pounding into shore seemed to increase. She asked, "Is the world coming to an end, Doctor?"

"Our world is."

"I heard that over sixty years ago when I came to Illyria as a bride."

He scowled, and a lock of fair hair, bleached almost white by the sun, fell over his forehead. His shirt was open at the neck and showed the springing blond hair of his chest. "What's the feeling abroad?"

"Perhaps not overly optimistic."

"And you, Grandmother? How do you feel?"

"I'm a very old woman, Theron. I've learned that if a problem is not settled in one—or even several—generations, it doesn't mean that it never will be."

"You can still say that? When Grandfather has just been killed?"

Her voice was cold and quiet. "He has hit by a stray bullet." There was a waiting silence in the car. She closed her eyes as though in pain. "Theron, my dear, as far as your grandfather was concerned, it was a merciful bullet. We knew that he didn't have long to live, and that his last months were going to be painful, and probably far too long-drawn-out. Your modern medicine is not always kind."

"What are you trying to tell me, Grandmother?"

"I wrote you that he had cancer, Theron. It would have been a slow and humiliating end for his body. As it is, he functioned fully as a human being up until the last minute. He was a good public servant, and he died doing his duty. In the fifteen or so years since his official retirement, how much time did we have at Illyria?"

"Not much."

"And there's a kind of—" she hesitated, then said, "cosmic justice in his being sent, in the end, to Africa, to Kairogi again. These assignments meant a lot to him; he liked mediation. At least one small crisis has been averted because he was there." She opened her eyes and looked down at her hands, small and delicate and only lightly gnarled. The veins were raised and blue, but they gave an effect of fragility rather than age. On her ring finger was a plain gold wedding band. The Renier ring, entwined serpents with ruby eyes, had gone to the young man beside her, when he was married, to put on his wife's finger. "Is all well with you and Margaret?"

"She's cross with us. With me."

"That's not what I asked."

Now he smiled. "Yes, Grandmother. All is well with us. All is very well. We're having another baby in the winter. The family grows, and so does our love."

"Then the world is not coming to an end." She reached out and patted his thigh lightly. He wore white drill shorts, white socks and tennis shoes; he was still a young man, and his world—ending or not—was utterly different from the world of her youth. Nevertheless they had always shared a special ability to communicate, beyond chronology, beyond miles, and this was not only because he reminded her of his grandfather, for whom he had been named. "Theron Renier," she said softly. "I'm old and I've lost count. Are you the fifth or the sixth?"

"More like the seventh."

"Is it a burden?"

He laughed. "I don't think about it very often."

Smiling, she looked out the windshield. Despite the noisy efforts of the air-conditioner, despite the rising wind, the sun beat hotly against the black roof and heated the interior of the car. The blue of Theron's shirt deepened between the shoulder blades, under the arms. Her grey linen traveling suit felt hot and sticky, and she longed to get at the light cotton dress in her suitcase. She brushed her carefully groomed white hair back from her face, the delicate bone structure showing strongly now in old age. She was not unaware that she was, as an aging woman, still beautiful, but she took this fact lightly, as she had learned to do most things. Still smiling, she turned from the ocean to look inland, past her grandson to the dunes laced with wild grape vines, topped with golden sea oats and giant palms. The sea oats were flattened against the dunes by the wind; the dry fronds of the palms flailed like windmills. A flock of gulls rose into the air, beating with difficulty against the wind.

As they passed the crumbling end of a sea wall, the dunes became less wild. Weather-beaten cottages appeared, and then, when the old sea wall turned into a modern cement-and-shell bulkhead, they drove by new and ostentatious houses surrounded by lawns kept passably green with constant sprinkling. Palm and magnolia trees, azalea and camellia bushes, all were carefully trimmed and tended. Around houses and lawns was frenetic activity: shutters being closed and fastened; low plants and bushes covered with canvas; buildings and gardens battened down against the impending storm.

"We saw flashes of the funeral on television," Theron said. "The children were very impressed. It made them realize that 'the old Renier' was important for more than being their great-grandfather."

"He had a full life," Stella said softly, "and a useful one. I was proud of him, too."

Farther up the beach the houses began to crowd together on small plots, became dingy, less cared for. The bulkhead showed breaks against which broken cement slabs had been placed as a holding action against the sea. "Let's hope they stand through this storm. It's going to be a big one." He frowned, sighed. "We're in for another kind of storm in this country, aren't we, Grandmother? Perhaps that's why it seems so incongruous that Grandfather should have been killed in a riot on the other side of the world. And yet it was somehow——"

"Justice?"

He shook his head fiercely. "I don't understand about that kind of justice. Or revenge, or reparation, or any of that stuff. I don't think anybody does, any more. But the Reniers have never been loved by extremists of any persuasion." He tried to smile. "I believe it's family tradition."

"It's a good one, Theron," she said gently.

"Even when it ends with a bullet?"

Houses, hotels, boarding houses, gave way to a shabby amusement park with a rickety wooden roller coaster, a ferris wheel, a merry-go-round with paint-peeling horses. It looked desolate, and empty, except for men nailing boards up against kiosks, tying tarpaulins over the merry-go-round.

"There are worse ends." Stella's light body was shaken by

a shudder. "Only on love's terrible other side is found the place where lion and lamb abide."

"What's that?" he asked sharply.

"Something of Mado's. Marguerite Dominique de la Valeur Renier." She drew out the syllables lovingly. "My husband's grandmother. Your great-great-grandmother. Love's terrible other side. The other side of the sun. You can't go around it, Theron. You have to go through it."

He looked at her obliquely. "There are literally hundreds of telegrams waiting for you."

"They will wait."

"There was one which used exactly those words. It struck me when I read it—you did tell us to open everything—"

"Of course. Do you remember who sent it?"

"Yes. Ronald Zenumin."

For a moment her eyes filled with tears. But when she spoke, her voice was calm. "I'm glad. I'm very glad."

"Grandmother, how would a Zenumin be able to quote something of Mado's?"

"That's a long story. But it's possible. I suppose some of the Zenumins are still living back in the scrub?"

"Quite a clan of them. They seem to be almost more gypsy than black, now."

"They were always what you might call a mixed bag."

"You knew them well?"

"I knew them. Yes, I knew them."

He looked at her probingly. "You never actually knew Mado, though?"

"No. She died before I came to Illyria. But—I did know her, Theron. Her presence was still very strong."

The amusement park petered out into a series of bath and boarding houses. Then came, abruptly, a high wall of Spanish Bayonettes in full bloom, each fan of green rapiers topped by a fountain of blossoms whipped unmercifully by the wind.

"We're here." He nosed the car in from the beach and stopped before a white coquina ramp which crossed the boardwalk and bulkhead and led over a jungle of scrub myrtle, dwarf palms, scrub oak, to the front steps and veranda of an enormous, rambling old house that rode the tops of the dunes like an unwieldy ship.

"Illyria," Stella murmured. "Illyria." She made no move to get out of the car. "If I can manage to forget the boardwalk it looks just the way it did all those thousands of years ago when

I first saw it. Thank you for understanding, my dear. I have to come here and get my bearings before I can go into town and face the tribe."

"They don't understand." He walked around the car to help his grandmother out.

The hot wind struck her like a wave. "That air-conditioner was more effective than I gave it credit for. I long to see the children. But I'm simply not strong enough yet to cope with the rest of our kin. I've got some private grieving to get through—I can't—"

"I know, Grandmother. It's all right. I understand. I don't like the buzzards, either."

She pulled herself together and pointed to the ocean's edge where another flock of sandpipers pecked placidly. "Don't worry about the hurricane. As long as the birds aren't frightened, then I'm not, either." She leaned on his arm and they started slowly up the ramp, her old joints stiff from the long hours of travel. "I know the family wants me to decide about the house, and I can't do that, except here."

He put one arm about her slight body to help her up the incline. "You don't have to decide anything now, Grandmother. And Illyria's your house. Don't let anybody push you."

"What do you think?"

"It's your house, it's what you want."

"Nonsense," she said briskly. "What do *you* want?"

"Illyria's always been the special place for me."

They climbed the shallow wooden steps, bleached silver by sea and sand. Despite his help, the effort made the old woman's breath come in light, thin gasps. "Let's sit on the veranda for a minute."

He pulled up two old wood-and-wicker rocking chairs, green paint peeling. She sat, gratefully, leaning her head against the high back. "If you want Illyria, we'll keep it. No—I don't want to promise yet. It all depends...on the angels."

He smiled, hitching his chair close to hers. The pounding of the surf was loud now, and the rattling of the hot wind in the palms. "I'm the only one who wants to keep Illyria. Everyone else says the place was ruined when the amusement park was built."

"Yes, Theron, but what about you?"

"I've never known Illyria without the amusement park, and that's always been part of its charm for me—who'd expect a house like this in the midst of merry-go-rounds and kewpie dolls and ferris wheels? But it's more than that—Illyria is magic. I'm a doctor, a scientist; I'm usually reasonable, but I love this place just because I *don't* feel reasonable about it. It's special—magical—and my children sense it, too. But I don't want to influence you, Grandmother."

Her laugh pealed out. "My dear Theron, no wonder you're a successful doctor! You should have been a psychiatrist."

"Grandmother, really—" he started, then laughed, too.

The afternoon sun, pushing through the clouds, struck against the fragments of shell in the coquina ramp, and the old woman put up her hand to shield her eyes.

"Sorry to take you out of the air-conditioner. Are we getting soft, Grandmother? Margaret and the children and I are the only ones who come to Illyria any more. The others won't because it isn't air-conditioned."

Inside the house the phone began to ring. "Don't answer it," Stella said.

"But—"

"It will just be someone insisting that you drive me right back to Jefferson. And I am not going into town, Theron. I am going to stay here."

He rose. "Then I must go in and tell them that." He struggled for a moment with the heavy front door, swollen from damp, then went in. She could hear his voice, at first calm and firm, reasonable, then authoritative and sharp. He came back to the veranda. "Even Margaret is annoyed with me. I am not to allow you to stay in Illyria. The power will go out, and the phone—and they're right about that, they always do go off during a hurricane."

"I'm used to Illyria without electricity or phone. And I've been here for any number of hurricanes. Help me check the shutters—make sure that I have plenty of candles and supplies, and go on back to your family before Margaret divorces you."

"You underestimate Margaret."

She smiled in satisfaction. "How can I make a decision about Illyria if I don't stay here? How can I know about the angels?"

"What about the angels, Grandmother?"

"Poor old Grandmother, old age has finally caught up with her. That's what you're thinking, isn't it?"

He sat beside her again. "I'm an internist, but I deal with my patients' minds as well as their bodies. I believe in angels.

Devils, too. You used to tell me about Illyria's angels when I was little, and I've always felt them here."

"Still?"

"I don't know. Grandmother, I don't think I should let you stay. It really is madness."

She stood up. "I'm going in to make my bed. Why don't you buy me some candles and enough food to keep me going for a few days?"

"You're impossible! I'll stay with you tonight, but tomorrow we'll have to drive into Jefferson. I've made arrangements to be out of the office and the hospital today, but tomorrow I must be back."

"Of course. I've been here alone before."

"It's not just the storm, Grandmother. It isn't safe for you to stay alone. There's a rough element about the boardwalk and in San Feliz. It isn't the safe little village it was in the old days."

"It wasn't very safe in the old days. I remember on my very first evening in Illyria, when I wanted to go for a walk so that I could be alone, I was warned to walk up the beach rather than down, because there was a rough element in San Feliz." She paused at the screen door. "Just to prove to you that I know that discretion can sometimes be the better part of valor, I'll sleep downstairs in Aunt Olivia's old room instead of going up to the third floor. Which room do you and Margaret use?"

"I'll sleep downstairs tonight, too. Take it easy till I get back from San Feliz, will you? And we'll discuss what you'll do tomorrow when tomorrow comes."

She laughed, as the screen door slammed behind her.

They ate scrambled eggs and bacon for supper, sitting in the large kitchen which faced west and was somewhat protected from the northeast wind which flailed about the house, shaking the shutters. The electricity flickered several times while they were eating, but did not go out. The air was oppressive and weighed heavily on the house. After they had washed up their few dishes they went back to the veranda. Clouds had covered the sky. Waves pounded up to the bulkhead.

"Just be grateful you arrived at low tide," Theron said. "Tides are running high because of the storm, and we couldn't possibly have driven on the beach at high tide." He sat on the veranda steps, leaning against the worn rail. Just behind him, his grandmother rocked contentedly. All about the house the insects were shrilling out warnings against the storm. In the dark lagoon behind the house the frogs boomed back and forth. Incongruously, a mockingbird sang, outdoing the nightingale. Theron let out a gusty sigh.

She reached out to touch his hair. "What is it?"

He shifted position so that he could lean against her chair. "Questions."

"Go ahead and ask them."

"One of your reasons for coming to Illyria was to avoid questions."

"Will your questions be the ones the others would ask, Terry?"

"Terry—that was your name for Grandfather, wasn't it?"

"Yes." There was sudden, bleak pain in the response.

To try to ease it, he asked, "Do you remember your rhymes, Grandmother? The Kings of England rhyme, and then the Theron Renier rhyme?"

"Of course. I taught Terry the Kings of England, and then he made up the Theron rhyme for me in exchange."

Together they recited,

> "Willy, Willy, Harry, Ste,
> Harry, Dick, John, Harry Three,
> One, Two, Three Neds, Richard Two,
> Harry Four, Five, Six, then who?
> Edward Four, Five, Dick the Bad,
> Harrys twain, and Ned the lad.
> Mary, Bessie, James the vain,
> Charlie, Charlie, James again.
> William and Mary, Anna in Gloria,
> Four Georges, William, and Victoria.
> Edward Seven was next and soon
> We'll put George Five upon the throne."

"I was the only medical student who could recite the Kings of England—that is until 1910. After George V, I had to put them in without rhymes." He began to intone again, schoolboy fashion:

> "Theron the ambassador
> Went to France before the war;
> Doctor Theron, his young son,
> There met Mado, loved and won,

But lost the War Between the States,
1861 to '65, the dates.
Theron and Mado had a son
Known as Therro by everyone.
Therro's son was then called Terry:
English Stella, fair and merry,
Married him in 1910,
And came across the ocean then.

"And then we added when I married Margaret,

"Terry and Stella birthed their Theron,
Remember, Theron rhymes with heron.
Theron in turn produced a boy
Who married Margaret to his joy."

"And all the Therons," her voice was calm again, "are long-legged as herons. I hope the silly rhyme was as helpful to Margaret as it was to me. I couldn't have kept the generations straight without it. What did you want to ask me, my dear Theron?"

He leaned back against the old woman's knees. "I suppose I want to separate fact from fancy, truth from fairy tale. That telegram was important to you."

"Yes."

"Why?"

"If there can be reconciliation between the Reniers and the Zenumins, then perhaps, after all, the angels—" She let her words drift off.

"I don't know all that's gone on between the Reniers and the Zenumins."

A gull screamed, a raucous, angry cry. "I don't suppose anybody knows all of it. I know only the smallest part."

"Tell me."

"I told you years and years ago."

"When I was a boy. I know you never bowdlerized the way everybody else does, but you must admit you omitted."

"Did I? Perhaps I did. But I'm not sure any more what really happened. People aren't as good as I thought they were—or as bad."

"How old were you when you came to Illyria?"

"Nineteen. Everybody else was old—the great-aunts, Honoria and Clive, Cousin James. Everybody except Ron. . . . It never occurred to me that one day I would be as old as Aunt Olivia and Aunt Des. Even now I really don't believe in my own antiquity. But I am old, and I'm not sure that I can tell you the truth, not because I'm not willing to, but because I'm afraid some of it may have been lost somewhere in the past. I don't think it's possible to remember without the burden of hindsight. Think. You're still a very young man—"

"Not so very."

"A man in his thirties is very young to someone in her eighties. Try to remember something important that happened ten years ago. Can you remember it as it truly was? Or is your memory distorted by what you know now? All my memories are colored by the person I've become. And I'm a most opinionated old woman, as you have cause to know."

Theron smiled into the deepening dusk. "If it's too difficult for you, Grandmother—"

She gave a sharp yank to his hair. "How well you know me. All right. I'll try. I'll talk, and I'll think, and I'll remember, and maybe I'll dream a little—I'm very tired. But you have a right to know something of what it was all about."

He closed his eyes as her gentle fingers moved over his hair. The waves battered against the bulkhead; palm fronds rattled in the rising wind. "Being here with you like this—it's worth having the family dithering because Theron and Grandmother are off doing something crazy again."

"Is it crazy? Maybe that's what people think of all the essential actions." Far out at sea the beam from the lightship swept across the stormy darkness. "Perhaps going all the way through the sun, all the way through the fire, does tend to make people a little mad." She closed her eyes. There was a ripping, cracking sound as the arm of a palm was torn from the tree. The wind howled. The veranda seemed to shake, but the old woman realized that this feeling was as much from her overworked heart as from the gale. For a moment she thought that she, too, might be dying, and this did not disturb her. She leaned back and let her past wash over her as the waves washed over the beach.

TWO

I

THEY were here on the veranda waiting for me when I finally reached Illyria, the four women: Honoria, tall, powerful, purply-black; the two old great-aunts, small and pale; Aunt Irene, half the age of the other three—but when one is nineteen, middle age is old. Honoria stood calmly aside as the others, twittering like birds, palm-leaf fans fluttering, rose to greet me. Aunt Irene held out her plump hands. "Stella! It *is* Stella, isn't it?"

"Who else would it be?" one of the old ladies whispered.

I felt the eyes of all four probing me. I was being measured, judged. I smiled brightly to hide my discomfort.

"Stella, honey, welcome to Illyria. I am your Aunt Irene." She drew me to her. Her voice was bright-pink crushed velvet and she smelled of heliotrope. She called herself 'Ant Ah-reen' and, probably because I was so keyed up, I almost giggled.

"And this is your Great-aunt Mary Desborough, and your Great-aunt Olivia."

The two old ladies moved forward. Unlike Aunt Irene, who looked like a fashion plate, they were dressed in rusty and old-fashioned clothes, with their hair parted in the middle, and their ears poking out in the fashion (I learned later) which had been popular during 'The War.' "Welcome, child," one of them pecked me on the cheek. "We welcome the new Mrs. Theron Renier. I am Aunt Mary Desborough."

"And I'm Aunt Olivia," the other old lady said, and reached to kiss me. She smelled lightly of lemon and lavender; the old-grey watered silk of her dress rustled as she moved, and her voice was like it, a dry, gentle rustling.

"Clive! Clive! Ronnie!" Aunt Irene called. "Oh, there you are. Please see that Miss Stella's things are taken to her room so that Honoria can unpack them."

The old colored woman moved to me; there was something majestic about her; she took my hands in her very strong ones

17

and looked into my face. I felt like a child instead of a married woman. "We welcome you, Miss Stella."

This, then, was Honoria. I knew that Honoria was important. Immediately after Mado's death it was Honoria who saw to it that her ring came to my Terry for his bride.

The Renier ring. Touching that ring got me through a lot of bad times. Not that I thought it had any magical properties, although I was to find that many people did indeed believe this. It was just that the ring always made me know who I was: Mrs. Theron Renier. I touched it now, a heavy ring, made of two beautifully etched gold serpents, entwined like those on a caduceus, with rubies for eyes.

'It came to Mado from Honoria,' Terry had told me when he first showed it to me the night he asked me to be his wife.

'Mado—'

'My grandmother. Marguerite Dominique de la Valeur Renier. She was always called Mado.'

'And Honoria?'

He hesitated. 'I suppose you might call her Mado's house-keeper. I love her almost as much as I loved Mado. Maybe as much, because they belonged together.'

My husband, of all the Renier men, was the one who was most full of laughter, but when he took the ring out of its velvet box to give it to me, he was totally serious. 'It carries a responsibility,' he said, 'a responsibility of healing. The serpent isn't always a symbol of evil. You remember that the twined serpent is the doctor's emblem, and my Grandfather Theron was a doctor.'

> (Doctor Theron, his young son,
> There met Mado, loved and won,
> But lost the War Between the States...)

I looked at the ring, fingering the rubies. 'How would a housekeeper get a ring like this?'

'Honoria was born in Africa,' Terry had said, as though that explained everything.

Honoria withdrew to the side of the veranda as Aunt Irene fluttered about me. "Honey, sit down. You must be exhausted. Was it a terrible, terrible trip?"

I didn't know whether she meant the ocean voyage or the

long drive from Jefferson to Illyria, so I just said, "It was beautiful," and sat in the rocking chair Honoria pulled up for me.

Aunt Olivia, moving with difficulty, lowered herself into her chair; she was crippled with rheumatism. A silver-handled cane lay on the floor by her chair. "Honoria will bring you something to cool you off. I can see that you need it."

"Livia," Aunt Mary Desborough reprimanded. But it must have been wholly obvious that I was hot, wrinkled, and travel-worn.

"Stella isn't used to the heat," Aunt Olivia said, and smiled at me with eyes faded to a soft kitten's blue; everything about her was a little faded: her ash-blond hair was the color of bleached sand; her skin was soft and finely wrinkled; the once rich material of her grey moiré dress was faded, too. "They have *snow* in England. Don't you, Stella?"

"Yes, but not in summer."

"Here, lovey, this will help." Aunt Olivia handed me a large fan made from palm fronds. Aunt Mary Desborough and Aunt Irene were slowly swishing similar fans back and forth against the sluggish air. Honoria reached behind one of the shutters and brought out another fan for Aunt Olivia.

The old lady nodded her thanks. "What do we have to give Stella, Honoria? Do we have some sangaree?"

Aunt Mary Desborough sat down briskly, though I guessed her to be the elder of the two old ladies. Her voice was dis-approving, rusty brown like her dress; she looked, I thought, like a little brown owl. "Livia, you know Hoadley doesn't like us to imbibe anything with spirits until he arrives." Her dress might be frumpy and out of style, but her fingers bore two magnificent rings, and the pendants which hung from her ears were, I was sure, real pearls.

"Sangaree is hardly spirits," Aunt Olivia said. "I'm sure Hoadley wouldn't object." Her gnarled and twisted little fingers could not support rings, but the throat of her dress was fastened with a superb brooch.

Hoadley was Aunt Irene's husband; it was Uncle Hoadley and Aunt Irene who had taken Terry into their home after his parents were drowned in a boating accident.

"I think she'd like some strawberries," Aunt Olivia said. "Don't you think Stella'd like some strawberries, Des? Straw-berries and cream."

"Strawberries aren't in season."

Aunt Olivia snorted, "Daz it. Strawberries and cream taste even cooler than sangaree."

"How about a little claret lemonade?" Aunt Irene suggested.

"But—" Aunt Mary Desborough demurred.

"I wanted something special to welcome Stella," Aunt Olivia said. "I wish we had some strawberries."

"If wishes were horses—" Aunt Mary Desborough started.

"Beggars would ride," Aunt Olivia finished. "Anyhow, that doesn't count, Des. We're playing Shakespeare today. And in any case, just because thou art virtuous, shall there be no more cakes and ale?"

"*Twelfth Night*. Sir Toby Belch. Point for me."

"You'd have been pretty silly if you hadn't identified *that* one. What about figs? There's nothing nicer on a hot day than a cool bowl of figs and cream."

"Livia," Aunt Mary Desborough pursed her lips. "You know perfectly well the fig tree hasn't borne since the year Mado died."

"Virtue!" Aunt Olivia cried, undaunted. "A fig! 'tis in ourselves that we are thus, or thus. Our bodies are our gardens, to the which our wills are gardeners."

"Shakespeare, of course." Aunt Mary Desborough huddled into herself in thought, so that she looked more owlish than ever. "I know! *Othello*!"

"Daz it,". Aunt Olivia said.

"Stop swearing."

"I just said daz. That's not a swear word. I made it up myself."

"You made it up to use as a swear word."

"But it isn't one, and you can't scold me for it. Daz. Daz. Daz it, Des."

"Livia!"

"Miss Olivia," Honoria said softly, sternly, "that is enough."

"Daz anyhow."

"Hush." Honoria held up her large, strong hand, night-black on the back, a soft wrinkled pink on the palm and the insides of the fingers. "Hush and listen."

The two old ladies in the rocking chairs leaned forward, suddenly alert as sea gulls: I listened, too. I heard the wind rustling the palms with a sound like paper; I heard the soft slur of sea against sand; that was all.

"What?" Aunt Mary Desborough asked impatiently.

"The wind has changed!" Aunt Olivia cried. "That means the storm tonight will cool things off. That'll be nice for you, Stella. I hope the storm will come soon. There isn't much time."

"Time for what?" Aunt Mary Desborough asked crossly. "Don't sound silly."

"Don't raise your voice. It's not polite. That time when thou shalt strangely pass and scarcely greet me with that sun, thine eye."

"Oh—something obscure like *Titus Andronicus*, I suppose."

"It is not. It's the Sonnets. Point for me. You're losing your memory."

"Aunties," Aunt Irene chided.

"Are you sure the fig tree didn't bear this year?" Aunt Olivia asked.

"*Now* who's losing her memory!"

"There are people," Aunt Olivia said, "who can make fig trees bear."

"*If* you re*mem*ber," Aunt Mary Desborough said with heavy emphasis, "that particular fig tree did *not* bear. And it got blighted."

"So? That was only one fig tree. What about all the others?"

I managed to get a word in. "What I would really like is a cup of tea, and then to change out of these clothes into something cool."

Honoria moved quietly across the veranda, opened the screen door, and went into the house.

"Now, I call that a sensible suggestion," Aunt Mary Desborough said approvingly.

What Honoria tried to keep simple, the aunts managed to make complicated, but we did have tea, with milk for Aunt Mary Desborough and me, and thin wheels of lemon stuck with cloves for Aunt Olivia and Aunt Irene. There were cucumber sandwiches—it didn't taste like English cucumber—and thinly sliced raisin cake, but I wasn't hungry, and I was relieved when Honoria came to the screen door and said that she had unpacked a few things for me, and perhaps I would like to go to my room.

Aunt Irene started to rise, but Honoria said, "I'll see that

Miss Stella has everything she need." Her voice was unlike any of the other strange, warm Southern voices I had heard. It was deep and guttural, with a quality like some dark metal dug deep out of the center of the earth.

I followed her into a vast, dusty, wind-swept room, or, rather, two rooms, one leading into the other, so that there was an open sweep from front veranda to back. The front room, shuttered and dim, contained the kind of ornately scrolled bamboo furniture which came from India or China or maybe both, I'm not sure. There was a day bed covered with an Oriental rug, and above this a huge portrait in a great gold frame of two young women in Empire dresses. One was singing, the other accompanying her on a harpsichord, and though they must have been long dead, they reminded me of Aunt Olivia and Aunt Mary Desborough.

I did not notice the dog and kitten on the day bed until Honoria said, "Now! This minute!" I turned, startled, thinking she was talking to me, then saw an elderly Irish wolfhound and a small amber kitten slither to the floor, both looking guilty. "Finbarr," Honoria said. "Minou. Just because my back is turned and Miss Stella is arriving don't give you no right to sit where you don't belong. Remember who and what you is, and the time is dark." She glanced from the animals to the portrait, fondling the old dog's ear. "That Dr. Theron's mother, singing—Miss Mado's Dr. Theron—and his aunt, Olivia Hugeot. Painted by the younger Mr. Peale when he visiting Charleston."

There were other portraits in the front, or living room, and also in the rear, or dining room; and I anticipated studying them and getting further acquainted with my husband's family: these people on the walls would be the ancestors of our children. I felt past, present, and future swirl around me like the sea breeze which came through the screen door and brushed against my hot cheeks.

> (Edward Seven was next and soon
> We'll put George Five upon the throne
> Theron and Mado had a son
> Known as Therro by everyone)

Between the two rooms was a wide staircase, which Honoria and I mounted; then we climbed another, narrower flight of

stairs and went down a long, winding passage and into a large
and airy room that I knew at once I was going to love. It was
five-sided because one corner was cut off by long French windows that led to a triangular balcony overlooking sea and dunes.
A tall brass bedstead, brightly polished, with a white Marseilles
bedspread, stood to the left of the French windows, and over
it, attached to a brass ring, was a roll of white netting, which
my husband had told me I would have to let down at night to
protect me from mosquitoes. A dark mahogany highboy was
opposite the bed, a magnificent piece of furniture which had
never been intended for ocean damp: the delicate veneer had
cracked and buckled in several places. In one corner of the
room, over a rattan chaise longue, was a daguerreotype of a
young man and woman in sailing clothes, proudly displaying
an enormous swordfish. Sun had burnished their skins, bleached
their hair. They were smiling, and their eyes had the narrowed
look I had seen on people who had spent many years in India
and become accustomed to half closing their eyes against the
glare. The young man with the engaging grin might almost
have been—but was not—Terry. They were, I guessed, my
husband's father and mother, Therro and Kitty. I would have
to learn to know them, these grandparents my children would
never know. How long after that happy picture was taken had
their little boat been caught in a swift and unexpected storm?
All I knew about my husband's parents was that they had loved
the sea and died in it.

There was a sound outside my door. Clive, Honoria's husband, and a young colored man came in with my boxes. Clive
and Uncle Hoadley had met me in Jefferson, and Clive had
driven me to Illyria, a drive so long and hot that despite my
delight in the lush strangeness of the scenery, I had slept most
of the way. Clive was considerably shorter than Honoria, thin
as wire; strong as wire, too, I suspected. The younger Negro—
he was much younger, was, perhaps, Terry's age, was tall and
thin, with steel-rimmed spectacles.

Clive lowered the heavy box he was carrying and smiled
his dignified smile. "Miss Stella, I like you to make the 'quain-
tance of my grandson."

The young Negro bowed. "I'm happy to meet you, Mrs.
Renier. I'm Theron James."

Theron.

It still came as a shock—although Terry had, in a sense,

prepared me—that this tall, dark-skinned man, with a face as austere as his grandfather's and a far more bitter twist to the mouth, should be another Theron.

'Here's another nursery rhyme for you,' Terry had said.

> 'Clive and Honoria, Honoria and Clive,
> Keep Illyria's light alive.
> They had a son whose name was Jim;
> Jimmy married, and from him
> Came Terence Ronald, known as Tron,
> Then little Theron, nicknamed Ron.'

Ron spoke to his grandmother. "I thought Miss Irene wanted Mrs. Renier downstairs."

"I prefer Miss Stella here," Honoria said.

Ron raised one eyebrow slightly.

"The room Miss Irene had in mind just across from Mr. Hoadley's, and Mr. Hoadley, he snore. Just put that box there, please, Ron, so's I can tend to it. If you'd like to bathe after your journey, Miss Stella, I'll prepare a bath for you."

A bath! Joy! I needed one.

Honoria left the room, simultaneously stiff and stately, indicating with one authoritative shoulder that Clive and Ron were to follow.

Ron paused in the doorway. "Mrs. Renier, if Honoria tells you to do something, do it. Honoria is to be taken seriously."

"Well, yes—" I said. "Of course." I did not understand him, or anything about him. Like Honoria, he moved like royalty, and he didn't sound like any of the soft and sultry voices I'd heard at the harbor in Jefferson or since my arrival in Illyria. His voice was cool and sounded strangely British.

"Miss Stella, since you're new here it might be better if you don't eat anything Honoria doesn't give you."

At my look of surprise, he began to talk about change of diet, change of water bothering some people, but it seemed to me that there was a definite edge of warning to his words. Before he closed the door behind him, he said, "Your trunks will be on the train with Mr. Hoadley. Train gets in at six. Miss Irene may want you to change rooms, but you needn't."

Again a warning? Perhaps not, but how strange! I moved from his words, opened the shutters, and stepped out onto the wooden gingerbread balcony which looked out over the jungle between Illyria and the beach. The sun was moving westward now, but the air was still molten with heat. I leaned on the balcony rail; the ornamented and carved wood was weather-worn silver-grey, and had the fine texture of driftwood. The brilliant expanse of ocean darkened as a cloud moved across the sun. Breakers moved regally to the shore, rising, curving, falling in a hish of green foam. Mingling with the constant crashing of waves was the breeze in the palms. A cumbersome and clumsy bird with a large beak waddled along the edge of the water; it was so ludicrous in its ungraceful movements that I almost laughed; then, suddenly, it raised its head and soared up into the air in a glorious arc: and I was shamed.

There came a rap on the open door to the balcony. "Your bath is ready, Miss Stella."

"Honoria, I just saw a bird, big and awkward and ugly, and then it flew—it was—it was one of the most beautiful things I've ever seen."

"That would be a pelican, Miss Stella."

I laughed with pleasure. "Oh, Honoria, I've never seen a pelican before except in the London zoo. I'd no idea they were like that!"

"Yes, Miss Stella. That is what a pelican is like."

2

HONORIA took me to a square room with a high, round window. In the middle of the floor was a big high-backed zinc tub from which steam rose. It was exactly like the tub brought to my nursery in Oxford when I was a small child. If I had been especially good, Nanny would let me soap the back and slide down it with a lovely splash into the warm water. I felt a great wave of homesickness, not so much for tidy and familiar England in this strange, wild land, as for my lost childhood. Suddenly I was not certain that I was ready to be a wife. It did not occur to me that all brides must feel like this, and particularly those who have to be separated from their husbands early in marriage, before they have had a chance to become accustomed to this new climate.

Honoria pointed out great fluffy white towels on a mahogany rack, and a bowl of powder on the low dresser. There was an oval cake of hand-milled soap in a china dish. "And here's a pitcher of cold water if you need it. Mr. Terry tell you about our sulphur water?"

Yes, Terry had told me, and the smell indeed assailed my nostrils. 'We're used to it,' Terry had said. 'As a matter of fact, I like it, but perhaps that's nostalgia. Some people say it stinks of rotten eggs, and I get the analogy, but that's not it, because it's a good, healthy smell. The Fountain of Youth—that's sulphur water. Maybe that's why Honoria and Clive never grow old. Illyria has its own fountain of youth. The old aunts don't seem to change any, either. So you stay exactly as you are until I come for you, mica, mica, parva Stella. Don't let anybody change you.'

I tested the water with my toes. I was lonely and strange and a little frightened. I was not quite certain I could bear it in Illyria without my husband. I cried a little then.

I was nineteen when I came to Illyria and I had been married less than two months. Theron Renier and I met at a dinner party. He had been sent to England by the Bureau of Navigation, the Navy's Office of Intelligence and one of the first peacetime intelligence organizations in the United States. We fell in love immediately, idiotically, romantically, like Romeo and Juliet, except that there weren't any family problems—not that kind. Perhaps the open enmity of the Montagues and Capulets would have been easier.

My father, who must have realized that his heart was giving out, gave us his blessing, and the Dowlers, distant cousins, but the nearest relatives we had, threw a magnificent engagement party for us. Terry and I had met at the Dowlers in the first place: Lord Dowler, my Cousin Octavian, was retired from the Foreign Office, but still did something or other for the government—perhaps the same kind of thing Terry himself was to do in his later years. Cousin Augusta was still a handsome, if not intelligent woman, and it was her pleasure to give small dinner parties for the bright young men who were sent from all over the world to consult with her husband.

The week after the engagement party my father keeled over while he was giving a lecture. It was exactly the way he would have wanted to die, and though I grieved, it was a clean and proper grief. In a few weeks Terry and I were married very quietly in St. Aldate's. Cousin Octavian gave me away, and I wore Cousin Augusta's wedding dress, and then Terry and I had a short honeymoon in Paris.

We had expected to have perhaps six months together before he was sent off by his government on an assignment. When we got back to England his instructions were waiting. If I arrived in Illyria with no preconceptions that's one reason— he didn't have time to give me any.

I tried not to cling, not to weep, but it was hard. He was being sent somewhere, urgently, and nobody, certainly not his bride, was allowed to know where. There was, as usual, trouble in the Balkans, and I knew that there were still problems in the United States left over from the Civil War. 'Wars like ours don't end when they're over, Stella,' Terry had told me. 'Think: aren't you still suffering from the time of Cromwell?'

I didn't want to think about Cromwell. 'You've been talking with Cousin Octavian!' I cried. 'And you've been studying Kairogian. Are you being sent to Africa?' Archaeology and Africa—particularly the section of Africa known as Kairogi— were Cousin Octavian's special fields.

'Stella. Parva Stella.' Terry held me close. 'Don't try to guess. It will just make it harder for both of us.'

He sent cables home to his family to confirm his long, preparatory letters, booked me a passage on the *Boadicea*, and left the day before I sailed. The Dowlers saw me off with a basket of fruit and trunks' worth of trousseau, and I waved and waved and left my childhood behind me in England.

For better or for worse, alone or together, I was married; I was Mrs. Theron Renier and I wore the Renier ring. I loved mu husband passionately; I hoped that I was already pregnant— of course one didn't talk about that kind of thing in those days, though my father had brought me up to speak freely on taboo subjects. Perhaps this atypical and un-Victorian—or even un-Edwardian—lack of inhibition was one thing which drew Terry to me. I understood, with absolute rapture, what it is to be one with another human being. Naturally we were married to the words of the English Prayer Book, and my husband did worship me with his body, and for me there was never any problem about obeying him—ever—even when I wholeheartedly disagreed with him.

'In Illyria,' Terry had said, 'you will learn to know me.' I did realize that my own family, which consisted of my father and the Dowlers, was incredibly simple in comparison with Terry's. I was an only child; my father had been an only child. The Dowlers had no children, and my father and I were the only relatives they claimed. But in the American South, Terry had told me, kin mattered. 'To the point of absurdity. People fill in whole evenings tracing relationships. It's a parlor game that doesn't cost anything but memory and time, and there's plenty of both in the South, and not much else. Just relax about it and try to think of the family as characters in one of those new Russian novels you're so fond of. We may not have patronymics, but all the ladies are "Miss" whether they're married or not, and Chekhov or Tolstoy would have been quite at home at one of the St. Cecilia Balls.'

But I was not a character out of Chekhov or Tolstoy, and I felt a stranger in an alien land as I lay back in the steaming tub Honoria had prepared for me, and tried to relax after my long journeying.

The strange-smelling water was deliciously warm (yes, it did remind one of rotten eggs); I even had to add a little cool water from the pitcher; and I learned early in Illyria that a warm bath is much more refreshing in hot weather than a cold one from which you emerge into the heat with an unpleasant shock.

Outside the bathroom door I heard a voice which I recognized as Aunt Irene's, warm and rhythmical and a little wistful. "Honoria, I thought I told you to put Miss Stella downstairs in the yellow room."

Honoria's voice was calm. "Mr. Hoadley snores, Miss Irene."

"He's only here on weekends."

"You be less disturbed this way, Miss Irene. Nobody walking about the halls when you take your afternoon nap."

"I know what you're afraid of, but surely that's all over now?" There was a long silence, then Aunt Irene said, "All right. I know there's no use arguing with you. So will you—" she dropped her voice—"will you read the cards for me after dinner?"

"You know I won't, Miss Irene."

"But I need—"

"No, Miss Irene. You don't. And don't go back to *her*."

"Why not, if you won't help?"

"Help? It's never led to anything but misery. Misery. You know that."

"But I'm frightened, Honoria. What else can I do?"

"You can pray."

Aunt Irene's voice went thin, and somehow hard. "Mr. Hoadley will want some ice before dinner, please."

"Very well, Miss Irene."

Their footsteps moved away.

When I returned to my room, wrapped in a great white towel, Honoria had unpacked for me. On the bed table were my books, the ones I had brought to read on the ship: the latest French translation of Tolstoy, *Anna Karenina* (the Oblonskys, I thought, were simple in comparison with the Reniers); one of my father's marked volumes of Plato; some poems. Under these was a book which was not mine: Pascal's *Pensées*. I opened it. On the fly-leaf, in firm but delicate hand, was written *Marguerite Dominique de la Valeur*. My husband's grandmother, his dearly loved Mado. Marking one of the pages was a slip of paper with some verses carefully copied out:

> In this parched place of desolate wilderness,
> This war-torn, hate-split world, oh, who will bless,
> Bless and redeem the blood-stained, tear-drenched
> ground
> So once again the healing sun will blaze,
> The small birds sing, the flowers be found,
> And lion and lamb in loving joy may graze?
>
> Who is there left the truth of love to guess?
> How shall we stand the violence of the sun?
> How hate redeem, how brother's love confess?
> What will be left when wind and fire are done?
> Only on love's terrible other side
> Is found the place where lion and lamb abide.

by Marguerite Dominique de la Valeur Renier, translated by Olivia Hugeot Renier.

* * *

I did not understand the verses, but I felt the pain out of which they had been written, and for the first time Marguerite Dominique de la Valeur Renier began to be a real person for me, and I could share my husband's regret that she had died before I had a chance to know her and be guided by her, for I, too, was Mrs. Theron Renier and in a strange land.

I lay down in the big brass bedstead, covered loosely by the towel, and slept.

Honoria called me a little after seven. "Your aunts and Mr. Hoadley are on the veranda, and would be pleased for you to join them."

I woke up, not quite knowing where I was, my conscious mind waking not to the present moment but to the conversation overheard between Honoria and Aunt Irene while I was bathing. "Honoria, is there some kind of problem about my room?"

"Don't you fret, Miss Stella."

I sat up, wrapping the towel around me. The old woman looked gravely into my eyes. I looked back, smiling just a little. At last Honoria's face relaxed into a wide, radiant return of my smile.

"Miss Mado right about you, Miss Stella."

"What?"

"Don't mind me, Miss Stella. Talking things over with Miss Mado the way I used to do is just one of my old woman's ways. There wasn't nothing Miss Mado and I didn't share. Nothing. We glad you come. Maybe now the angels will come back to Illyria." She smiled again, and left me.

I reached for *Anna Karenina* in which I had put the hastily drawn-up family tree which Terry had made for me.

'There's not enough time, Stella. I'm sending you to Illyria without any armor, except perhaps your very ignorance. If I try to tell you now, I'll just confuse and upset you. There are things you ought to know. All I request is that you ask your questions of Honoria and Clive. Not anybody else. You won't need to ask the great-aunts. They're bound to bend your ears with their nanny goats.'

'What!'

'Anecdotes, my darling,' and we collapsed into the wild laughter which was all that got us through those last hours of parting.

I studied the family tree now, written in my husband's swift and definite hand, preparing myself before going downstairs.

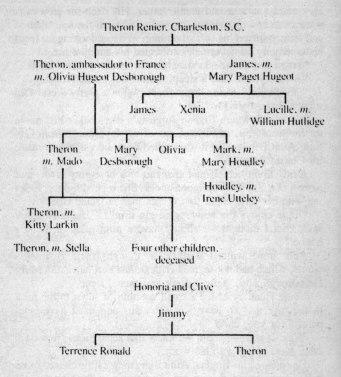

Theron Renier, Charleston, S.C.

Theron, ambassador to France
m. Olivia Hugeot Desborough

James, m.
Mary Paget Hugeot

James   Xenia   Lucille, m.
                         William Hutlidge

Theron   Mary   Olivia   Mark, m.
m. Mado   Desborough   Mary Hoadley

                                    Hoadley, m.
                                    Irene Utteley

Theron, m.
Kitty Larkin

Theron, m. Stella   Four other children,
                          deceased

Honoria and Clive

Jimmy

Terrence Ronald   Theron

When I got out to the veranda, Uncle Hoadley was sitting on a bamboo settee, a folded newspaper lying beside him. Honoria or Clive had drawn up the chairs around a huge brass tray on a low bamboo stand. On the tray were set out bottles of spirits and a cut-glass jar of fresh mint and a silver ice bucket. Uncle Hoadley was crushing mint with mortar and pestle, and the aunts sat hovering around him, watching the ritual.

At the sound of my footsteps he rose to greet me, and then returned to preparing the libation. He looked, I thought, as though he had stepped from a Renaissance painting, was, perhaps, a monk—no, no, at least a cardinal—performing his priestly oblations. I was grateful for Uncle Hoadley, overwhelmingly grateful, because he reminded me most comfortably of my austere and gentle father. His deep-set grey eyes were calm and thoughtful; the hot wind from the sea touched and faintly stirred his soft silver hair. Without looking up from his ceremony he nevertheless directed his smile at me.

"I trust you had an adequate rest after the long drive, Stella?"

"A lovely rest, and a sleep, thank you, Uncle Hoadley."

"Oh, Stella!" Aunt Olivia cried. "What a pretty dress! Did it come from Paris?"

It was one which Cousin Augusta's dressmaker had made for my trousseau, and it was one of my favorites. "From Oxford, Aunt Olivia. But it was copied from a dress Worth made for Cousin Augusta."

Aunt Olivia herself had changed to a blue-grey lawn, and wore a pendant set with moonstones. She rocked lightly, looking with her little smile first at me, then at Uncle Hoadley.

"Irene enjoys the newfangled gin drinks," Uncle Hoadley said, "but I thought we should have a mint julep in Stella's honor."

Aunt Irene winced slightly, as though Uncle Hoadley's words, which had not seemed critical, had hurt her. Aunt Mary Desborough said, "Gin! I don't understand Irene."

Uncle Hoadley added a small quantity of sugar to the mint in the mortar. "To have left Terry so soon must have been painful for you, child."

"Yes. It was—is. But we knew that separations from each other went along with his work."

He snapped his fingers. Aunt Irene rang a little chased brass bell. Clive, changed from his coachman's uniform to a white butler's jacket, came through the screen door with five frosted silver mugs.

Aunt Olivia clapped her tiny gnarled hands. "It's been ages since you made us a julep, Hoadley. O wonderful, wonderful, and most wonderful wonderful! and yet again wonderful, and after that out of all whooping!"

"Auntie!" Aunt Irene said. "Isn't that a little excessive? Or are you at that idiotic game again?"

"Celia, in *As You Like It*," Aunt Mary Desborough said.

"It's not. It's Rosalind. Point for me."

"I identified the play."

"I should hope so."

"Anyhow I still think it's Celia."

"Look it up, then."

I started to say it was Rosalind, then decided I'd better keep out of it.

"Ladies." Uncle Hoadley calmly passed them each a silver mug. "Aunt Olivia, I was talking with my medical man at the club this noon, and he thinks all the lemonade you drink in summer is bad for your joints. A little whiskey before dinner, yes. He suggests a tumbler of water with a tablespoonful of whiskey."

"Hoadley!" Aunt Olivia wailed. "You can't have more branch than bourbon. It would be vile. I'd vomit."

"Livia!" Aunt Mary Desborough reproved.

"Branch?" I asked.

"Water. Branch water," Aunt Olivia said. "Just ordinary water. Branch means the branch of a river. Ugh. It would be awful. I'd just be sick all over every—"

"Olivia!"

From my new and small experience with sulphur water I thought Aunt Olivia was probably right.

"Hoadley isn't telling *you* to drink it, and he'll make me, I know he will, just like old Moulton Barrett making Elizabeth drink porter—"

"Aunties. That will be enough." Uncle Hoadley was quiet, pleasant. "Your bickering can hardly be amusing to Stella on her first evening with us. Aunt Olivia, if you are going to be naughty, I shall tell you to stand not upon the order of your going, but go at once."

"*Macbeth!*" Aunt Olivia exulted. "Oh, Hoadley, it's such fun when you play, too!"

"That's better, isn't it?" Uncle Hoadley handed frosted mugs to Aunt Irene and me. "And I will make you mint juleps every Friday night, Aunt Livvy. That's a promise."

I sipped mine and it was as cool and refreshing in this tropical heat as spring rain. "It's lovely, Uncle Hoadley."

"Take it slowly." He raised his mug to me. "It's more powerful than it may seem. Any idea where young Theron is?"

I looked into the cool depths of the silver mug. "No, Uncle Hoadley."

"None?"

"He could be anywhere, things change so quickly. There was talk about an uprising in Kairogi, everybody was very concerned, but there was trouble in the Balkans, too. He could have been sent anywhere."

Aunt Irene poked at the sprig of mint in her julep. "Why

should a lot of black savages fighting each other in an unimportant country in Africa upset us so? What's it got to do with us?" She put her mug down with a clank. "Why can't we let them fight? Good riddance. Why do we always have to butt into everybody else's business?"

Uncle Hoadley poured a generous amount of whiskey into his mug and swirled it around. "If we want to emerge from the destruction of our recent troubles—" he smiled slightly, "—as a country of any power, then the world is our business, my dear Irene, and Kairogi is part of the world. We would be blind indeed if we chose to ignore Africa at this point in our history."

"Well, it's beyond me." Aunt Irene shoved her mug a little closer to Uncle Hoadley, but if he noticed it he gave no indication. "And all this about the Balkans—I do believe they're as savage there as in Africa."

"The Balkans are most definitely a cause for concern."

"Hoadley," Aunt Olivia clasped her hands, "you can't mean you think there's going to be war?"

"Of course there's not going to be war!" Aunt Irene said. "The world is far too civilized for that."

Uncle Hoadley sighed. "You were not quite as affected by our own war as the rest of us were, Irene."

Again, he had hurt her. "I couldn't help—"

He held up his thin, authoritative hand. "I am afraid the world will never be too civilized for war. If war is to be averted, it will be only because of the intervention of foresighted leaders. There are too many royal navies being massed and reviewed; this does not happen when peoples are not preparing for war."

"But that's in Europe—"

"Ron says," Aunt Olivia's faded eyes were sharp as she looked across the brass tray at Uncle Hoadley, "that there are a lot of boats in the yacht basin at San Feliz."

Uncle Hoadley laughed. "That is hardly a royal navy preparing for war, my dear Auntie."

Aunt Mary Desborough gave a funny, sad little laugh. "Please don't think I'm awful, but I was happy during the war, happier than before or since. Oh, it was all terrible, but when Mado and Theron brought us to Nyssa—that was our cousin James's plantation, Stella—and we turned the house into a hospital, I—I was of use. Oh, I saw terrible things, terrible, but I was of use. People need to be of use."

I took a new look at Aunt Mary Desborough. Terry had

tried to tell me something about the War Between the States. It did not mean much to me. 'But it does to the family,' he had said. 'If you don't know much abut the war now, you will. Wars don't end, Stella, particularly for the defeated.' 'But it was so long ago!' 'Not to the great-aunts. Not to any Renier.'

"Battlefields have changed, Auntie," Uncle Hoadley said, "and you are of use here."

She snorted. "Faddle."

"You tell me all the news of Illyria and San Feliz, and it gives me a sense of balance and proportion. I tend to forget that it is the little things which have always held chaos at bay: the new kitten; or what Finbarr has managed to steal from the larder; or the latest quarrel among the ladies of the Daughters of the Confederacy."

"Mado was asked to be the first president of the Daughters of the Confederacy," Aunt Olivia told me, "but she turned them down. She said we'd fought our war and lost it, and an organization like that could only make us hold on to resentments and keep our wounds from healing. She said for them never to come to her about it again."

"Mado was French," Aunt Irene injected.

"*You* are an Utteley," Aunt Olivia said.

At a time like this Aunt Mary Desborough evidently could be counted on to back her sister up. "Mado was an aristocrat. Olivia and I don't belong to the Daughters of the Confederacy. We don't need to. And as for you, Irene, you'd never have got into the Colonial Dames if it hadn't been for us."

"Auntie," Uncle Hoadley soothed, "come now, I was just complimenting you on keeping me up with the kind of news that keeps the stars in their courses. What's gone on in Illyria this week?"

"Nothing," Aunt Mary Desborough said.

"Stella's come," Aunt Olivia said.

Honoria came out onto the veranda.

"Honoria," Uncle Hoadley said, "did you do as I asked you to do?"

"Sir?"

"I asked you to change Miss Stella's belongings down to the room next to Miss Irene's as we originally planned. I don't like the idea of Miss Stella sleeping alone up on the third floor."

"But she's not alone, Hoadley," Aunt Olivia said. "She's with Honoria and Clive."

Uncle Hoadley ignored her. "Honoria: have you done as I asked?"

Honoria stood motionless, facing him, a tall and commanding presence. "No, sir, Mr. Hoadley."

"Why not?"

"Bin getting dinner."

"Then you will do it after dinner."

"Dishes to do. Ironing."

Aunt Irene spoke nervously. "Honoria reminded me that you snore, Hoadley, and your room's right across from the room we thought Stella—and you do snore, Hoadley, quite loudly."

"Honoria: do you intend to disobey me?"

"Yes, sir, Mr. Hoadley. My Powers told me what I has to do."

Uncle Hoadley rose.

I, too, rose. "Uncle Hoadley, I prefer to stay where I am. I'm very happy in my room and I do not wish to move." I tried to keep my voice light, courteous. It shook.

"Dinner served," Honoria said.

3

AT dinner it was as though the tension between Uncle Hoadley and Honoria had never existed—on the surface, at least. I was not sure what lay under Uncle Hoadley's pleasant manner, and Honoria's impassive face was even more foreign and unfathomable. Uncle Hoadley talked lightly, amusingly, as though there had been no warring forces out on the veranda (but there had been; there had been): "When I was a small boy I used to spend weeks at a time with my Hoadley grandparents, my mother's family. They had one of the fine old plantations in Summerville—that's just outside Charleston, Stella, and has some of the loveliest places in the South. Most fine houses were built with the kitchen and house-servants quarters connected to the main house by a latticed breezeway. For a long time it didn't seem quite decent to nice people to have either the kitchen or the bathrooms directly connected with the house, and certainly not *in* it."

"When you put it that way," Aunt Olivia interrupted, "you make me feel bourgeois not to go outdoors to perform my natural functions."

"Olivia!" Aunt Mary Desborough cried.

Uncle Hoadley continued, reaching out with one calming hand to press Aunt Mary Desborough's fingers. "I used to love to go through the breezeway to talk to my grandmother's cook, old Bounty. Everything about Bounty fascinated me. Grampa had an iron pump in the breezeway, where we got our water, and I remember seeing Bounty with a big tin dipper filled with cane syrup and kerosene, to which she added a little water from the pump. It was for her health, she said, and she lived to be over a hundred—nobody knew exactly how old she really was. I always wanted to try some of it, but she wouldn't let me. Just outside the dining room and pantry there was a big store-room for food. In one corner was a barrel of brown sugar—not the kind of dry rock we get today. It was always moist, and the sugar came out in chunks and oozing syrup. It was better than any candy and when I was good I was allowed a big spoonful..."

I listened, delighted, absorbing this strange world from which Terry had come, which had nourished him, patted and shaped him into the man who had made me his wife.

Finbarr, the old dog, walked through the dining room and paused beside Aunt Olivia. "No, Auntie. No, Finbarr," Uncle Hoadley said, and the old beast, with a wistful sniff towards Aunt Olivia's dinner, moved stiffly on out to the kitchen.

"Now, Stella honey," Aunt Irene said, "tell us all."

I smiled. "What kind of all?"

"Everything."

"Every thing, saith Epictetus," Aunt Olivia announced, "hath two handles, the one to be held by, the other not."

"*A Winter's Tale,*" Aunt Mary Desborough responded.

"No."

"Yes, it is, I'm positive it is."

"Look it up, then."

"I don't need to."

"Well, it's not. It's Robert Burton's *Anatomy of Melancholy.*"

"It doesn't count, then. We're playing Shakespeare."

"Aunties, a toast," Uncle Hoadley intervened, and raised his wine glass. "To Stella: welcome."

"To Stella: welcome," the aunts echoed.

Something in me relaxed at the warmth of their words and the kindness in their eyes. Aunt Olivia whispered to me, "All shall be well, and all shall be well, and all manner of thing shall be well."

Aunt Irene, smiling warmly at me, began asking eager little questions about my father, about the Dowlers. I soon learned that Aunt Irene enjoyed being able to talk about 'Lord and Lady Dowler, my niece's kin, you know,' or saying, 'My niece's father was a Fellow of All Soul's. That's in Oxford, you know. Oxford in England.'

I answered her as best I could that first evening. "I really don't know very much, Aunt Irene. Father and I lived alone, and he didn't concern himself about ancestors or family trees."

"Since we all came from the same trees originally anyhow," Aunt Olivia said, "I think your father was very sensible. It certainly doesn't seem to me to be very important which branch of ape one has descended from."

"Olivia!" Aunt Mary Desborough protested. "If you're going to be sacrilegious—"

"All right, all right, you go right on thinking you're an act of God created in his image, and I'll go right on thinking I'm descended from an ape. When you look in the mirror I should think you'd feel pretty discouraged; I wouldn't be happy to look at myself and think that *my* face is an Imago Dei. It wouldn't make me feel I'd done very well by God. But when I look in the mirror and think that I'm descended from an ape, I feel I've done remarkably well."

"Auntie! That is enough!" This was the first time Uncle Hoadley had raised his voice. And here he differed from my father, who would have been amused and delighted by Aunt Olivia.

She subsided momentarily, then pointed to the portrait over the sideboard, an austere-looking gentleman with white side whiskers. "That is our father, Theron Renier. He was ambassador to the court of France under the third Napoleon, before the war, of course. It was while we were there that our brother Theron met the young noblewoman, Marguerite Dominique de la Valeur, and married her."

"Olivia," Aunt Mary Desborough said, "for one who has

been discussing the unimportance of the family apes, you are showing an inordinate interest in genealogy."

"Who ever said apes were supposed to be consistent? We learn by paradox and contradiction. And why not get Stella acquainted with her new family? I'll wager all Terry did was confuse her."

"He didn't have time to do much else," I said. "He had to leave so much sooner than we expected."

"Did he tell you about James?"

"Yes, but I'm not sure who—"

"James is our cousin. He and Theron were like David and Jonathan."

"Nyssa belonged to James," Aunt Mary Desborough said wistfully. "You'll meet James on Sunday, Stella. He has a place a few miles up the beach from us—Little Nyssa."

"Nyssa is gone." Uncle Hoadley sounded sharp, a sharpness for which I was not prepared.

"No!" Aunt Olivia cried. "Not while Des and I are alive. Not while James and Xenia are alive. Not as long as Illyria stands."

Clive moved silently around the table, breaking the tension, holding a silver serving dish out to Aunt Olivia. "All Terry's favorite things," she said. "Honoria's eggplant—I do hope you like eggplant?"

"I've never had it before. This is magnificent."

"And stuffed mushrooms—we were always afraid Terry and Ronnie would find a poisoned mushroom some time and eat it, but they never did. Honoria picked these, didn't she, Clive?"

"No, Miss Livia. Ronnie pick them."

Aunt Irene turned the conversation back to my father. "You say he was considerably older than you, Stella, honey?"

"He was almost eighty-three when he died, though that was hard to believe."

"I'm eighty-three," Aunt Mary Desborough said.

"That's hard to believe, too."

"And he was in Holy Orders?"

Wherever did she get that idea? "He was a philosopher, Aunt Irene, and an atheist."

Aunt Irene looked shocked, but continued bravely, "Then your upbringing was a little—unusual?"

"It was happy."

"Clive," Aunt Olivia asked, "would you be kind enough to bring me a saucer of cream, please?"

"Auntie! What do you want cream for?"

"Not for me, Irene, I assure you. Nor for you. The kitten's hungry. He's nibbling my toes, and his little teeth are sharp."

Clive bent down to pick up the kitten. He whispered so that the others could not hear—but I was sitting next to Aunt Olivia. "Put you slippers back on, Miss Livia. At once."

I decided that I was going to enjoy getting to love this old lady.

In a louder voice Clive said, "I'll give the kitten something in the kitchen, Miss Irene." The kitten nuzzled into the old man's neck and they went through the swinging door.

Aunt Mary Desborough pointed to a charming portrait of a small boy in a sailor suit. "Look, Stella, that's Terry over the serving table. Aren't his eyes beautiful?"

I looked at the portrait of the blond and solemn little boy, at the vague, myopic eyes which came into focus only behind the thick lenses of his spectacles: the Renier shortsightedness hadn't been discovered until he went away to school. But yes: his eyes were beautiful; the child in the portrait was a promise of the man I had married.

"It was only this past winter, wasn't it," Aunt Irene pursued, "that you met Terry?"

I looked across the table to the portrait. "And I'm still meeting him."

"That's Hoadley over the sea chest," Aunt Mary Desborough continued, "when he was at Harvard Law School. Terry looks a little like him, don't you think? but all Hoadley's features are elongated, like that painter you like, Livvy."

"El Greco. What are we having for dessert? I do hope it's something special."

"Stella, honey," Aunt Irene said, "you do know, don't you, how happy we are to have you with us?"

"It's too bad there aren't any strawberries."

"Auntie!"

"But we do have such good strawberries, and I thought Stella would like—"

"I love strawberries," I said quickly, "and I do thank you, all of you, for taking me in this way, a stranger—"

Aunt Olivia rushed in, "—here in Gloucestershire: a stranger here in Gloucestershire: These high wide hills and rough uneven ways—"

"Shakespeare, and it is *Richard II*." Aunt Mary Desborough thumped the table. "I am a stranger here in Gloucestershire. Twenty points for me."

"Nineteen."

"Twenty."

Clive came in with a tray, which he set down on the sideboard; from it he took two saucers, the first for Aunt Irene, the second for Aunt Mary Desborough. Aunt Olivia peered at her sister's plate. "Oh. Pineapple ice."

Clive put another saucer in front of her, then, carefully, one before me.

"What's that?" Aunt Irene asked. "What are you giving Miss Stella?"

"There were just enough figs for one serving, Miss Irene," Clive said.

Aunt Mary Desborough half rose in her chair. "But, Clive—"

"Sit down, Des," Aunt Olivia said triumphantly.

Coffee was served on the veranda. We waved our palm-leaf fans back and forth, not so much against the heat now as against the insects which fluttered about, strange, delicate creatures with long legs and translucent wings, unlike anything I had ever seen in England.

"Sugar, honey?" Aunt Irene asked me. "Cream?"

Clive passed me the small white and gold cup. His jacket shone white; the rest of him faded into the shadows of the veranda.

"I'm going in to get my knitting," Aunt Mary Desborough announced. "No, Clive, I want to do it myself. I'll be right back. *Three* sugars, please, Irene. Two is not enough. You never remember."

Aunt Irene leaned across the coffee table to me. "The aunties," she whispered, "you'll have to forgive them. They're quite senile. Hoadley and I are only glad we can take care of them."

Aunt Olivia had been rocking placidly, slowly waving her palm-leaf fan to and fro. She stopped. "Clive and Honoria take care of us."

"Auntie—" Aunt Irene started.

"Clive and Honoria. Make no bones about that. This is Honoria's house, Irene. I wouldn't forget that if I were you. Honoria allows you to spend your summers here—"

Aunt Irene rose in agitation. "Auntie!"

Uncle Hoadley, lighting a cigar at the far end of the veranda, moved towards us.

"Miss Olivia." Clive bent to the old lady. "Your coffee. Half hot milk."

Illyria belonged to *Honoria*?

Aunt Mary Desborough returned to the veranda with her knitting. Heat lightning flickered over the ocean. The slow pounding of the waves mingled with a distant rumble of thunder—the storm Aunt Olivia had predicted was moving towards us. I sipped my coffee: it tasted odd: probably the sulphur water.

Beyond the shadows of the porch it was still light. The sun had gone behind the house, but the wet sand near the ocean shimmered with the rosy afterglow, and the ocean itself had a luminescent quality I had never seen in England. Honoria brought out a shallow dish of some kind of pungent oil with a wick in it and set it on the porch rail. The flame burned low, with blue-green flickerings.

Uncle Hoadley said, "I hope you don't object to the odor, Stella? It does help to keep the insects away. And my cigar serves somewhat the same purpose. You will allow me?"

"When we had the hospital in Nyssa," Aunt Mary Desborough said, "Mado brought in a woman from the town, from one of—one of those—places. We thought it was dreadful of Mado until she made us realize that Carrie was the best nurse we had. She had the gift of healing in her hands. She could touch a soldier who was delirious and screaming with pain, and he would become quiet and sleep like a baby all night— far more peacefully than if he'd been given morphine—and of course during the war drugs were hard to come by. After we'd had a particularly bad night Carrie used to smoke funny little brown cigarettes—it was your cigar made me remember, Hoadley—and they seemed to give her so much relaxation and pleasure, I envied her."

Uncle Hoadley pulled out an engraved silver case. "I got a fresh supply today at the club. Like to try one, Auntie?"

Aunt Mary Desborough gave a little shriek of pleased laughter. "Oh, Hoadley, you are such a one for a joke!"

"I'm serious, Auntie."

The old lady shrank back in her rocking chair. "Oh, no, Hoadley, I couldn't. Not now. It's too late." Then she said to me, with a note of defiance, "We nursed Union soldiers at

Nyssa, too. There was a lot of criticism, but Mado insisted. Everybody said there'd be trouble, but I guess when a man is badly enough hurt, he doesn't care who's in the next bed. Oh, we were happy there, all of us, we were a family, white and black, but we never got anything but brickbats. People are always suspicious of that kind of happiness."

Aunt Irene sighed impatiently, and I guessed that Aunt Mary Desborough often favored them with her reminiscences.

"Ron has it," Aunt Olivia said.

"Has what?" Aunt Irene asked.

"The gift of healing in his hands."

Aunt Irene sighed again. "That's enough, Auntie."

But Aunt Olivia leaned toward me. "Ron is a doctor, a qualified medical doctor."

"Ron? the one who carried my boxes upstairs?"

"A fine doctor."

"Auntie! I said that is enough." Aunt Irene's voice held a note of inexplicable malice as she asked, "And what did you do, Auntie, while Aunt Des was so busy nursing the wounded?"

Aunt Mary Desborough sprang in swiftly. "Olivia has always been frail. She did what she could."

My father, when I was a child, had tried to teach me perspective: I would need a lot of perspective to sort out all the unexpectedness since my arrival at Illyria. What, after all, had I expected? Something not quite so foreign and bewildering; something which would bring me closer to my husband. But the more I saw of this alien land and its people from whom he had come, the more he was becoming a stranger to me.

I needed, all at once, to be alone. I didn't want to suggest going to bed, in case the argument about my room should come up again. I had no intention of shifting rooms; if I felt certain of one thing only, it was that my room was meant especially for me.

I rose, "Is it all right if I take a little walk on the beach?"

Uncle Hoadley looked surprised. "Of course, my dear. Irene and I will go with you."

"No. Please. I would like to be alone." I could not help it if I was rude.

But Uncle Hoadley, bless him, understood, as my father would have understood. He smiled his tired and gentle smile. "All this must be strange and confusing to you. You'd like to walk on the beach and sort things out in your lovely little head, wouldn't you? Very well, my dear. But walk up the beach, rather than down, if you please. Sometimes we get an unpleasant element in San Feliz on weekends. And, Stella, don't be long."

"I won't."

"You'll get used to our summer thundershowers; we have one almost every evening. Sometimes they are more violent than usual, and we seem to be brewing a big one for tonight. But don't be afraid. We're so accustomed to them that we pay very little attention."

"I'm not afraid of storms."

"Also, my dear, night falls very quickly here, not like your long English twilights."

"Yes. Terry told me." I ran down the ramp to the beach.

4

I RAN down the ramp to the beach. The air was hot, heavy; new to me. I reached up and closed my fingers as though I could squeeze some of the steaming moisture from the atmosphere. When I got to the beach I sat down on the end of the ramp and took off my shoes and stockings. My feet burned in an acutely painful manner wholly new to me. The physical results of the Illyrian heat were going to take time for me to become accustomed to. I arched my feet, stretched my toes. I could not have stood shoes and stockings a moment longer. I buckled the straps of left and right shoes together, so that I could hang them over my arm. The soft sand at the foot of the ramp was still warm from the sun, and delicious as it sifted between my toes. I moved slowly to the firmer, damper sand at the ocean's edge, then walked along the beautiful coolness close to the sea. As the waves were sucked out into the ocean I could feel a strange suction beneath my feet. Terry had warned me about the tides, the undertow, the treachery lurking beneath the beauty. 'Check with Aunt Des about the swimming,' he had told me. 'She knows the beaches like the palm of her hand, where the undertow is dangerous, where the tide pulls hardest—at least she used to.'

I waded up to my ankles in the warm water, the undertow pulling strongly now. I bent down and dabbled my hot hands in the lacy foam. Splattering salt water I moved up the beach, then turned to look back at Illyria.

The old house was set back on the dunes, an extraordinary monstrosity—though I soon came to see it as beautiful—built up on stilts filled in with wooden latticework. There were towers and chimneys and wings and elbows and little balconies, and the great, many-angled veranda which surrounded the whole thing like a moat. The dunes raised themselves all about, so that the house seemed to float like an unwieldy ark on a sea of sand. The long wooden ramp, made of the same sea-grey wood as the house, led up from the beach, over a jungle of scrub and wild undergrowth, up onto the veranda.

Oh, Illyria, Illyria. The home place. The place of love. The place where living taught me something about dying, and where death taught me even more about life.

Illyria: always the smell of the sea, of mustiness. Always wind: the wind of the Spirit, even if it sometimes blew in odd nooks and crannies. Wind moving across the face of the water, over the great pale stretch of beach, through the veranda, and into the house, so that the heavy linen damask curtains stirred constantly, rugs undulated, doors slammed.

In the wet sea wind wood swelled. Everything was sticky. Doors were hard to open and close. Shoes left too long unworn became covered with green mold. Little beach ants ate our silk stockings unless we kept them in tightly closed preserving jars. Our clothes were always damp to put on unless they'd just come in out of the sun. In winter nothing dried. Clothes were constantly and ineffectually draped over the fenders, and the smell of warm, damp cloth added itself to the other Illyrian odors.

In the nature of my husband's work with the State Department we were away most of the time, in Africa, China, Rome, St. Petersburg, Paris, London. Our home leaves of course were spent at Illyria, but only our first child, our Theron, was born there, or even in the United States. But Illyria was always home, the place of love—and why? I have been more afraid, more filled with anguish, in Illyria than any place on earth. The answer has something to do with love. Love that has to go through darkness and pain and endurance and a stark acceptance before it can come out into the far light of the sun. Love I hadn't dreamed of, and wouldn't have wanted to dream of, before my husband sent me to Illyria to wait for him.

'Illyria is my home,' he had told me. 'Not Jefferson, not Uncle Hoadley's and Aunt Irene's pretentious house. Uncle Hoadley was my father's most intimate friend—that's why I went to him. But Mado was all the mother I ever knew or needed. And the great-aunts and Honoria and Clive are my true family—though Aunt Irene tried to love me, and I admire and respect Uncle Hoadley. They are your family now, Stella-Star; they'll take good care of you while I'm gone. And you take care of them. The old aunts need you. Aunt Olivia's letters— I'm worried. She tends to dramatize, but still I'm worried. And do whatever Honoria and Clive tell you to do. You must promise me this.' Over and over he had warned me: obey Honoria and Clive.

I will, I promised Terry silently.

The drumming of the ocean seemed to reiterate the warning.

Thinking only of Terry, I wandered from the water's edge towards the dunes, and walked directly into a swarm of tiny insects, almost invisible until I felt the fierce heat of their bites, heard the shrill of their cry. No wonder mosquito netting was needed in Illyria! I ran back to the ocean and into the water, dabbling my toes in the foam. Relieved of the stinging cloud, I looked up from the small, lapping waves. Far ahead of me on the beach a man was walking with the strange, a-rhythmic gait which was peculiarly Terry, which was uniquely and only Terry. I began to run along the ocean's edge, trying to call, but my voice was caught somewhere within me, lost in the frantic pounding of my heart.

Terry, here!

I ran to meet him, stumbled, righted myself, ran faster.

It was not Terry. It was someone with black hair, dark skin: Ron James.

He turned, saw me, stopped.

I slowed down, my heart pounding in my throat, my mouth dry. Swallowing hurt as it might with a very sore throat.

"Mrs. Renier," he said, "is something wrong?"

I tried to laugh. "I thought you were—were my—husband—"

He waited.

"You walk the way he does. I've never known anybody else walk that way."

Ron's voice was harsh, as though he were angry with me. "Mrs. Renier, I have nothing in common with your husband but our rather distinctive name. And I don't walk differently from anybody else."

My heart was still banging painfully. "People—people do walk differently. Like—like different rhythms in music. Aunt Olivia walks like the old dog, Finn—Finbarr. My father walked like a stork. So does Uncle Hoadley. Terry and—and you—" I was stuttering in reaction. Ron waited. I managed to swallow, to take in a great gulp of fresh salt air. "Please. Let's sit down."

We walked a few yards up the beach to where a broken-down half dock jutted out from the bulwark across the sand; on a dark piling crouched an even darker bird. As we approached, it jumped down and hovered over something on the beach which looked like the remains of a fish. The bird stretched out a long neck, pink, repulsively bare of feathers. I shuddered. "What's that?"

"A buzzard. Better get used to them, Mrs. Renier. There are plenty around."

"But pelicans, too?"

He walked past the dark piling on which the bird had brooded, and leapt up onto the remains of the dock. He held his hand out to help me. "Perhaps."

I sat beside him on the rotting wood, still swinging my shoes and stockings over my arm, totally unthinking of my bare feet and ankles. There were no insects here on the dock, except for a small and unexpected galaxy of fireflies. Ron held out his hand, cupped one, let it go. He did not look in the least like Terry. Terry was stocky, with a kind of golden, lion-like strength. Ron was not only a Negro, he was taller than Terry, thinner, more graceful. To have fancied that he walked like my husband was only a mirage brought about by my longing.

"Why did Terry send you to Illyria?" he asked.

"Where else? My father's dead."

"What do you make of us?"

I thought for a moment. My heart was beginning to beat normally. "I don't suppose I *make* anything of you."

"Stop it, Mrs. Renier. Let the old ladies have the games. The rest of us can't afford them."

I said on impulse, "The great-aunts and their game—What country, sir, is this?"

He responded without hesitation, "This is Illyria, madam."

"And what should I do in Illyria? My husband is in—where, Ron? Kairogi?"

He was suddenly tense. "Why Kairogi? What would he be doing there?"

I did not understand his reaction. "It's—it's just one of a number of places he might be."

"But you don't know that he's there?"

"I haven't any idea where he is. I really don't. I just—I just said that."

"Mrs. Renier, maybe it's safe to go around just saying things in England. It isn't in Illyria." He made an odd noise, half groan, half anger. "How did you meet Ter—your husband?"

"Through the Dowlers. They're cousins, though not very close ones, and friends of my father's. Lord Dowler was with the government, and did a lot of archaeology. He spent years in Africa, and he's one of the experts on Kairogi. I think that's why Terry was sent to talk to him. I'm not sure."

A firefly lit briefly in Ron's short, crinkly hair, and almost seemed to illuminate his thin face with high cheekbones and finely arched nose. "Mrs. Renier, when you go putting two and two together, no matter what number you come up with, keep it to yourself."

"Why?"

"Innocence!" Ron said loudly. "Is that what Terry thought he was sending us? Innocence? It is not innocence. It's blind idiocy."

"I am capable of learning."

"Who's going to teach you?"

"You?" He did not respond, and I said, "Terry told me about you. You've been in England."

"I'm not in England now."

"But you were. Why? Terry didn't tell me—we had so little time."

"My grandmother—Honoria—saw to it that I got away from my mother when I was very small." The bitterness in his voice was dull and dry. "I was sent to England to school—to Lancing, by a patron who wished—wishes—to remain anonymous. I was given a white man's education, much good may it do me. I stayed on, after Lancing, went to Durham, then St. Andrews, and all for what? No white man's hospital will let me darken its door. As for your husband, we haven't seen each other since we were small boys playing together under the chinaberry tree and in the bamboo grove. Terry—sorry—Mr. Renier—"

"He calls you Ron."

"I imagine your father called his valet by his first name."

"My father's valet was not a doctor. I'm glad you and Terry like each other."

"Why? What difference does that make?"

"I like you."

He stood up on the rotting wood of the dock, towering over me. "But I don't like you, Mrs. Renier. Please let us get that straight. I have been back in Illyria for six months. You, too, are in Illyria now. You and I can have nothing in common."

"Illyria?" I asked, getting to my feet. "Affection for Terry?"

"You must not allow me to be rude to you, Mrs. Renier." He jumped to the sand, helped me down. "Good night."

"Good night."

He made me a courteous bow; set off rapidly for Illyria. I knew that I should follow him, that it was time for me to go back. Although the sky was still light, the fireflies were brightening. Night was hovering somewhere behind the dunes. Nevertheless I turned from Ron and walked farther up the beach.

And then night fell.

It came as Uncle Hoadley had warned me it would, like a clap of thunder. It had been light, a soft, pearly light, light enough for me to see Ron with ease. And then it was night. Utter and absolute. The fireflies blazed. From far out over the ocean a star pulsed. Then, on the very edge of the horizon where the darkness of water almost lost itself in the darkness of sky, I could see a faint, luminous glow, a red streak almost as though far out at sea there were fire. Then the redness began to have edges and the look of fire left and the upper circumference of a huge circle pushed itself out of the water, the color of blood.

I had never seen a moon look like this. It frightened me.

I walked along the edge of the water, comforting myself with one of Terry's rhymes:

> *Clive and Honoria, Honoria and Clive,*
> *Keep Illyria's light alive.*
> *They had a son whose name was Jim;*
> *Jimmy married, and from him*

Came Terence Ronald, known as Tron,
Then little Theron, nicknamed Ron.

I said it over, meaninglessly, several times, then began to
wonder about Terence Ronald. Where was he?

As swiftly as night had come, the great sphere—it was
nearly full—leapt from the sea, free of the horizon. The blood
on the moon faded; it turned to burnished gold, seemed to take
another leap up into the sky, and shone silver. It was, at last,
the familiar moon I knew, the moon under which I had walked
with my husband. Was it shining on him somewhere now?

I held my hands out to its light, as though to cool them.
Then, aching for Terry, trying to hold back foolish, forlorn
tears, I walked still farther up the beach.

Far ahead of me I saw two little figures dancing under the
light of the moon, turning in slow, erratic circles. Up on the
dunes warm yellow light came from a small cottage. The heat
still bore down oppressively; I felt damp all over; and yet I
was grateful for the comforting warmth of that light.

The two figures moved together, closer; then, circling still,
began to play a clapping game.

The thought of children out playing on the beach reassured
me, and I hurried toward them through the velvety tropical
darkness.

"Pease porridge hot," I heard them chanting, "pease porridge cold, pease porridge in the pot, nine days old."

They were not children. They were little old men.

As I approached them in the increasing brilliance of the
rising moon, I could see that they were no more than five feet
tall, with laughing, wrinkled faces, white, softly curling hair,
and white beards. They looked like something out of Grimm's
Fairy Tales.

"Ashes, ashes, and we all fall down!" one of them shouted
suddenly, and they tumbled onto the sand. The moonlight emphasized their gnomishness, the soft silver of their hair.

I sighed with a kind of resigned terror.

They saw me, and suddenly they were running towards me,
arms held out. They were so like children that I could not be
frightened.

"Pretty lady! Pretty lady!" they cried, and came running
along the sand to meet me, tumbling into my arms.

They were, I realized, the Illyrian equivalent of village idiots,
affectionate and harmless. The middle-aged son of our elderly

porter in Oxford was such an idiot and looked very much like these two little men, with the same wrinkled, vulnerable face and round eyes with an expression which combined innocence and an ancient, painful wisdom. He used to follow me around like a dog, and I was fond of him, and not in the least afraid.

"Miss—?" one of the little men inquired.

"Mrs. Renier," I replied, still bemused by the joy of the new name.

"The new lady!" he cried. "The new lady at Illyria! Joy! Joy!" They joined hands and danced around me in glee. I could not help laughing.

They loosed hands, and one of them pointed, first to himself: "Willy." Then to his brother: "Harry."

"Hello, Willy." I held my hands out to them. "Hello, Harry."

They took my hands in theirs, warm and dry as tissue paper, bobbing and nodding their pleasure.

Willy pressed my hand, and his expression of happy welcome changed to one of anxiety. "Pretty lady, we don't want Honoria and Clive to go away."

"Don't let them go away," Harry whispered. "Away, no, no, no."

I stood there in the moonlight, Willy holding on to my left hand, Harry to my right. "I don't think Honoria and Clive are going anywhere."

But they repeated, nodding their top-heavy heads, "Away, away."

"Where did you get that idea?"

"We heard," Willy said.

"Heard what?"

"Heard *her*."

"Who's *her*?"

"The Zenumin. Bad, bad, bad," Willy said.

"We listen. Nobody knows. But we listen: we hear: we see. Dark and bad," Harry said.

"What's a Zenumin?" I asked.

"Her."

"Where does she live, this Zenumin?"

Willie pointed up the beach and inland. "Back. In the scrub. The Bad Clearing."

"Could I find her if I walked?"

The two little men got excited, both crying, "No, no, no! Don't go find! Never. Never. Bad bad bad to take Honoria and Clive away."

"Just Honoria and Clive? What about Aunt Olivia and Aunt Mary Desborough?"

"No, no, Honoria and Clive," Willy said.

"Don't let them," Harry pleaded. "Stop it. Stop."

I remembered how the porter's idiot son sometimes got all excited and upset over nothing. I tried to comfort Willy and Harry. "I won't let anyone take Honoria and Clive away."

"Promise?"

"I promise." I had the sense to add, "I'll do my best." I left the two little men and started back to Illyria.

5

THE lights of the cottage disappeared behind a dune. Moonlight drenched the beach. The arm of the lightship swinging protectingly across the ocean was dimmed by the brilliance of the night.

"Ma'am!"

I stopped, looked around, saw only a shadow beside a palm tree atop a dune. The shadow moved, revealed itself to be a woman, tall, slender, graceful. She ran lightly down the dune, across the sand, and stood facing me. An odor came with her, an odd mingling of herbs and spices, neither pleasant nor unpleasant.

"Mrs. Renier?"

"Yes."

She held her hands out to me, smiling. In the moonlight she was incredibly beautiful, and I understood for the first time that the freshness of youth cannot hope to compete with the beauty of maturity. I had no idea how old she was; I only knew that I was callow and unformed in comparison. I held my hand towards hers, but she drew me to her in a quick and unexpected embrace. I was both surprised and touched.

"Welcome," she said. "Welcome. I am Belle."

"Good evening." I slid my hands out of hers. "I'm happy to meet you. How did you know—"

"Everybody at the beach knowed the new Mrs. Renier was coming. Everybody know Belle Zenumin and her boys."

"Except me," I said. The moonlight touched her delicate features, glanced off her dark skin. The rising breeze whipped her skirts about her long thighs. Her skirts were considerably shorter than mine, and revealed her feet and ankles. She wore a laced bodice, gypsy-style, but she had a delicacy and a darkness I had never seen in a gypsy.

"You ain't met my Ron?"

"Honoria's and Clive's grandson? Yes. Of course."

"Ron be my son. Ron been away from home a long time."

"Yes. In England."

"Mr. Hoadley tell you that?"

"No. Ron did."

"You met my other son yet? My Terence Ronald?"

"No. Not yet."

Suddenly her moonlit face looked infinitely sad. She held her arms close about her breasts as though in grief. "They took Ron away from me. They took him to Illyria. When him but a baby. For his own good, everybody tell me that. But it be hard on a mother to lose a boy. My other son, he stay back in the scrub with me. He a Zenumin. Oh, never think, ma'am, that I would have held my Ron back. But it was hard, hard." The moonlight showed me that there were tears in her dark eyes, and one rolled down her fine, high cheekbone. "Oh, Mrs. Renier, ma'am, I didn't mean—I'm sorry—" Suddenly her face cleared and she laughed, high and clear, like a bell. "Time for grieving's over. You and me is going to be friends. I can feel it. Lonely for you, coming this way to a strange land, and your man so far away. Belle know what loneliness is like. Lost my husband, lost my Jimmy, and then my baby Ron was taken from me. Belle knows what it like to be lonely. Ever you need a friend, you call on Belle."

"Thank you." I was touched by her concern for me, and that it seemed to outweigh her own trouble.

Her smile embraced me. "Come. I got a gift for you." She held out her hand again, and I took it. She led me up over the moon-drenched dune, past a giant palm lifting dark wings against the sky, down a narrow path which ran between a tangle of vine. I could still hear the ocean, but I could no longer see it behind us. "Where are we going?"

"Just back to the creek. Creek runs into the scrub. Zenumins live in the scrub." She sighed. "Zenumins. Some good, some bad. Like most everybody else, I guess. People say we no good because we live in the scrub, because we black, because we different. Why different no good? You coming?"

"Yes." The path was so overgrown and narrow and dark that I had begun to pull back; but Belle's last words had assured that I would follow her. My father had been very emphatic that there was no reason why other ways of living, ways we call primitive, should be considered less valid than our own just because they were different. It's the old error, he told me, of equating like and equal.

So I let Belle take my hand again. "Friends. Belle needs a friend. Belle gets lonely. Belle different. Like my Ron. It not easy to be different, Mrs. Renier."

The narrow path ended at a river; the water was so dark that the moonlight did not penetrate its surface. Trees with heavy, gnarled trunks, and great uncovered roots, leaned over the darkness, so that the moonlight scarcely filtered through, and it was not until I heard a voice that I saw an ancient canoe at the water's edge. It was an old voice and it came from what looked like a bundle of clothes in the canoe.

"You found her."

"Yes, Granddam."

"Told you she'd walk on the beach tonight. Told you she'd need to be alone. Bring her close. Want to see her."

"Mrs. Renier, ma'am," Belle said, "this be my grandmother. It make her right proud to meet you." She gave me a gentle push.

I leaned over the canoe and looked into the wrinkled black face of an ancient woman—though crone, rather than woman, was the word that came to mind. She peered at me with a small cackle, whether of amusement or pleasure I did not know. "Evening, Mrs. Renier."

"Good evening."

The old woman looked past me to Belle. "She'll do, won't she? 'Pon my word, I do think she'll do."

Belle pressed her hand lightly on my shoulder. "The Granddam be very hard to please. She likes you."

The old woman held her hand out to me. I found her rather frightening, but didn't want to hurt her feelings, so I offered her my hand in return. She took it, but not to shake; instead, she held it, palm up, moving it so that the moonlight, shafting through the trees, shone directly upon it. She peered and peered, nodding in satisfaction. "I see—oh, I see so much, so much. I will tell you—"

"No, please—" I tried to pull my hand away, but her bony old fingers held it in a tight grip.

"What's the matter, little Missy Renier? Don't you want me to tell you what I see?"

"No, no, please—" I was afraid of fortune tellers, inordinately afraid. I had had one experience in Oxford with a gypsy, an experience I would never forget—I tried to stem my panic, to speak calmly. "Please. I really don't want to have my fortune told."

"I see a baby," she said cajolingly. "You got a wish about a baby right now, ain't you? And your wish is true."

Her words filled me with happiness, but even so I found that I did not want this old woman to know how much I wanted to bear Terry's child. I did not want to hear it from her. And I did not want her to tell me anything else.

"Never knew your mother, poor little thing," she said. "She too old for birthing. Pain and blood, very much blood, and a little baby, and then death."

I felt Belle's reassuring hand on my shoulder. "But that's not Mrs. Renier, is it, Granddam? That's her mother."

The old woman spoke slowly, deliberately, spacing her rhythmic words. "Mrs. Renier going to be very old lady. Very grand. But first there be fire. There be blood. And death. There be death."

"Granddam! What's wrong with you?" Belle Zenumin was respectfully reproving. "You're frightening Mrs. Renier."

"Didn't do nothing to frighten her."

"You didn't mean what you said, did you, Granddam? The bad things?"

The old lady cawed like an old crow. "Could change it. Maybe. If she be good. If she do what she told."

"Come on, Mrs. Renier, ma'am," Belle said. "We go back to the beach. When the Granddam gets in a black mood, best to leave her be. Let Mrs. Renier go, Granddam."

My hand was released. Belle helped me along the path. The sharp grasses cut at my feet. I realized that I was no longer carrying my shoes.

Belle said, as we climbed the dune, "I'm sorry she got angered with you. You shouldn't have been frightened, ma'am. She just wanted to tell your fortune."

"But I don't want to have my fortune told!"

Belle was all full of apologies. She had thought it would be a welcoming gift for me. She was so happy that I had come, she wanted to give me something special. Her grandmother had the power of foretelling, and people came to her from all over. She was revered and respected. "You ask Miss Irene," Belle said. "Miss Irene come to the Granddam whenever she in need."

I could only say, "But I'm not in need, Mrs. Zenumin."

We were on the crest of the dune now. The ocean lay before us, the wide path of moonlight brilliant from horizon to shore.

Belle, her body seeming to move like a reed in the ocean breeze, looked out across the water. "Mrs. Renier, ma'am, it all my fault. It not good to have the Granddam an-angered at you. But Belle calm her down. Belle try." Quickly she grasped my hand and turned it palm up in the moonlight. Against my will I was compelled to look at her face, trying to read there what she saw in my palm. But her beautiful features were expressionless. "Belle has the gift, too," she said, "though not the Big Gift, like Granddam, or like—that why I took you— oh, Mrs. Renier, ma'am, all Belle wanted was to offer you a token of friendship—" Again in the moonlight I could see the glint of tears.

"Don't worry." I withdrew my hand gently. "I've lost my shoes somewhere. I don't remember whether I dropped them on the beach—or maybe it was on the path, or by the river—"

"Shall we go back?"

"No, no, I'll find them tomorrow in the daylight. I don't need them to walk along the beach."

"Belle will look. Belle will bring them if she finds them."

We slithered down the dune. "Good night, Mrs. Zenumin. And thank you for being kind."

"Oh, ma'am—Mrs. Renier, ma'am." Her voice broke. "It not fitting for you to call me Mrs. Zenumin. I'm Belle. In my heart you be Stella, my friend, but Mrs. Renier on my lips. Belle know her place. And names—Belle know names be important. When my baby Ronnie went to Illyria, to Honoria and Clive, he took their name: James. Dr. James. Oh, that be wise, Mrs. Renier, ma'am. Who go to a Dr. Zenumin? Dr. James. That be a fine-sounding name. But I ask myself in my heart: can my boy *be* that fine-sounding name? Who going to tell me? My other boy, my Tron, he a Zenumin. He don't change on me."

"But your husband—" I started. "Jimmy—"

"In the Zenumin part of the scrub, once you be a Zenumin, that what you always be. A man marry a woman, or a woman marry a man, don't make no never-mind. You marry a Zenumin, that what you be. You all right now, Mrs. Renier? They'll be looking for you in Illyria."

"I'm fine. Sorry, I didn't mean to be silly about—please apologize to your grandmother for me."

"Yes, ma'am. Belle going to try."

> *"The farmer in the dell,*
> *The farmer in the dell,*
> *Heigh, ho, the derry oh,*
> *The farmer in the dell."*

The two piping cracked voices came over the top of a dune, and Willy and Harry slid down the sand, onto the beach.

> *"The mouse gets the cheese,*
> *The mouse gets the cheese,*
> *Heigh, ho, the derry oh,*
> *Ashes, ashes, and we all fall down!"*

and they landed at my feet, looking far more like children dressed as grownups, in their bell-bottom trousers and red and blue neckerchiefs, than the white-haired adults they were.

Belle pressed my hand quickly. "Good night, Mrs. Renier. My friend." Then she whispered, "Mrs. Renier, ma'am, be careful of the idiots. They won't harm you, but—"

Willy and Harry picked themselves up out of the sand, and Belle, with a quick glance at me, turned and went swiftly up the dune.

"Not nice to call us idiots," Willy said.

"Naughty lady. Naughty, naughty." Harry shook his finger at the disappearing figure. "Naughty lady going to be ashes, ashes," he chanted, "fall down, fall down."

"Ashes, ashes." Willy shook his head. "Zenumins. Bad. Bad."

"All Zenumins?" I asked.

Willy puckered up his little face, shaking his head. "Not all. Some good."

"Good night, my dears," I said. "I must go back to Illyria."

"Good night," Willy said. "Good night. Good night."

"Honoria and Clive," Harry reminded me anxiously. "You promised. Pretty lady promised."

"I won't forget. I don't want Honoria or Clive to go anywhere, either. But I don't think there's anything to worry about. Will you be all right?"

"Boys all right," Willy assured me.

"*Good* boys all right," Harry added. They held up their nut-like faces for my good-night kiss.

Very aware that I had been away from Illyria too long, I began to run down the beach. The damp sand felt glorious against my feet, and I concentrated on this physical pleasure in order to hush the wholly irrational fear the old Granddam had roused in me.

I was carrying Terry's baby? Surely that ought to make me happy. Had I been a praying person, it would have been my prayer. As it was, it was my wish and my desire.

The lightship swept its secure and comforting finger across the sea.

Ahead of me on the beach, coming towards me, were two figures, and one of them started to run, leaving the other behind. The runner was Ron, Dr. Ron James, and he was furious.

"Mrs. Renier, you have upset everybody! The great-aunts are hysterical. Where have you been all this time?"

"I'm a grown woman. I needed to be alone," I said.

"For an hour and a half? The aunts are worried about you, and quite naturally."

"What's natural about it? Or is there something I don't know that I ought to know?"

Ron's voice was cold, controlled: a doctor's voice. "Perhaps we aren't as civilized around Illyria as you are in Oxford."

"Why? What do you mean?"

"There are some—rough characters—in San Feliz. Not that there's any real danger, yet, but we didn't expect you to be gone for so long and we were afraid you might have been frightened."

"By what?"

"Buzzards," he said bitterly. "My grandfather has gone back to calm everybody down."

"I've lost my shoes," I said.

He looked down at my feet. "Your skirts are long enough. I doubt if anyone will notice. Where did you leave your shoes? I'll go get them."

"I don't know. I don't remember when I dropped them. Somewhere on the beach, I suppose." I did not tell him about meeting his mother and going with her to the old crone: I was too angry, too guilty, too confused.

"I'll go look for them."

"Don't bother. I'll find them in the morning."

"I'm walking up the beach anyhow. Go on back to Illyria now, please, Mrs. Renier. Good night." He bowed.

I returned the bow, equally cool. "Good night."

Illyria loomed above me on the dunes, like a house in a dream. Not only the house: the whole walk on the beach had had the quality of a dream: completely logical and realistic while it is being dreamed, and yet incredible—and foolish or frightening, as the case may be—when one wakes up. But the splintery wood of the ramp of Illyria was not a dream, nor the insects as I turned in from the ocean. Does one ever get stung by mosquitoes in dreams?

Uncle Hoadley was on the veranda, waiting for me.

"Uncle Hoadley, I'm terribly sorry. I walked farther than I realized. And dark did come more quickly than I'd expected. I'm sorry Ron and Clive had to come looking for me."

Unlike Dr. Ron James, Uncle Hoadley was gentle with me. "I ought to scold you, but I think I understand. All of this— all of us—must be overwhelming to you." In the moonlight he looked at me sharply. "Are you all right, child?"

To be called child that way again: I felt a wave of grief for my father. And I wanted to tell Uncle Hoadley all about the horrible old Granddam who had frightened me so, but something—perhaps pride—prevented me. But I could ask him about the little men.

"Oh, the twins. I hope they didn't frighten you."

"No, they were sweet."

"Tragic about the twins," Uncle Hoadley said. "Their father was the captain of my father's boat. We used to spend long holidays on it when we were young. The Captain's poor little wife died when the babies were born, and he almost went out of his mind with grief. We've always assumed responsibility for them—their father served the family well and it seemed the least we could do. The twins aren't a great deal older than I am, and I used to play with them sometimes when I was little. As a matter of fact, I loved nothing better than to be allowed to spend a day with the twins. They were more fun to be with than anyone else I knew—except Therro, of course. Your husband's father, the one real friend I have ever had in my life." I wanted to reach out and touch him in a gesture of comfort, but his voice lightened. "The twins play now exactly as they did when we were children. You'll be seeing something of them, because they often come to Illyria to be fed, though they have their own little cottage we built for them. Ready for bed, my dear?"

"Yes. Thank you. Very ready." Around the house I could hear a wild cacophony of insects shrilling and chirring. I might have expected this in Africa or India: I hadn't, in my husband's home in the United States of America. I would have given a lot to be able to slap at my bare and itching ankles.

The sky over the ocean was split by a blinding fork of lightning. I waited for thunder, counting the seconds as my father had taught me to do when I was a little girl, to see how many miles away the storm was. But there was no answering crash. The wild electrical power that had opened the sky was beyond the reach of sound.

Uncle Hoadley held the screen door for me and we went into the living room. Aunt Olivia was seated at the piano, the old dog by her, his gaunt head on her knees. Aunt Irene and Aunt Mary Desborough were at a small table in front of the fireplace, playing backgammon. I made my apologies immediately, stopping their twittering before it really got started. Aunt Mary Desborough and Aunt Irene returned to their game. Aunt Olivia gave me a sharp look, started to say something, shook her head, smiled at me, and then held her hands out in front of her, working her arthritic fingers. "I used to play well. It's terribly frustrating. Look: they're nothing but talons."

Aunt Irene handed the dice cup, ebony, set with mother-of-pearl, to Aunt Mary Desborough. "Go *on*, Auntie. It's your turn."

"Age." Aunt Olivia fondled Finbarr's ears. "I can't wear my rings any more. They hurt. We turn back into animals when we grow old. Our beautiful human hands become claws. Our aristocratic noses turn to beaks or snouts. People shouldn't be humiliated by getting old and doddering in this undignified manner. I'd rather have died young, like Therro. Your husband's father, Stella. Oh, everybody thought it was a dreadful thing for him to be cut down so young. But he's still and forever a young man, and handsome and joyous and talented, while I—while I—but you see, when I remember Therro, then

I'm young, too. Or, rather, I'm not any age at all. I'm me. Olivia. Myself. Not an old woman. How old are you, Stella?"

"Nineteen." I looked away from Aunt Olivia to the Chinese vase filled with beach grasses which stood in the summer-empty fireplace. There was a musty smell to the house, and the woven grass rug was prickly under my shameful bare feet. I hoped that Ron was right and that my skirts were long enough so that no one would notice.

Aunt Irene and Uncle Hoadley, not looking in the direction of my feet at all, bade me a courteous good night, and Aunt Irene shook the dice cup. "*My* turn now, Auntie."

Then, out from under the sofa cushion, peered the kitten. He looked at Aunt Irene and Uncle Hoadley, at the old aunts, at Finbarr, at me, and then jumped, landing, claws extended, on my toes. I dug my fingernails into my palms, determined not to cry out and reveal my shame. I bent down and loosened the kitten from my skirts and picked him up. Attack successfully completed, he began to purr loudly, and patted my cheek with a sheathed paw, soft as velvet. Nobody, I thought, had seen.

But Aunt Olivia put her hand up to her mouth to keep from laughing. "Oh, Stella, I'm *so* glad you've come! At last I've been granted a friend in my retreat."

"What's that?" Aunt Mary Desborough looked up from the backgammon board. "I didn't get it. Say it again. I can't guess if you mumble."

"Maybe your ears aren't as sharp as they once were."

"My hearing is perfectly good. Say it again, properly."

> *"But grant me still a friend in my retreat,*
> *Whom I may whisper—solitude is sweet."*

"I know it, I know it," Aunt Mary Desborough said. "Obviously not Shakespeare."

"Obviously."

"Oh, botheration, I give up. One of your obscure madmen, I suppose. Who is it?"

"William Cowper."

"All right." Aunt Mary Desborough clucked in annoyance. "Point for you, then. But I'm still ahead. However, Irene, I concede this game of backgammon." She rose. "Good night, Livvy. Good night, Stella. Good night, dear Hoadley. And Irene. See you in the morning."

"One hopes," Aunt Olivia whispered to me. "One hopes.

Not that Irene will see us, but that we will see Irene. That we will see."

Aunt Mary Desborough paused at the stair landing, holding her candle aloft so that it made long, wavering shadows. "Go to bed, Livvy. I'm not playing any more this evening. Give up. I've won for the day."

"Daz it," Aunt Olivia said, "I thought we were brought up that ladies do not gloat. Go on, Stella love. I'm unconscionably slow, and my room's down here. I can't manage stairs any more."

"Good night, then, Aunt Olivia."

"See you in the morning," the old aunt said anxiously, as though it were a ritual.

"See you in the morning." I took my candle and went upstairs.

6

HONORIA had turned down my bed and lowered the mosquito netting which was now tucked carefully all around the mattress. The lightweight blanket was folded down to the foot. On my bed table the lamp was lit, turned down low. A moth was fluttering against the glass chimney, trying to get to the flame. I turned up the lamp and blew out my candle. I did not want a moth burning his wings in the open flame.

The windows to the balcony were now opened wide, and I stepped out. Was the breeze rising? I wiped the still sandy back of my hand across my mouth where perspiration beaded my upper lip. A mosquito shrilled past my ear and I swatted at it. The old wood of the balcony floor still held the heat of the sun. I hoped that Honoria had unpacked the trunk in which I had put my shoes.

The lightning had now become a constant tremor in the sky. The sound of the waves seemed to increase, the slow, inexorable rolling of the surf, the waves breaking as they neared the shore, followed by the sucking sound of their return to the deep, dark water, pulling sand with them, and shells, grinding everything with dispassionate consistency. It seemed suddenly a cruel sound, and I would willingly have changed it for the bells of Oxford. Out over the ocean the lightship beam, brighter than the throbbing lightning, flashed out, swung round, disappeared. If moths were attracted by the tiny flame of lamp or candle, would they not also be drawn to the rhythmic beam of the lightship? And what about lightning? Would they fly into that violent flame in which they would instantly be incinerated? Why are those lovely, fluttering creatures so fascinated by the source of their destruction?

I shivered, watched and waited for the more comforting beam of the lightship, which my husband had loved when he was a small boy staying in Illyria with Mado. He had sat in her lap on the veranda, and she had sung to him while he watched the slow turn of the light and drifted into sleep. I held the thought of him close to me, as his grandmother had held him, and waited for the light to swing past me again, and again. Then I looked about, up and down the beach: night, the quiver of lightning, the dark line of dune and scrub, the lighter stretch of beach curving around the horizon until it met the sea. I leaned my elbows on the balcony rail. The breeze was feverish against my cheeks; it did not have the cooling breath of the night air to which I was accustomed. It reminded me hotly that I was not in rational and reasonable Oxford but in Illyria, where all sorts of strange things seemed to be taken for granted. And I, the newest Mrs. Theron Renier, would have to get acclimated to them during these weeks until my husband's mission was completed and we could begin our married life together.

Down below my balcony, out of sight, came the sharply radiant song of a bird. A nightingale had sung in just this way the night Terry and I were married, sending us into laughter and joy; so I was comforted. But this was not a nightingale; it was a mockingbird.

The mockingbirds, the redbirds, all the flora and fauna of Illyria, the ilex bushes, scrub oak, moonvine, persimmons, scuppernong grapes, ligustrum hedges, four-o'clocks with their sweet, heavy smell, cape jessamine with its shiny, dark leaves and easily bruised waxen petals—I remember them all as though I'd always known them. But when I first came to Illyria they were all foreign to me, and it was a long time before I became familiar with their names. And yet this took less time than accustoming myself to the inner atmosphere of Illyria, the heart of the conch shell.

The angle of my balcony was such that from it I could see the long walk which meandered about the house. Someone was pacing the walk, moving slowly, steadily, the small light of a cigar brightening, dimming, brightening as he moved.

Uncle Hoadley.

He moved quietly, but there was no peace in his pacing.

Sometimes my father had paced like that. Once, after an evening with Terry, he had walked up and down half the night. I knew that Terry must have told my father something which he had not seen fit to tell me, something disturbing. This was a memory I had tried to put away, like a chest under a bed, or dust under the carpet.

A small flame curved over the walk and went out in the sand. Another flame appeared, brighter, a match flaring as another cigar was lit; and the pacing began again.

I turned from the balcony and went to my bed. Under the delicate and pure-white mosquito netting lay the kitten, curled up in a soft, striped ball on my pillow. I was comforted to see him. I undressed and got into bed, but did not blow out the lamp. I was too tired and confused, and—yes, let's admit it, Stella—too full of presentiments and fears to be sleepy. A large moth clung to my netting, looking strangely fierce seen from its underside. Other insects brushed by, fluttered against my lamp. I heard the whine of a mosquito. I made a small opening in the netting and reached out towards my pile of books. There were several which had not been there earlier, notebooks covered with marbleized paper that had browned and spotted from age and damp, almost as though from burning. I picked one up and opened it carefully; if I did not touch the pages with extreme gentleness they would fall apart in my hands. But if the notebooks had been placed on my bed table, they must have been put there for me to read.

On the flyleaf of the one I held was written in the same delicate penmanship I had seen in the Pascal, *Marguerite Dominique de Valeur Renier. Charleston, South Carolina.* I turned the pages tenderly. They were filled with the beautiful clear writing, still completely legible despite the brown fading. I began to read at random, grateful for Mademoiselle's patience in overcoming my reluctance to learn French: "Croyez-vous qu'il arrive jamais à un ange de se faire du souci parce qu'il n'est pas un archange? ou de penser que s'il travaille un peu plus dur ou se fait des amis, il pourra s'élever dans la hiérarchie céleste? C'est de la folie: mon ange gardien est l'égal, du point de vue de rang, de n'importe quel archange. C'est nous, les gens de la terre, qui ne voyons pas qu'il y a une différence d'essence et non pas de rang. Et de toute façon cela n'a pas d'importance, parce que mon ange gardien est complètement ce qu'il est, et remplit entièrement la fonction pour laquelle Dieu l'a créé. En ce moment, il veille sur moi. Après ma mort, on lui commandera peut-être de balayer de la poussière d'étoile du coin du ciel. Mais parce qu'il fait ce pour quoi il a été créé, lumineusement, joyeusement, quelles que soient les difficultés que je lui crée, je peux saisir une partie de sa joie. O, sans la joie de mon ange, où en serais-je?"

("Do you suppose it ever occurs to an angel to worry because he is not an archangel? or to think that if he works a little harder or makes the right angelic friends he'll get elevated in the heavenly hierarchy? That's nonsense. My guardian angel is equal, as far as rank goes, to any archangel. It's we earthlings who've lost sight of the fact that it's a difference in kind, not in degree. And anyhow it doesn't matter, because my guardian angel is fully what he is, performing wholly the function for which God has created him. At the moment, this function is to watch over me. After I die, he might be assigned to sweeping stardust out of a corner of the sky. But because he is doing what he is created to do, radiantly, joyfully, no matter how difficult I make it for him, I can catch some of his joy. Without my angel's joy, where would I be?")

Smiling, I lowered the book. Guardian angels were not part of my father's cosmology, but they had belonged in the world in which my nanny moved. I caught myself hoping that my guardian angel had managed to cross the Atlantic with me, and come with me to Illyria.

I turned to another notebook. This was evidently a later one, and was written in English. "There has been, of course, gossip and worse about our coming to Illyria. And sometimes I wonder if Honoria and I are right. Dare we try to redeem what Claudius Broadley built? At any rate, James completely agrees with me that Honoria must not give up the title to Illyria. It is the only title she has left, and nobody must take it from her."

Here it was again: Illyria belonging to Honoria. In the midst of my curiosity I was overwhelmed by a wave of sleep. This kind of sudden sleep has always been one of my body's safeguards—sleep and laughter. When I have had more than I can manage, my body simply goes to sleep and there is nothing I can do about it. It has happened in far more inconvenient places than in a room in which I am already in bed. I blew out the lamp and fell into sleep.

But after the first drench of sleep I slept lightly, as though listening for something; I would wake up, then drift back into sleep as into shallow water. When the waves of the night-breathing ocean began to make a different sound, I woke up completely, pushed aside the mosquito netting, and went to my balcony.

But it was not the ocean which was making the pounding sound; it was a group of horses galloping along the ocean's edge. They were ridden by hooded figures like something out of All Hallow's Eve. They galloped up the beach, growing smaller in the distance, as small as sandpipers strutting along the sand. Finally they disappeared from sight, a vanishing cloud of dust. They were like something strange and sinister out of the Middle Ages; they did not belong in the twentieth century. They were an Illyrian nightmare. I was not entirely sure they were real. If I had been given to fancies I would have thought—

A large insect flew by, its wings brushing my cheek and frightening me. I left the balcony and went back to bed; the kitten was gone. I tucked the netting in carefully. In its filmy protection I felt comforted, as though I were a small child. I tumbled back into sleep.

I woke up when the storm broke. Now that it was here there was no need to count between thunder and lightning; crash followed immediately upon flash. The storm was directly over Illyria. Around the house the palm fronds rattled in the wind; the great fans, shaken and brushed against each other, sounded like driving sheets of rain, so that the rain when it came was simply an added hissing across and against the roofs and turrets of Illyria.

At first, so noisy was the storm, I did not hear the gentle scratching at my door. The scratching turned to a soft, insistent knocking. I pushed at the soft cloud of mosquito netting, found the opening, reached for matches. The room was lit by a brilliant green flash of lightning, so that I was blinded in the following dark and fumbled with my fingers over my bed table: where were the matches? Where was my candle?

The knocking became louder, almost frantic. I heard a muffled, urgent bark. Lightning exacerbated rather than relieved the dark. I found the matches. As I struck one the door burst open and the old Irish wolfhound slid, cowering, belly dragging, across the floor and under the bed.

"Oh, Stella!" came Great-aunt Olivia's voice. "Oh, Stella, I'm so frightened!"

"Aunt Olivia!" I managed to light another match, and then the candle.

Flash.

"Come in!"

Crash.

Aunt Olivia was in my arms. I held the old woman as though she were a baby: what an extraordinary resemblance there is between the very old and the very young. To Aunt Olivia's faded hair, to the folds of the long-sleeved, high-necked nightgown, clung a soft odor of milk, of powder, of lavender. The old woman's breath was sweet and smelled faintly of pomander. On her cheeks there were tears. I brushed them away in a wave of tenderness, a kind of gentleness which was wholly new to me. I murmured endearments, marveling at the softness of the wrinkled skin.

"Cucumber." Aunt Olivia answered my unspoken thought. "It does marvels for the skin. And I rest my elbows each in half a lemon every night when I say my prayers. Do you think God minds? I think he wants us to be our best for him. And that includes not having leathery elbows." Flash. "Irene's elbows are like horn." Crash. The dog under the bed yelped. Aunt Olivia clutched me more tightly. "For all she's half my age. Her skin's like a turtle's who's left its neck out too long, and sometimes I think—oh, Stella, hold me tight, I'm so glad you've come!"

I held the old great-aunt close until there was a lull in the storm. "But we can breathe quietly for a few minutes. And I'm not afraid while I'm here with you. Is there anything you want to know, lovey? Is there anything I can tell you while we're waiting for the storm to pass?"

"Yes. Please, Aunt Olivia. I don't understand about Illyria belonging to Honoria."

"Terry didn't tell you?"

"There was so little time—we'd expected at least six months together."

How much did Great-aunt Olivia tell me that night during the violence of the storm, and how much did I learn later? I remember Honoria's story all of a piece, but surely she can only have hinted at it in the breathless intervals between lightnings. It was an ugly story, though she took pains to assure me that it wasn't unique: there had been old man Kingsley at Fort George Island, off Jacksonville, and other men, too, who like Claudius Broadley had been successful slave traders. 'He was successful,' Aunt Olivia had said, 'because the Africans were nothing but animals to him, or less than animals, really. Half of them died on the ships coming over to America. He'd have treated animals better.' Honoria had not come over in the hold with the slaves because she came as Claudius Broadley's wife. In Africa she had been a princess, and exotically beautiful. No one knew precisely why the slave trader had bothered to marry her, but her power must have been as magnetic then as when I first met her. Perhaps he knew that here was one human being he could never beat down. In his own way he must have loved her.

'So,' Aunt Olivia said, 'she was never a slave. And the chief captain answered, "With a great sum obtained I this freedom." And Paul said, "But I was born free."' She looked at me expectantly. Candlelight flickered over her face, blurring the lines of age; she looked young and eager. But her words made no sense to me and for a moment I thought that Aunt Irene was right about the great-aunts; then I realized that she was playing her game. "I suppose it's from the Bible. Sorry, Aunt Olivia. My father considered the Bible great literature, but I know Plato lots better.'

'Acts.' Aunt Olivia cringed against a flash of lightning, waited for thunder. 'Acts, 22. Honoria, like St. Paul, was born free.'

Born free, and never a slave, but ostracized, scorned, sometimes abused. Broadley was often away from home on his hideous business, and the young black princess almost died of homesickness.

'When was all this?' I had asked.

'A long time ago. A lifetime ago. Fifty, sixty years. It was before the war.'

My candle was burning low, so I lit the lamp and blew the candle out.

Not long after Claudius Broadley brought his African princess to Jefferson, Theron—Dr. Theron, Mado's husband—was asked to come to Jefferson to start a hospital. It was assumed by the family that they'd be in Jefferson only a year or so, just long enough to get the hospital on its feet, and then they'd go home to Charleston. But the war changed everything. And by then Mado and Honoria were fast friends.

When Mado and Theron came to Jefferson they heard—of course they heard, it was a scandal and a source of gossip—about Claudius Broadley and his bride; and Mado, breaking all precedent, went to call on Honoria. They were both young brides far from home, come to live in a strange land; from the beginning they were drawn to each other. And Aunt Olivia made it clear to me, that night during the storm and later, that Mado knew the difference between compassion and pity. 'When you pity someone,' she once said, 'you are concerned with their problem, but you don't share it. Mado somehow shared. And that's compassion.'

About once a week Mado had herself rowed down the river to the Broadley plantation. It must have been quite a sight, the young Frenchwoman in her best Paris clothes, holding an elegant silk parasol, sitting in a little tub of a rowboat. As I came to know more about Mado, I learned that she had the kind of arrogance that comes with the absolute assurance of knowing who you are, the assurance of true aristocracy. She couldn't have cared less what Jefferson society thought. When people criticized her, she simply laughed her beautiful, joyous laugh. But Claudius Broadley and Honoria didn't get off so easily. He was cut dead whenever he appeared on the street in Jefferson, and people threw stones through their windows.

'Why?' I had asked.

'Because Honoria was black. And free. And a princess. And Broadley was crude and filthy rich. But when money was being raised for the hospital in Jefferson he was one of the biggest benefactors. Did it even ever bother him that if Honoria were ill she wouldn't have been allowed in Mercy Hospital? Merciless Hospital, Mado sometimes called it. She saw that things were impossible for Honoria in Jefferson, so she talked Claudius Broadley into building Illyria for his wife.' All she had in mind was a cottage, but Broadley insisted on building the great Gothic folly which was to become so dear to me. In those dim days before the war it was the only house on the beach, and could be reached only on horseback and by boat. San Feliz was entirely postwar, and the little railroad and the yacht basin didn't come till after the turn of the century. Illyria was a safe place for Honoria, and Mado used to visit her there, and who knows which one taught the other more?

Aunt Olivia spoke through a rumbling-off of thunder: "The beach is becoming fashionable now, alas. A Negro wouldn't be allowed to have a house here today, even if he could afford it."

"What happened after the war? How did you come to Illyria?"

With a seeming non sequitur she replied, "Claudius Broadley was a beast. We all loathed him. Though why people who bought and kept slaves thought they were morally superior to a slave trader I'm no longer quite sure. Was he any more of a beast than William Hutlidge?"

"Who?"

"Oh, someone you needn't fret about, lovey. He's dead, thank God. James's brother-in-law. His plantation bordered on Nyssa. Let's forget him. Even if Broadley was a beast, he was a shrewd one. And no one is wholly bad. Not quite. Broadley's gains may have been ill-gotten, but he did provide for Honoria. Maybe he wouldn't have if Mado hadn't pushed him, but no matter why, he did. He built Illyria, and he made investments, and after the war Honoria had what—for us here in the South— was a good bit of money. And then there was Honoria's treasure."

"Treasure?"

"Her *dot*—her dowry. The precious stones and jewels she brought with her from Africa. Your wedding ring. Oh, and I don't know how much else. No one knows. Some people think she still has a fortune in precious stones hidden somewhere. Remember, she was a princess."

I didn't know much either about treasure or about African princesses. I looked at the ring again; in the lamplight it shone quietly.

"After the war, Honoria managed to get a message to Mado and James that she was in trouble. She made it look as though we were doing her a favor, all of us, by coming to Illyria to live with her. And in a way she did need James and his legal protection. And Clive. If Claudius Broadley made marriage a farce and a tragedy, Honoria and Clive made it what it ought to be and seldom is. People in the South right after the war weren't—still aren't—apt to be generous or even honest with a black person who has money when whites are starving. So Honoria did need James. Claudius Broadley died of apoplexy in a fit of rage during the war, and Honoria'd have been wiped out, ruined, perhaps worse, if James hadn't managed everything for her. And she made the rest of us feel that she needed us, too. So, because of Honoria's friendship with Mado, we fared a lot better than most people. And we were a family. We all shared, the good things and the bad. The only reason Des and I still have a bit of jewelry left now is that everybody had jewels, and we couldn't always find a market for them. Diamonds, yes: all the diamonds went to get the Charleston portraits back." She yawned.

"Don't you want me to help you back to bed, Aunt Olivia?"

But even as I spoke, the room was lit again by lightning; and the thunder, following immediately, made the old dog under the bed yelp anxiously. Great-aunt Olivia clutched to me. "Not till the storm's—and there's something I want to say. It must seem odd to you, the way we live, as though Honoria were the servant, and we the—it all happened slowly, inevitably, the world being the way it is. Mado understood it better than the rest of us. I tried to quarrel with Honoria about not eating at table with us, but Mado said that we had to let Honoria do as she saw fit. And she reminded us that there are—that there are precedents. For whether is greater, he that sitteth at meat, or he that serveth? is not he that sitteth at meat? but I am among you as he that serveth." She paused.

"Sorry, Aunt Olivia. I suppose it's the Bible again."

"St. Luke. It bears thinking about. And so does the verse that precedes it: He that is greatest among you, let him be as the younger; and he that is chief, as he that doth serve." She looked at me with the sudden sharpness that could come to her gentle blue eyes. "I suppose all this must seem very confusing to you? Oxford's not a jungle, is it? Was life reasonably tidy and ordered for you there?"

"Reasonably, I suppose."

"It used to be for me, too, when I was nineteen. I didn't understand about the jungle, then—not the jungle around Illyria, but the one in our hearts and lives. The pattern is all overgrown now, for all of us. The past ought to be past, so that we can get everything all tidied up and start again. Maybe that's what we're all hoping you'll do for us. Push us into a present that leads to a future. But the past doesn't ever seem to be past. It moves up and intrudes into the present. And it threatens the future."

Lightning and thunder shook the house again, and again the old woman clutched at me like a child. "Did you see—did you see the journals?" she gasped. "I had Ron put them on your bed table. Mado's journals. I thought they might help and comfort you. You'll find more about Honoria in the—"

"Miss Olivia. You here?" Honoria herself stood in the doorway, revealed in a brilliant flash of lightning, wrapped in an old blue and white seersucker robe. Below it hung her white cotton nightgown, and below that were her dark ankles and large feet in men's felt slippers. The amber-striped kitten followed her. "How you get up those steep stairs?"

The thunder almost obliterated the question. "I came up on my bottom," Aunt Olivia said. "I butted my way up. Is Illyria going to be struck?"

Honoria's voice was scolding. "You want to fall and break your hip?"

"I was scared. This isn't just a regular little old thunderstorm. This is a—a cosmic thunderstorm. I called you, Honoria, I called, and you didn't come."

"I is here." Honoria pushed the netting farther side, reached in and disentangled Aunt Olivia's arms from their hold on me. She picked the old woman up as though she were a small child and stood by the bed, holding her. "You all right, Miss Stella?"

"Yes, I'm fine."

"Miss Olivia didn't frighten you?"

"Of course not." Lightning lashed across us. The house trembled.

"Why would *I* frighten Stella?" Aunt Olivia asked indignantly. "I thought she might need me." Then she giggled. "That's one of my poorer lies, isn't it?" Thunder roared, and in the following silence Aunt Olivia said, "That's immediate retribution for you."

Honoria started toward the door, but Aunt Olivia cried, "No! Not yet! I want to stay here in Mado's room."

"Hush," Honoria said, but did not argue. She sat in the rocker near the windows. The next flash of lightning seemed to lick around the chair.

Creak, went the rocker. Creak. Creak.

Thunder overrode it. It seemed as though the storm would never leave us. But there had been a slow count of three between flash and crash, so it was, in fact, beginning to move over. I could feel a relaxing of the tension in the air, in Aunt Olivia, in and around Illyria.

"Why is it a cosmic storm?" Aunt Olivia asked sleepily. "It's almost as though the elements are angry because of Stella's arrival."

"Could be," Honoria said. "Darkness don't like the light."

"Did Minou come tell you I needed you?"

"Could be," Honoria said again.

"Minou's a Guardian, like Finbarr, n'est-ce pas?"

"Speak English, Miss Olivia."

Aunt Olivia shifted position in Honoria's arms and looked at me. I sat up in bed, my arms about my knees, and looked back at the extraordinary picture of the gaunt black woman in the rocking chair, cradling the old great-aunt. "Oh, Stella," Aunt Olivia said, "we're all terribly curious about you. You are aware of that, aren't you?"

"I'm curious about all of you, Aunt Olivia."

"Irene's going to go on asking you all kinds of semi-polite questions as though her only reason were—oh, solicitude and hospitality. Though of course you had impeccable references, you might say, from Lord and Lady Dowler."

"They wrote you?"

"Of course. You don't think we'd let Terry marry someone we didn't know about, do you?"

No, I supposed not. I had been aware only of my father's establishing the fact that Theron Renier was a suitable person for *me* to marry.

"I'm not going to be like Irene," Aunt Olivia said, "skirting around questions. I'm too old for that. There isn't time for games. Except Shakespeare. Terry's working for the government, and we're all proud of that, though when he was at Chapel Hill classics was his field, and he always put puns in Latin and Greek in his letters. Des and I called him our Lancelot Andrewes. It's odd to think of him involved in some kind of hanky-panky."

I smiled. "It isn't hanky-panky, really. Just—special and confidential."

In the next flash of lightning—but gentler, now, not the searing, tearing brilliance of the storm when it was directly over Illyria—I saw Aunt Olivia's smile of satisfaction. "So what he's doing now is a deep, dark secret?"

"Yes."

"You're not in the least like Delilah with Samson, are you? Aren't you curious? Couldn't you have wormed something out of him?"

I made one attempt, at which my husband sternly, and not very gently, let me know that I was not to question him. It was a side of Terry for which I was not prepared, and which I did not want to provoke often.

The old lady gave her small girl's giggle. "All right, lovey, I won't try to pump you. I know you've been trained never, never to ask questions."

True: and I would never forget my nanny and the reprimand I got, physical as well as verbal, when, aged five or thereabouts, I asked a distinguished visitor if he wore a wig.

"So was I. So were we all. But the older I grow the more I lose the proper veneer, like the furniture in Illyria. I'm like the sideboard and the highboys, buckled and cracked. Just you wait: it's amazing what being on the further side of eighty does to freeing a body from the shackles of civilization. How did Terry and your father get along?"

"Superbly—probably because they're so different. Terry's no philosopher, he's a—a person of action. But he admired my father's books."

"Do you have any with you?"

"Yes, of course. Would you like to read one?"

"Oh, Stella, I would! It would make you closer if I could read something of your father's. I'm so glad you've come! Usually storms don't frighten—Illyria's stood through many a storm. But I'm afraid for Illyria now. The angels have gone, and there's nothing to keep the weather at bay."

"Hush, Miss Livvy, hush." Honoria's voice was calm and firm as a rock. "The storm done gone by. Hush now." She began to sing, softly, caressingly; her old voice was deep and smoky.

> "Dreamland opens here,
> Sweep the dream path clear.
> Listen, child, now listen well
> To what the tortoise may have to tell,
> To what the tortoise may have to tell."

I lay back, the listening child, against the pillows.

> "Dreamland opens here,
> Sweep the dream path clear.
> Listen, child, now listen awhile

> *To the song of the crocodile,*
> *To the song of the crocodile.*"

This low, slow lullaby belonged to Illyria, to palmettos and pelicans; it was totally unlike the nursery rhymes with which Nanny had sung me to sleep. But it, too, gave me a sense of pattern, a promise of order in the chaos of the unknown. And now the air was lighter. A soft breeze, rather than gusts of hot sulphur, came through the open windows.

> "*Dreamland opens here,*
> *Sweep the dream path clear.*
> *Listen, child, now close your eyes,*
> *In the canebrake the wild cat cries,*
> *In the canebrake the wild cat cries.*"

"You didn't shut the windows," Aunt Olivia said sleepily. "Why didn't we shut the windows?"

"Nothing bad going to come in," Honoria said. "Maybe something bad go out."

"What would keep the bad things from coming in?"

"Miss Stella," Honoria said.

Lying there in the big brass bed, half asleep, I wondered: what kind of responsibility is Honoria trying to put on me?

Aunt Olivia stirred comfortably in Honoria's strong arms. "My bones feel better. How lovely it is when they don't ache! Mado used to write in this room. It was her room, her special place where she could be private. Only the children were allowed in."

A last, distant growl of thunder rumbled on the horizon.

"Do you know anybody who can call up storms?" Aunt Olivia asked.

"Hush."

"Or quiet them down? To still a storm. That's better, I think."

"Hush."

I stopped listening. Despite the fact that Honoria seemed to be handing me a responsibility which I did not understand and certainly was unprepared to accept, the mere presence of the old colored woman in the rocker gave out a warm sense of strength and comfort.

I slept.

THREE

I

IN the morning I wakened to the plaintive mewling of sea gulls and the far more demanding mewing of the kitten who was announcing in my ear that it was time to rise. I untucked the mosquito netting to let him out; in the daylight I could see that in several places the netting was meticulously darned. "And small wonder," I remarked to the kitten, "with claws like yours around." The kitten looked at me with enigmatic, Oriental eyes. "You won't catch me without shoes today," I promised it, "even if my feet burn right off. Where do you suppose my shoes are, kitty? I must go look for them right after breakfast. Where's my husband, this morning, Minou? In darkest Africa? I wish he were here in darkest Illyria." Then I felt ashamed for having called Illyria dark. I yawned and stretched, pushed the mosquito netting aside, and went to the balcony.

The early-morning light scattered gold over sea and sand. The peaks of the waves glinted. There was more movement in the ocean than there had been the day before. The wind ruffled up white horses; the waves pranced into the beach, rearing up and back, then curving over in a concave arc of green, breaking, scattering foam. The panaches of the palms shook with royal dignity. The sun touched bits of shell on the beach which threw back sparkles of glittering light. A sea gull, stark white against the early blue of sky, flapped past my balcony. There was nothing dark about Illyria this morning, and despite the interrupted night I felt rested and refreshed: in the light of daytime reason I would find some simple explanation for my fears the night before—not the storm, there had been no terror in the storm—but my inordinate reaction to the old woman back in the jungle. If I believed in witches—but to believe in witches is superstition.

I turned back to the room where my light-dazzled eyes could see nothing but shadows. I closed my eyes, breathing quietly, resting, preparing myself—

I wanted to know more about Honoria from Mado's point of view. I sat on the edge of my bed and riffled carefully through the journals, pausing when I saw Honoria's name.

"I have been innocent where Honoria is concerned," I read, "and this is inexcusable. Innocence has no place in this evil world. When I was a child, it was one thing to be innocent. But now I am married to Theron, and I have a child of my own, and in me, now, innocence is in effect a form of sin. Theron should have someone beside him who was prepared for the world, not someone who all her life has been protected from it. He will not find my stupidity charming for long; it is his magnanimity which enables him to love me despite my ignorance not only of his country and his people, but of human nature. Naïveté is no quality to be desired in a wife. He will not want it in the mother of his children.

"I blame myself for my sense of shock, of outrage, at what has happened. Theron got so exhausted the first week the hospital was opened that it brought back his malaria, so off we went to Nyssa to stay with James and Xenia till he was better. The night we got back to Jefferson I knew that Honoria needed me, I felt her calling me, my skin tingled with the strength of her cry. It was too late to go to her, or even to send her a message. But in the morning I went. I thought we would never get there. When we finally arrived, I found Honoria's little maid hovering about, waiting for me. 'We knowed you'd come, Miss Mado, we just knowed you'd come.' I found Honoria half conscious, so badly had Broadley beaten her, not for anything she'd done, this time, but because a group of young blades had come out to the plantation and tried to get Honoria for themselves. They were—of course—drunk, and kept shouting: Why should old Claudius have all the fun with the beautiful African princess? So—typique—after he'd driven them away, and then proven to himself that Honoria is his possession (thank God he does not seem able to give her children), he beat her. I must get him to take Honoria away from Jefferson. Perhaps if he were to build her a small place by the ocean she would be safe there. So I must not antagonize him. I must not be innocent and outraged. Everything in me cries out against playing up to Broadley, smiling and laughing and being coquettish. But is this not what I must do? There is no longer any role for the innocent in this world."

I closed my eyes against Mado's and Honoria's pain. Was I, too, unpardonably innocent? Ron had accused me of being so. If I were innocent, was I then without a role to play in Illyria? I did not understand what Mado meant by this. I turned the pages of the journal until again I saw Honoria's name. "The trip up-river was woefully hot," Mado wrote, "and then there was the drive past the slave quarters to the plantation. I sensed a strange quiet as we started up the wide road between the live oaks, and then I heard a long-drawn-out animal scream. The coachman turned around in his seat and gave me a level look, but said nothing. I had automatically put my hands to my mouth as though to stifle a scream of my own. The scream came again, ending up with a horrible, frothy, bubbly sound, as though it were coming over blood. Probably it was. Everybody knows that Broadley beats his slaves, and nobody does anything. Honoria sees to it that the slaves get proper food— Broadley used to starve them as well as beat them. But if she tries to stop the beating, then she, too, gets beaten for her pains. I pray that Broadley will get Illyria built before he beats her to death. Why couldn't he have been satisfied with a simple cottage? But no, he must have this mad, magnificent monstrosity."

I let the journal drop onto my crumpled sheet. I felt sick. What kind of an insulated, nonexistent world had I grown up in? Why hadn't my father taught me about the real world? No, that's not fair. It is an enormous ocean that lies between Oxford and this strange jungle which must become my home.

Mado, too, had known nothing about slaves when she first came to Illyria, except those in history books, those of the ancient world, a world which need not touch us today. Did anybody question the right to own slaves in Greece or Rome? Not Plato. Not Aristotle. Were slaves beaten in ancient Greece? Probably. In any case, one does not have to be a slave to be beaten. I remembered my own sense of outrage when Cousin Octavian's groom beat a stable boy for no reason. Had I felt, then, rushing to the defense of that scrawny, sniveling child, the way Mado felt about Claudius Broadley?

"Oh, God," Mado wrote, "how can your world be so beautiful and so terrible? Why do we betray and destroy your creation?" And then, a few pages later, "Today before lunch Honoria offered to run the cards for me. I asked her how she had learned such a thing. She told me that it was on the ship on the long voyage to the States. Honoria had a small cabin for herself and her maid, but she could hear the cries and groans of the slaves in the belly of the ship. She knew that many of them were dying. She made friends with an old sailor with a gold ring in his nose and tattoos all over his body, and got him to send extra bread and water down to them, and old gunny sacks to use as blankets—it was stifling hot by day, freezing cold by night. The old man had a pack of cards, and he must have sensed Honoria's powers, because he taught her how to use them. Honoria did not understand why I got so upset, why I refused so violently to let her ask the cards about my future. Neither did I—though I am quite convinced that my guardian angel would disapprove most strongly of anybody, even somebody like Honoria, trying to manipulate the future. And isn't that what running the cards really is? It's more than just asking. The Greeks call it hubris, and it leads to disaster."

I did not want to think about running cards, or fortune tellers. I put the journals carefully back on my bed table, and dressed in the fashionable but cumbersome bathing outfit which was part of my trousseau: bloomers, skirts, stockings, shoes, buttons and more buttons—it hardly made swimming easy, and certainly seems laughable now. But I was very proud of it then, and felt wholly fascinating in it.

I descended the stairs, hearing soft clinking sounds from the kitchen and sniffing the fragrance of coffee as I walked softly through the empty living room. A shaft of sunlight struck the portrait of the two young girls, the two young musicians. I turned to look at another portrait, of a young man standing near a wintry tree, holding a book in his hands. He had dark hair and eyes and so he completely surprised me by reminding me painfully of my husband.

"Up early, Miss Stella? That's nice. Going for a swim? You'll enjoy that."

I turned to smile at Clive, in a rusty black alpaca jacket, an apron tied about his waist, polishing a crystal decanter.

He pointed to the portrait. "That's Miss Mado's father. Favors Mr. Terry, don't it? for all Mr. Terry's so fair. Mr. Hoadley's crazy mad to get it away from the beach. Also the picture of Miss Mado painted by Mr. Jean Dominique Augustin Ingres—" (How lovely, how gentle the names as he said them) "—which come with Miss Mado all the way crost the ocean. You seen it?"

"No. Where is it, Clive?"

"In the library. Maybe this morning you wants to wander round and look at things?"

"Yes, that's exactly what I want to do."

"It look zackly like Miss Mado, that picture. Even when she grew to be an old lady she still had that look, expecting, like watching a sunrise. Mr. Hoadley say the sea wind crack and kill the paint and the canvas. He want to take all the portraits away. Miss Olivia and Miss Des say it no better in town. Wind from the river come just as damp as wind from the sea. Miss Olivia clean the portraits every autumn and spring, the way Miss Mado show her. Miss Mado left the portraits to Miss Livvy and Miss Des, but then they is to go to you and Mr. Terry."

I looked at the portraits with a difference: the unexpected fact that they would one day belong to Terry and me, that we would look at them all the days of our lives, pulled me in closer to Illyria, made me more indubitably Mrs. Theron Renier.

Clive gave me his quiet smile. "You go on in the water, Miss Stella. Miss Livia and Miss Des just gone and they was hoping you'd be along."

The sun had not yet warmed the ramp from the drench of the storm, and the wood was cool through the thin soles of my bathing slippers. The dark leaves of the jungly undergrowth, stunted myrtles, palmettos, scrub oak, were clean and shiny. A dragonfly, a startling shimmer of blue, brushed by me. The sand at the foot of the ramp was firm and wet from the rain, and I hurried across the beach and into the shallow waves where the great-aunts were waiting. They greeted me affectionately. Aunt Olivia made no mention of the night before, so neither did I. Aunt Mary Desborough did not mention it, either; perhaps from her point of view storms were so commonplace at Illyria that they were not worth mentioning.

"The beach is glorious this summer," Aunt Olivia said. "When we walk out past the first file of breakers, there's a lovely slough, a deep one, over our heads. There hasn't been a slough like this since the year we all came to live in Illyria. The ocean floor shifts and changes all the time, and Hoadley says we're going to have to put in a proper bulkhead soon because the high tides are nibbling at our shoreline. Beyond the blessèd slough there's a sand bar, and then the ocean proper. You have to watch out for undercurrents there."

The shallow water was stinging, even through my bathing stockings; the waves were full of shells ground fine from the pounding of the night before. Then the sand sloped abruptly and I slid into cool, deep water, so that my searching feet found no bottom: this, then, was the slough. Beyond it the water was a lighter color where the sand bar rose, and waves were breaking as though on a separate beach. I rolled onto my face, blew bubbles, opened my eyes to the sting of salt water, took in an accidental mouthful, spat it out, rolled over onto my back and lay there, arms and legs stretched loosely, rocking in the swells as Aunt Olivia had rocked in Honoria's arms the night before.

(. . . As Terry had held me in his arms our last night together in Oxford. 'It is all right.' The sea brought me the echo of his loving, persuasive voice, 'Because I am you, and you are me, and we are one.'

My tears had been salt, salt as the water which slapped now gently against my face. 'Then how can we be torn apart?'

'Dear love, we aren't,' he had said. 'I take you with me, and me with you. Mica, mica, parva Stella, you knew when you married me that . . .'

I could not hear. The tears covered my face and I licked the brine from my lips. My nose was running and I fumbled under the pillow for Terry's handkerchief. But it was in the pocket of his nightshirt which lay in a crumpled heap on the floor.

He kissed my tear-blurred face. 'Wait for me in Illyria. Time is magic there, and before you know it I'll come for you. Illyria's a joyful place; there's a blessing on it, put there by Mado's angels. And, my sweet wife, there is a blessing on you, too.'

'Me? How?'

'Because you are my Star, my mica mica parva Stella. Because you'll be able to look on Illyria with fresh eyes, free from preconceptions. The way you look at me.')

"Stella," Aunt Mary Desborough splashed over to me, "is your ring tight enough? There isn't any chance of its slipping off, is there?"

I held up my hand, with the entwined golden serpents firmly binding my finger. "I think it's all right. The ring is quite tight. I'm sure it's safe."

Aunt Olivia put her hands up to her face, speaking through her fingers. "When Therro and Kitty were drowned—oh, God, Honoria and I went with Mado to identify the bodies. It was only the ring on Kitty's finger which made me sure—" Her voice was muffled with pain.

"Hush, Livvy," Aunt Mary Desborough said. "It doesn't

do any good to remember horrible things like that. It's over now."

"Things like that are never over," Aunt Olivia said.

I touched the ring again, and shivered, for the first time fully realizing that it had been worn before Terry put it on my finger when we were married. The ring not only symbolized the beginning of our marriage; it also contained the past.

I slid both my hands under the water.

Aunt Olivia paddled contentedly in the gentle wavelets of the slough which, in summer, never lost the healing heat of the sun, letting it ease her painful joints. Old Finbarr came loping across the beach, breasted the waves into the slough, and swam protectively beside her, holding his grizzled head up out of the water.

"Come with me, Stella," Aunt Mary Desborough said, and led me out of the slough, across the sand bar, and into the open sea. "But never without me, please." When Aunt Mary Desborough talked about the ocean there was an authority in her voice which it lacked at other times; the small down-scaling of self-pity disappeared. "The tide is coming in now, and if we swim directly opposite Illyria there's no undertow, but down by San Feliz there are eddies that have swept people out to sea. And always watch out for sharks. There haven't been many this summer, but you can't ever relax and forget about them. A steadily gliding triangular fin: that will be a shark. A fish that flashes is a dolphin and you need never worry then. When the dolphins are flying there won't be a shark around. Somehow dolphins and pelicans belong to Illyria, and sharks and buzzards to—" She caught her breath.

"To what?"

"To all the hate and anger left by the war, people wanting to eat each other like sharks. I understand wanting revenge; I suppose I want it myself. But not—not burning and hanging and lynching. Please God we will never see a lynching again."

I did not know what a lynching was. I did not understand her anguish. But she pushed it away, briskly. "Come, now, and I'll teach you to ride in on the breakers. I can't do it myself any more, too old, but I'll teach you how."

I could feel her approval, though she took care not to show it, as I learned to plunge at precisely the correct moment into a wave and ride with it into the sand bar. I laughed in exhilaration. I had never experienced anything as delightful as this. I mistimed a wave and was rolled over and over against ground shells and pebbles and sand, scrambled up and went rushing back to Aunt Mary Desborough to try again.

Then we heard Finbarr barking, and the old woman said, "That's enough for this morning, Stella. Time for breakfast."

I realized that I was ravenous.

The old aunts led me out of the ocean and to the right of the ramp down a tiny path, pressed in by Spanish Bayonettes, palmettos, and scrub myrtle, to the under-regions of the house. They explained that Illyria, like most houses of its period and place, was built up off the ground on columns of coquina.

"Coquina is ground shell that turns into a sort of natural cement," Aunt Olivia told me. "I suppose it grows the way coral does. Just think Stella, all those tiny shells you see in it have been there for hundreds and hundreds of years, just waiting to be the foundation for Illyria. Building a house up this way keeps it much drier; things don't mold as quickly. And it's cooler."

"And snakes, Livvy," Aunt Mary Desborough said. "Building a house up off the ground helps keep the snakes out."

"Don't wander around in the undergrowth," Aunt Olivia warned. "Clive keeps it as cleared as he can, but we do see an occasional snake. Most of them are harmless, but we saw a coral snake this spring, and Clive heard a rattler last week. And the twins—you'll meet them—say there are some of the stinging jellyfish coming in with the high tides. When Mark brought his boat to the inlet—our brother Mark, our younger brother, Hoadley's father—and the Captain, the twins' father—"

"Olivia." Aunt Mary Desborough used her warning voice.

"I'm just telling her about the poisonous jellyfish."

"Don't frighten her! We've lived in Illyria for decades and we've never been bitten by anything worse than a red bug."

"We're still not very civilized, for all Hoadley's got his yacht basin down below San Feliz. Sounds very grand for what's only a lagoon with an arm that lets out into the sea. But all kinds of people from Jefferson seem to be bringing boats in this summer. I think Hoadley's got something up his sleeve."

"The idea of a yacht basin keeps Irene happy," Aunt Mary Desborough said. "Let's not ask questions."

The areas of under-Illyria between the white coquina columns were filled in with wooden latticework which had once been painted dark red but which now showed mostly sea-bleached silvery wood. Aunt Mary Desborough unhooked a latticework gate and we went into the twilight where she fumbled around until she found a hanging lamp, which she lit. The flame flared high, and the lamp swung, making great, grotesque shadows. Finbarr rushed into the darkness under the house and disappeared. The old lady turned the lamp down. In its flickering light, shadows moved back and forth over a series of wooden stalls.

"Dressing rooms," Aunt Mary Desborough said. "Good, Honoria's already given you this one and put towels and dry clothes out for you. This is your very own cabin now, Stella, right by Livia's and mine. You can make you a willow cabin at our gate and call upon your soul within the house—"

"Viola. *Twelfth Night*. A somewhat garbled version," Aunt Olivia said. "Point for me."

"If you missed something as obvious as that, you *would* have to worry about losing your mind."

"I'm glad *you* were able to remember it."

"What else is under here?" I asked.

"Lots of things," Aunt Olivia said. "Honoria keeps her preserves here. She puts all kinds of things up in jars, vegetables and fruit and meat and fish. And Clive keeps his gardening tools—" Aunt Olivia put her hand up to her mouth to try to contain her laughter.

"What's the joke, Aunt Olivia?"

"Olivia!" Aunt Mary Desborough said. "Don't you dare."

"But, Des, it was so funny! Clive heard somewhere that urine is good to use as fertilizer on certain kinds of plants in the spring, so he began to save his in Honoria's empty preserving jars, and Irene—"

"Olivia!"

At that moment Finbarr came yelping out of the shadows and pressed, quivering, against Aunt Olivia, who bent down to fondle him. "What were you hunting, Finny? And did it scare you?"

Finbarr whined, leaning with all his bony weight against the old lady.

"Come on, old Finny, you're all sandy. You can get under the pump with me."

"Olivia, that's not decent!"

"Egad, you have a filthy mind. At your age! Come, Finbarr."

Glowering at each other, forgetting me, the great-aunts disappeared into two stalls where pumps raised up on wooden standards made primitive showers. Aunt Olivia, recalling first, peered over the wooden barrier. "We won't be long, Stella. And I'm sure you dress more quickly than we do." The smell of sulphur was strong. Aunt Olivia called, "When you want to wash your hair, Honoria has a pump on the back veranda with rain water." She began to sing,

> *"Dead men's hair*
> *And dead men's bones*
> *Have no care*
> *For sticks nor stones.*
> *Buzzards pick*
> *Eye sockets bare*
> *Dead men never*
> *Need to care."*

"Olivia! Stop that awful song!"

> *"Dead men make*
> *No never-mind,*
> *Eat no cake*
> *Nor melon rind,*
> *Sing no songs,*
> *Feel no ache,*
> *Have no heavy*
> *Heart to break."*

Aunt Olivia's normal speaking voice was clear and precise despite its gentle Southern rhythm, but now she was singing with a nasal drawl, more marked than Aunt Irene's.

"Olivia! Stop it!"

"Don't you throw water at me. You'll get my hair wet."

"Then stop it! You know I hate that song."

"Scares you, doesn't it?"

"Be quiet."

"Timor mortis conturbat te."

"Et tu, Olivia?"

They had been shouting over the sound of splashing water. Now they stopped and came out, not even seeing me. I went into the stall Aunt Olivia had used and began to pump sulphur water over myself, wondering why it was preferable to leaving on salt water. There was silence under Illyria except for the sound of splashing. I didn't stay under the pump long. It was going to take time before I was used to the smell, and I didn't feel washed. I dressed quickly and was ready before the old ladies, so I went out into the morning sunshine to wait for them, blinking at the brightness. Despite the flickering lamp it had been dark as Hades under Illyria.

By the time we got to the dining room I was starved. Clive seated the old ladies, asked me, "Coffee or tea, Miss Stella?"

"Coffee in the morning, please. Terry converted me."

On the sideboard was a pitcher of orange juice, moisture from the cool liquid condensing in delicate drops. There were covered silver dishes of bacon and eggs, hominy, which I had never tasted before—I had tried unsuccessfully in Oxford to find its equivalent to please Terry—fried green tomatoes. I helped myself liberally.

Finbarr whined and scratched at the screen door and Clive let him in. "How old is Finbarr?" I asked Aunt Olivia.

"Ancient. He's even older by dog standards than I am by people, aren't you, Finny? According to my calculations he's a hundred and thirty-seven years old. That's how old Ishmael was when he gave up the ghost and was gathered unto his people."

Aunt Mary Desborough looked up from her eggs. "And they dwelt from Havilah unto Shur, that is before Egypt. Genesis, 25. Point for me."

"Oh, daz it, Des, I really wasn't playing then, and anyhow it's a Shakespeare day."

"That isn't fair."

"It is, too. We've already started with Shakespeare."

I suggested, "Why don't we just play quotations from anybody today so it'll be easier for me?"

"You mean you want to play with us?" Aunt Mary Desborough asked.

"Of course I do. Do you mind? My father would have loved this game."

Aunt Olivia's face was radiant. "Of course she wants to play with us; didn't I tell you she was one of us? Of course we'll play Free Quotations today. Oh, Stella, what fun!"

"Very well, then. We'll play Free today. But I declare Bible for tomorrow."

"You can't declare a day ahead. It's against the rules."

Before I could intervene again a tolerant voice came from the landing. "Aunties! Aunties!" and Aunt Irene, dressed in a fashionable skirt and blouse which emphasized the frumpiness of the old aunts' clothes, came downstairs. However, Aunt Irene gave no impression of youth as she sauntered towards us; I felt a far greater chronological gap between us than I did between Aunt Olivia and me.

"Aren't you going swimming?" Aunt Mary Desborough asked.

"Not this morning, Auntie."

"Why not?"

"I just don't feel like it."

"But it's a perfect day for a swim and you always take a dip before breakfast."

"Not today, Auntie."

"The custom of women is upon her," Aunt Olivia said. "And he searched, but found not the images. And Jacob was wroth."

"Olivia!" Aunt Mary Desborough reproved.

"It's perfectly all right," Aunt Olivia said airily. "It's in the Bible, and you aren't implying there's anything improper in the Bible, are you?"

"You are using the Bible to mention things which ought not to be mentioned."

"If the Bible can mention them, why can't I? Anyhow, point for me."

"It is not. I know perfectly well where in the Bible it is. Genesis. All that nasty bit about Jacob and everybody trying to outsmart everybody else. It's immoral."

"Who said the Bible's supposed to be moral? History isn't moral. It's—"

"Please," Aunt Irene cut in. "Can't we have one day without these eternal bickering games? Let's give Stella a chance to get her bearings."

I was eating hominy and bacon gravy with gusto. Aunt Irene helped herself to a single rasher of bacon, a scant spoonful of eggs, carried them back to the table and said, "Oh. Willy and Harry." Her voice betrayed mild annoyance. "What do you want?" She put down her plate and went through the front room to the screen door. There stood the two little old men I had met the night before, gnome-like and rosy-cheeked, nodding and smiling. "What is it, boys?"

They mumbled something of which I could hear only "yes'm," and "please'm," bobbing and giggling through their words.

Aunt Irene's voice, unlike the gentle murmurs of the old men, carried clearly. "Go round to the kitchen and Honoria and Clive will give you breakfast. Oh, boys, wait a minute! Come here." She opened the door wide and they stepped into the living room, bowing apologetically as they crossed the threshold and followed Aunt Irene to the dining room.

"Stella, these are, uh, Willy and Harry. Boys, this is the new Mrs. Theron Renier. Now, boys, let's show her something. What is—oh, say, one thousand four hundred and ninety-two times seven hundred and thirty-three?"

Willy and Harry looked ecstatically at the ceiling as though they were reading the answer. Then, almost in unison, Harry a fraction of a beat behind Willy, they chorused, "One million ninety-three thousand six hundred and thirty-six."

"Good boys! At least I suppose it's right. . . . Isn't that cute, Stella, hon?" She beamed. "Run round to the back now and get some breakfast, and if you behave nicely Honoria might give you something to take home."

The white-haired gnomes bobbed and smiled and nodded, peering at me with their bright little eyes. I felt that they were memorizing me, and corroborating for themselves the final, unalterable judgment they had made the night before.

Aunt Irene clapped her hands. "Willy! Harry!" They scuttled off. "Honestly, Stella, it's amazing the way those idiots can do almost anything with numbers as long as it's complicated, but they can't make change to buy an egg."

Aunt Olivia said, "I wish you wouldn't call Willy and Harry idiots."

"They are idiots." Aunt Irene sat down at her place, lifted her coffee cup to her lips, and set it down in distaste. She rang a small silver hand bell. "Of course they're quite harmless." She spoke with the same casualness with which she had referred to the great-aunts as senile. "People think the twins ought to be put away, but as long as they don't cause any trouble Hoadley doesn't see any reason they shouldn't go on living in their little cottage. We certainly couldn't have them here. But I suppose we have to be responsible for them simply because their father worked for the family. Mado was like a mother to them—frankly, I think she overdid it, and they thought she really was their mother. Of course nobody expected them to live this long, idiots usually die young—"

"Ma'am?" Clive stood in the kitchen doorway.

"Oh, Clive. Willy and Harry are here and want food. And my coffee's cold. Please take it away and bring me a fresh cup and saucer. And Clive—"

"Ma'am?"

"Did my paper come?"

"Yes'm, Miss Irene. I'll fetch it." He took her cup and returned to the kitchen.

"Willy and Harry must be pushing sixty. They'd know to the minute, of course. When we were little, Hoadley's father had a lovely yacht and Willy's and Harry's father was captain. Of course he was only a cracker from back in the scrub, but he was a good sailor and Hoadley's father insisted on calling him Captain, giving him biggety ideas. In the summer Cousin Mark used to come down from Charleston and anchor in the inlet, where the yacht basin is now—"

"We've already told her," Aunt Mary Desborough said.

"Of course, Auntie. I should have realized. You would. Anyhow, Stella, we young people used to have glorious house-boat parties. They were all the rage, and an invitation to Cousin Mark's yacht meant that you'd really been accepted. He was Cousin Mark to me, that is. Hoadley and I are cousins of a sort. Third cousins twice removed, I think it is. I had to have it all figured out for the Huguenot Society and the Colonial Dames. Even after we all grew up, the twins used to spend hours playing ball or catching butterflies on the beach, just like children, but they were good clammers and fishermen, and they used to wash the decks and help with the painting, so Cousin Mark encouraged them. Oh, thank you, Clive. Willy and Harry not bothering you?"

"No'm." He laid a folded paper by Aunt Irene, then went to the sideboard to pour her fresh coffee.

Aunt Irene opened the paper, turned to an inside page and read quickly, eagerly. "Oh, dear. The stars are bad for Capricorn this month. No wonder I woke up with a headache. I get this paper from Atlanta; it's only a few days late, and they do the stars for the whole month. The Jefferson paper here yet, Clive?"

"Not yet, Miss Irene."

"Takes almost as long for the paper to get to San Feliz from Jefferson as it does my paper from Atlanta. Oh, well, the news is all bad anyhow. When I'm at the beach I think I'm due a little peace. All I really want to see the Jefferson paper for is the obituaries, anyhow. Seems to me everybody I know is dead or dying."

"Still eating, my dears?" It was Uncle Hoadley.

"Where have you been, Hoadley?" Aunt Irene demanded. "You're late."

"There was some work I had to do before breakfast. I wish I could leave problems in town for the weekend, but they follow me here."

"You bring them," Aunt Mary Desborough said. "And you shouldn't. Can't you leave all the shooting and looting and hate behind you for a few days? They say old Judge Larkin— not one of our Larkins, of course, he was from Texas—was shot last week in front of the courthouse. Oh, Hoadley, it isn't safe anywhere any more."

"Creation groans," Uncle Hoadley said, smiling tiredly.

"It's like the fall of the Roman Empire. Hoadley, you look so exhausted, can't you get some rest?"

"That's why I'm here, Auntie. Honoria's cooking and your loving are an ever present help in time of trouble."

"Remember one thing, Hoadley," Aunt Olivia said. "You can't stop the Roman Empire from falling all by yourself."

"I'm really not trying to, Auntie."

"I think, Hoadley, the trouble is that you are."

2

AFTER breakfast the old great-aunts retired to the small writing room which opened off the south side of the living room. Aunt Irene went upstairs to put a cool cloth on her forehead. Uncle Hoadley inconspicuously removed himself. I went out to the kitchen to get permission to explore the house before going up the beach to look for my shoes. Permission from Honoria and Clive? Yes: after all, it was Honoria's house.

But when I got out to the kitchen Willy and Harry and Dr. Ron James sat at the kitchen table eating corn bread and syrup. All three rose as I entered, and Willy handed me something wrapped in an old paisley scarf. I opened it: there were the shoes and stockings I had lost the night before.

"Thank you, Willy! I was going to have to go look for them this morning. Did I drop them when I was with you?"

"No, no." Willy shook his head. "Bad to let Zenumins get. Bad."

"Hurt, hurt," Harry warned.

Willy put his arms around me, kissing me gently on the cheek. He smelled of tobacco and fish and the oil used for the insect repellent; it was not an unpleasant smell. "We like you."

Harry was immediately behind him. "Want to kiss the pretty lady, too."

"Leave her alone." Ron's voice startled me with its Englishness.

"No, it's all right, we're friends. I met them last night on the beach." I turned my cheek to Harry. The twins were dressed this morning in faded blue trousers and what had once been red and white checked shirts, and could be told apart by their neckerchiefs, Willy's blue, Harry's red.

"Willy," Ron said, "if I have five apples to sell at five cents each, and you buy two, how much do you pay me?" Willy bowed his head, unable to face disappointing Ron. "Don't know. Too hard."

"Can't afford apples nohow," Harry said.

"Maybe if it was oranges?" Ron suggested.

Willy shook his head. "Still too hard. Oranges, grapefruit, kumquat, still too hard, too hard. Can't do apples."

I smiled, remembering when I was a small girl and my father was trying to teach me arithmetic. We, too, had had our problems with apples, when he tried to teach me that nothing times something equals nothing: a simple mathematical fact, but totally incomprehensible to me. $0 \times 3 = 0$. It was as impossible to me as five apples at five cents each to Willy and Harry. I actually succeeded in annoying my father—which wasn't easy—with my obtuseness.

'$0 \times 3 = 0$ is a fact,' he said.

'But, Father! Take three apples. I can see that if you have no apples, and you multiply them by three, you still have no apples. But if you already have three apples, and you multiply them by nothing, that doesn't make them go away, does it?' My father told me rather brusquely that he was trying to teach me mathematics and not metaphysics. 'But, Father, if it's true in metaphysics, it has to be true in mathematics, doesn't it?'

'I never said it was true in metaphysics.'

'But if you *have* three apples—'

'Stella, for the time being you will have to accept that $0 \times 3 = 0$. The entire multiplication table is an agreed-upon fiction to make life more convenient, and you will have to bear with it.'

Odd: I couldn't. I never had any trouble with complicated equations; for instance, when we were studying astronomy, my father taught me to determine the distance between the earth and the moon by observing the size of the earth's shadow on the moon during a lunar eclipse, this being the method first suggested by Aristarchus of Samos around 250 B.C., and this had not confused me in the least. Perhaps the difference between my understanding of mathematics and the twins' was one of degree, rather than kind.

It took me a great deal of pain and fear before I learned that my father was right. After a while he stopped trying to make me understand that 0×3 does indeed equal 0, because— I'm sure—he knew that only experience can teach the truth of that particular mathematical fact. It's not a pleasant rule, but it has to be accepted. You can have something—even if it's only three apples—and if you multiply them by nothing, then you don't have them any more. But this was something I still had to learn as I sat in the dappled sunlight in Honoria's big kitchen on my first day in Illyria.

As though to make up for failing us over the price of apples, Willy pushed back from his chair, smiling and beckoning. Harry followed him, and they went out onto the kitchen porch, bobbing, calling, "Come, pretty lady, come. Come, docdoc."

Out on the veranda hung a straw basket. "Sunflower seeds for the birds," Ron said, "and for—wait."

Willy reached into the basket and came out with a little green wriggly lizard which he held on the gently curled palm of his hand. The lizard, interrupted from its morning nap, puffed up in fear like a little balloon, and Willy began to stroke it with a gentle finger, and I could see the little creature calming down, returning to its normal size. When it was completely relaxed and comfortable, lying in Willy's steady hand, it began to roll its eyes.

"Loves us! Loves us!" Willy cried joyfully.

Ron said, "I read once in a scientific textbook that when a lizard wants to express affection it rolls its eyes. But I've never seen it happen except with Willy and Harry."

Willy held his hand towards me. "Pretty lady."

This was both gift and test: I held out my hand, and the lizard was slid onto my palm. For a moment it puffed up; then, as I took my finger and stroked it as Willy had done, it shrank again. Its tiny claws tickled my palm as it wriggled slightly. It felt cool, the way jade does, no matter what the weather. I looked down on the little thing, tender green with jeweled eyes, beautiful and innocent, and laughed slightly with the pleasure of this new experience. "Oh, thank you, Willy!" I returned the delicate little creature. Willy slid it back into the hanging basket and beckoned again, tiptoeing around the veranda to a great brass pot which contained a geranium plant, the most enormous and luxuriant geranium plant I have ever seen. Curled up around the plant was a little green snake.

"Shh!" Willy held one finger to his lips. "Sleeping."

"Nice dreams," Harry whispered, "oh, pretty, pretty."

Ron spoke reassuringly to me. "It's just a garden snake, Mrs. Renier, and the geranium pot is its favorite bed. And of course, where there are snakes there's never any problem with rats."

The little snake curled around the plant reminded me of the snakes on my ring. The twins either caught my thought or had it, too. Willy put out an exploratory finger to touch the ring. Then he smiled up at me. "Love."

Harry, too, touched the ring. "Strong."

"Not soft," Willy said. "Stern. Just. Always." He turned away, skipping across the worn boards of the veranda. "Hungry!"

Harry clapped his hands. "Hungry!"

I followed them back to the kitchen.

Harry sang in his rusty voice, "Oranges and lemons, say the bells of St. Clement's. Honoria, ma'am, please—" He held out his plate. "A little corn bread to finish my syrup—"

Willy held out his plate. "A little syrup to finish my corn bread. . . . When will you pay me, say the bells of Old Bailey?"

Harry, wiping corn bread and syrup around on his plate, said, "When I grow rich, say the bells of Shoreditch."

And Willy, fork to his mouth, "Here comes a candle to light you to bed. Here comes a chopper to chop off your head."

Harry spoke through a mouthful. "Glad the pretty lady's come. Stop the chopper."

"Glad, glad," Willy said. He reached his hand towards mine and gently touched my ring. "Good lady."

I took my shoes and stockings up to my room and put them away, wondering where the twins had found them.

I stood out on the back veranda. A redbird sat in the chinaberry tree and screamed at me. Minou, the kitten, came pouncing around the corner and spat at the redbird, who flew off. I started down the back steps and Minou twined himself around my ankles, then swished down the steps, tail erect and quivering, looking back over his shoulder as much as to say, "Come along, I have something to show you." I followed him down the path of old, pale-pink bricks set in a zigzag pattern. At the foot of the kitchen garden was a windbreak of bamboo, and just in front of this was an ancient fig tree, old and gnarled, many of its branches bare of leaves. One branch alone was fresh and green and heavy with fruit. Minou sat down under it, curled his tail about himself, and began washing his face.

The sun beat down on my head. I turned back to the house and exploration. Throughout Illyria was the smell of sea, of mustiness, almost a fungoid smell. The rolling of the breakers surrounded the walls of Illyria, so that it was as though I were walking within an enormous conch shell, winding my way from chamber to chamber.

And birds: sea gulls screamed, and again I heard the mockingbird's pure and underisive song; surrounding it was a constant chittering of birds I could not identify. The wind rattled in the palms. Loose shutters clattered.

Downstairs, the main body of Illyria consisted of the two big rooms, living and dining; adjoining these were the small writing room and Aunt Olivia's room—I peeped in the half-open door to see an enormous mahogany four-poster bed with dotted-Swiss summer curtains. There was a massive mahogany bureau and a highboy even larger and in poorer repair than the one in my room; a large mahogany rocking chair; a dressing table; a wardrobe with a speckled mirror. Everything was massive, dark, too heavy for the tiny, delicate old lady who would be lost in that huge bed. On the walls were seascapes of storms, dark still-lifes. I moved on to look in the other major ground-floor room, the library, a square room, the walls covered with books, books piled on tables, on the floor: I choked over the smell of leather mold and paper dust. A portrait hung over the mantelpiece, a young, brown-haired woman, elegantly dressed.

It must be the portrait of Mado which Clive had told me about, Mado holding a flute so that it did not quite touch her lips, lips puckered slightly as though for a kiss, rather than as though she were about to play. The eyes were blue, a darker blue than Aunt Olivia's—they were, in fact, very much the same color as mine. And yes, they did look expectant, as though she were watching a sunrise.

"Oh, you're lovely," I said to her, "and someone should take care of these books or they'll all fall apart." I sneezed.

Rubbing my nose, I leaned against a section of bookcase and was startled to have it swivel around under my weight to reveal a large, beautifully proportioned ballroom. Spider webs threaded delicately through the prisms of the chandelier and bound a few rickety gilt chairs against the wall. Long windows, looking out to sea, led onto a kind of promenade. I pushed at one of the windows, but damp had stuck them tight. The promenade, I realized, was where Uncle Hoadley had been pacing the night before.

I moved through the ballroom and out the far door, climbed a rush-carpeted staircase, and went down a long hall with rooms on either side. Most of the rooms were at least sparsely furnished; some had matting on the floors, others threadbare Persian or Chinese rugs. The walls all had paintings, seascapes, still-lifes, a series of faded prints of native flowers, or at least I assumed them to be native; and everywhere were portraits, portraits looking at me with following eyes, accusing, wistful, occasionally sinister, but usually welcoming eyes: hello, newest Mrs. Theron Renier, wearer of the ring, we are your family, you belong to us.

And you to me, I extended my welcome in return. One day you will hang on our walls, Terry's and mine, and I will say to the children, 'This is your Aunt Olivia. This is your cousin James.'

Terry had promised me that Illyria was a joyful house. I stood still, sniffing, sensing. It was, I thought, a waiting house. There was a feeling of expectancy about the rooms. There was, I thought suddenly, a demand: a demand of me.

I did not want it.

I turned away. Terry had talked to me about the comfortable pleasure of sitting in the kitchen with Honoria and Clive, drinking milk and eating cookies, and then, when he was older, tea or coffee. That's what I would do, I decided, needing comfortableness; I would go find Honoria and Clive.

It took me a few minutes to realize that I was lost. I had run down a flight of stairs, thinking to find the kitchen, but the rooms it led to made a separate wing to the south of the main house. I found another flight of stairs; this led me to what I took to be the north wing, mostly bedrooms with tables and chests which looked as though they had been brought from China, some definitely Chinese vases, and then a glass case full of porcelain horses which I was sure must be infinitely valuable. I went on up the stairs to the third floor, the floor I shared with Honoria and Clive. I was, perhaps, not far from my own bedroom, but the wings of the house did not seem to connect up on the third floor, and I could see no way to get from this cul-de-sac to the part of the house with which I was familiar. There was only an iron ladder leading to a skylight almost obscured by cobwebs.

I was not quite frightened. If I did not feel the joy which my husband had led me to expect in Illyria, at least I felt no threat, no evil, only the waiting, the expectancy. I opened a door with a white china handle.

But here was a room which was used. The walls were covered with maps in which red- and green-flagged pins were stuck. A large table in the center of the room served as desk and was piled with papers. Spread out on the desk was some kind of plan.

This was a War Room. I had a sudden anxiety that someone would come in and see me where I had no business to be. The War Room did not want me. I was an intruder. I backed out, running away before I was caught.

I ran down the stairs, pushed open the door on the next floor which would be directly beneath the War Room, ran through it—a pretty and peaceful bedroom with French furniture—found a flight of stairs, ran down them and half fell into the library, knocking over a pile of books in a cloud of dust.

There was nobody in the kitchen.

Only the heat, filtering through the shutters, moving sluggishly in the breeze.

I wanted Honoria and Clive.

I ran upstairs, the familiar stairs to the third floor, past my room, knocking at closed doors and opening them to find first a bedroom; then a big box room—there were my emptied trunks; another bedroom; and finally Honoria and Clive.

They were standing facing each other across an old iron bedstead with sagging springs. I was embarrassed and apologetic over having blundered in on them this way.

But they welcomed me, turning from each other to the door and saying, "Come in, Miss Stella."

I entered, awkwardly. Theirs was a big and airy room, sparsely furnished but full of wind and light. Besides the bed there were two old and comfortable but extremely shabby chairs, evidently retired from the main house, one on either side of a rosewood table. In one corner, above a large chest of drawers, was a mirror framed in seashells.

Clive looked at it affectionately. "Jimmy made that for us one Christmas—with a lot of help from Therro, of course."

> *(Clive and Honoria, Honoria and Clive,*
> *Keep Illyria's light alive.*
> *They had a son whose name was Jim—)*

"Your son."

Clive said, very quietly, "Yes. Jimmy was born here at Illyria."

Beneath the mirror was a framed daguerreotype, browned and speckled with age and sea damp, a picture of seven boys, ranging in age from fifteen or sixteen down to a toddler, a little black boy with great innocent eyes and a winsome, wistful smile, sitting on the lap of the eldest boy, the boy I recognized as Therro, blond and stocky and cocksure; and a baby, a tiny black button, held by a tall, thin boy I was sure was Uncle Hoadley.

"That was the children the way we was then," Clive said, "Therro, Mr. Hoadley, the twins, Jamie, Jimmy, and Honor."

"Jamie and Honor?" I asked.

Honoria answered with a quiet and stark acceptance I did not understand. "Jamie was Miss Mado's youngest; Honor, Clive's and my baby. They died of scarlet fever that next spring after the picture was taken. All the children took it; the others pull through, with long nursing. It were a killing fever that year. It be good we have the picture. Miss Mado had it made for us."

It was a charming picture; all the children were handsome and appealing, with the fey exception of the twins, already their full size, already gnomish, shorter than Therro and Uncle Hoadley. Odd: I thought of my husband's father as Therro; but

Uncle Hoadley, even as a slight, rather melancholy-looking young boy, I still thought of as Uncle Hoadley. Jimmy was the kind of wide-eyed, wistful child people would immediately want to pick up and cuddle; it was difficult for me to imagine him a grown man, the father of Dr. Ron James.

Holding the picture, I said, "Jimmy—he's sitting on Therro's lap?"

"Yes, Miss Stella," Clive answered. "Mr. Therro's shadow, we called him. Therro was very patient with Jimmy. He was good with the twins, too. They was about his age, but acted more like Jimmy, and Therro would spend hours with them, teaching them to swim, going crabbing or digging for clams." He spoke slowly, carefully. It seemed as though he were deliberately trying to find kind things to say about my husband's father. "Or donax; you ever had donax soup, Miss Stella?"

"No. What's donax?"

"Next time you walk on the beach, look for little bubbles in the sand; that mean donax, and you can just dig with your hand down in the sand and pick them up, little shellfish no bigger than your fingernail, all pinks and blues and lavenders. Honoria, you make Miss Stella some donax soup soon, hear?"

"I'll do that," Honoria said. But they were not thinking about donax.

"Jimmy," I said again, then stopped.

"James Theron James," Clive said. He paused; then, "You see, Miss Stella, slaves didn't have no names, excepting what their masters give them."

"No names? No names of their own?"

"Like a horse or a dog, Miss Stella." He was stating a fact. "But that's not the way it was at Nyssa, and I was born at Nyssa. I always knowed who I am. I grew up always knowing Mr. James and Mr. Theron. When a slave was freed by his master—"

"If," Honoria said. "Not many were."

"—he had to have a name, and often he would take the name of the man who freed him. Sometimes out of honor, sometimes because it was easiest. When my mother had me baptized she give me the name of James, Clive James, after Mr. James, and I always been proud to bear it, and give it to my sons. Mr. James the best man I ever knowed, Mr. James and Mr. Theron, and the best friends to me, and to each other. Renier men understand friendship."

"Or used to," Honoria said.

Clive turned to her. "Mr. Hoadley love Mr. Therro. That a fact."

I asked, "And Jimmy and Therro were friends?"

Clive said slowly, "Our Jimmy was many years younger than Mr. Therro and Mr. Hoadley. It all right when they still boys, but when they grew to be young men they moved into different worlds."

"Did they?" Honoria asked. Her voice was deep, harsh. She looked at Clive as she had been looking at him when I came into the room.

"In the nature of things," Clive said gently.

Honoria was not gentle. "The black world and the white world. But there is a shadow world that overlaps."

In Honoria, who had never been a slave, I sensed a smoldering anger.

To try to ease the tension I said, "I met Jimmy's wife last night."

It was as though my innocent statement had turned me into Medusa and Clive and Honoria to stone. For a long, frightened moment—I had no idea what I had said or done—I thought they would never move or speak to me again.

Then Clive sat down on the edge of the bed, the creak of rusty springs loud as thunder in the silence, took a Bible from the bed table, and turned it, turned it in his dark fingers, as though seeking strength.

Honoria rose. She towered over me; she seemed to have grown taller, as she had with Uncle Hoadley on the veranda. "Where you hear about Jimmy and Belle Zenumin?"

"I didn't! I met Belle last night when I went for my walk up the beach."

"What she say?"

"I don't—she was very kind to me, very friendly—"

"Where she take you?"

I looked from Honoria's stern face to Clive, still turning the Bible in his hands. He saw my consternation. "Honoria. Be gentle with Miss Stella. She don't know."

Honoria repeated her question, but her voice was less guttural and strange. "Where she take you?"

I answered reluctantly, "We went back behind the dunes to the creek."

"Who was there?"

"Belle's grandmother. She—oh, Honoria, she frightened me."

"Miss Stella. When you went on your walk last night—tell me: tell me everybody you see."

"Well, I saw—I saw Ron, first. And then I walked on farther, and I saw the twins. And then Belle and her grandmother. Everything was all right except the Granddam and I don't know why she frightened me so, she just—" I wanted Honoria to reassure me, to comfort me as she had comforted Aunt Olivia during the storm the night before.

But she turned to Clive. "It is the Rule of Three. Ron. The twins. The Zenumin. One is not chance, two is not coincidence, but three mean—" She sat down, withdrawing herself, holding her arms about herself and rocking slightly back and forth. Again she spoke only to Clive. "I told you what I saw. I told you. It will happen again. We cannot prevent it. And I am too old now, I cannot carry enough pain, it will be unbearable—"

"Honoria." Clive put the Bible back down on the table. "Miss Stella, it is not good that you should go near the Zenumin."

"God," Honoria said. "Oh, my Lord."

I could not reach out to touch Honoria. She had gone to some cold, dark place beyond human comfort. Clive was not offering her comfort. He was, in a strange sense, giving judgment.

Honoria rose, ponderously. For a moment she stood, silent, motionless, while strength and dignity returned to her. "Better go downstairs now, Miss Stella." I was not being dismissed because of what I had said or done: I did not know what it was only that it had brought an agony almost too great to be borne.

I followed them down to the kitchen, feeling shaky, and strangely chilled.

The kitchen was empty. The old enamel coffee pot was still on the back of the stove, and Honoria poured me a cup of the cold and muddy brew, then went to the old stone sink and began washing rice in a colander. Clive sat down across from me at the table and continued with his work of polishing silver. "Sulphur water blacken the silver. Have to keep at it every day. Ain't never done."

The outer door slammed, and Ron came into the kitchen. He spoke to me courteously, and asked if I had been enjoying the morning.

"Yes. Thank you." I looked round the big kitchen. The back veranda deflected some of the fierceness of the sun's rage, and light shifted through the vines in shifting, dappled patterns on the worn floor. The wooden shutters let in whisperings of breeze. Finbarr lay snoring lightly under the large black range, which was used only in winter. "I've been exploring the house," I said, and waited.

There was a small pause. Then Honoria spoke calmly and without apology, "Most of the house excepting the main building is pretty dusty."

I gazed at the unappetizing dregs in my coffee cup, asking after the fact, "Is there any place I oughtn't to go?"

Ron James gave a small smile. "Like Bluebeard's wife? Most Southern families—"

"Most families," Honoria amended.

"—have skeletons in cupboards."

The doctor's smile had been turned inwards, not towards anybody, but I directed my smile straight to him. "And a closet full of Bluebeard's dead wives?"

"You should have asked your husband that, not me."

"Thee-*ron*." Honoria swung round from the stove. "You go anywhere you like, Miss Stella. We even got a secret room in Illyria if you can find it. Mr. Claudius Broadley thought he might have to hide me out. Don't you pay no mind to Ronnie's humor. It's ugly, ugly."

"Somebody threw a flaming brand at the twins' house last night, Grandmother. They were struggling to put it out when the storm broke and doused it for them before any real damage was done."

"Why the twins?"

"Why anybody?" Ron countered.

"Was it because of you?" Honoria asked him.

"Who knows? The back stoop was burned off, but that was all. This time." He turned to leave.

Clive asked, "Where you going, son?"

"There's fever in one of the clearings back in the scrub. They asked me to come."

"What kind of fever?"

"Probably typhoid. Don't worry, Grandfather, I won't bring anything back to Illyria."

"When you be home?"

"By this evening."

When he had gone I said, "Honoria, when I was in the library I leaned against some books and they moved—"

"Yes. They be a revolving door. Lead into the dancing room."

"I went in. It's a lovely room."

"Don't know what Mr. Claudius Broadley had in mind when he build him a room like that. But we used to have dances there after the war. Not balls, like in Jefferson, but Virginia reels, and all the young people laughing, and everybody able to forget, for a while. Miss Mado, she dance like a butterfly even when she an old lady. They's been some happy times in Illyria. Miss Stella, your great-aunts was asking for you. They in the writing room."

3

I soon learned that writing letters was more than an occupation with Aunt Des; it was a vocation; it held the family together. She wove the webs of her letters and patiently threw them to the cousins in Charleston, the cousins in Winchester, the cousins in Raleigh. With Aunt Olivia it was more haphazard. She wrote to whom she chose, when and if she chose, sometimes leaving a gap of years and then picking up the correspondence as though only a few days had gone by. I stood, now, in the doorway to the writing room, watching them. They sat, backs to each other, at writing desks on opposite sides of the room. The scratching of their pens on paper was counterpoint to the wind in the palms, the roll of the breakers.

"May I come in? I'd like to start a letter to Terry."

"Come in, lovey," Aunt Olivia welcomed. "My gracious, Stella, you look pale."

"She's not used to our heat," Aunt Mary Desborough said.

I was offered a small rosewood lap desk by Aunt Olivia, note paper by Aunt Mary Desborough, pen and ink by both. I took Aunt Olivia's pen and Aunt Mary Desborough's inkwell. My heart was so full, there was so much to write about, that I could say nothing. I looked down at the pale blue paper, finally told my husband how much I loved the strange and rambling house, the ocean, the dunes, how I already loved the old great-aunts, Honoria, and Clive, respected Uncle Hoadley as well as loved him. And I talked to him about Ron James, and my determination to make friends. "I wonder why he ever came back? Perhaps it's because there aren't many doctors around the beach and he feels that he's needed." I chewed my pen again and then wrote about the storm. "Before the storm I heard a noise, different enough for me to get up and go to the balcony. And there was a group of horses ridden by hooded men." I looked up from the page and asked the great-aunts, "Last night before the storm broke, were you asleep, or did you see the men on horseback?"

"What men?" Aunt Olivia asked sharply.

"Galloping along by the edge of the water—men in hoods."

Aunt Olivia stood up angrily. "How dare they! How dare they come near Illyria!"

"Don't tell Hoadley." Aunt Mary Desborough nervously rolled her pen between her fingers.

"Of course I'm going to tell Hoadley! He's got to put a stop to it! I wouldn't have the Night Riders near Illyria! You know what Mado thought of them. I'll get my guns. If they come again I'll shoot, I'll kill them, I'll—"

"Olivia, don't make threats you can't carry out."

"Oh, can't I? You think I wouldn't dare? Well, I would. I'm an excellent shot. I—"

"Sit down," Aunt Mary Desborough said. "It's none of our business."

"If they come near Illyria it's our business."

"Who were they?" I asked.

"I suppose they were the Klan." Aunt Mary Desborough dragged her words reluctantly.

"The what?"

"The Ku Klux Klan."

"Daz on them," Aunt Olivia shouted, and the small word was now definitely a malediction. "Daz, daz, daz. They've been outlawed—it's illegal—"

"Olivia."

"They get around it by calling themselves something else— the Great White Riders or whatever it is. How can you say they're not our business. After what they did when—"

Aunt Mary Desborough did not allow her to finish. "Let Hoadley take care of it."

"Hoadley didn't take care of it before."

"He couldn't, then. That's why he—"

"Somebody's got to stop them from—oh, God, not again, not again—"

"Why should anything happen again?"

"I don't know, I don't know. I'm afraid. All that is required for the triumph of evil is that good men remain silent and do nothing."

"Edmund Burke. Point for me."

"I wasn't playing! This is serious!"

I asked, "Were the Riders the ones who tried down to burn down the twins' house last night?"

"Oh, God," Aunt Mary Desborough whispered.

Aunt Olivia said, "Do you suppose it's because Ron's taken care of some sick people in the twins' house?"

"Better there than here," Aunt Mary Desborough said. "We can't have people coming here."

"Why not? Where better? Have you forgotten Nyssa?"

"Olivia, we can't! Not today!" Aunt Mary Desborough's voice rose to a wail. She asked me, "Who told you about the twins' house?"

"I was in the kitchen when Ron told Honoria and Clive."

"But what happened?" Aunt Olivia demanded.

"The storm broke and the rain put the fire out. I don't think it did any damage. I'm sorry, perhaps I shouldn't have mentioned it."

"Of course you should have mentioned it!" Aunt Olivia said. "Never be afraid to tell us things, Stella, lovey."

"If you're going to throw a fit and talk about shooting people," Aunt Mary Desborough said, "she certainly isn't going to tell you things."

Aunt Olivia stared at her sister. "Would you stand by and let anybody hurt the twins?"

"I don't feel about the twins the way you do. They give me the creeps."

"But would you? Come now, Des, give me an honest answer."

"No."

Aunt Olivia turned to me. "We are responsible for the twins. And not only because the Captain worked for us. I loved him—"

"You didn't," Aunt Mary Desborough contradicted. "You're romanticizing. Anyhow he wasn't anything but a cracker."

"You sound like Irene." Aunt Olivia winked at me. "Both you and I are old maids, Des, because we were so inordinately afraid of marrying beneath our station. But one thing that age, if not wisdom, has taught me is that one can't marry beneath one's station. If one does, then one is. And, conversely, one can't marry above one's station. If one does, then one is."

"Livvy, stop chattering nonsense."

I folded and addressed my letter, if one could call it addressing: it was in care of an office in Washington, and I could only trust that the letter would get to my husband. I put the little lap desk on the floor. Aunt Mary Desborough was sealing her envelope. Aunt Olivia was looking at me, as though waiting for something.

"Tell me about Mado, please," I asked. "She was so important to Terry, and I know so little about her—"

Now they both smiled. The tension created by my reference to the hooded riders eased. The old ladies, like children, were easily diverted.

"She was a de la Valeur," Aunt Mary Desborough said, as though that were all that needed saying.

Aunt Olivia's silver laugh pealed. "But nobody in Charleston or Jefferson knew who the de la Valeurs were. You'd think nobody was good enough for a Renier. The first Theron Renier settled in Charleston a generation before the Revolution."

"The American Revolution," Aunt Mary Desborough specified, as though I, being a foreigner, might not know. She was not far wrong. "The de la Valeurs went back to Charlemagne. Or do I mean Richard Coeur de Lion?"

"Both, silly." Aunt Olivia's amused, child-like laugh came again. "Mado spoke perfect English, she had no accent, but there was always the French music behind her voice making the words sing. She had courtly manners. She accepted everybody."

"Sometimes she carried that too far," Aunt Mary Desborough said.

Aunt Olivia snapped, "We wouldn't have a home in our old age if she hadn't."

"But that was different."

"Why? Oh, Stella, it must have seemed so strange to Mado, coming from the French court to Jefferson. Jefferson wasn't—isn't—a typical Southern town. It's completely different from Charleston, where we were all born and raised. Even before the war a lot of Northern families had moved to Jefferson, mostly because it was supposed to be a healthy climate for people with weak chests."

"But it's a beautiful town," Aunt Mary Desborough said. "You'll see. On the west side of the river are the old Southerners, and that's where Mado and Theron had their house—though Mado lost it, of course, after the war, like everything else she had—though we do have the furniture in Illyria. Stella, do you have any idea how awful it was right after the war? Nobody who was anybody had money, and there was Mado with small children, and the carpetbaggers descending on us like the barbarian hordes from the North—"

"The barbarians always come from the North," Aunt Olivia said. "And it was hell for the emancipated slaves—"

"Olivia."

"It was *hell*, there isn't any other word. Nobody took any care of them, and they were shoved into positions for which they had no training and then blamed because they couldn't do the jobs. Oh, Stella, slave-owning was bad, was evil, we did learn that, but so is everything that's been done since the emancipation. It's worse, because it bears a label of being good. And then there are people like—well, like the Utteleys—"

"Aunt Irene said she and Uncle Hoadley are cousins. How is that?"

Aunt Mary Desborough snorted in annoyance. "Isn't that just like Irene to claim kinship? Irene's father was an Utteley from *Chicago*, and her mother was nobody. Nobody who was anybody would have married an Utteley. Her mother was an offshoot—very far off—of the Winchester Pagets—Winchester, Virginia, you know, it was one of the hotbeds of the Confederacy. Nobody *we* knew from Winchester would have married an Utteley."

An Utteley: it sounded as generic as a Zenumin.

Aunt Olivia gave an enormous sigh. "Oh, Des, I feel about them just as you do—but we'd be a lot worse off than we are without Utteley money."

"We've never had *that* much of it, just what Hoadley—" She put her hand to her mouth. "After all, dear Hoadley did marry—"

Aunt Olivia giggled.

Aunt Mary Desborough, the defender, continued, "Irene was the most ravishingly beautiful young girl I've ever seen—you know she was. I'm sure Hoadley didn't give a hoot about Utteley money."

"Certainly not," Aunt Olivia affirmed, "or at any rate not

much of a hoot. But we've all been a great deal more comfortable because of it. Though it's been Honoria—"

"Honoria's taken care of us," Aunt Mary Desborough said. "Hoadley's never taken anything from her."

"But we have. We've taken everything."

Aunt Mary Desborough spoke with dignity. "We were forced to. And we didn't take it for granted."

"Didn't we? I'm afraid a lot of the time we did. Or at least I did. And still do."

We heard a yelp, and Honoria stalked into the writing room, dragging a reluctant Finbarr by his collar.

"He may be old, and he may be aristocratic, though he don't look it, like some others I could name, but he got no call to put those big paws of his up on my kitchen table when my back is turned and take that long tongue of his and eat up all the cookies I made special for Miss Stella."

Finbarr slipped from Honoria's grasp and flung himself at Aunt Olivia. "Finny, you didn't! Finny, that's naughty! Honoria, I'm sorry, I'll make some more cookies."

"Ha."

"I can too make cookies."

"No more butter."

"Irene."

"Not asking Miss Irene Utteley for nothing."

Aunt Olivia leaned forward to whisper to me, "When Honoria calls Irene 'Miss Utteley' it means she's extremely angry. I wonder what Irene's done now?"

Aunt Mary Desborough went to the window, pulling open the shutter so that a glare of heat struck the room. Her voice was bitter. "Without you, without Utteley money, where would we—"

"Miss Des," Honoria said. "Hush."

"It doesn't make sense!" Aunt Mary Desborough cried to the ocean. "I was happy at Nyssa during the war, and look where it got us! I've outlived my time. I ought to be dead."

Aunt Olivia's voice was suddenly gentle. "Des. Des, come. Don't, Des."

Aunt Mary Desborough slowly closed the shutter.

"Honoria, are we going to have hot bread for lunch?"

"For every question there is a good moment and a bad moment."

"Honoria, please, for Stella?" She gave me her radiant smile.

"Stella knows how to keep Des and me from squabbling, just like Mado."

"For that, then," Honoria said, "I will make corndodgers."

"But corndodgers aren't—" Aunt Mary Desborough protested.

"Honoria's corndodgers are. They're better than biscuits. Honoria, what's this about the twins' house?"

Honoria seemed suddenly older, more gaunt. Her voice was dark. "Ronnie went over. The fire burned off the stoop, but that all."

"But who did it, Honoria? Who would want to burn the twins' house?"

"There was lightning last night," Honoria said impassively.

"No, Honoria, that won't do. Is it because Ronnie's seeing his patients in the twins' kitchen?"

"Could be."

"Stella saw the Riders going up the beach before the storm."

Honoria thought about this for a moment in silence, then asked, "Miss Stella—the Riders: was they dressed in black or white?"

I tried to remember, and was amazed to find that I couldn't. My memory of them was more emotional than visual. Whether they had been robed in white or black I could not tell.

"Black?" Aunt Olivia asked.

"Miss Olivia. Miss Des. It better if you don't say nothing."

"Not even to Hoadley?" Aunt Olivia asked.

"Not to nobody. Least said, least harm done."

"I'm sorry," I apologized, accepting, on more than one count, the rebuke. "I saw the men riding on the beach before the storm last night, and I asked the great-aunts about them."

Honoria said nothing. But her silence spoke to me as clearly as words. I thought of Ron mentioning Bluebeard's closet. Perhaps it had been real warning, rather than questionable humor.

"Stella, lovey," Aunt Olivia said, "did you say anything to Irene?"

"No."

"Then we can just keep this between ourselves. Irene gets excited about things."

Aunt Mary Desborough asked, "You're not going to tell Hoadley after all?"

"Not if Honoria doesn't want me to."

Aunt Mary Desborough held out her hand. "If you'll give

me the letters I'll give them to Clive to take to the depot this afternoon. Then I'm going out to the garden. There's work to be done."

Aunt Olivia and I were left alone in the writing room.

"Oh, Aunt Olivia! Terry tried to prepare me for the family and all its—its ramifications. But I'm vastly confused." I looked at my fingers, counting my confusions: Ron, with his strange English speech, causing someone to try to burn the twins' house because he saw patients there; the old Granddam, terrorizing me about the future; the Riders, be they white or be they black; the War Room, unlike Cousin Octavian's map room an evil room; Belle Zenumin and Jimmy James, and whatever it was which caused Honoria and Clive unbearable pain: five fingers' worth of confusion, a hand's worth.

"And well you might be confused, lovey. Southern families like ours—we're by no means unique, much as some of us would like to think so—are almost Chinese in our ancestor worship. But everything else was taken from us in the war. Who we are is all we have left." She fingered the silver head of her ebony cane. "I don't know how much Terry told you, but we do have forebears to be proud of—as well as some to be ashamed of. Our great-grandfather was one of Adams's early appointees to the Supreme Court. We seem to run to lawyers in the Renier family. Our brother Mark is a lawyer, a fine one, one of the most respected judges who has ever sat on the bench, and for a Charleston lawyer that, my dear, is quite an accolade. And Hoadley is a lawyer, of course. And you'll meet dear James on Sunday."

I laughed. "First thing we do, let's kill all the lawyers."

Aunt Olivia gave what was practically a shriek of pleasure. "Shakespeare! *Henry VI*, part II."

"I'm sure that's right," I said. "All I remember is that it's Shakespeare."

"Stella, Stella, you came just in time. Oh, bless you, bless you."

I was, as always, uncomfortable with this kind of exuberant gratitude. "I didn't mean to interrupt. Tell me about your great-grandfather. Another Theron?"

"Yes; from Charleston, naturally. Jefferson didn't even exist in those days, except as a sort of outpost, called Santa Ana. Anyhow, our great-grandfather almost got himself run out of Charleston, because he fought in the courts for the legal rights of free Negroes. Not the kind of thing apt to make him popular, but it *is* the kind of thing that runs in the family. Of course he's not highly popular in the Confederate States, but Union children learn about him in their history lessons. *I* don't happen to think this is a disgrace, but I've learned to keep my mouth shut on the subject. Another of my favorites is Justin Renier; he lived maybe a couple of centuries ago in France, I'm not good about dates, and he was burned at the stake. Sometimes it strikes me as our only safety, that we have a saint in the family, though I'm too Occidental and too Huguenot to pray to an ancestor, even an oblique one. Of course, being a priest, he had no direct descendants—or if he did, we don't know about them. You name me one great family which has no descendants of the left hand, as it were, and I'll—I'll swim the Atlantic tonight. Or am I making excuses for us? Here in the South it's more complicated being in the left hand than it is in Europe, because there's usually a touch of the tar brush."

"The what?"

"You British have the same problem in a small way with your Eurasians, don't you?"

I really didn't know, except through gossip.

"Don't let it all overwhelm you, lovey. Remember, Mado went through the same thing. Tout ça change, tout c'est la même chose." I must have looked doubtful, for she said, "I know it must seem different to you; Mado did have her Theron with her. And she had Nyssa."

"Nyssa seems so important to everybody, and Terry did mention it, but I don't really understand."

"Of course not. Practically nobody understood Nyssa. The plantation came to our cousin James when he was twenty-one, from his maternal grandmother. If everybody in the South had done what James did with Nyssa we might never have had a war. Nyssa was an experiment in a kind of freedom most people couldn't understand—that was why they were suspicious of it—and of us. And even if Nyssa failed—no! Who knows, really, what failure is? Nyssa was a community where we all lived and worked together as a family. James freed all the slaves when he left Charleston and went to live at Nyssa, and the ones who stayed—and many of them did—stayed because they wanted to, of their own free will, not because of fear, or because any pressure was put on them. James has two sisters, you'll meet them tomorrow, but let's not talk about Lucille before we have to. I can't stand her, never could. Xenia went to Nyssa with James and did all the—I suppose you'd call it administrative work. Clive got his education in Xenia's school; he was born at Nyssa so he's always been one of us, because we share the same memories of places and people. I believed in God until Nyssa was burned. We were always joyful there, even in the midst of war, of horror, because we were together."

"Honoria, too?"

"Oh, no. Honoria was in Illyria all during the war. She was alone most of the time—Broadley was dead by then. She'd have been killed if she'd been anywhere but Illyria. The twins and the Captain and some of the little people of the scrub brought her food, though the scrub people were afraid of her because—well, all the herb teas she makes, and the kinds of poultices she uses for my joints—all the wisdom she brought with her from Africa. Sometimes I wonder how much Honoria remembers of Africa? More than she says. And I think she misses it. She learned English from Broadley's slaves, and sometimes she comes out with a touch of Mado, but that funny guttural sound of Kairogi comes out in her voice whenever she's moved. It's a little like Gullah, but more—more austere. Funny: if it hadn't been for that beast Broadley she'd never have met Mado, and she wouldn't have wanted to miss that friendship. Or, all things considered, would she? I don't imagine Honoria would mind in the least giving up the *things* of civilization, but I don't think she'd want to lose the wisdom she's learned. The question I ask myself is this: is it the wisdom of civilization? I'm not sure. But I think it's a kind of wisdom she wouldn't have learned in Kairogi. Clive has it. Mado had it. It is more to be desired than gold."

"Do you have it?" I asked.

Aunt Olivia's face lost the youthful animation that lit it when she talked. Her eyes looked bleak and old. "I? I am a fool."

4

Aᴛᴛᴇʀ coffee that night I excused myself from the veranda, promising that I would not take as long a walk as the night before. But I made it clear, I hoped, that I needed time alone, that I would be gone more than a few minutes. With the realistic ruthlessness of youth I simply removed myself from my husband's family and set off up the beach.

There had been a brief thundershower—no more than a few minutes—during dinner, and the atmosphere had lifted. Beneath my feet I saw a delicate bubbling, bent down and plunged my fingers in wet sand and came up with a handful of sand and tiny shells. I let the sand sift through my fingers until I could see the shells clearly, rainbow-hued and no bigger than my little fingernail: donax, just as Clive had described them. I held them in my open palm, not knowing what to do with them—I certainly did not have enough for soup—and finally put them back down on the sand, where they were immediately sucked in, and fresh bubbles appeared.

I walked on, along the water's edge. This evening there was a brilliance to the air, so sparkling that I could feel it against my skin, a touch totally different from the oppression of the night before. It was also considerably later, for we had lingered over dinner and coffee. The moon was already up, and above me the stars were coming out in profusion, stars curving down to tip into the black rim of sea, the curved plumed hills of dunes, stars in and among the dunes—

I ran across the beach: fireflies, a festivity of fireflies. I held my hands out to cup one as Ron had done the night before, remembering also Terry telling me about running on the beach with a preserving jar when he was a little boy, catching fireflies to make a lantern. 'But then I would always let them go,' he told me. 'I tried one night taking them up to my bedroom to keep me company and light my dreams, but they wouldn't shine for me there.'

I lay down in the gentle curve of a dune and looked up at the soft velvet of sky, very different in texture from the English skies. I lay quietly under the calm of stars, then closed my eyes and listened to the sea, the wind moving in the beach grasses, the salty, fragrant odor of the vines clinging to the sand. I opened my eyes and the whole sky was slightly tilted, at a different angle from the summer sky in Oxford. I felt a moment's dizziness as though the earth had shifted on its axis.

I sniffed. Sniffed again: it was the odd, herbal odor which had accompanied Belle Zenumin.

She appeared from behind a clump of palms, a beautiful silhouette against the sky. "Mrs. Renier, I hope I didn't startle you." She dropped lightly to the sand beside me.

"Belle!"

"I hope you don't mind. I wanted to see you tonight, and Granddam said you'd be walking on the beach again, and later than last night, so I presumed to come."

I sifted sand through my fingers and said nothing.

"Mrs. Renier, ma'am, did you find your shoes and stockings?"

I looked up. "Yes, thank you. The twins found them and brought them to me."

In the starlight I could see a frown move across her face like a cloud. Then she gave her clear laugh, like glass bells blowing in the wind. "The twins—magic, ain't they, with numbers? How you suppose they do it? Suppose it's like my Granddam? Just knowing things other people can't know, out of the stars, like?"

"Astronomers do have to be mathematicians." I deliberately misunderstood. I did not want to talk about the Granddam.

Belle put one of her slender dark hands, devoid of rings, down on the pale sand. "That not how the twins do it, nor my Granddam, neither. Mrs. Renier, did she scare you right bad? That what I wanted to see you about tonight." I shook my head in a negation that was a lie. "If you'd come with me and see her again, Mrs. Renier, ma'am. I don't want to discommode you, but it not good to make the Granddam an-angered, to have her turn her powers against you. I think if you would come—"

I fought down panic. "Not tonight, please, Belle, I'm very tired, and everybody was cross because I was gone so long last night."

"Oh, not tonight, ma'am. But in the daytime, when you

can see the beautiful waters of the creek winding into the scrub.
The creek's black from cypress root, smooth as glass, full of
flowers and birds—you will love it, Mrs. Renier, ma'am. You
will come?" She leaned towards me, awaiting my reply.

"Yes, but I don't want her to read my palm or tell my
fortune—"

She touched my hand comfortingly. "Nothing you don't
want, Mrs. Renier, ma'am. Belle be sorry. It were meant to
be a gift. But iffen it not pleasing to you . . . It just be good if
you make my Granddam understand you wasn't slapping away
her gift. Belle understand, but Granddam be an old woman."

"I didn't mean to hurt her," I said. "Truly."

"Oh, *I* know you didn't, Mrs. Renier, ma'am. You be good
and kind. And we friends. So I make bold to ask—Mrs. Renier,
people been talking to you about my Ronnie?"

"No. But I've talked to him. I like him. And I'm sure he's
an excellent doctor."

"But people been talking, ain't they?" She reached her hands
anxiously towards me.

"Not really, not much."

"There's something I want to tell you about my Ronnie
before anybody else—" She sighed, slowly, deeply. "It be hard
on a young girl, growing up back in the dark of the scrub,
coming out maybe once or twice a year. It be hard to live in
the dark and be young and full of life, and knowing nothing
about the world outside, knowing nothing about men. I didn't
even know they was white folks like you till I was a grown
girl. Whites in the scrub, they not like you, and they don't mix
with Zenumins. Scared. I was kept in our own clearing. Nobody
come in who don't stay in. Once in, don't go out." She took
my hand, my ring hand, in both of hers, and held it tight,
whispering. "This be hard to say. I didn't think it was going
to be so hard."

I returned the pressure of her fingers. "It's all right, Belle.
Don't be afraid to say it. Go ahead and tell me, whatever it
is." I was proud to have her confidence.

"Mrs. Renier, ma'am, Miss Stella, people going to talk to
you about Ronnie. Someone, sooner or later, someone going
to tell you Mr. Hoadley be Ronnie's pappy. Don't you pay
them no mind. Ain't true."

If my words earlier that day had turned Honoria and Clive
to stone, so Belle's words struck me. "Uncle Hoad—"

"Ain't true, Miss Stella. Don't you listen to nobody. Mr.

Hoadley and I, we never. Not once. Maybe Mr. Hoadley might have wanted to—I was right beautiful—but he never. He a man of honor."

I asked in consternation, "But why would anybody say that Uncle Hoadley—"

"Miss Stella, you seen Ron. You seen he got a white man's education. How you think a nigger get to go to England to school? How you think a nigger go on after school and study for to be a doctor?"

"I don't know. I hadn't thought—"

She released my hand and lay back on the dune, looking up at the sky where the stars bloomed, thick as daisies in the spring. "What happen if you think?"

I, too, lay back. The moon looked down at us with impersonal clarity. "I suppose—I suppose somebody would have to send him, would have to pay for it."

She reached out and caught a firefly, but instead of releasing it as Ron James had done, in her tension she crushed it, then wiped her fingers on the sand. "Why would anybody take a twelve-year-old black boy and send him across the ocean to a biggety school?"

"My cousins at home—the Dowlers—saw to it that a number of deserving young men were educated."

"For why?"

"Why? Because the boys deserved it, and the Dowlers were interested."

"For why?"

"Well—it matters, doesn't it, that people should be educated? And if—if people can do something about it, isn't that their responsibility?"

"These be black boys your kin send to school?"

"No. But we—we don't have many Negroes in England."

"It make a difference, Miss Stella, leastways around here. No one aiming to educate a nigger out of the goodness of his heart. White folk don't want niggers educated. If a white man send a black boy to school, got to be a reason behind it."

"What kind of reason?"

She laughed again. This time it sounded like glass breaking. "Who you think send my Ronnie to school?"

"I suppose—" I looked away, out over the dark, inscrutable face of the sea. Moonlight touched the whitecaps with brilliance, making a shining swath across the water. "I suppose Uncle Hoadley?"

"Yes. Mr. Hoadley. That why people think Mr. Hoadley be Ron's—that why people talk about Mr. Hoadley and me. But we never. Not Mr. Hoadley. I don't mind the talk; don't make no matter to Belle. Belle used to talk. For what Mr. Hoadley done for my Ronnie, people can talk about Belle. Belle be grateful to Mr. Hoadley for what he done. But you must know it ain't true, Miss Stella, because you is my friend, and it would pain me most grievous to have you think that I— and for Mr. Hoadley, too. It ain't fair for you to think that he—"

"But I wouldn't! He couldn't! Not Uncle Hoadley!"

She sat up and put her hand lightly on my knee. "You just a baby, ain't you?"

"I'm nineteen."

"Tron, my first, were born when I were sixteen; Ronnie when I were seventeen. But you still wet behind the ears. Ain't going to be easy for you in Illyria. Listen. Listen to Belle. Things get too much for you, come to me. Belle will help."

Things were too much for me right then. I scrambled to my feet, spattering sand. "Thank you, Belle. I appreciate it. I won't forget."

"I won't forget, neither, Miss Stella. Belle never forget. And, ma'am, ever you need Belle, just follow the path behind the big dune. But when you come to the fork, remember to go to the left hand. Right hand lead to Mr. James's house." She held her hand out to me. I did not want to take it because, despite the heat, my hands were sweating cold sweat. I seemed to be standing in a stagnant pool of dirty, icy water. I felt in the pocket of my dress, my beautiful dress made for my trousseau, and pulled out a handkerchief, rolling it between my palms.

Belle put her hand lightly on my shoulder. "Forgive me, Miss Stella, ma'am. I come bringing the gift of friendship in my hands, and all I give you is fear. Don't hold it against me. Better you hear it from me, better you hear what is true, than all the mud people been slinging around. Some of it going to hit you. Give me your pretty little handkerchief and I take it home and wash and iron it for you. Let Belle do at least that little thing."

It was a handkerchief Terry had given me. I held it in a damp ball, tight in my fist. "No, it's all right, thank you, really."

She bowed her head, as though I had hurt her, but accepted

it. "I know you will be good to my Ronnie. Belle don't matter. Only her boys." She stood in front of me on the dune, raised herself up on tiptoe, and stretched her arms up to the sky as though to pluck a star. "Don't forget, Miss Stella, ma'am, you going to come see my Granddam. Be important. She want to like you, but iffen you don't let her and her heart turns dark against you, oh, I would be afeared for you then. You will come? You will?"

"Yes. I'll come."

"And soon. It be urgent."

Ron James, leading a red horse by the halter, crested the dune, silhouetted against the moonlight. "Mother, Mrs. Renier."

Belle, to my surprise, drew back. "Ronnie."

"What are you up to, Mother?"

"Talking with Mrs. Renier. With my friend. I go now, son. The Granddam be calling. Take care where you go with that horse. Scrub ain't safe for you no more, black scrub nor white scrub."

"I can take care of myself. Good night, Mother."

Belle smiled, curled her fingers in a small gesture of farewell, ran lightly towards the scrub. Ron stood, one hand resting on the red flank of the horse. Silence lay between us. To break it, I said, "That's a nice horse."

"Yes. Thales used to belong to Miss Olivia. She gave him to me when I came back to Illyria. He's old now, and can't do much beyond a steady walk—he has rheumatism, too—but he's a big help when I have to go see someone back in the scrub. Thales can go places I couldn't possibly manage on foot. No wonder some of the people have never left their little clearings in their lives."

I held out my hand, palm up, and the horse snuffled into it, pulling back his lips and showing his long, yellow teeth, but not at all ferociously. "What did you say his name was?"

"Thales. After Thales of Miletus. Ionic philosopher. He predicted the eclipse of the sun in the reign of the Lydian King Alyattes, and he maintained that water is the origin of all things. It is water out of which everything arises, and into which everything resolves itself. Well-educated, aren't I, Mrs. Renier?" I thought of my conversation with Belle and did not answer the bitter question. "I'll walk you home, Mrs. Renier. Forgive me for interfering again, but it might be as well if you don't see too much of my mother. Her powers are not like Honoria's, but neither are they to be taken lightly."

"You believe in these—these powers?"

He pressed the toe of his English shoe against the wet sand, so that water oozed about it. He wore an English riding habit, shabby but still quite presentable. "You expect me to say no, don't you?"

"I never know what to expect from you, Ron."

We walked along the water's edge, down the beach towards Illyria. "A belief in Honoria's powers, or my mother's, was not included in my education and medical training. It would have been laughed at as savage superstition. But I can't say an unqualified no, Mrs. Renier. Perhaps it's because I'm a Negro, because I have one foot still in Africa."

—But only one foot, I thought, looking at him, at the milkiness underlying the darkness of his skin. If I had grown up in the South I would have realized immediately that Ron's father, if not Uncle Hoadley, was a white man. "Ron, I don't have one foot in Africa. Why do I take it seriously?"

"Perhaps it's because you love and trust Honoria."

"But Honoria's afraid of her powers, isn't she?"

"No, Mrs. Renier. Fear isn't the right word. But my grandmother has seen powers misused and abused. When she was a girl in Kairogi they were all mixed up with witchcraft. And here in this country it has been even worse, because she has seen powers deliberately used for evil."

"By whom?"

Without answering, he led me to the broken-down dock on which we had sat the evening before, helped me up. Water lapped against the barnacled pilings. I waited for him to speak until I thought that he would not. But he said, as though there had been no pause, "Mrs. Renier, I've spent most of my life away from Illyria. When I was in England I thought of myself as being wholly a black American; or perhaps an Illyrian would be more accurate. But when I returned to Illyria I found that I had almost forgotten my own country, and particularly the scurb, where I was born. I had almost forgotten my mother and the Granddam. I remembered Honoria and Clive and the old ladies and conveniently forgot all the rest. It was a grave error."

"Why? What kind of an error?"

"An error or underestimation. If I take Honoria's powers seriously, it's a mistake to forget the powers of the scrub."

"I don't understand."

"I know you don't, Mrs. Renier."

Again there was a silence, in which I felt condemned for my obtuseness. "Please. If you'd try to tell me—"

He kicked his heels against the rough piling. "It's something you have to understand through your pores and in your blood, not with your mind. I had forgotten that, too. I had thought that my mind was capable of coping with my background. But I'm half Zenumin, and I would do well to remember it. When you came to Illyria, Mrs. Renier, there wasn't anybody in the scrub who didn't know about it."

"But how—"

"The people of the scrub have a way of communication which is more effective than the telegraph. It's the way of the jungle, and it's been forgotten in England. But it's real. It works. It is not to be taken lightly. Honoria knows this. And she knows that the dark people of the scrub fear her, as well as respect her."

"Why would they fear her?"

A wave broke against the end of the dock with a sound like a sigh. "Because of her powers. Because she will not lend her powers to the Zenumins. Because she knows the kind of things that go on in the dark clearings. Most of the people in the scrub are simple, decent, God-fearing people trying to scratch a living out of the ground and maintaining a kind of integrity which civilization has forgotten. But there are dark things in the scrub, too."

"Dark things?"

His voice was suddenly savage. "You want an example, Mrs. Innocent Renier? All right, I'll give you one. Where there are already too many babies, there is no sentimentality about them. There isn't enough food for those who survive, which may be why I don't get more angry when babies are brought to me too late; if I save their lives, what am I saving them for? If they grow up at all it will be to be hated, abused, and sometimes obscenely murdered. But there are other obscenities. Babies have been sacrificed in the dark clearings, because the inebriated god likes to get drunk on human blood."

"Ron—Ron—no—"

He jumped down from the dock, splashing into the small waves of the incoming tide. "Does that seem so strange to you, Mrs. Renier? How different is the altar of the scrub from your Christian altars? Isn't blood part of the sacrifice there, too?"

"But that's different—it's different—"

"Why? To kill a baby for sacrifice is one of the more merciful ways of death. Their throats are slit quickly. It's not like the long-drawn-out agony of a lynching done by Christian white men."

"Ron, I was brought up an atheist, I don't understand these things, but it's not the same, it can't be! Ron, you don't really mean it, do you? Not babies—" I looked at him in anguish; in the moonlight his face was impassive, austere; he wore an expression I had seen before only on Honoria.

He spoke slowly, thoughtfully, the rage drained from his voice. "Mrs. Renier, for my grandparents' sake, for Terry's sake, I feel a sense of responsibility for you. I wish I didn't. Because I don't know how I'm going to keep your youth and your idiotic ignorance from leading you—and the rest of us—into danger. Because the air smells of danger. We both know that. And part of the danger is your innocence. You don't understand, for instance, that I'm a Negro. You don't understand that I'm a doctor, and that I'm hamstrung. You don't understand that Illyria is my grandmother's house and I would give my right arm to use it as a hospital, and instead we can live in it only as servants. To bring my patients there would be to endanger everybody."

"Why? Why, Ron!"

"The Riders wouldn't stand for it, for one. I'd be lynched. You ever seen a lynching, Mrs. Renier?"

"No—no—"

"You should. Makes that baby sacrifice that upset you so look like child's play. I'll tell you about a lynching. Jimmy. Honoria's and Clive's son, Jimmy, went after a man with a knife. It wasn't the first time my mother'd pleasured herself with somebody else, but it was the first time he caught her at it. So he went out to kill. But he got drunk first, and he wasn't quiet about it, and the Riders were waiting for him. They lynched him. They rolled him in burning tar. Do you know what hot tar on a man's flesh smells like, Mrs. Renier? It smells like roasting beef. Delicious."

"Stop—stop—you can't possibly remember—"

"I wasn't born till three months afterwards. No, I don't remember Jimmy's lynching. But he isn't the only Negro around here who's been lynched. I saw a man strung up simply because he was a Zenumin. If the Granddam is filled with hate, she has plenty of reason. They tarred Jimmy, the noble Riders, and they feathered him, and then they dug out his eyes. They did other things to him, too. I won't tell you those. Then they took the bloody, screaming pulp which was all that was left of what had once been a man and they hanged him on a tree and left him there swinging. Mado went and cut him down. She was a small woman but she carried him in her arms to her carriage and brought him back to Illyria."

I rolled over on the rotting boards of the dock and pressed my face against the wood.

After a long time I felt Ron's hand on my shoulder. "You're like the twins. Everybody thinks the twins are idiots. In the world's eyes they are. So people laugh at them and show off their little tricks. I'm no better than anyone else. They have fantastic memories, even for dates before their time. As what hour and on what day did Claudius Broadley start the building of Illyria? When did Honoria first come to the beach? What was the dark moment when evil entered the scrub? Go on back to the house, Mrs. Renier, before they send Clive out to hunt for you again."

"Was it true?"

"Yes. Quite true."

"I'm sorry—I'm sorry—I didn't mean—"

"Forget it." He helped me down from the dock. The tide had moved in, and we had to splash through the lacy criss-crossings of wavelets to get to dry sand. The beach around us was vast and empty.

"Where's your horse—Thales—"

He looked up and down the empty beach. "Either gone back to Illyria or up to the twins' cottage. Most likely up. Will you be all right to walk home alone?"

"Yes. Thank you."

He gave me a small bow of farewell (Did he indeed wish me to fare well? I believed, against the evidence, that he did), turned, and ran up the beach towards the small and comfortable warmth of the twins' cottage.

I could not run. I walked, slow as Aunt Olivia, back to Illyria.

Nothing had changed.

Uncle Hoadley was reading. Aunt Olivia was playing the piano, Finbarr at her feet. Aunt Irene and Aunt Mary Desborough were bent over the backgammon table. The kitten, curled up on top of the piano, announced my presence by leaping onto the keyboard with a crash. Aunt Olivia pulled him into her lap. "Hoadley, you've got your lamp turned up too high. I can smell the mantle burning."

"Much obliged, Auntie." Uncle Hoadley turned down the guttering flame. It lit up his delicate and austere face, and I wanted to put my arms around him, both as a request for comfort and as an affirmation of faith in him. But nobody would understand such wild and impulsive behavior.

I sat on the old day bed, covered with the beautiful but scratchy Oriental rug, and listened to Aunt Olivia playing Scarlatti, to Aunt Irene and Aunt Mary Desborough rattling dice, watched Uncle Hoadley quietly turning the pages of his dark, dry-looking legal tome. As Aunt Irene and Aunt Mary Desborough finished their game and Aunt Irene started to put it away, Aunt Olivia turned from the piano, swinging around on the stool, which gave an anguished creak. "You know who I thought about today? General F. X. Everard."

Uncle Hoadley looked over his book; his wire-rimmed reading glasses had slid halfway down his nose. "Do you still have his pistols, Auntie?"

"Yes. I do."

"Where are they?"

"I keep them in a safe place. When the children were little—Therro and Jimmy, and you, too, Hoadley—I was afraid one of you might get hold of them. Do you remember him—the General?"

"Of course, Auntie." He looked at me, generously drawing me into memories I did not share. "General Everard was Treasurer of the United States for a while, Stella child—he was appointed by Lincoln. I don't know where he was from originally, or how he happened to come to San Feliz."

"He had money," Aunt Des said reprovingly. "He wasn't quality. His daughter built a house in San Feliz, but he chose to live on top of a dune in a big tent, which fascinated the boys—didn't it, Hoadley?"

"It did indeed. We wanted to live in a tent, too."

Aunt Mary Desborough, putting backgammon pieces in an inlaid teakwood box, clucked in reminiscence. "He began to study Greek after he was eight, and Mado said he had a brilliant mind. I suppose he was considered an eccentric."

"That's doubtless why he pitched his tent near us," Aunt Olivia said.

Aunt Mary Desborough bristled. "I, for one, do not consider myself eccentric."

"Perhaps, Auntie," Uncle Hoadley spoke in his calm way, "all Aunt Olivia means is that the General knew that you would not criticize him, or make unkind judgments."

"Know ye not," Aunt Olivia murmured, "that ye shall judge angels?"

"One Corinthians, chapter six, point for me. Eighteen to twelve," Aunt Mary Desborough triumphed. "And it is hardly pertinent."

"Why not? You ought to be used to angels, having lived in Illyria as long as you have. General Everard looked like a great, dark, fallen angel in his big black cape. It had a black fur collar, and he always wore it in cold weather, and we used to wonder how he kept warm in his tent—it does get cold at the beach in winter, Stella, though that's hard to believe in August. I wasn't frightened of the General the way you were, Des. I thought he was grand."

"He was a horrid old man."

"Why? Because he saw us all as women? One morning I was talking to him, standing on the dune by his tent—I'd gone to pick scuppernong grapes and he came out to chat, and we saw Mado walking to the beach in her bathing suit, and he said, 'Mado has damn fine legs, and she knows it.' First I was shocked—people didn't swear in front of ladies in those days the way they do now—and then I giggled, because it was true. She did, and she did know it." Aunt Olivia rose from the piano stool, took her case, and limped over to the day bed, sitting beside me and putting her hand firmly on my knee. "Touch.

He loved young people, and was fascinated by us—because to him we were still young, then, Mado and Des and I. He had a theory that if he touched us—or, what was much better, the truly young, Therro or the little boys, if he put his hand on their knee, like this, or held on to us while he walked on the beach—an electric current would pass into him and invigorate him and prolong his life."

"I never let him touch me," Aunt Mary Desborough said. "He was a lecherous old roué."

"Daz it, he was not! Why do people always have to put horrid interpretations on things that are simple and innocent? He loved youth, and he was young at heart, but there wasn't anything sloppy about it. The little boys loved him, and he was wonderful with them. When he gave me the guns it was with the understanding that they were to go to Therro. But Therro never used them. General Everard lived in his tent till he was way up in the nineties—so maybe his theory did work after all, Des—and one winter's morning Mado went to take him some fruit, and he was stone-cold dead."

"It's not nice to touch people the way he did," Aunt Mary Desborough reiterated.

"Oh, daz it, of course it is. Fear not to touch the best; The truth shall be thy warrant."

"Is it Shakespeare?"

"It is not Shakespeare. I'll give you the next two lines. Go, since I needs must die, And give the world the lie."

"I am well aware that we all must die some day, but I fail to understand why you harp on it so constantly."

"I don't harp. The quotation was, Fear not to touch the best. Don't change the subject. You don't know what it is."

"All right, I don't know. At least I admit it when I don't."

"You're accusing me of not admitting it when I don't know?"

"You never admit it. You always make some wild guess."

"Half of any game is intelligent guessing."

"Ha. You identified something this afternoon as *Henry IV*, part I, and it was *Romeo and Juliet*. If it had been part II, or even *Merry Wives of Windsor*, I might have called it intelligent guessing. But you were just pretending."

"Aunties." Uncle Hoadley banged his book against the arm of his chair. "That will do."

Aunt Olivia broke into her giggle. "Sorry, Hoadley-love. Really. It was Sir Walter Raleigh, Des."

Aunt Mary Desborough said rather stiffly, "I'm sorry, too, Hoadley."

Uncle Hoadley opened his book again. "Apologies accepted." He smiled. "I think I would be inclined to be a little anxious if you two played your game without squabbling. As long as we have a hot game of Shakespeare going on in Illyria, I know that the world is still going around."

With these words of reassurance I was able to say good night and go upstairs to bed.

When I was undressed and washed and in my thinnest nightgown, I stood again on my balcony, looking at the comforting light from the lightship. The next morning we were all to go to Cousin James's beach cottage for "church." That is, Aunt Olivia told me, Cousin James would read Morning Prayer, since there was no church in San Feliz and the trip into Jefferson was thought to be much too tiring for the great-aunts. After "church" we were to have dinner at Cousin Lucille's.

I sighed, and went to bed, under the mended mosquito netting. A large, many-legged insect with gossamer wings walked up the netting and peered at me, waving two long forelegs. The kitten was waiting for me, curled up as before in an amber-striped circle on my pillow. I took Mado's journals from the bed table, then tucked the netting in and shivered against the heat: odd reaction. But I found that the extreme heat made me break out in goose-flesh the way extreme cold does. I was tempted to shove the stifling mosquito net aside, but the curious night insects fluttering about the room stopped me.

I turned to the journals, arranging them in chronological order. Only the first was in French, and towards the end there were entries in English. The second was in English, with occasional French words or phrases. I held it in my hands and felt a sudden and terrible alienation from my husband. When we were in Oxford, when I had been able to touch the golden healthiness of his body, to see his open and direct regard, it had seemed only admirable to me that he was able to do secret work for his country, work he could not share even with me. But now I wondered if it were not the very honesty of his myopic blue eyes which made him so useful in intelligence work. And: if he could keep state secrets from me, could he not also keep other things? things I ought to know? I ought not to have had to hear about Jimmy's lynching from Ron—

I opened the first journal. It was written by a young girl, joyful and in love. I was filled with a wild envy, because Mado went with Theron wherever he went: why couldn't I have gone with Terry?

Life in the new country was strange for Mado, too, but she never lost her sense of humor. There were servants to do everything for them, and of course she had her own maid, a young girl from Nyssa who had been educated by Cousin Xenia, and it was she who often read aloud to Mado in the evening, as well as dressing her hair, taking care of her clothes. "I had thought," Mado wrote, "to teach my maid something about reading and writing; instead I am the one to be taught."

There were balls and dinner parties and Mado loved Charleston, though the heat bothered her. Then came the move to Jefferson, and heat even more oppressive than that of Charleston. They took a house, nevertheless, and people flocked to them and they were happy and busy. I had a mental image of Mado sitting at a beautifully appointed table and drawing everybody to her by her beauty and gaiety, and of course she was able to be beautiful and gay because her Theron was at the head of the table, they were together . . .

She described one of the ball gowns she had brought over from Paris, black lace over a scarlet underdress, very daring. "People are buzzing about it," she wrote, "and say I am a French hussy, no better than I should be. Theron says all women are wildly jealous. He doesn't realize that people are jealous of him, too, because he's handsome and brilliant and from Charleston. Jefferson is raw and rough in comparison to Charleston; there's an unfinished quality to it. But it has—or could have—its own beauty and ambiance if only people would stop trying to imitate Charleston mores and patterns. People from the West and North live on the far side of the river, and even if they build magnificent houses, they are looked down on. I think I shall go call on some of them and see what they're like."

Then Therro was born, and Theron began talking about the inevitability of war, and a more serious note came to the pages of the journals. "I am afraid of war," Mado wrote, "not for myself, but for the baby. What kind of a world has he been born into? And I am afraid for Theron. He says that he will not fight; he is a doctor, and he has been trained to save life, not to take it. James has warned me that if there is a war it will not be easy for Theron—and, it just now occurs to me, for James, either. A lot of people hate Nyssa, hate James."

Mado and Theron and the baby made frequent visits to Nyssa to get out of the heat, and I learned that every possible impediment had been put in the way when James freed his slaves; he succeeded only because he was a lawyer and a Renier; he had money and influence. And he was hated and called a maniac. A rumor went around that he had drugged and hypnotized his freed slaves to keep them working for him.

Mado wrote, "When the war comes—and now it is *when*, not *if*—Theron says the children and I are to go to Nyssa." There was a second baby now, another little boy. I knew from Terry's chart that he must have died. "Olivia and Des will leave Charleston and come to Nyssa, too. Yes, that is best. Nyssa is a tiny island of sanity in this sea of madness. I did not understand at first what James was doing at Nyssa. I thought it was the old heresy of a Utopia on earth, man presuming to think that he can return, of his own virtue, to Eden. But James is not a blind dreamer. I am not sure how long he will be able to keep Nyssa going, simply because Nyssa is in the world, and worldly people always want to destroy those whose true home is heaven. Nyssa succeeds, I think, in a far more realistic way than Little Gidding, or any of the Utopian colonies attempted in New England. It has the structure of worship and prayer to outline and define the day that Little Gidding did, but it is far more possible in a thousand acres in North Carolina to be self-contained than it was in either England or New England. All the food needed for the community is grown right at Nyssa. Every man and woman there works hard, but lovingly. Every man is free, not just in the sense of being, legally, a freed slave, but in being free to work with love. James has an extraordinary capacity for leadership; he knows how to love with open hands, and to take his own importance as head of Nyssa both factually and lightly. And he knows how to delegate authority, too. Xenia is magnificent. She runs both house and school completely and capably. People—his younger sister, Lucille, being a prime example—would like to provoke jealousy between Xenia and James, but I don't think they're likely to succeed . . .

"We begin and end the day in prayer, the entire family. It gives meaning and dignity to everything that is done. The work in the fields under the blazing American sun is hot and hard, but there is singing and laughter. There is always singing at

Nyssa. Unless it rains, most meals are eaten on long trestle tables under the live oaks; the food is not elegant—at least it would not be considered so by most of the people we know—but there is plenty, and I always eat enormously when I am at Nyssa. After everyone has eaten there is more singing. There is a beauty to the rich voices of James's people I have never heard anywhere else. It is joyful singing, in natural harmony, and the closest I can come to describing the quality is that it is like music I heard at the Imperial court in Russia. When there is so much love and so much beauty at Nyssa, why do people hate it so? I thought Theron was being oversensitive, that he was imagining it, until I went into town yesterday to get supplies. I wanted to buy several bolts of gingham, and the shop woman spat on me. I was spat on! I did not want to tell James and Theron, but when we returned to Nyssa without the gingham, I had to. But Theron said calmly that we were self-sufficient at Nyssa in most ways, and the solution was to spin our own thread and weave our own cloth. He and James called a meeting of the community, and everybody was enthusiastic about the idea. And angry for me. I did not like being spat on; it was one of the most disgusting things that has ever happened to me. But the concern of the community, the love I felt from all of them, more than made up for it, and I was undressed, bathed, gentled, as tenderly as though I were a baby. And that evening, eating out under the trees with the moonlight coming through the dusty, autumn leaves, we were all unusually close and happy."

Mado was a sporadic journal writer. While Therro was a baby she wrote seldom. There was an occasional cry to her guardian angel if something upset her, or if she felt particularly joyful. She and Theron took Therro and the new infant and a few servants and went out to the Western territories for several months because Theron had been asked to try to break up an epidemic of yellow fever.

I looked up from the journal, suddenly listening, aware of something more than the usual creakings of an old house. Silence. Then footsteps climbing up to the third floor. Footsteps moving down the passage, moving softly to my door, stopping. I waited, but there was no further movement, no knock on the door. Nonetheless I felt a presence waiting outside. I listened: listened: heard a small creaking of the floorboards. It was not my imagination. There was someone outside my door.

The kitten moved from his place between my feet, stalked

over me, planting his tiny paws deliberately and disdainfully upon me, and curled up in the curve of my arm, giving a yawn and starting to purr, his warm sides vibrating with pleasure.

The footsteps left my door, moved back down the hall, down the stairs.

I was afraid, and I did not know of what—or of whom. Heat and darkness and an awful sense of the unknown surrounded me like mosquito netting. I turned, almost frantically, back to Mado's journal. But what I read was hardly comforting.

"O my angel my guardian, come to me tonight and return me to myself. I would that Theron were beside me so that I could sleep. But he is in Jefferson, and I am in Nyssa because of the babies. The heat has been intense, even here, and the malaria has been worse than usual, and now Jefferson is filled with dengue fever, so Theron sent us here into cooler weather. Children are dying in the heat of Jefferson; I should feel only grateful that I am able to bring my little ones to Nyssa. Instead, I feel guilt and anguish. How can I love myself, or let God love me, or you, angel, guard and protect me, while evil is done around me and I stand still and do nothing to prevent it? Today, out of duty, I went to call on James's sister, Lucille Hutlidge—would that I had not. I saw William Hutlidge, the beast she calls her husband, beat a man with a whip, and I, myself, bear the marks of his whip. I ran, I threw myself between the whip and the slave, there is across my back a strange and painful welt—now at least I share this with Honoria—but it did more harm than good. I am sure that the slave's beating was the worse for my interference, that Hutlidge gave extra lashes because I infuriated him. How can I love Hutlidge? But I must. If I cannot love William Hutlidge I cannot love myself, I cannot love God. Not only do I not love him: I do not want God to love him. It is all right for me to thrust William outside my loving forgiveness, but not to want him outside God's. I am dark with anger."

In the next journal I read, more quietly, "In our differing ways Honoria and I are both aristocrats. There are not many around. When I come to Illryia to stay with Honoria for a few days I feel that at last I have found my proper level. This is a dangerous feeling, particularly for me in this raw country which is about to explode; and a total lack of understanding of levels is one of the reasons we're not going to be able to avoid the explosion. Theron understands how to bend, Theron, my darling, the real aristocrat, who is able to bend down to people.

And let me be quite clear with myself: true aristocracy has to do with personality rather than birth, or social group, or class, or caste. Honoria is an aristocrat because she is Honoria, and not just because she is a princess. I am an aristocrat—no need for false humility in these pages—because I am Mado, not because of my forebears. Aristocracy is not a right or a privilege; it never makes demands on others; it gives; it is in itself an obligation. Theron and James try to answer the demands made on them. I suppose what Theron and James want to do at Nyssa is to make every man there an aristocrat—Clive, for example, certainly is one! It is not, as the Hutlidges and their ilk think, that Theron and James want to lower themselves, to descend, but that they want to go down in order to bring up. That's it! It's like the water level in a reservoir! And every loving and giving and aristocratic act raises the level. Perhaps Theron and James and Xenia are ahead of their time. Perhaps the world is not ready for them, or for Nyssa. The world can sometimes tolerate dreams of Utopia, but it cannot bear the brilliant flame of reality. But we cannot wait until the world is ready! Meanwhile it is right and proper that I should enjoy this breathing spell here at Illyria with Honoria. Theron and the babies and I are going to Nyssa next week; James needs Theron. Darling James, I wish he'd find a wife."

I had a strong feeling that darling James would not, because James loved Mado.

When I ran across the beach the following morning, Uncle Hoadley was there before me, wetting himself in the shallow waters at the edge of the slough. He stood and waved. In his long dark woolen bathing suit he looked old and ascetic; his somewhat sallow skin had tanned only lightly on Illyrian weekends; there was a parchment-like quality to the sparse flesh over the long delicate cage of bones which spoke of self-denial.

"So you and I are the early risers this Sunday, Stella-child?"

"Hello, Uncle Hoadley. Good morning."

He gave a long, sweeping gesture with one arm, taking in the expanse of sea, sand, dune. "On a fine morning like this one I think that Illyria is the most beautiful place in the world. As a matter of fact, I know of no place more beautiful, though there are those who claim the blue hills of Kairogi to be the spot on earth closest to Eden."

"Have you been to Kairogi!"

"I've done a good deal of traveling in my day, child. But

Illyria has a kind of peace I've never felt anywhere else. So you think Terry may be in Kairogi?"

I was resting in the gentless of the water and now I rolled over and stood up. "No, Uncle Hoadley. It's possible he may be there, but it's also possible he's anywhere else in the world. I have no idea where he is."

"My dear," he said mildly, "there's no need to sound so defensive: I am merely interested. After all, Terry has filled the place of the son Irene and I were never able to have. He is very close to our hearts."

"Sorry, I didn't realize I was sounding defensive. Perhaps if I knew where Terry was, if I could imagine him in some particular place, then he wouldn't seem so—so very far away."

"Poor lamb, of course. Terry can see you in his mind's eye here in Illyria, and you have no setting in which to visualize him. I think I understand how particularly painful this is." He held his fingers up and yawned, delicately, then smiled. "Last night was a white one for me, I have them rather frequently, and around two o'clock in the morning I left the house and walked for miles up the beach. The wind was blowing across the sea, and I lay in the sand of a far dune and it had been cooled by moonlight so that it was almost like lying in a snow-drift. The wind blew over the sea oats and over my body and the moon swung across the sky and poured its clean cold rays over me and all the insects hushed and listened. When I walked back to Illyria I thought I saw a light in your room?"

"Yes, Uncle Hoadley. I couldn't sleep either."

His voice was gentle. "If you will love Illyria, and all it has to offer you, then I think you can be happy with us. Perhaps it's a good thing for your relationship with Terry, in the long run, that you are given these weeks in which to become ac-climated. Try to learn not to ask too many questions, child. There are problems which need not concern you. Do try to remember that." He gave me a small wave of his fingers and splashed into shore, then raised his head, gazing while a flock of pelicans broke against the sky. I, too, followed their passage. When I looked again, Uncle Hoadley was going along the narrow path by the ramp into under-Illyria.

6

AFTER I had pumped sulphury water over my salt-soaked bathing costume, the sun was already steaming the air, and I dressed hurriedly and went into the cool of the house. Aunt Olivia was in the living room, under the stairs where the piano stood. The lid was up, and she held a lighted lamp over the strings, singing softly.

> *"I do not see them here, but after death*
> *God knows the faces I shall see,*
> *Each one a murdered self, with low last breath.*
> *'I am thyself—what has thou done to me?'"*

I recognized it: Rossetti. And told her so. "Point for me, Aunt Olivia," and we both laughed.

But Aunt Mary Desborough, coming down the stairs, shouted, "Olivia, stop it! And why aren't you in your bathing dress?"

"It's Sunday; I'll need all my strength to face the day."

"A swim would refresh you."

"I'm too tired."

"But you're supposed to move. It's not good for your joints to stay still. They'll lock and you'll be crippled."

"Daz it, I will not let my bones lock. I'll die first."

"How do you know you can?"

I intervened, "What are you doing to the piano, Aunt Olivia?"

"The dampers stick in the beach damp. I'm trying to dry them out with the lamp."

"You'll set them on fire. For goodness' sake be careful," Aunt Mary Desborough said. "And I'm going swimming even if you aren't."

"Oh, jolly dee." Aunt Olivia limped into the dining room.

135

"The water's lovely this morning, Aunt Des," I said lamely, and followed Aunt Olivia.

"Hungry?" she asked me.

"Famished. I don't think I was ever this hungry in Oxford."

"You didn't have Illyrian air. Or Honoria's cooking." She poured coffee and hot milk, peered into covered dishes. "Sherried kidneys. For Hoadley. I love them, too."

"Shall I take your plate?"

"No, thank you, my dear. It's very kind of you. But it would be far too easy for me to let people do things for me. Then my bones really *would* lock. When you go to James's this morning you'll see the kind of living death that terrifies me." She looked at me imploringly. "I talk too much. . . . But I don't mind your knowing about me."

I smiled. "Are there things that are mindable?"

Balancing her plate precariously, leaning heavily on her cane, Aunt Olivia limped to the table. "To how many people do we want to reveal our secret selves? Do you think I want to make myself wholly vulnerable to—oh, Irene, for instance? Or to most of my dear friends and relatives, most of whom are more dead than if they were six feet under? Death: what a strange thing it is. Some of our kin you'll be meeting sooner or later are far more dead than Mado will ever be."

"Mado." I brought my filled plate to the table and sat next to the old great-aunt. "Last night I read in Mado's journals, mostly the parts about Nyssa. What happened to the little boy who was born after Therro?"

"He died at Nyssa, during the war, before we came to Illyria. There wasn't enough to eat, and nobody had resistance against illness. A great many children died in those years." Aunt Olivia leaned on one elbow, looking rather tiredly at the sherried kidneys on her plate. "I'm sure you realize that Mado was far more than sister-in-law to me. She was the one true, real friend of my life. So many people loved her, and it never occurred to the little ones to call her anything but Mado; I think they thought the name Mado meant grandmother, that all grandmothers were mados. To me it meant the one who saved my life. I think I felt this as strongly as Honoria, though perhaps with less obvious reasons."

"How did she save your life, Aunt Olivia?"

She made a self-deprecating little gesture. "Just in small, everyday ways. By making me feel that I—that I existed. It was Des who saved my life dramatically when I got caught in the undertow and was being dragged out to sea. Not that I would have cared—or would I? I don't know. Sometimes I'm of two minds about death. But it was too close to Therro's and Kitty's drowning."

I fetched the silver coffee pot and milk pitcher from the sideboard and refilled our cups.

"Hoadley kept telling them their little boat wasn't sea-worthy, but they wouldn't listen. Therro was arrogant about the sea—as about everything else. He thought he could outwit it. And then one of those sudden storms came up—at least there was a storm, and nobody even mentioned that it might have been anything else."

Aunt Olivia answered my look. "It wasn't that bad a storm, and Therro was as good a sailor as he thought he was. So was Kitty." She gave the polished tabletop a sharp slap. "If we're going to be friends, Stella, we can't have secrets from each other. At least I can't. I haven't had anybody to talk to since Mado, and Mado and I were the only ones who admitted Therro and Kitty might—and even we asked it only once, when we were walking up the beach catching fireflies. Oh, Stella, they had been so gay and so in love, Therro and Kitty, and always parties and dances and music. There was a glamour about them, a brightness, as though the sun would never stop shining. They had a handsome house in Jefferson, and Therro and Hoadley were doing wonderfully well in practice together. It was be-cause of Therro that Hoadley left Charleston and his father's law offices and came to Jefferson. And Hoadley was pushing him—Therro had a lazy streak, but everybody said that if he wanted to go into politics here he'd be governor before he was forty. We were so proud of them—and then everybody came to Illyria for the summer as usual and there was nothing but quarreling, and Kitty rushing off crying and nobody knew why, and if you asked what was wrong you got your head snapped off. Jimmy was living back in the scrub with Belle then, but when he came around he flew into violent rages for no reason whatsoever. Honoria stalked through the room cleaning every-thing four and five times over. Clive sat and read his Bible. I got underfoot, as usual. And Mado—she tried to keep laughter in the rooms, but she had no idea what was going on, and I suppose we should be grateful for that. It would have killed her. And then there was Jimmy's death and that—" She stopped abruptly, and there was the dark hole of Jimmy's death like a chasm between us.

"Aunt Olivia, please forgive me, but there's so much about your country I don't—why was Jimmy lynched?"

She put her coffee cup down on the saucer so sharply that it overturned. She ignored the coffee spilling across the table, dripping on the floor. "Did Terry tell you that?"

"No. Ron."

"Ron told you? How much did he tell you?"

"That—that Jimmy was lynched—"

Silence came between us, strange and dark, pushing us further and further apart. At last Aunt Olivia said, moving her hands as though to try to close the chasm, "I will try to explain it to you, Stella. But not today. Jimmy was—he was my baby, my boy—" She tried to control the tears which welled up in her faded blue eyes, reached into the folds of her skirt for her handkerchief, blew her nose, then said quite calmly, "Sorry to be such a fool. Jimmy gave me the illusion that I was alive, and Honoria let me mother him. Most of my life I haven't been alive. Nothing's ever happened to make me be. I've never even been in love, except with dreams. I mean, I was never in love with a real person, the way he actually was, instead of the way I dreamed. The nearest I've ever come to being in love with someone real was with the twin's father, but of course I'm not supposed to mention that. Des knew. I don't know how, but she did. That's why she tries to shut me up if I mention the Captain. Afraid I'm going to embarrass her. To look at the twins you'd never guess that their father was one of the handsomest men you could possibly imagine. For all he was nothing but a cracker, he looked like a prince." She gave a laugh which was half sob. "That's the story of my life. The man I loved was another woman's husband, and the babies he counted on turned out to be—to be the twins. And as close to being a mother as I've ever become was with someone else's baby. Manqué, manqué, all the way. But I didn't make Jimmy up. I knew him, all his lovingness, and all his faults and weakness, everything that led to—I wonder if I made up the Captain? Just because I needed to love a man? I wonder if I imagined someone to put into the flesh of the visible man I saw? Only partly, I think. Most of the people who live back in the scrub are people of honor and integrity—very different from the Zenumins."

"Ron—he's half Zenumin, isn't he?"

"Honoria and Clive raised him. They're far more his parents than—"

"But Belle, his mother—"

I had stepped on forbidden ground again. For a moment Aunt Olivia looked angry; then she said, "I can tell you this much now: Jimmy was very young when Belle Zenumin seduced him. Some say she bewitched him, and I'm not denying that's possible, but beauty in itself can be bewitching. Look at Irene."

"She's still beautiful."

"Not any more. You should have seen Irene twenty years ago. Irene has not aged well."

"Not Aunt Irene. Belle Zenumin."

She drew back. "How would you know? You haven't met her and I hope you never will."

"But I have."

"How? When?"

"Both evenings when I've taken my walk."

"Stella, keep away from her—"

"But why, Aunt Olivia?"

"Stella, believe me, please, I beg of you, believe me, Belle is bad, bad all the way through. Why do you think we took Ron away from her? It's not a light thing to take a child from its mother."

"What about her other son?"

"Jimmy's boy. He was a year older. Things were different."

"Why do you say 'Jimmy's boy' that way?"

She looked away. "Who knows who any Zenumin's father is? I shouldn't have wiped up the coffee with my napkin. Honoria will be furious. Tron looks enough like Jimmy so that we all go on the assumption that Jimmy was, in fact, his father. Stella, I must ask you please not to say anything about all this to Des. I got in far deeper than I intended."

"I've asked too many questions. I do apologize."

"No, no, Stella, it's I who have—you have every reason to—just don't ask—oh, don't ask Hoadley, or tell him."

"I won't. I promise." It was an easy promise.

She relaxed a little. "If you're just *around* Des you'll find she'll tell you things. More than you want to know. Both of us do. Maybe all old people— Have I been boring you?"

"Boring me? It's all part of my husband's world, what makes him Terry."

She nodded. "We are part of one another, aren't we? Would you get me another piece of toast, please? I know I ought to make myself do it, but we have a long day ahead. . . . I'm much obliged. . . . I don't have the kind of stamina Mado did, and Honoria. . . . How did they bear it all? Mado lost her husband, four of her five children, and then Therro, her first-born, was drowned, and she had to accept—Stella, how did she bear it? When I look back on her life it was one tragedy after another, and yet she was the most joyful person I've ever known. It's strange how vividly I remember the past. It's all so clear to me, clearer than the present. It's not so much that I'm living in the past, as that the past is moving up to meet and engulf the present."

"Ladies." Uncle Hoadley bowed slightly as he came in and went to the sideboard for coffee. "Where are Irene and Aunt Des?"

"Getting all primped up for Morning Prayer," Aunt Olivia said.

"I suggest that you and Stella do the same, then, Auntie."

I left the table and climbed the stairs. As I neared the third floor I heard voices from my bedroom, first Honoria, saying, "Miss Irene, you are not to go in there."

I stopped on the stairs.

Aunt Irene's voice was high. "But I only wanted—"

"Miss Irene, I warn you. Keep out of Miss Stella's room. You been seeing Belle Zenumin again, ain't you?"

Aunt Irene spoke in a strange and awful wail: "You're not accusing me of wanting to harm Stella, are you?"

"Don't meddle in things too big for you."

"You ought not to speak to me that way."

I cleared my throat and firmly mounted the stairs.

Aunt Irene raised her voice. "Are you sure there are enough towels, Honoria? Or would you like Mr. Hoadley to bring more in from Jefferson?"

"Plenty of towels."

As I entered the room, Aunt Irene's voice returned to its usual warm drawl. "Good morning, Stella, honey. All through breakfast?"

"Yes, thanks. I've just come to finish dressing."

She gave me a little pat. "We'll meet on the veranda in about half an hour."

It took me only a moment to collect gloves, bonnet, a fresh handkerchief, so I went to my balcony; the ocean stretched, calm and unimpressed by my ignorance and arrogance, out to an almost invisible horizon. A woman came into my line of vision, leading a pale horse. It was Belle Zenumin. She looked up and saw me, raised her hand in greeting.

I waved back.

A dark shadow flew between us. It was a buzzard, in sudden descent to a fish washed up on the beach. It was an ugly sight.

"Miss Stella." There was a light tap on my door. "You ready?"

I turned from the balcony. "Coming."

Honoria was waiting in the hall, gloved and bonneted, prayer book in hand. "Miss Olivia on the veranda. She say maybe you like to come sit with her a spell."

"Honoria, I just saw Ron's mother on the beach with a pale horse."

Honoria's hands in their black lace gloves tightened over her prayer book. She stood very still, peering at me as we stood in the summer dimness at the top of the stairs.

I said, "Yesterday morning when I asked if there were any place I oughtn't to go while I was exploring, Ron said—"

Honoria drew herself up. "Don't fret, Miss Stella. If God wants you to open doors we have kept closed, the key will be given."

"The Zenumins—"

"Don't fret," Honoria repeated, and I thought she was saying it more to herself than to me. "I didn't have no call to speak the way I did yesterday. But I ask you, Miss Stella, to stay away from the Zenumins."

"But why?"

"Zenumins—" She looked down at her gloved hands. "Zenumins ain't nobody. They some of everybody, and this sum adds up to nothing. If a body don't love nobody, a body become nobody. You got to understand this, Miss Stella. Zenumins don't love. They live together back in the scrub not because they a family, like some folk in the clearings; but because they hate everybody not Zenumin. They bow down and they kiss Hate and they worship." In the dusk at the head of the stairs I could sense, rather than see, her strain. Her shadow loomed behind her, elongated and austere. But Honoria seemed even taller than her shadow, a dark, foreboding force. "Now, Miss Stella, we go down to Miss Livvy. She waiting." She drew back to let me go down the stairs ahead of her.

AUNT Olivia was sitting on the veranda in her favorite rocker. Like Honoria, she wore an old-fashioned bonnet, the kind Cousin Augusta had worn when I was a child but which had long gone out of fashion. Her prayer book was clasped loosely in her hands; her kid gloves were yellow with age. Honoria took a palm-leaf fan from behind the shutter and waved it slowly back and forth so that we all benefited from the gentle stirring of the air. Two carriages were drawn up in front of the house, the horses waiting patiently, occasionally stamping softly on the sand or shaking their heads against the insects.

"I dreamed about Theron last night." Aunt Olivia gave a pleased laugh. "I just remembered! It was lovely. My brother Theron, that is, Stella. I wish you could have known him."

"I wish so, too. Was he killed in battle?" That sounded right, Mado's Theron leading a victorious charge, galloping his horse uphill, his flag aloft, and a bullet piercing his heart . . .

Honoria, slowly moving the fan, gave me a long look. Aunt Olivia said, "No. Being a doctor, he didn't have to fight. As you know, he and James turned Nyssa into a hospital, but Theron also had a hospital set up in a mobile tent and he went out into the battlefields, so I suppose he might easily have been killed that way, but he wasn't. He was murdered."

The old woman spoke these words perfectly calmly, far more calmly than she had talked about Jimmy, but again Honoria stopped waving the fan. The breeze, too, seemed to have died down. Everything was still. A yellow jacket humming over the ilex bushes sounded louder than the ocean.

"Murdered?"

"To do William Hutlidge justice, I don't think he was really party to it himself—I couldn't bear to believe that. Theron came to Nyssa on leave, and he was sent for on a trumped-up call to take care of one of the Hutlidge slaves who had a fever. Mado took Therro, and drove Theron over. He was terribly tired, and it was a good five miles between plantations. When they got to the Hutlidge gates, the overseer was there to let them in, and right there at the gates they shot him. They shot Theron. Mado caught him as he fell. Therro saw. He saw his father killed."

Despite the heat I felt cold. Aunt Olivia, like Honoria, was staring out over the ocean, as though only thus could she continue.

"Mado turned the carriage around, whipped the horses and galloped back to Nyssa, but Theron was dead. Therro held his father all the way. He would not believe his father was dead, and he had nightmares from that day on. The whole state was in an uproar. Some said Theron had been rightfully executed as a traitor to the Confederacy. That he was not, ever; and many people came to mourn him. The day after he was buried—oh, Stella—someone set fire to the house, and before anyone knew what was happening the place was a blazing inferno. James and Clive and some of the other men managed to get almost everybody out. Therro helped carry stretchers— we got all the wounded men out safely and into the old slave quarters—and his hands were badly burned; he carried the scars until he died. The two baby girls, Olivia and Lucy, and their nurse, were trapped upstairs. Clive's brother died trying to get them out. Mado—she had baby Jamie in her arms, but it was only Clive's holding her that kept her from rushing back in after the little girls. Stella, Stella, we have known so much pain and grief together. If Therro bore the scars on his hands, there were other scars that did not show, no matter how wildly he tried to forget them. And Mado—Mado had scars, too, not physical ones, but scars of the heart. No: scars of the soul. And yet I was the one to rage and rebel and deny God. Mado was never bitter nor resentful, never."

Honoria turned from her contemplation of the ocean. "Never, Miss Livia? Miss Mado, she got through the darkness. She knowed love has to work itself all the way through the dark feelings; you can't go around them; they has to be gone through, all the way through."

"Only on love's terrible other side," Aunt Olivia said softly, "is found the place where lion and lamb abide." She reached one small gloved hand towards Honoria. "They did well, didn't they, Honoria? The people we have loved. They were lights to lighten the darkness. And I—I cannot sleep at night without leaving a candle burning."

I made an impulsive rush to Aunt Olivia, kneeling on the veranda beside her rocking chair. She put her hand lightly on my head. "Don't fret, lambie. I'll probably be cross and repulsive the rest of the day—that's my usual reaction to pain— and make you suffer for it. I'm not good about my fear and pain the way Mado was, I give in to it, I always have, and now death is just around the corner, and it's time I came to terms with the past."

"Remember Miss Mado," Honoria said. "She will teach you."

"Honoria, when we were all young you used just to call her Mado."

Honoria gave her strange, disturbing smile. "When I was a chattel of Mr. Claudius Broadley I called my friend Mado. When I became my own self I deemed it necessary to call her Miss Mado."

"Why?"

"Don't you know?"

"I can guess," Aunt Olivia said, and then, fiercely, "I hate the world, Honoria! Why do things have to be this way?"

Aunt Irene, looking like a fashion plate from *The Queen*, swept out on the veranda, letting the screen door bang behind her. "What's the matter, Auntie?"

"Out of the north an evil shall break forth upon all the inhabitants of the land."

"Jeremiah." Aunt Mary Desborough came around the corner of the veranda, dressed in ancient and rusty brown, carrying prayer book and gloves. "Chapter two."

"All right. Your point. Daz it. The trouble is that the evil breaks forth out of our own hearts. We'd like to blame it on the north, but it's everywhere, like the plague."

"Miss Olivia," Honoria said, "let us go to the carriage."

We drove slowly along the beach, two carriages, one behind the other. Uncle Hoadley led the way with Honoria in his small phaeton. The great-aunts and I, driven by Clive, followed. Aunt Mary Desborough, shiny with heat, decided to instruct me on Jefferson, "because you'll be going in with Irene when she goes to get supplies. Olivia and Honoria and Clive and I manage perfectly well in the winter, but Irene can't get on without all kinds of fancy city foods."

"Not at all, Auntie." Aunt Irene sat stiff and straight and over-corseted. Her face looked flushed in the light which filtered through the fringed canvas canopy which protected us from the sun. "I notice you and Aunt Olivia enjoy the delicacies Hoadley and I provide."

"Remember it's Sunday, Des," Aunt Olivia said. "We must be patient."

Aunt Irene twirled her furled pink taffeta parasol. "*I* am not the one likely to forget it's Sunday."

"Has it ever occurred to you, Irene," Aunt Olivia asked, "to put your light back under a bushel?"

I said swiftly, "Do tell me about Jefferson. I look forward to seeing it."

Aunt Mary Desborough slipped happily into her reminiscing voice: "Social Jefferson is divided by Ecclesiastes Street, Stella. East of Ecclesiastes is ante-bellum South, and west of Ecclesiastes are the carpetbaggers and people from other states. Sometimes I wish we could go back to Charleston. I don't think Charleston is changing the way Jefferson is."

"The whole world is changing," Aunt Irene said. "At least Jefferson is keeping abreast of the world."

"Is that a good thing?" Aunt Olivia demanded.

"Perhaps it's all right for you aunties to live in the past. But Hoadley and I have to think of the future. So does Stella."

Aunt Olivia rapped on the floor of the carriage with her pearl-grey parasol, as she sometimes banged for emphasis with her cane. "The day I stop thinking of the future, Irene, you can put me under. But I think about it with my reason. I don't go running to tea leaves and cards and stars."

I asked, "How long a drive is it to Cousin James's?"

"Three miles," Aunt Mary Desborough answered. "When we pass the twins' house we're halfway. How Livia and I used to love Uncle James—dear James's father—when we were little. Their house was out on the river—the Ashley—a lovely, lovely place. Uncle James had a long brown beard flecked with grey and he used to let us children pull it. On our birthdays he always drove into town in his buggy and brought us presents."

"This was in Charleston?"

Aunt Irene patted my knee. "Don't worry if you take a while to get things straight, honey. The aunties often get things confused."

Aunt Olivia started to retort, then shut her mouth, murmuring, "Sunday."

Aunt Des leaned forward, whispering loudly, "Irene has one of her headaches."

I thought that it was a good thing that Cousin James did not live far away. "Aunt Olivia has been telling me a little about Nyssa, and how Terry's grandfather was killed."

Aunt Irene patted my knee again. "You must remember, Stella dear, that the aunties exaggerate."

"Death," said Aunt Olivia, "cannot be exaggerated."

Aunt Irene smiled tolerantly. "Uncle Theron may not have been quite the hero his sisters make him out to be. But Hoadley and I feel that if they are a little blind on the subject it doesn't do much harm."

"If we were blind it would do untold harm!" Aunt Olivia's eyes flashed. "I told Stella precisely what happened."

Aunt Irene's determined smile was like cracked china. "It's only your interpretation that I question, Auntie."

"How would *you* know?"

"I may be too young to have been there, Auntie, but I *am* married to your nephew, and he *is* your brother Mark's son."

"That still doesn't make you one of us."

Aunt Irene's voice began to rise. "I've never had to apologize for my family's treatment of the slaves—"

"Neither have we, since we had none to apologize for."

"Your brother Mark had slaves, and would still have them if it weren't for the war. Are you criticizing him?"

"Mark stayed in Charleston, and we are not discussing Mark. It's James and Theron you're criticizing, because they treated the people who worked and lived with them as—as human beings. Not as though they were chattels, or—or things. They treated them as persons."

"And you think it was oh, so noble of them, freeing their slaves? setting them loose in a world where they couldn't take care of themselves? You think that was treating them like human beings?"

Aunt Mary Desborough cried, "Theron and James did not just set them loose, like—like horses. They stayed on at Nyssa and worked with—with dignity and honor."

"Yes, and what happened to them after the war?"

"If more people had been like James and Theron, and like Mado too, there might not have been a war."

"Well, then, Aunt Des, how would you like it if Stella—" Aunt Irene's angry smile was turned on me "—came to us from England and criticized the way we do things and got Terry to overturn a society which has been stable and workable for a number of years?"

Aunt Mary Desborough clenched her ringed fingers. "Mado did not do that, Irene! Nobody needed to tell Theron what to do!"

The anger in the carriage had built to an alarming degree, and at least part of it had been caused by my blundering. Aunt Olivia grasped her parasol as though she were going to strike Aunt Irene with it. "How could one young girl from France have started the war? Do you think she personally stood on the Battery and fired that first cannon? Because that's what you're accusing her of doing!"

"Don't be idiotic, Auntie, I'm doing no such thing!"

Aunt Mary Desborough began to cry. "You're being vile, Irene, and in front of Stella, absolutely vile as only an Utteley can be. I suppose you think William Hutlidge was right to stand by while Theron was murdered."

Aunt Irene shot back, "If Theron had been a loyal—"

Aunt Olivia stood up.

"Sit down!" Aunt Irene shouted.

Aunt Olivia sat, and turned to her weeping sister. "Don't, Des, dear Des. Don't pay any attention to that utterly Utteley." Then, back to Aunt Irene, and in the singsong drawl she occasionally affected, she said, "You lie, your feet smell, and you don't love your Jesus."

Aunt Mary Desborough's sob turned into a hysterical laugh.

Aunt Irene was furious. "There were some people who felt they had reason to call Dr. Theron Renier a coward and his wife a—"

Aunt Olivia stood again and raised her parasol.

"Clive!" I shouted, and grabbed the parasol.

Clive stopped the horses.

Had Uncle Hoadley heard the commotion? He, too, drew to a halt. Clive sat, impassive, holding the reins lightly. Uncle Hoadley jumped down onto the sand and walked back to our carriage.

Aunt Mary Desborough started to cry again. "Irene's vile, absolutely vile."

All the pink had gone from Aunt Olivia's cheeks. She was white with rage. "Irene has gone too far."

"Ladies." Uncle Hoadley spoke sharply. "I'm surprised at you. All of you. Irene, I think you had better apologize to the great-aunts."

"I? Why should I be the one to apologize when it's they who—"

"Irene."

"We wouldn't be having all this trouble with the nig—"

"*Irene.*"

She subsided.

"*I* apologize." Uncle Hoadley made me a small, courteous bow. "Irene, you will kindly go sit with Honoria."

"But—"

"You will do as I say. Clive, you will please drive them."

"Yes, sir." Clive climbed down from his high seat. Uncle Hoadley took his place, waited until Clive had started, then slapped the reins lightly against the horses' flanks, and we clopped placidly along the beach. The old ladies were silent, except for Aunt Mary Desborough's hiccuping sniffles. Aunt Olivia fished in her handbag and gave her sister a handkerchief. Aunt Mary Desborough blew her nose with a loud honk. Silence.

Uncle Hoadley turned slightly. "You see, Stella, peace does not necessarily follow the cessation of war. I presume you were firing on Fort Sumter again?"

Aunt Mary Desborough put her handkerchief into her reticule and clicked it shut. Aunt Olivia carefully rested her parasol across her lap.

"You see, Stella—and please don't interrupt, Aunties—my Uncle Theron thought he could solve problems by brushing them aside as though they didn't exist. But they do exist, they still exist, and unless responsible people do something about them, our land is in for fresh disaster, brother against brother, black against white. Perhaps our government in Washington would like us to concentrate on the troubles in the Balkans so that we won't notice the troubles in our own back yards. I, for one, do not intend to have my attention deflected. Dear Aunties, Irene was silly enough to argue with you precisely because she shares my grave concern about the future."

"So do we," Aunt Olivia started.

"Auntie, I told you not to interrupt. I'm not trying to undermine your love and admiration for Uncle Theron. But you must allow me my considered opinion that he acted against his time. There is always a right time for things: remember your Ecclesiastes, the Good Book, not the street. To every thing there is a season, and a time to every purpose under heaven; a time to be born and a time to die; a time to plant and a time to pluck up that which is planted; Uncle Theron tried to reap crops before the seeds were even planted, and that is always fatal."

"He did not—" Aunt Olivia started, but Uncle Hoadley held up his thin hand for silence. He had turned completely around now and was facing us, holding the reins loosely. Despite the shade of our parasols the heat beat down on us, and my entire body felt drenched with perspiration.

"There is a time to keep silence and a time to speak, and Uncle Theron and Aunt Mado often spoke when silence would have been wiser."

"Who doesn't?" Aunt Olivia asked. 'I hate old Ecclesiastes, anyhow. He didn't believe in eternity, and as far as I'm concerned that means he didn't believe in God."

"Auntie. Wait. There is a time to love and a time to hate; a time of war and a time of peace; but we must know our own time and not be afraid of it. But we must know it. We must know the right moment. To misjudge is fatal."

"But Theron—"

"I am not talking about Uncle Theron now. I'm talking about myself." He turned back to the horses.

Ahead of us Clive brought the phaeton to a stop, and we pulled up behind him. High on the dunes was a low house of soft grey wood, half hidden by trees. I helped the old aunts out, Aunt Mary Desborough climbing down from the carriage briskly and standing blinking in the sunshine; Aunt Olivia leaning heavily so that I almost lifted her down—she was feather-light.

"In the old days in Charleston," Aunt Mary Desborough said, "there was a palm-leaf fan with each prayer book and hymnal. It always means God to me, the sounds of hundreds of palm-leaf fans being waved in unison, like the sound of waves, or the rushing of wings."

"Angel wings," Aunt Olivia said. "Where are they now?"

Cousin James's house was much smaller than Illyria, built Spanish-fashion, a red-tile-roofed rectangle with an open central court. Cousin James awaited us in the open doorway, an old man with white hair and Vandyke beard, his white suit a little loose on his bones, as though he had shrunk since buying it. His lightly trembling hand was raised in greeting, his wrinkled face alight with welcome.

I liked him, I liked him immediately, a gentle man, simultaneously shabby and elegant, radiating warmth and joy. After the first rush of greeting and welcome, he suggested that he take me to meet his elder sister, Xenia.

"Oh, good, James, it will mean so much to Xenia," Aunt Des said.

"It will mean nothing to Cousin Xenia," Aunt Irene whispered to me, "but it is a duty you might as well get over and done with."

Cousin James led me off. "We will have Morning Prayer in Xenia's room, because she is bedridden, and has been for several years, but she is considerably more aware of what is going on than may be easily apparent." He called back to the others, "Go into the courtyard and relax in the breeze, dear friends, while Stella greets Xenia. Come and join us in five minutes."

The large room to which he took me had the same musty smell as Aunt Olivia's room, a smell of times past, of old winds held within the walls and mingling with the very present smell of salt, of living ocean. It was a paradox of openness and enclosure: dusk was enclosed to keep out the heat of the sun, yet there was a feeling that the shadows stretched into

infinity. We stood in the open doorway and I could see across
the room to a high bed which was turned so that it faced the
window. A plain young woman sat by the head of the bed,
reading aloud. Cousin James put his lightly palsied hand on
my arm and we stood, listening.

> Then being is distributed over the multitude of things,
> and nothing that is, however small, or however great, is
> devoid of it? And, indeed, the very supposition of this
> is absurd, for how can that which is, be devoid of being?
> In no way.
> And it is divided into the greatest and into the small-
> est, and into all kinds of being, and is broken up more
> than all things; the divisions of it have no limit.

Plato? I recognized the general style.

> True. Then it has the greatest number of parts?
> Yes. The greatest number.
> Is there any of these which is a part of being and yet
> no part.

(Like those apples? Like Cousin Xenia?)

> Impossible.
> But if it is at all, and so long as it is, it must be one
> and cannot be none?

Cousin James led me into the room and up to the bed. The
young woman closed the book on her finger, gave us a shy
smile.

"Miss Harris," Cousin James said, "I want you to meet Mrs.
Theron Renier, our new cousin from England who has come
to pay her respects to my sister. Stella—"

I stepped up to the bed, shook hands with Miss Harris, and
then looked down at an old woman whose strong bone structure,
showing sharply through the pale and wrinkled skin, belied the
blank emptiness of her expression. Her steel-grey eyes were
open, but they were not focused. She was covered with a sheet,
and her liver-spotted hands lay motionless upon it. This was
the Xenia who had run the school and the hospital at Nyssa,
who had been Mado's friend, who had been young and brilliant

and alive. I reached down and took her inert hands into my own. "Cousin Xenia, I'm Stella, Terry's wife."

I thought the hands moved slightly in mine, so I bent closer and held them to my face. The fingers uncurled in response and I held them to my eyes, my nose, my lips. "Here I am, Cousin Xenia. Stella. Feel me." I felt a pain deep within me so sharp that I almost cried out with the hurt of it. Not my pain. Cousin Xenia's. It flowed between us. After a moment I could contain it no longer and I returned her hands to the sheet.

Cousin James had been watching closely. Now he put his arm around me and led me from the bed. "Terry is most dear to me. I am glad he chose you. Glad." He pulled out a white lawn handkerchief and blew his nose. "Xenia had a beautiful and brilliant mind. I am convinced that it is still there, trapped by the paralysis which imprisoned her body when she had her stroke. I am certain that she hears. Certain. And this is all I can do." He gestured towards Miss Harris, still marking the place in the volume of Plato.

I took Cousin James's hand and held it. I loved him very much.

The clan gathered in Cousin Xenia's room. Honoria and Clive stood near the door, beside an elderly black woman in a neat grey dress with white collar and cuffs. I moved back to stand with them, but Honoria pushed me gently forward, whispering, "Stand next to the great-aunts, Miss Stella."

Cousin James read the office of Morning Prayer with authority and courtesy, and I was not embarrassed. I felt that even my father, who found all churches a blasphemy, all prayer a self-indulgence, would not have been offended. What Cousin James was doing was wholly real; I did not know why; I only knew that I believed and trusted him. They all sang "O God, our help in ages past," and then we all went out to the courtyard and sat on rough wooden benches around the fountain. The trellised vines and the water cast a coolness around us, and the aunts all waved palm-leaf fans. Honoria and Clive had disappeared, and sherry was served by the old woman in the grey uniform, who was introduced to me as Saintie, from Nyssa.

"What is Cousin Xenia hearing this week?" Uncle Hoadley inquired. "As I recall, Miss Harris was having a little trouble with Racine. Her French was not up to him."

Cousin James seemed preoccupied, so I said, "I think it was Plato, Uncle Hoadley."

Cousin James gave me his brilliant smile. "You recognized it. Yes. Plato's *Parmenides*."

"Of course she recognized it," Aunt Mary Desborough said. "Terry grew up with blue-stockings. He wouldn't have married a ninny."

"And she plays Shakespeare with us!" Aunt Olivia clapped her hands in pleasure.

"Miss Harris also reads Xenia the *Tribune* paper from New York," Aunt Irene said. "Of course it's a week late, but I don't suppose that makes much difference."

Aunt Mary Desborough, perhaps trying to make peace, nodded. "Xenia was always a great one to keep up with the news, but does it really make much difference if she hears what's happening in Bishop Potter's college in Virginia a week after it's happened or not?"

Aunt Irene was not as generous as Aunt Des. "Bishop Potter's a damn-yankee, and it is not his coll—"

Cousin James rode across this, bathing Aunt Irene and Aunt Des with his smile as though they were in complete agreement. "We're sorry to hear that Olivia's rheumatism is being troublesome."

Aunt Irene shook her head. "We pray that it will not make her bedridden."

Cousin James put his hand on Aunt Olivia's small shoulder. "I don't think Olivia will be bedridden, Irene. Not Olivia. Excuse me, dear friends, and I will get my hat." He disappeared into the house.

"Who'd have thought Cousin Xenia'd ever be bedridden?" Aunt Irene asked. "Of all people—and look at her, three years next month in that bed. All that reading aloud, and she doesn't hear a word. It seems a waste."

"It would be a waste if it were you!" Aunt Olivia cried. "James knows precisely what he is doing. And it is none of your business." She turned to me just as Uncle Hoadley was opening his mouth, and whispered, "There are times when I simply don't understand why Xenia doesn't die of humiliation. Thank God she has a brother who keeps the hope that somewhere in that inert lump there is still a flame to be nourished."

Cousin James returned, carrying his broad-brimmed white Panama hat. "Come. Let us go to Lucille's."

* * *

Saintie handed us our parasols and we walked out what would have been the back door at Illyria, onto a white sand road. Uncle Hoadley took my arm. "I do apologize again for my wife and the great-aunts."

"It's all right, Uncle Hoadley."

"No, it's not. And I can see that this kind of squabbling is new to you. At least in Jefferson there is more of the tribe; the animosities are diluted. And I'm sure you realize that underneath the barbs is an unbreakable loyalty. We may cavil amongst ourselves, but we present a united front to the world." He smiled. "You are a Renier now, and you will have to get used to our Renierities." He pressed my arm and changed the subject. "Terry's present work is a great source of pleasure to me. We have a long tradition of public servants in our family. Not only our ambassador to France through whom Mado came into the clan."

> Theron the ambassador
> Went to France before the war;
> Dr. Theron, his young son,
> There met Mado, loved and won,
> But lost the War Between the States . . .

"The very first Theron Renier in Charleston was a noted Federalist, and his son, also Theron, went to the Supreme Court. Like the other Therons he was an idealist, rather than a realist. I have tried to teach Terry that it is the realists who clean up after the idealists."

Cousin James moved up beside me, and Uncle Hoadley stepped back to walk with Aunt Irene. Cousin James looked at me from under his white eyebrows, saying, "Child, I'm glad you're in Illyria. You'll be safe there."

It seemed to me that Illyria was tottering on the brink of a precipice, so I looked at him questioningly.

"The warning is oblique, my dear, but it is a warning. You are obviously far too intelligent not to realize that there is little safety left in our world today. Sometimes I listen to Miss Harris reading to Xenia, or I go to Lucille's cottage for a quiet game of cribbage, and I wonder if the ancient Romans thought that when they had defeated Spartacus they had solved their problem. Stay in Illyria, Stella, and do whatever Honoria and Clive tell you to do. You should be safe there when the storm breaks."

"What's that, Cousin James?" Uncle Hoadley came abreast

of us, and I understood quite clearly that Uncle Hoadley and Cousin James, under the careful veneer of courteous cordiality, disliked and distrusted one another.

"It's going to storm," Cousin James said.

"Not tonight, I think," said Uncle Hoadley.

Cousin Lucille's cottage was scarcely visible through the trees and bushes which grew around it and choked it. Spanish moss hung thickly from everything, from the wistaria vine which climbed the porch, the rain-water spout, the crape-myrtle trees which crowded together, from the oaks whose interlocking branches obscured the sky. Azalea bushes pushed untidily up to the trees, tangled with cape jessamine, turning brown and dry from the long summer.

Cousin James pushed aside branches and tendrils of the uncontrolled jungle growth as we made our way down the path. "Lucille pinches pennies to pay a yard man, but she doesn't give him any supervision. I sometimes wonder why Lucille comes to the beach, because she never leaves the cottage. The heat, of course. If you are feeling the heat here, and I can see that you are, it's a good thing that you were not asked to endure a summer in Jefferson. I must speak to Lucille about the yard again. It's one thing to let wool grow over the house, as it were," he plucked a long beard of Spanish moss from a bush, "but another to let it grow over her eyes. It is all, I suppose, part of our crumbling. Mado—your husband's grandmother— had a lovely belief in guardian angels, assigned by the Heavenly Powers to each of us. Perhaps if we all believed in our angels we might not do all the self-centered and possessive and jealous things which hurt and separate us. Our angels haven't been around for a long time. Mado used to say that we could make them go away, and we seem to have done just that."

His voice was infinitely sad. I looked at him, his eyes shaded by the wide brim of his hat, his neatly groomed mustache and beard concealing the set of his mouth. He saw my glance, and I turned my eyes away, shifting my parasol in my embarrassment.

He gave me his swift, sweet smile. "Mado always said that the angels would come back. She was an extraordinary woman. Of course I loved her," he added simply.

We climbed the splintering steps to a paint-crumbled porch supported by Doric columns, and entered a large, dark room which appeared to be the entire ground floor of Cousin Lucille's beach cottage. It was crowded with far too much furniture, chairs, sofas, couches, love seats, tables, cases of porcelain, *objets d'art* and bric-a-brac, rug piled on rug on the floor, almost as though everything in all of Illyria had been jumbled together in one room. The walls were smothered in pictures so that the ornate plum-red wallpaper hardly showed. I felt suffocated.

Wishing for one of the palm-leaf fans, I looked around the dark and cluttered museum of a room, trying to find Cousin Lucille, and finally saw a huddled, black-garbed figure in a maroon velvet wing chair. It sat blinking like a large black toad: Cousin Lucille. Her yellowed white hair was bunched on top of her head. From her long and wrinkled earlobes dangled diamond pendants. Her rings made Aunt Mary Desborough's look insignificant. She gestured to me with fingers gnarled as parsnips. "Louder!" she shouted, though no one had said anything. Cousin James gently shoved me towards her. "Louder!"

Cousin James spoke slowly, clearly. "This is Terry's wife."

"Who?"

"Stella, Terry's wife. Remember, you invited her for the midday meal."

"Yes, of course I remember, James, I am not an idiot. Who was she?"

"Stella North."

"I don't speak to Northerners."

"She is from England," Uncle Hoadley said.

Cousin Lucille sucked long, yellowed teeth. "Nonsense, Hoadley. Northerners don't come from England. The English were on Our Side. Don't contradict James. Show some respect for your elders, young man. She's pretty, isn't she? Now who does she remind me of?"

"Mado," Cousin James said.

Cousin Lucille shook her head, setting the diamond pendants swinging. "Too young. Too pretty."

Cousin James gently shoved me a step farther forward. "She is more than pretty, Lucille."

One of the claws lifted from the black dress and reached for my hand. I had wanted to give myself to Cousin Xenia; from Cousin Lucille I wanted to withdraw. I reminded myself that she, too, was Cousin James's sister, and I managed to let her take my hand, and found myself looking past grey, wrinkled skin, past little beady eyes, being drawn in deeper, deeper, through layer after layer, to where a small light flickered feebly.

"Welcome to the clan, child," Cousin Lucille shouted at last. "No. You aren't like Mado. You are like me."

I could make no response to that, though I knew it was meant as the highest of compliments.

"Cousin Lucille," Uncle Hoadley shouted, "show Stella all your lovely pictures."

"Lights!" Cousin Lucille shouted back. "Lights!"

Aunt Olivia moved to stand close to me, whispering, "Lucille brings all her Lares and Penates with her when she comes to the beach. The pictures all belong in her house in Jefferson, and so does practically everything else here."

An elderly butler in a frayed white jacket came in and lit the candles in a large silver candelabrum, which he held up to illuminate the pictures. In heavy gold frames, they not only took up all the wall space, some of them overlapped each other. Bundled together that way, they looked like bad copies of the masters, the kind of thing art students spend hours doing in museums.

Cousin Lucille heaved herself up out of her chair and reached for the cane which she needed to support her immense weight. She waved it towards one of the darker oil paintings. "That's my Rembrandt," she said, "and that's my van Eyck. William and I lived abroad after the war; he was a great lover of art."

Cousin Lucille brandished her cane. "That's my Cranach, and that's my Thomas Eakins." The cane continued to tremble, then pointed at the portrait of a glorious golden girl. "That's the picture Winterhalter did of me while we were in Europe."

I looked from the portrait to the fat toad of a woman pointing at it, then closed my eyes in a reflex of pain. Had time destroyed Cousin Lucille? Or had she helped to destroy herself? Aunt Olivia was still, I suddenly realized, beautiful.

Aunt Mary Desborough raised her voice so that Cousin Lucille could hear. "Our portrait of Mado in the library is by Ingres, and the big portrait in the living room is by the younger Peale."

"Hush, Des," Cousin James said. "You and Olivia do not need to compete with Lucille."

Cousin Lucille's ears caught this. "Ha! They ought to know better than to try, but they never learn. *I* married William Hutlidge, for all Mary Desborough would have liked—"

"I couldn't stand him," Aunt Mary Desborough snapped. "He was a swine."

Cousin Lucille smiled placidly. "But a man, Des, which is something you've never known."

The old butler announced, "Dinner is served."

I was seated next to Cousin Lucille, who would occasionally reach out to give me an exploratory poke in the ribs. Dinner was fried chicken, rice, baked squash, hot bread, home-made peach ice cream.

"So you married young Terry, hey?" Cousin Lucille shouted, dropping rice and gravy over the front of her black dress. The butler took a clean napkin and quietly wiped it off. "How did you hook him?"

"I rather thought he hooked me."

Cousin Lucille gave a snort. "And you come from where? Who was your father?"

"I was born in Oxford, and my father was Benedict North."

"The philosopher," Aunt Olivia said.

"A philosopher, hey? I don't approve. Philosophy has caused my brother James all kinds of folly."

Uncle Hoadley spoke in his calmest manner. "Cousin James, you have undoubtedly read Benedict North's work?"

Cousin James, stroking his neat white beard, smiled. "Not only have I read it, Hoadley, but only last winter Miss Harris read Xenia his book on guilt."

"Guilt," Cousin Lucille snorted. "What has Xenia to be guilty about?"

"Less than you have," Aunt Olivia said.

"Always loyal, n'est-ce pas, chère cousine?" Cousin Lucille said. "I, at least, regret nothing."

"We were not speaking of regret," Olivia said.

"I have no sense of guilt, either, if that's what you're referring to. And William worked as hard as any of you. Nobody can say he had a lazy bone in his body."

"Nobody's saying it. It took energy to swing that heavy whip."

"Auntie." Uncle Hoadley, seated next to Aunt Olivia, put a restraining hand on hers.

"Stella might as well see us as we are."

Cousin James spoke calmly. "Like everybody else, a mixture of good, bad, and indifferent."

"Only fools feel guilty, brother," Cousin Lucille overrode him, "and that's because they do things without knowing what they're doing and regret them afterwards."

Aunt Olivia, irrepressible, said, "I'd hate to think that William knew everything he did."

"And if guilt isn't regret," Cousin Lucille shouted, "then what is it?"

Responding more to Cousin James's gentle smile than to Uncle Hoadley's warning hand, Aunt Olivia spoke quietly. "To accept guilt means to accept responsibility." She looked to Cousin James for corroboration. "It takes nobility to accept guilt. Not many of us can do it."

Cousin James nodded, setting down his water goblet with lightly trembling fingers. "But it's a shared guilt, dear Livvy, not just a private one. That helps. We, here at this table, all have a share in one another's actions. Lucille, like it or not, had a share in all that went on at Nyssa. And I had a share in every slave William bought on the auction block." Before either Cousin Lucille or Aunt Olivia could speak, he turned to the old butler. "And I would like some more of that superb chicken, please, Eben."

Eben brought the platter of chicken. He was old, and he moved slowly. Cousin Lucille began to complain loudly about his laziness and shiftlessness and thievery, as though he were deaf. I had heard Cousin Augusta speaking in front of her servants as though they were not present; it was, as it were, an agreed-upon fiction; but she had never been unkind, or said anything they could not or should not have heard. I was embarrassed, more for Cousin James than for the old butler, who continued imperturbably about his duties, finally coming in from the kitchen with a damp cloth to clean Cousin Lucille's front.

"I suppose you had Clive and Honoria with you for Morning Prayer?" Cousin Lucille asked.

Aunt Irene surprised me by saying, "It is the custom, Cousin Lucille."

Cousin Lucille brushed Eben's hand away. "Honoria and Clive are no doubt at Little Nyssa now, James, feasting with your Saintie?"

"They are eating together," Cousin James said quietly.

"It's bad enough, all the Nyssa niggers putting on airs, but Honoria pretending to be royalty is carrying things too far."

"Honoria *is* royalty," Aunt Olivia said.

"I notice you don't have her eat at the table with you."

"That is Honoria's choice. We would be honored."

"James!" Cousin Lucille shouted. "Something will have to be done about the twins."

"Why?" Aunt Olivia demanded. "The twins are fine."

"They've been coming up the beach and crabbing in front of my house."

"Why not, Lucille?" Cousin James asked. "Undoubtedly the crabs are better up here this summer than down towards San Feliz."

"I will not have them coming around my place and spying on me."

Cousin James said, "I really don't think the twins are interested in spying on anybody."

"They were peering in my windows the other night. I won't have it. If you don't put a stop to it I'll report them to the authorities and have them put away. I should have done it long ago. They're a menace."

"Lucille." Cousin James spoke before Aunt Olivia could get a word in. "I will speak to the twins. I really doubt if they were looking in your windows. They are not curious."

"Someone was peering in, and if it wasn't the twins, who was it?"

"Your imagination?" Aunt Olivia asked.

"Nonsense. I have no imagination."

"True enough."

"I warn you, James, I will not be spied on. And don't just talk to the twins. I want action. Talk is a waste of time."

"I wasted time," Aunt Mary Desborough said, "and now does time waste me." She held up her hand to stop Aunt Olivia and looked expectantly at me.

"*Richard II*, Aunt Des."

Aunt Mary Desborough looked like a headmistress whose pet pupil has just done well on an exam. Aunt Olivia gave me her shining smile, much like Cousin James's. "Xenia would have loved you."

"Xenia does love her," Cousin James said.

"Eben, you may clear now," Cousin Lucille ordered.

9

Uncle Hoadley, Aunt Irene, and I drove home in one carriage; the old aunts, Honoria, and Clive in the other; Uncle Hoadley was precluding further argument. Our carriage followed, and when Clive had turned in towards the sheds behind Illyria which served as stable, Uncle Hoadley continued along the beach.

"Where are we going?" Aunt Irene asked.

"Something I want to see. We won't be long."

We passed the cluster of coquina and cypress buildings which made up San Feliz, and continued on down the beach. Aunt Irene asked again, "But where are we going, Hoadley?"

"To the yacht basin. I called a meeting of the Yacht Club officers last week in Jefferson; it occurred to me that it might be pleasant to have a regatta of sorts at the beach."

A sharp note came into Aunt Irene's velvet voice. "I dare say you'll find a way to mingle some new money with the old?"

"There's not much old money left, my dear, but that is not what I had in mind. Just a gathering together of people with like interests. Most of our friends have boats of a sort, and we're also concerned with certain irresponsible actions all over the state, and intend to do something about it."

Aunt Irene smoothed her skirts impatiently. "How can having a regatta help?"

"More than you might think. You will have to trust me, Irene."

"Why should I?"

It was the first time I had seen overtly the antagonism which I instinctively felt lay between them.

"Irene, my dear," he said calmly, "you are sounding like Kitty."

"With the same cause?" Her hands shook on the handle of her parasol.

"Perhaps if Kitty had trusted Therro more, the things which happened might never have happened."

"Therro was a Renier," Aunt Irene said tightly. "And so are you."

"Irene, haven't we given enough displays of ill-temper and ill-manners in front of Stella for one day? Try to remember that you and I share all our interests in common."

"Do we?"

"We are closer than you know."

The carriage drew up in front of a long, semi-enclosed body of water filled with an assortment of small craft. The water was separated from the ocean by an arm of low dune, covered with vine and sea oats. A narrow opening, protected with low coquina walls, led from the basin to the ocean.

Uncle Hoadley did not get out of the carriage, but sat and looked across the arm of dune to the boats, as if he were counting them. But when he spoke, it had nothing to do with yachts. "Irene, you must try not to argue with the great-aunts. You live in two different worlds."

"And you, Hoadley? Which world do you live in?"

"Perhaps I have one foot in each. Right after the war, Stella, we quite literally did not have enough to eat, but were willing to give up some of what little we had in order to have a ball once a year, because it gave us a feeling of identity. For at least one night a year people like the great-aunts knew who they were."

"I apologize," Aunt Irene said stiffly, "for not having starved as a child."

"Irene, Irene, I am simply explaining that I understand the great-aunts a little better than you do. And I am enough of a Renier to share the responsibility which Uncle Theron and Cousin James had for the slaves—though not their solution. We did bring the slaves over from Africa, and we are responsible for this."

"When we lost the war, we lost the responsibility, too. Let the carpetbaggers cope."

"Do you really mean that?"

She shrugged.

"Now, Irene, don't you think a regatta might be a splendid change of pace?"

"I suppose it could be quite pleasant. Would we have Japanese lanterns and dancing?"

"We're just beginning to make plans, but I think I can

promise that at the very least there will be excitement and change."

Aunt Irene twitched her shoulders and gave a moue and I saw in her an echo of the beautiful and perhaps tantalizing woman she had once been. "If you are good I will save the first and last dance for you." She tapped him lightly on the sleeve, as though with a fan.

"And trust me, Irene," Uncle Hoadley said. "For once, trust me."

It was after four when we got back to Illyria. The old aunts had gone to their rooms to rest.

"We'll just have a light supper around nine," Aunt Irene announced. "I am exhausted. And I'm sure Stella is, too. After everything she's seen and heard today. We must seem as savage to her as anyone from Kairogi. I'm sure Lord and Lady Dowler don't behave the way we do. I apologize, honey. I apologize for us all."

She and Uncle Hoadley went upstairs. I followed, and continued on up to my room. I wasn't sleepy, but I was hot and tired, and I took off my stiff Sunday clothes and put on a light negligee and lay down. A large and somnolent water bug was clinging to the shutters and slowly folding and unfolding his bronze wings. I picked up Mado's journals.

During the early stages of the war, when the whole family was gathered together at Nyssa, there was an active peace and joy to the pages. Mado was well aware that Theron and James would soon be leaving Nyssa, Theron to set up field hospitals, James to take charge of his regiment, that it would be up to the women to run the community, and these weeks when they were together held a kind of radiance I did not understand. She was pregnant again, with one of the little girls who would die with Nyssa. Now I was reading with pre-knowledge, and Mado's joy was almost unbearable to me.

James left, and then Theron. They knew that James was often in the midst of the fiercest fighting; and Theron, too, going after the wounded, was in danger. But he used to get back to Nyssa fairly frequently. Sometimes he or James sent them soldiers to hide. Once, when Theron was back at Nyssa for several weeks, Mado was perturbed because he spent so much time with Olivia. Lucille, even then, had a vicious and jealous tongue, and there was gossip. 'Renier men are all the same,' Lucille told Mado. 'I'm glad I'm married to a Hutlidge.

William hates his sister. There will never be any incest in the Hutlidge family.'

"I do not have Theron's peaceful nature," Mado wrote. "Not that I put any credence in Lucille's malign words, but I know other people will. Anything will serve, no matter how absurd, to get back at Theron and James for Nyssa. And incest is not unknown in Southern families. Lucille sat and drank several cups of our precious tea—the supply is running very low—patted her golden curls, and remarked upon Olivia's beauty. 'Yes,' I replied, 'we do have a plethora of pulchritude at Nyssa.' 'You and your French words,' Lucille drawled, feigning stupidity. She kissed me and went out to her carriage, unfurling her parasol like a banner at battle, and was driven triumphantly back to the Hutlidge plantation.

"Olivia came tonight as we were all getting ready for bed—Theron was in the library, writing—and sat perched on the foot of the bed, chattering away, mostly about her love for the captain of Mark's yacht. It was her way of reassuring me."

A few weeks later Mado wrote, "There is something afoot, and I do not know what. Olivia has gone off on a visit to some distant cousins in Raleigh. Theron says that she is not well and the pace at Nyssa is too much for her; he has sent her away for peace and quiet. This he announced to us all at breakfast. Everybody else seemed to accept it, but it does not ring true. We may work hard at Nyssa, but there is a peace here I have never felt anywhere else, except at Illyria with Honoria, and Olivia obviously blossoms here. I have never seen her look better."

For the next several months Mado wrote only of life at Nyssa, of the development and delight of her children, of her deepening friendship with Clive and others of the community. "Clive is teaching me the Bible. He knows it far better than I do. He is a well of clear, pure water. One must go deep to find it, but it is more than worth the descent." Then she wrote, "Now at last I know what was going on between Theron and Olivia. I know what Olivia's visits to various relatives really have been about. But I cannot write it."

I put the journal down, slipped into a thin, dimity dress, and went down to Aunt Olivia's room. I opened the door quietly and peeped in, in case she was sleeping, and found her struggling to walk round the bed.

"Aunt Olivia, what's the matter?"

"If I stay still my joints will lock. I won't let it happen."

Tears of pain stood in her child's blue eyes. "You saw Xenia, didn't you? I couldn't bear to be like that, I couldn't bear it."

"But Cousin Xenia had a stroke."

"I've seen people become vegetables simply by staying in bed. No, Stella, no, not for me. I'd rather die. And for someone who has a reaction of panic at the dissolution of this flawed and failing body, that's quite an announcement. I think I would like to die a holy death, Stella. Does that give me away as being hopelessly old-fashioned? I suppose I am. But perhaps our death is the one strange, holy, and unique thing about us, the one thing we can *do*, as *ourselves*. Maybe in dying I will at last become me." She held one of the footposts of the bed to support herself. "I've always been a coward—" She gave a small gasp of pain. "I'll get into bed now."

I helped her. She leaned back against the pillows, breathing quick, shallow breaths, finally a deep sigh. "I do get very angry at God. Maybe it's better just to be angry at Lucille. Lucille and I have always been like cat and dog. And saying that I've been in a lot of pain all day is only alibi-ing. I'm very sorry."

"No, Auntie."

"I could have behaved better. And I didn't. Deliberately. We were all at our worst. Which I suppose means we behaved as usual. But we weren't always like this. Times around our table were our most beautiful and blest. Particularly when it was just—well, when it wasn't the whole tribe. 'We' were Mado and Theron, James and Xenia. And me: Olivia."

"And Aunt Des?"

Beckoning to me like a child inviting a playmate to a game, Aunt Olivia indicated that I should climb onto the bed. Then she drew the dotted-Swiss curtains about us and we were enveloped in a soft white world that reminded me of snow. "Now!" she said with satisfaction. "We're safe! About Des: Des was the one who tried to keep the gaps closed—or at any rate to keep them from widening. Mado and Theron were the only people in the world who could get Des to laughing, not just social snickering, but real hilarity. She didn't share their passion for justice, but she quite honestly couldn't see anything wrong with having slaves."

"And you, Aunt Olivia?"

"Mado had an extraordinary way of making me see things through her eyes. She came here as Theron's bride—just like you—and she saw things we'd always taken for granted, and suddenly I couldn't take them for granted any longer. Slaves—

we hadn't seen any difference between having slaves and having servants. We treated our slaves a lot better than most people treat their servants. We didn't see anything wrong. We all buy and sell people as well as things every day. It's just more apparent when you call people slaves than when you hire them and then overwork and underpay them and cheat them whenever you can.... Stella, believe me, it wasn't any of it cut and dried, black and white. The war wasn't about slavery, not really. That was the smallest part of it."

"Aunt Olivia, why did you give me Mado's journals to read?"

She sighed. "Because I'm a coward, I suppose. I knew you'd have questions, and that the questions ought to be answered. I thought if you read Mado's journals I wouldn't have to tell you, or perhaps she'd answer enough of your questions so you wouldn't ask the other ones. But go ahead and ask, Stella, and I'll tell you what and when I can. Did you come down to ask me something special?"

"Yes. When Mado was writing about all of you being at Nyssa during the war, there was something about you, Aunt Olivia, she couldn't explain."

Aunt Olivia looked relieved. She had expected me to ask something else, and perversely I wished I knew what it was, so that I could ask. She relaxed back against her pillows. "Mado didn't put everything in the journals, I'm well aware of that. What was it you wanted to ask?"

"Mado said that during the war you used to go off on visits to various relatives and there was some mystery about this."

Aunt Olivia sat up, pushing the pillows against the headboard; she pulled her knees up and put her arms around them. "It's not what Lucille—"

"I didn't think it was."

"Of course Lucille managed to get tongues wagging—and *she* talks about family loyalty! I want you to know about it—for all the wrong and selfish reasons—so that you'll think better of me, I suppose. So that you won't think I'm nothing but a bickering, childish old woman, afraid to die. For what it's worth, I've never told anybody. Mado guessed, and went to Theron, and after that she helped me, in that she always gave me enough courage to—but I never told Des. There's nobody living who knows except Clive and James. And I imagine Clive has told Honoria. Why do I want you to know, after all these long years of silence?"

Then she gave her small, surprising giggle. "It's one reason I was so amused and pleased to have Terry involved in hanky-panky myself, though a much less dignified kind. I was in a small and not very important way a courier. I took messages. During a war messages don't get very far in a proper diplomatic pouch. So—remembering that bushel—I did cross battle lines. I was under fire. The presumption was that I was going to visit relatives, as Des and I had been wont to do before the war, because I wasn't strong enough to do the hospital work at Nyssa. Sometimes when there wasn't a safe place for me to sleep, I slept under haystacks, got soaked with rain—that's probably how my rheumatism got started. You see, lambie, it was easy for me, because everybody thought I was silly and ineffectual. I was the last person anyone would have thought of as a dispatch bearer, so I could go unsuspected into places where anybody else would immediately have been caught and shot. I almost did get caught, several times, but I always managed to fumble my way out. My tongue may be foolish, but it's glib."

"But why couldn't Mado write about it in the journals?"

"Because if Nyssa had been taken by Union soldiers, if the journals had been found, I'd have been shot, and Theron and James, too. The way Mado phrased it, if anybody had checked over the journals, it would have looked as though my hanky-panky had been with my own brother. It wouldn't have been the first time in the South. But it's not in the Renier tradition. Does that clear it up for you? Anything else you want to ask?"

"How did the journals come to be saved when Nyssa was burned?"

"They weren't in the house. They were in the old building we used as a school, where we all used to go when we wanted to write or be alone. Mado kept her journals in one of the desks. Oh, dear, why have I told you all this about myself?"

"Because I asked you to."

"Thank you. But it's also to make you think less poorly of me. But I don't need to buy your love, any more than I needed to buy Jimmy's."

"You have my love, Aunt Olivia." I leaned across the bed and embraced her. For a few moments she clutched at me almost as she had during the storm.

We heard a knock on the door, and Aunt Mary Desborough's voice. "All right, Olivia, open up, I know you're there. Is Stella with you?"

Aunt Olivia reached for the cord and pulled aside the curtains so that she could peer at her sister. "What business is it of yours?"

"Hoadley says you're not to monopolize Stella."

"I'm not."

"You are, too. There are Things to Be Done."

"What?"

"I," said Aunt Mary Desborough righteously, "am going to help Hoadley and Clive in the garden."

"And I," said Aunt Olivia, "am going to stay behind my mosquito netting and be a lily of the field."

There was a sudden wistfulness in her voice, and Aunt Des sprang to her sister's defense. "Olivia has always been delicate. Come and see our garden, Stella. Mado planned it. What are you really going to do, Livvy?"

"I am going to read Darwin," Aunt Olivia said.

10

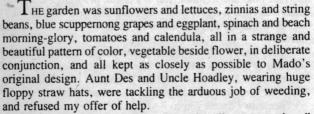

THE garden was sunflowers and lettuces, zinnias and string beans, blue scuppernong grapes and eggplant, spinach and beach morning-glory, tomatoes and calendula, all in a strange and beautiful pattern of color, vegetable beside flower, in deliberate conjunction, and all kept as closely as possible to Mado's original design. Aunt Des and Uncle Hoadley, wearing huge floppy straw hats, were tackling the arduous job of weeding, and refused my offer of help.

"Not until you are more used to the climate, my dear," Uncle Hoadley said. "Even this late-afternoon sun is too hot for anybody except us natives, and we ourselves can't take it for long."

I wandered back into the house. I was filled with a sense of unease, the kind of feeling in the air which warns of a storm—and yet the sky was clear and hot, and I did not think that what I felt hovering over me was physical thunder and lightning. I turned my steps to the library, drawn, called to the

War Room, the inhabited room in the uninhabited part of Illyria, the room which had given me no welcome. I pushed the revolving wall of books and crossed the ballroom, not at all sure that I could find the War Room again.

Fine grains of sand which had blown in through the closed windows, through the very walls, held the prints of my soles. I moved upstairs and down, in and out of rooms, past butterfly cases, walls of Oriental weapons, chinoiserie, portraits, porcelains, sand constantly gritting under my feet.

Footprints other than mine.

There, in front of me, was a door with a white china knob. I pushed it open.

Behind the large table in the center of the room stood a young man, bent over a spread-out map, marking it with a compass. At first I thought it was Ron James, but, as he raised up and looked directly at me, I saw that it was a stranger, a little darker than Ron, not as tall, but with a striking similarity of bone structure and expression.

He regarded me, startled at my presence, perhaps, but not surprised, and smiled in welcome. "Mrs. Theron Renier, the newest?"

I acknowledged this with a small nod.

"I'm Tron Zenumin—no, Tron's not a nigger nickname for Theron, my name is Terence Ronald. My half brother, Ronnie, is the Theron in the Zenumin nest. I'm honored to make your acquaintance, Mrs. Renier. My mother has talked to me about you, and how you've already made friends."

"Your mother has been very kind to me."

"Why wouldn't she be? Zenumins have a big debt to pay the Reniers. Me, for instance. I talk half Illyria, half scrub, because Mado taught me to read and write. We're all anxious to make you feel at home, Mrs. Renier. By the way—please excuse my asking you—who told you about this room, and that Tron would be here?"

"Nobody." I looked around me, then across the desk, past Tron to the big map on the wall. It was, I thought, a map of Africa, but I was far more interested in Tron than I was in the map.

"Then how you happen to be here?"

"I was exploring—exploring Illyria."

"Why, sure enough, Mrs. Renier, Illyria will be yours one day, won't it? Course you want to look it over."

"Mine? Whatever gave you that idea?"

"Yours and Terry's. Why not? Who else Honoria going to leave Illyria to but Terry?"

"You and Ron?"

"Me? You don't know my grandmother, Miss Stella, if you can think that. Maybe she might want to leave it to Ronnie. He her pet. But she can't."

"Why not?"

"Riders."

"What could they have to do with it?"

"Burnings or lynchings or other merry pranks." He came from behind the desk and drew up a chair for me. "Won't you be seated, Mrs. Renier?"

I took the offered seat. "Do you live here?"

"Me? Not little old Tron. I live back in the scrub like my mother. Maybe Tron be the link between Illyria and the scrub. Illyria's in my blood, sure enough. And right now I'm doing some work for Mr. Hoadley. Miss Stella, ma'am, it not my place to make suggestions to you, but it be best if you don't talk to nobody about this room, or finding Tron."

"All right. I won't say anything if you don't want me to."

"Nothing wrong. Nothing wrong about my being here. Tron got some right to be in Illyria. But Mr. Hoadley, he might not want it known. Mr. Hoadley, he do special work, very special, and he allow me to help him some. But he say Tron not to tell anybody. Nobody knows about this room, or about his work, not Miss Irene, not the old ladies. So if you could see your way—"

"I won't say anything."

"Thank you, Miss Stella, ma'am. That make me feel easier. I knowed I could ask you, because of what my mother say about you. Now, ma'am, if you would so kindly go downstairs, I finish up what Mr. Hoadley done ask me to do."

I left him, shutting the door carefully behind me, and found my way back to the library with only a few false turns. I stood amidst the fusty smell of books and listened: the house was quiet, was warm with peace. I went towards the kitchen, seeking the comfort of ordinariness, of a stove, a sink, a pump, pots and pans. Seeking the comfort of Honoria and Clive.

They were there, sitting at the kitchen table with Ron and the twins, drinking glasses of cold tea.

"Don't get up," I said swiftly, and moved to an empty chair that was pulled slightly back from the table as though waiting for me.

There was about Dr. Ron James and Terence Ronald Zenumin the same veiled look to the eyes, the same fine flare of nostril. Tron had disturbed and intrigued me almost as much as his brother, with his odd speech, slipping from the educated cadences of Uncle Hoadley to the dark rhythm of the scrub. There was in the two young men none of the peaceful strength that was so powerful in their grandparents. Nevertheless I felt an intense desire to know both of them better. And perhaps peace had not come easily or early to Honoria and Clive.

Honoria put a cool glass in my hand.

"Thank you, Honoria! That tastes wonderful."

"Wonderful," Willy said.

"Wonderful, wonderful," Harry echoed. They held out their glasses for more.

"Willy and Harry," Ron said, "there was a total eclipse of the moon on Good Friday, April 2, 1865. The next eclipse of the moon on Good Friday will be April 12. What year will it be?"

"1968," Willy said.

"1968," came Harry's answer a fraction of a beat behind.

I asked, "But twice six divided by three is too difficult?"

Ron James smiled gravely, "Much."

On impulse I turned to the two little men. "Willy, Harry, what's 0×3?"

The two tea glasses were lowered simultaneously, set down on the scrubbed surface of the table. Willy closed his eyes. His face was expressionless. But Harry screwed up his round, wrinkled face, grimacing as though in pain.

"Nothing," Willy whispered. "The answer is nothing. Nought."

"Nothing," Harry echoed, and then, "I don't want it to be nothing!"

"But it's nothing!" Willy shouted in sudden excitement. "Nothing! Nothing! Nothing!"

Ron pushed his chair away from the table. "Sit down, Willy, drink your tea. Be quiet." He took Harry in his arms and held him close. "Hush, Harry. It's all right. Don't be frightened." As Harry relaxed in the young man's arms, Ron looked over the white head at me, moving his lips silently: "No, I don't know what's wrong."

"A keg of powder," Honoria murmured. "It was a keg of powder. Why?"

* * *

$0 \times 3 = 0$. It had annoyed me; it had seemed unreasonable, and I did not like unreason. But the twins' reaction frightened me. There was fear in the kitchen and I left it and went out onto the back veranda, taking comfort in our bathing dresses kicking on the line, looking almost like marionettes. There were tea towels on the line, too, and old linen napkins, worn and darned.

When I heard Tron's voice I did not want to go back to the kitchen. But I was curious. I stood in the shadow of the chinaberry tree where I could hear.

"Tron." Honoria's voice did not sound welcoming. "What you doing here?"

"Where Miss Stella?" he asked.

"Gone to her room to rest, probably," Honoria said.

"All right, Tron, what you want? What you doing here? Clive sounded austere and unwelcoming.

"I want Grandmother to run the cards for me."

"You can want," Honoria said.

"What I want to know doesn't have only to do with me. It's you and Grandfather, too. If what I aim for to do not come to pass, then we die, all of us. Please. Help me."

"I do not run the cards."

"Grandmother, the Granddam is afeared. Run them now. The Granddam send me."

"If the Granddam be afeared, why don't she run the cards?"

"She run them. She afeared of what she see. And she don't have the gift like you do. Sometimes it play her false."

"How come she got the reputation, then? And the clients?"

"Granddam live on it, Grandmother. How else? It as good a living as any for a Zenumin. And she don't cheat. If she don't see, she don't tell. She see enough. She on the edge of the gift, like my mother. But you right in the center."

"Those with the gift do not take money."

"Grandmother, when did you last ask the cards something?"

There was a cold silence; out on the veranda I felt the cold; and then a cracked voice singing, "Ashes, ashes, we all fall down." The twins backed out the sagging screen door and almost fell over me.

"Boys, I—" Guilt and confusion made my face hot.

Willy held his finger to his mouth. "Sh." He stood beside me.

"But we oughtn't—"

"Sh!" Willy was vehement. "Listen. Learn."

Honoria's voice came harshly to us. "Get out of my kitchen, Tron. You made trouble when you was a little boy. You make trouble now."

"Grandmother—"

"Go back to the Granddam. Or your mama. Maybe she won't make you pay, though I never know her do anything for free."

"She done a lot of loving."

There was contempt in Honoria's voice. "Her?"

"We wouldn't be in this kitchen without it, Ronnie and me."

"It don't take love to make a baby. Would God it did."

I tried again to move, to reveal myself, but again the twins hushed me. "You tell Honoria," Willy said. "Tell her you hear."

"Scared of Tron," Harry said. "Got to find out. Listen. Tell later."

Tron's voice came out to us, loud and bitter. "Grandmother, you just don't want to understand me, do you? What I done you should always say me no? I should have known better than to ask for something now the favorite is home. Ronnie, *he* live in Illyria. Tron, he just go back to the scrub. Teach me Illyrian ways and send me back to the scrub."

Clive's voice was cold. "You made the choice, Tron."

"Grandmother be scared, just like the Granddam, only more, because she seen something. What you see, Grandmother?"

"Tron. Sometimes I has the gift of knowing what is going to happen in time that is to come. Sometimes the Lord tells me what is going to happen."

"How? How he tell you?"

"He just tell me. It like seeing around a corner of the sky. The sky opens, there comes a crack, I see through. That is the gift. It is given, and it is up to the Lord to tell me how to use it. If I run the cards—if I try to find out that way what the Lord is up to, then I be trying to manipulate him."

Tron laughed. His laugh was very like his mother's. "Maniwhatsit: that's not your word, Grandmother. That's old Mado."

"So."

I had forgotten Ron was in the kitchen until I heard his voice. "It's superstition."

"What be superstition?"

Honoria said, "It's something that gets between you and God."

"You think you can keep things from coming between you

and God, Grandmother? You just listen to little old Tron. You didn't take me out of the scrub the way you did my baby brother. You never live in the scrub yourself. Maybe Tron could learn you something."

"Go," Clive said. "Leave us, Tron."

"I understand I not wanted. But not why."

"Because trouble come with you."

"Nobody from Illyria going to send love to my—our—mama?"

"You are not a bearer of love, Tron."

Suddenly the twins grasped my arms, hurried me around the corner of the veranda. We were hidden by the shadows, by the ludicrous swinging bathing garments. Tron ran swiftly down the back veranda steps, along the pink brick path, past the fig tree, vaulted over the Spanish Bayonettes and disappeared into the jungle.

"Now," Willy said, "you tell Honoria and Clive."

"Now. Tell Honoria. Tell her you hear," Harry said.

"Boys listen. Don't tell. Pretty lady must tell."

"Goodbye, lady. Good lady. Tell all. Boys go home now."

The kitchen smelled warm and safe and familiar. From the black pot on the stove came the good, solid smell of meat and onions. Honoria was shelling peas into a dented colander. Clive was at the sink washing the glasses. Ron was still sitting at the table. He rose as I came in and pulled out my chair.

"Please let me help with the peas," I said. "Please."

Honoria handed me a sack of peas, put an old newspaper on the floor beside me. "You can throw the pods here. I cook the English peas with lettuce and a little onion, the way Miss Mado show me."

I wanted to say that the twins had made me listen, had made me stay on the back veranda when I wanted to stop eavesdropping. "The twins—" I started. I took a pea pod and ran my finger through it. The small green pellets bounced into the colander. Bending over the colander, I told them what I had done.

There was a grey, empty silence. They did not say any of the things they might have said.

"Ron told me not to be like Bluebeard's wife. I was worse. Please forgive me."

"Miss Stella," Honoria said dispassionately, with no condemnation, "I grew up a long way from here. I never went to school. I learn to speak English from the slaves, not from

Claudius Broadley. He wanted for me to be the African princess, beautiful and silent. It was Miss Mado who taught me to read and write. She teached me sometimes with words, and sometimes with silence. We could sit for hours and never speak a word, and yet we were talking with each other all the time. When I wanted to run the cards for her, she wouldn't let me. It was never that she doubted my power to read the cards. But to do it, to ask the cards what is going to happen, this is wrong. How can I tell you what I mean? Supposing when Ronnie, here, was little, he ask Clive could he do something, and Clive say him no; and then supposing Ronnie he turn around and ask me over Clive's head: that would be wrong, wouldn't it?"

Ron had been listening intently, and now he gave the most spontaneous and free laugh I had heard from him. "Which is precisely what I used to do. Over and over. Anything to get my own way. And both of you made me realize that it was wrong to try to play you off against each other that way. Maybe my bottom learned the lesson before the rest of me, but I did learn. Though I still like to get my own way." He ran his slender fingers through his short-cropped black hair (I had never before seen hair of the strange consistency of the Negroes', and I wanted to touch it, to see what it felt like to my fingers).

Honoria regarded him gravely. "So if I ask the cards, it's like you going over Clive's head. I'm going over the Lord's head."

"Why, Grandmother?" I was glad that he was taking her seriously, that he was not laughing at her.

"Why do I have to ask the cards, son? Why can't I ask the Lord? If I ask the cards over the Lord's head, then I'm believing that the cards know better than he does, aren't I?"

"Not necessarily, Grandmother. You're just being a child trying to get around him."

"But I am not a child, son. I have not been a child for a long time. If I have something I want to know, I'll ask the Lord, not the cards."

Ron drained his glass, added it to those he had taken to the old stone sink. "Thanks for the tea, Grandmother. It helped." He hesitated, pumped water so that it splashed into the glass. Then, "Was Tron right when he implied that you have, in fact, run the cards recently?"

Honoria bowed her head. "Yes. God help me."

"You asked the cards something?"

"Yes." She sat down, putting her face into her large, strong hands, bowed over in shame and grief.

Outside the kitchen window the mockingbird in the chinaberry tree began to sit inebriatedly. A yellow jacket hummed against the window; I looked out over the flowers bordering the brick path to the vegetable garden and the bamboo grove, to the protecting swords of the Spanish Bayonettes, and the fig tree with one live branch.

Clive pulled the shutters closer to keep out the heat of the sun, which was dipping westwards. And I felt cold. I could not see the garden, or the fig tree.

And in this strange, chill shadowiness I could no longer push back the memory of Cousin Augusta taking me with her to the gypsy. It happened when I was about fourteen. Cousin Augusta was going through one of her periodic enthusiasms; this time it was for spiritualism and the occult. One spring she arranged to have me go with her to a strawberry tea; she was making one of her periodic efforts to have me take part in what she considered normal life. I enjoyed the afternoon and the other girls and boys. It was one of those rare spring days when a picnic by the river was perfection. There was a striped awning to keep out the sun, or an unexpected shower, and we played battledore and shuttlecock, and croquet, and I laughed and got hot and happy, and when the carriage came to take us home I was sorry to leave.

On the way back, on the outskirts of the city, Cousin Augusta had the driver turn down a mean little street, to a house set back in the shadows. 'Since we are so close,' she said, 'I thought we'd stop off for a moment. I've heard there's a marvelous gypsy here who tells one absolutely extraordinary things.'

There was a sign outside the house with strange symbols on it, and within was a dirty old woman who had a pack of greasy cards, gold loops swinging in her ears, and dark hairs springing out of ears and nostrils. The place smelled of sweat and filth and incense. I was both repelled and fascinated.

Money passed between Cousin Augusta and the old woman.

Then the cards were run, spread out on a rickety table. The gypsy told Cousin Augusta all the usual things, and perhaps a few which were unusual, for how could she have known of Cousin Octavian's frequent trips to Africa, or his interest in primitive civilizations? She flattered Cousin Augusta, mentioning her beauty and talents as a hostess. But it was all done by rote. She was not interested in what she was saying, though Cousin Augusta hung on every word.

Then the gypsy turned to me and asked to see my palm.

Cousin Augusta pushed me forward. 'Go on, child. Don't be shy.'

The gypsy took my hand in her dirty old claw and looked at it intently. I tried to pull away, mumbling that I didn't have any money, knowing that one is supposed to cross a fortune teller's palm with silver.

The gypsy cut Cousin Augusta short. 'I do not take money for this one.' She studied my palm for a long time, not speaking, and then she began to spread the cards on the table; it was all quite unlike the indifference with which she had regarded Cousin Augusta. In the end, as I try to reconstruct it, the gypsy told me very little. She said that in a few years I would make a long journey across the ocean; that was not in any way extraordinary; isn't that what gypsies usually tell people? But she did tell me that the man I would marry would come from far away, and that I would go to live and bear my children among strangers. 'But the Guardians will care for you, if you recognize them for who they are.' I had no idea what she was talking about; the smell in the dirty room made me nauseated.

Holding my young, cold hand in her old, grubby one, she said, 'The Guardians always watch over the Star Changers. But there will be others who will try to catch you in their web. Beware of spiders. Beware of fire. I see—I see that you will play with fire and that you will be burned. Fire. I see fire, and a young man dead, a young man you love. You will change the stars, but this I still see, the young man dead—'

Honoria's voice slapped across my fear. "What is it, Miss Stella?"

I told her only that Cousin Augusta had taken me to a fortune teller and that it had frightened me. My terror had been so irrational that I had run out of the house, past the waiting carriage, down dark and unfamiliar streets, not even caring that I was lost, knowing only that I must run before I heard anything more.

"All alone," Honoria said. "You poor little thing."

"My father and Cousin Octavian were furious with Cousin Augusta, and Cousin Augusta was furious with me; she said that I had behaved like a little ninny, that there was nothing to be frightened about. Maybe there wasn't. One does not always get frightened for logical reasons. Of course it was the end of Cousin Augusta's occult period. It was a long time before she forgave me."

Ron had been silent. Now he asked, "And your father? What did he have to say?"

"Funny. He said a lot of what Honoria's just said. And he told me how primitive people used to worship gods who fought among themselves, and really didn't care for the people whose gods they were, so they had to be sacrificed to."

Honoria nodded. "Yes, Miss Stella. That is how it is where I come from. We made sacrifices to still the anger of the gods."

I looked at her in astonishment. All that my father had told me seemed to be about the dim past, about civilizations long buried. I thought of it in terms of Cousin Octavian's archaeological diggings, his piecing together of artifacts found in ancient tombs and temples. So now I did not stop to think that what I was saying might be offensive—or even apply—to Honoria. If you were a savage, my father had said, you could try to go over the heads of the gods. If your god didn't do what you wanted him to do, you could get mad at him, or you could appeal to Fate—a blind, impersonal, unconcerned fate, a fate more powerful than the god.

"When Miss Mado and I became friends, I tried to forget the old gods. Miss Mado taught me to give up my gods and to believe in God."

Ron's laugh was savage. "I don't have the—the spiritual sophistication to believe in a God of love. I'm a scientist, and I see no evidence of one."

Honoria spoke slowly, a reminiscent echo of the Mado-sound in her voice. "When I come to believe that the gods is God, then I understand that I may not read the cards. Or go looking to the stars. I had to stop asking over God's head. It not easy to stop doing something you can do. I can go over God's head and ask. I can find things out that way. God will not stop me."

"If you can do it, why not?" Ron shrugged.

"You're not sure I can. I can. If I want to know ahead, I can ask the cards, and the cards will tell me. And this is grief."

"It's superstition, Grandmother. That's all it is. And coincidence. If you could really know everything ahead of time, then you wouldn't have any free will."

"If I understand what you talking about, son, that's just what I been trying to tell you. If I asks the cards, then I be trying to see the future before it happen. And if I see it, then what I done is to close the future so it can't change."

Ron was leaning forward, his hands dropped loosely between his knees, wholly attentive. "So this is final, then? You set the pattern of your future and it can't be changed?"

Suddenly I understood. "It's only final if you believe it. But who goes to a fortune teller with complete skepticism? People wouldn't go if they didn't believe—at least a little. And that's enough." I took a deep breath. "Honoria, listen: *I* don't know what you saw in the cards. So nothing has to be set."

Clive stood up. "Miss Stella, you is right. The stars obey they Lord. Honoria, old woman, it is in your prayers you has to ask things. Not the cards, not the stars. Now you has to go to God and repent."

"God will not always undo what we have done," Honoria said.

I heard again the terrible echo of the old English gypsy's voice telling me that a young man I loved would die.

Ron looked at me sharply, a doctor's probing look. "Mrs. Renier—"

I pulled my handkerchief out of my pocket and wiped my face, dried my wet palms.

Instead of asking me, as I expected, if I felt all right, Ron said, "Do you believe in God?"

"I don't know," I whispered. "I don't know. Do you?"

He shrugged. "Why would I?"

Clive looked coldly at the young man. "Is this what all your fine English education fitted you for? I expect more of you than this, son."

Ron moved the pump handle up and down so that water ran into the already rinsed glasses. "Faith—superstition: I can't see much difference between Mado's angels and Tron wanting Grandmother to run the cards."

Clive slapped his thin hand against his thigh. "Then you cannot be a true doctor. Healing be more than book learning. It be what Dr. Theron had in his hands. Dr. Theron could look at a sick or hurt man and put his hand on him, and his hand would tell him what be right to do and what be wrong. Other people had the same learning as Dr. Theron, but it were he who got called to come to Jefferson to start Mercy Hospital. It were he who got called all over the country when there were yellow fever. Healing be a gift over and beyond anything you ever could learn in all those fancy schools of yours. You watch out, son, or all your learning will get in the way of healing. Miracles aren't made in medical schools."

"Who's looking for miracles?" Ron asked.

"What's a Star Changer, Honoria?" I asked.

Honoria did not answer. Her lips moved soundlessly. I thought she was praying.

Ron licked his lips as though they were dry. "If you have three apples and you multiply them by nothing, how many do you have?"

I fled.

11

UPSTAIRS in my room I fell onto my bed and dove into sleep as I dove into the slough in the morning. I could not have slept long when I was wakened by a knocking on the door and Aunt Irene's voice. "Stella, honey, there's cold meat and salad waiting downstairs. Did I disturb you? I thought you'd be through your nap."

"I am." I sat up. The bed felt damp from my body; my hair was moist around the temples: I would have to get used to the constant dampness of perspiration, of heavy, humid air. The sun seemed only to sizzle the moisture, not to dry it. My bathing dress felt clammy in the mornings, though Honoria put it out in the sun to dry.

Aunt Irene sat on the bench to my dressing table, looking at herself in the sea-specked mirror. She made a puckering face and pushed at the little lines on either side of her mouth and at the corners of her eyes; then she began fingering my things which Honoria had laid out on the dressing table; I had my mother's silver set, comb, brush, mirror, powder jars, oval tray; but I didn't have much in the way of paints, pomades, or powders.

"You have such a beautiful complexion, honey," she said. "You really don't need to do anything to it at all. I suppose the color in your cheeks is natural?"

"All mine."

"It's such a struggle to find a satisfactory rouge. They all seem to turn orange."

I sat on the edge of the bed, my hot bare feet on the floor, and felt for my slippers.

Aunt Irene removed a long chestnut hair from the tortoiseshell teeth of my comb. "You don't know anything about the Renier men, do you?"

"All the Therons are nearsighted."

"Very. How well do you know your Theron?"

"Well enough to have married him."

Aunt Irene sighed and smiled, traced the monogram of the back of my hairbrush with one finger. "You're very young, my dear. Did you know many other men?"

"I was brought up in an Oxford college."

"That's not quite what I meant. You did live a very protected life, didn't you?"

"In a way, I suppose—yes." I knew about Thermopylae, but I didn't know about Bull Run. I knew about evolution, but not the American Revolution. I had read Thucydides and Tacitus and Gibbon but she was right: I didn't know much about young men.

"Honey, please don't misunderstand me, but I think it may help you a little if I tell you something about the Reniers— Renier men, that is. They've been distinguished, that's for sure. I used to think people had to be good to be distinguished: I learned the hard way. Renier men have been judges and governors and bishops. They've served this country well, there's no denying it. When you married Terry you didn't marry someone no-count. The best entree into Charleston society is to have Renier connections."

She laughed her little social trill, and I thought that she had not come upstairs to tell me what a distinguished family I had married into.

"I wonder would it have made a difference if Hoadley and I had had children of our own? Hoadley takes such a great interest in young people." She paused. I waited. "Of course Hoadley doesn't like it talked about—he's so modest—but he's responsible for young Ronnie James's education."

"Yes. I heard."

"And what else did you hear, honey?"

"Why—nothing. I think it was splendid of Uncle Hoadley. The Dowlers help a number of young men get their education."

"And what kind of thanks do they get?" She was winding a hair from my comb around her finger. The long hair broke. "Of course it was fine for Hoadley to do what he did. He needn't have done anything about it at all. It would have been more discreet. Sometimes Hoadley's more like his Uncle Theron than his own father, and of course Uncle Theron always had Mado pushing at him. What right did she, a foreigner, have telling him what was right and what was wrong?"

I sat on the edge of the bed and looked at the golden snakes circling my finger; their ruby eyes glinted in the evening sun. Terry didn't need me to tell him what was right and what was wrong; we'd agree, anyhow.

"And James! I know more about Cousin James than most people do. And Therro—Terry's father, my husband's dear, darling, beloved friend—Therro had his reputation, too. That was the whole trouble between Therro and Kitty, that's what broke up their marriage."

"What?"

Her voice was sly. "Therro wasn't above liking his piece of poon-tang," she said.

Honoria's voice crashed from the doorway. "Miss Utteley!"

"I'm Mrs. Renier, thank you, Honoria."

"No Renier talk like that."

Aunt Irene stood up furiously. "What do you mean by coming in without knocking?"

"I knocked, Miss Irene. You didn't hear me." Honoria went over to Aunt Irene, looked briefly across my dressing table, then down at Aunt Irene's hands. She reached out and took the broken strands of my hair from Aunt Irene's fingers. "Miss Stella sure got pretty hair," she said calmly. "But you used to have the prettiest hair that ever was, Miss Irene."

Aunt Irene peered into the mirror. "All the red's gone out of it. Pink-brown, that's what it is now, pinky brown, and dull, not lustrous, like Stella's—though that kind of brown hair turns grey early. I'm losing my looks, Honoria."

"You're still a handsome woman," Honoria said.

Aunt Irene fluttered her hands in front of her face, as though she could change the image in the mirror. "Come on, Stella. Time we went downstairs. They'll be wondering what's become of us."

* * *

After the tensions of the day, dinner was relatively uneventful. Aunt Olivia had been reading one of my father's books, and was in a philosophizing mood.

"The Egyptians," she announced, "never separated astronomy from astrology, so they never separated philosophy from the myths of their religion. There are times when I wonder if your father was right to separate them, Stella? Perhaps they can't be separated."

Uncle Hoadley said, "But they must be separated, Auntie. Stella's father is entirely correct."

"*I* think," Aunt Olivia said, "that what happens if we separate philosophy from myth is that we separate our minds from our hearts, that we're saying, in effect, that there isn't any truth in storytelling and games and fun."

"Livia, you're showing off again," Aunt Des said.

"I'm not! I'm thinking."

"That is a mistake."

"Let me not think on't, then: frailty, thy name is woman!"

"That's *Hamlet*, of course," Aunt Des said. "Point for me. What's *Hamlet* got to do with anything?"

"That's just it!" Aunt Olivia was triumphant. "If you separate philosophy and myth, then you have to say *Hamlet* isn't true. Or *Twelfth Night*, or *The Tempest*. Or at least half the Bible."

"Olivia!" There was genuine anguish in Aunt Des's shock.

"Auntie," Uncle Hoadley reproved, "please do not be foolish."

"But I'm not, Hoadley. This is life and death."

"Then don't jest about it."

"I'm not jesting. I don't think that accepting the entire Bible as not personally directed by God from a cloud is any worse than Irene opening it and sticking a pin in for a message. Or consulting the stars. What did your paper say about Capricorn today, Irene? You've been edgy ever since you read it. And badgering Honoria."

Aunt Irene pushed her chair away from the table. "Hoadley. I have to talk to you. Alone."

"After dinner, my dear."

"Now."

"That is hardly courteous."

"Hoadley. Please."

He put down his napkin in resignation. "Very well, Irene. Ladies, we'll see you out on the veranda for coffee in a few minutes."

When we had heard the screen door open and close, Aunt Des said, "Well! What was that about?"

Aunt Olivia said, "For mine own part, it was Greek to me."
"Julius Caesar."

"Right. Point for you. Thank you, Des. Let's play, oh, let's play. When we stop playing games then everything will be over, everything!"

"Livia," Aunt Des said, "perhaps you're a little feverish tonight."

"Perhaps I am. I hope it's that. Let's go out now and see what's up."

Uncle Hoadley was in his usual place on the bamboo settee, smoking. Aunt Irene was not there. We asked no questions. Aunt Des sat beside Uncle Hoadley and poured the coffee. Aunt Olivia beckoned to me and we took our cups and went to lean on the porch rail and watch the moon rise.

Aunt Olivia balanced her cup on the old and splintery wood. "I've been sitting too much today and my back hurts. I'll be better if I stand for a while. Here comes the moon: look!" Lopsided and red, inordinately large, it sprang from the sea. Aunt Olivia reached for my hand. Hers was hot and very dry; I thought she probably did have fever. "The moon looks so old. Even older than I am. It's like a moonrise at the end of the world when all human beings are dead and only a few post-historic beasts are left to watch." She shivered. "How silly to frighten myself with my own fancies."

We went back to our chairs and Aunt Olivia took a swallow of her coffee and made a face. "My God, that coffee is enough to gag a maggot. What on earth did Honoria do to it tonight?"

It was, I thought, no worse than the usual after-dinner coffee made with sulphur water. I rose and slipped away from them, tiptoeing down the steps of the veranda. I could sense that Finbarr was following me, and then he was pressing against me. I put my hand on the comforting roughness of his head. We ran down the ramp and into a cloud of insects buzzing around us, hot, swarming, stinging. I tried ineffectually to brush them off with my hands, running blindly across the loose wooden boards. I jumped down onto the sand and hurried to the water's edge. Finbarr splashed into the frothy spume, then loped on up the beach ahead of me, occasionally looking back in his protective manner to make sure that I was following.

We came to the forlorn remains of the old dock. I climbed

up and sat, waiting for the swinging arm of the lightship to break across the darkness.

"Mrs. Renier."

It was Ron. I realized that he spoke my name in order not to frighten me, in order that I would not think he was spying on me. And perhaps the old dock was for him, too, a place to sit and think and find perspective and proportion. Finbarr came loping across the beach to be caressed by him. Ron stood, leaning against a barnacled piling, looking not at me but out over the quiet sea, until finally I asked, "What was this afternoon in the kitchen all about?" He did not answer. I sighed, kicking my heels against the barnacles; through the leather of my shoes I could feel the sharp little shells; they would cut the heels of my slippers. I stopped. "Tron—it's odd, his name sounding so much like Theron."

"It was my mother's way of getting back at the Reniers. Or maybe it was her idea of a joke. Stay away from my mother, Mrs. Renier. And don't ask about my father. Honoria and Clive are my mother and father. After Jimmy was lynched I became their son. They are my parents. You ask too many questions, Mrs. Renier. For a woman coming into the Renier family this is not a good idea."

"Why not? Why isn't it perfectly natural?"

"Questions again."

And so I asked another. "Ron, what are you doing in Illyria?"

"Nothing much. I'm not earning my keep, that's for sure. But I still think maybe I can be of use here. People are beginning to come to my little surgery in the twins' cottage, to send for me back in the scrub. Mostly they can't pay me anything. And mostly they want miracles. They aren't used to doctors. There aren't any around today who'll bother with blacks, the way old Dr. Theron used to. So they go to a Zenumin. Then if the witch doctor doesn't work, they come to me. Talk about superstition, Mrs. Renier, how do I break through it? They probably wouldn't come to me at all if I weren't half Zenumin."

I sighed. "You're an enigma."

"No. I am a nigger."

That silenced me.

After a while Ron said, "When Tron was little he got hold of a magnifying glass somewhere. There was a nest of ants on the brick path leading to the fig tree, and Tron shone the sun down on them through the magnifying glass and roasted them alive. I saw him doing it and I lit into him and ended up with a bloody nose and a black eye. I'm almost two years younger than he is and I was a lot smaller then. Maybe now I'd just let him burn the ants."

"No. No, Ron."

"Why not?"

I wanted to answer: because there is love in the world, and laughter, but the words stuck in my throat.

Blown to us on the wind came a faint snatch of song: the twins. I asked, "What about Willy and Harry?"

"What about them?"

"They're—they're special, aren't they?"

"Why? The idiot-savant is recorded all through history. The kink in their strange brains isn't unique."

"Yes, I know that. But in the Middle Ages, at any rate, the idiot-savant, or even the plain idiot, *was* regarded as special, almost a little holy."

"Every age has its own ignorances."

I looked across the wrinkled darkness of water. "Why was Harry so upset by $0 \times 3 = 0$?"

"Why indeed?" He held out his hand to help me down from the dock.

12

FINBARR, standing beside me on the dock, gave his coat a great shake. I was covered with sand. Holding Ron's hand, I jumped down, brushing sand off my dress, from my face, spitting sand. Ron said good night, walked up-beach towards the twins. "All right, Finny," I said. "Let's go home."

Uncle Hoadley had waited up for me. He pulled out his gold watch and looked at it.

"Sorry, Uncle Hoadley. We didn't eat till so late—sorry, I didn't mean to keep you up."

"The ladies have all gone to bed. Aunt Olivia asks that you go in and say good night to her."

The old lady greeted me from the great bed. "Did you have a good walk, Stella-love?"

"I met Ron."

"That's good. Did you talk, the two of you?"

"In a way."

"In a way. Yes, that's about all anyone can manage with Ronnie. Except, I suppose, Honoria and Clive. And who knows what they talk about when they're not with us."

"What about his mother?"

"Whose mother?"

"Ron's."

Aunt Olivia made a distasteful grimace, as over her after-dinner coffee. "I think of Honoria and Clive as Ronnie's mother and father. I suppose, biologically, Belle Zenumin is. It's easy enough to understand that she's Tron's mother. Tron frightens me. He's all Zenumin. There's none of Jimmy in him, or Honoria and Clive. He belongs to the Dark Clearing. Mado tried to rescue him, to take him out of the scrub. She taught him to read and write and talk, and he's bright enough—but he prefers darkness to light. But Ronnie belongs to Illyria. I love Ronnie, even though he won't let me, most of the time. He's a good doctor, too, like Theron."

I wanted to hear it from Aunt Olivia. "How did he happen to get educated in England?"

She said quietly enough, "Hoadley saw to it. On Utteley money, of course. But he's not the first young man the Reniers have sent to England for an education. James and Theron educated several promising boys before the war—Xenia would say, This one needs more than I can give him, and this one. One of the Nyssa boys, Burton James, a cousin of Clive's, became an actor and played with the Salvinis, both in Europe and America. But of course there was trouble when the company came to Southern cities, and eventually he settled in Rome."

"Why was England chosen? I mean, as the place for education?"

"I suppose it could have been anywhere in Europe, but there wasn't any language barrier in England, so it seemed the logical place, and we still have connections there. We always sent our boys to Lancing. It became a tradition."

"But why not the United States? Aren't the schools good? Sorry, I know I'm ignorant."

"Sometimes, sometimes I think the very fact that you don't have preconceptions—well, I don't suppose you've ever heard of the insurrection in Charleston in 1822?"

"No."

"Denmark Vesey—he was a free Negro—tried to get the slaves to revolt and take over Charleston. I sometimes wonder what he'd have done if he'd succeeded? He very nearly did. Most of the slaves were ready to go along with him—who can blame them? The extraordinary thing is that so many of them refused to kill their masters. It was one of our Desborough cousins' slaves who betrayed Vesey, because he wouldn't go along with the bloodshed. But we whites didn't have the same qualms. Slaves were executed. Idiotic, rigid rules were clamped down, curfews of Negroes, nightly road patrols. And white people were forbidden to teach their slaves to read or write: don't let them learn anything or they'll become troublemakers. James almost got thrown out of Charleston because he took the education issue to the Supreme Court. He said it was unconstitutional. But he couldn't break prejudice and its power, and the rule stayed. So that was another thing about Nyssa that was resented, that everybody was given schooling. So you see why we had to send our boys to England."

"Even after the war?"

"The war really didn't change anything. We have all the same problems; we just give them different names. People still don't want Negroes educated."

I felt abysmally sad.

"Ever since Ronnie came home last Christmastime, I haven't let another doctor near me, which doesn't please Hoadley. If it weren't for Ronnie I'd be tied to this bed, I'd become like Xenia. Oh, never, God, please, never let me be like Xenia, let me die first. When Ronnie came home I was much worse than I am now, I had much more pain. At first I'd see him just in the kitchen—he'd make suggestions to me there. And then one morning when I had an attack—I wake up sometimes with my joints all full of fever and abominably sore—I made Honoria bring Ronnie to me instead of sending for that fat idiot friend of Hoadley's. Sometimes Ronnie forgets who he is and talks to me like a human being. Mado might have been able to reach him. I can't. Not any more."

"Why not?"

The old woman closed her eyes. "His mother's a Zenumin, and he's had a white man's education, and he's trying to be a doctor in a world that doesn't know what black and white is, and doesn't know what it isn't, either. He's brilliant, but he's got chips on his shoulders the size of mountains. No wonder he stoops. I'm old and sometimes I can take a hatchet and chip away at them. But not often. Only when I remember Mado—" She reached with difficulty into the drawer of a small chest on one side of the bed and pulled out a notebook similar to Mado's journals. "Here. This is mine. Not a journal—it's translations of Mado's poetry. She always wrote poetry in French, and French poetry is impossible to translate, so it's not very good. But you might like to glance at it."

"Very much indeed. Thank you, Aunt Oliva."

"I miss Mado's angels. Sometimes I think it might almost be easier to believe in angels than to believe in God. But I wonder—if there are angels at all, why are they necessarily all good guardian angels? What about the fallen angels? Evil angels? If God in his infinite compassion has given us each a guardian angel to love and help us, what about the devil? Is he going to sit by and take that and do nothing? Do you suppose Satan has assigned an angel to each of us, too? An angel of darkness, constantly spilling his poison into our hearts?"

Honoria, in her nightgown and wrapper, came padding into the room, carrying a bottle. "Miss Olivia, I rub you now if you ready."

"Oh, Honoria, bless you, how did you know I need it?"

"You has fever tonight."

"Do I?" Aunt Olivia touched her cheek with the back of her hand. "Yes, I guess I do. And my joints hurt so much. But I want Stella to stay. Please?"

"Of course, Aunt Olivia." Still holding the book of poems, I sat in the tall rocker by the bed.

"Angels—maybe it's only because of Mado that angels seem quite reasonable and logical to me. So does the devil. If you'd been around the South for as long as I have, you wouldn't have much trouble believing in the devil. I wish believing in God were that easy. Read me one of Mado's poems while Honoria rubs me—"

I opened the book at random. Aunt Olivia's writing was much like Mado's, probably deliberately. The ink was her usual purple, still unfaded.

Honoria peered under the bed. "You there, Finny?"

"Of course he's there."

"Mr. Hoadley say he to sleep in the kitchen."

"Don't tell, then. Hoadley doesn't get scared at night the way I do."

"Don't he?" Honoria asked softly. She turned the old lady

over in the bed, pulling up the long white nightgown to reveal a back as tender and delicate as a young girl's.

"Honoria's liniment smells terrible," Aunt Olivia grumbled. "She makes it out of herbs. Can you stand it?"

As Honoria uncorked the bottle a strong, pungent odor filled the room, a mixture of eucalyptus, mint, lavender, and some other less identifiable and less pleasant herbs. 't reminded me of something—of Belle Zenumin. Honoria's mixture was different, perhaps less musky, but definitely reminiscent.

She looked at me. "You takes what grows, and you mixes a little of this and a little of that, and depending on what and how you mix, you can use it to help, or you can use it to hinder. Like Miss Olivia said, we has a choice." She poured a little of the oil into her hand.

"Honoria sets great store by her liniment, and Ronnie says it can't hurt, but I think it's Honoria's fingers have the healing in them. Maybe Ronnie got his healing hands from Honoria. But—oh, dear—" She clapped her hands to her mouth, then said quickly, "Read one of the poems, please, Stella."

I looked down at the fine handwriting.

> *"If and that we grow apart*
> *Earth's orbit shakes.*
> *With the rending of one heart*
> *All heaven breaks.*
>
> *Steadfast love, like gravity,*
> *Keeps stars in place.*
> *Enduring love's hilarity*
> *Burns bright with grace.*
>
> *If and that our love is pain,*
> *So does love grow,*
> *That heavenly Love's bewildering reign*
> *Earth's hearts may know.*

"Why, it's beautiful, Aunt Olivia! How much of that is Mado, and how much is you?"

"Oh, the thought, the feeling of the poem is all Mado's. I apologize for the faults in translation. 'Gravity' and 'hilarity' don't rhyme, and there's one syllable too many in 'bewildering,' but anything else changed the meaning. I've never had that kind of joy about the hurts of love, though Mado tried hard enough to teach me."

"It seems," I said tentatively, "an odd kind of poem for a young French girl to have written."

"She wasn't so young when she wrote that. And Theron encouraged her. For all he was a totally dedicated doctor he loved music and painting and poetry. He and James both played the violin. Xenia had a beautiful contralto voice, and I could play the piano in those days, and Mado was a soprano, so we often made music together. Rub around my hip a little more, Honoria, gently, that way. Oh, good. Thank you."

Honoria picked Aunt Olivia up, pulling the nightdress down over the smooth white back, laying the old woman against the pillows. She slid down in the bed, pulling the sheet up under her chin. "Good night, my dears, good night."

"Good night, Aunt Olivia."

"See you in the morning—" she said anxiously.

"See you in the morning," I responded firmly, then followed Honoria out.

"Miss Stella," Honoria said, "come to the kitchen and I fix you a posset." At the kitchen door she paused, "How you say it, Miss Stella? If *you* do not know, then maybe I has not seen things the way they *has* to happen?"

Honoria would not be as easily diverted and comforted as the great-aunts. I tried to sound strong and certain. "The future is still open."

She poured milk from the jug into a little saucepan and put it on the stove, looking down at it somberly. "Miss Stella, since Miss Mado died I have had no woman friend to talk with. You mind me of Miss Mado."

I could not say thank you to this enormous compliment. All I could do was look at her, and smile a totally inadequate gratitude. We remained in silence, but it was a good silence, and I remembered Honoria speaking about how she and Mado often communicated without words.

I looked away from the stove and towards the windows. The shutters were open now to get the benefit of the night breeze. Insects fluttered in and beat about the flame of the candle burning comfortingly on the kitchen table. I felt relaxed and happy. Then, in the darkness just outside the window, I saw a face. As quickly as I looked it was gone. I had no idea who it was, I could not possibly have described it. I was certain it had been there.

"Honoria—" She turned from the stove. "Honoria, there was a face at the window—"

She strode to the window, looked out. "Don't see nothing."

"But there was—I'm certain."

She did not doubt my word. "Was it white or black?"

"I don't know. I just saw a face, and whoever it was ducked down and disappeared. But it wasn't imagination. There was someone there. And Cousin Lucille was complaining today about a face at her windows. She said it was the twins."

"It was not the twins," Honoria said.

The twins might be listeners, but they were not peeping Toms. "I know it wasn't. Who was it?"

Honoria shook her head. "Best if you don't say nothing, Miss Stella. Don't want nobody frightened. I'll tell Clive." She poured the hot, fragrant milk into a cup and handed it to me.

The face at the window had destroyed my peace. "Honoria, I don't mean to meddle. But things are happening, and I'm part of them."

"I want you out."

"Can you keep me out?"

A film seemed to come over Honoria's eyes. "I can try."

"But when I first came—"

"Miss Stella, I asked for help. And I thought you had been sent to us by God as well as by Terry. But if I have—if I have brought you, by my prayers, across the ocean and into danger—"

"Your prayers didn't have anything to do with it. Where else could Terry ask me to wait for him?"

"Your kinfolk—"

"My only living relatives are the Dowlers. I'm fond of them, and I suppose if I hadn't married Terry I might have stayed with them. But I am Terry's wife, and my place is with my husband's people."

Honoria said slowly, "You have the ring—"

I touched it. The golden snakes felt cool, as though they were constantly touched by a breeze I did not feel, or were lying on a rock beside a cool stream.

There was a knock at the outside door and I jumped. But Honoria went calmly to answer it. A little black boy stood there, his eyes and teeth shining white in the moonlight. Had it been his face at the window? No, it had not been a child's face.

"Honoria, ma'am, please, where Dr. Ron? The baby not

coming like it should and my mama she screaming and screaming—"

"Who with her?"

"Papa and the Zenumin. Then Papa send the Zenumin away
and say get the doctor. The baby like to kill my mama."

"Ron not here," Honoria said. "He up at the twins'. Run,
child, and you find him there."

I was sad, and frightened: was this what childbirth was like?

"Yes, Honoria, ma'am, thankee." The little boy turned and
disappeared into the night.

Honoria said, "The ring come from my people. It mean that
two are one, and justice must be done, and prayers prayed,
and reparation made . . ."

"Why did you give it to Mado?"

"Claudius Broadley and I weren't never one. He just knowed
the ring always went to the princess, so he bound to have it.
On my finger the ring burn like fire. Claudius Broadley took
me, stole me, like a thief. He come with his guns and his glass
beads—what his beads mean to us when we had the real thing?
He no fool—he saw that and put his broken glass away. But
he cause us to fear his guns. We knowed about precious stones,
the fire that come out of the earth. But we didn't know about
the fire that come out of the black mouth of guns, the fire that
kills. Mr. Claudius Broadley, he shoot to kill. When he kill
enough, he make bargain with my father. Honoria the price—
my flesh and blood and a big dowry. He want both. Then he
willing to spare my tribe—what he'd left of it. My father
knowed he mean what he say. Better I should die for the white
man's lust and greed than the entire tribe roped together and
hauled into the ship for slaves. Better I die. To my father I be
dead. There no other way. I bring with me jewels, many jewels.
I bring the ring. The ring on my finger be a lie. On Mado it
once again be truth."

"What about when you married Clive?"

"The ring, once given, stay given. Or it lose its virtue." As
usual, Honoria seemed to know what I was thinking. "There
no magic in the ring, Miss Stella. Virtue be not magic. But a
thing may hold within it something of them who make it, or
who touch it, or wear it and give it grace. Then it be no longer
a thing. But this be not magic."

But at nineteen I did not know that essentially there is no
such thing as a thing. I fingered the ring, turning it on my
finger.

Honoria said, "You want to ask something, ask it."

"The ring—did it help Kitty?"

"I said the ring not magic, Miss Stella." She rose, and her shadow with her, stretching enormously up the wall and across the kitchen ceiling in the flickering light. "With Miss Kitty— as with others—there be too many questions. Too much talk. Too much darkness." She looked down on me. "I feel you asking, Miss Stella. You want to know about Jimmy."

"I don't know," I whispered. "Yes, I suppose I do. But I don't want to cause you pain, Honoria."

Honoria stalked over to the window where the face had been. I did not know what she was seeing as she stood there looking out into the night. "We name Jimmy after Mr. James, but he turn from the name and went out into the land of anger and greed and hate."

I turned away from the look in her eyes and looked down at my cup.

"He tell Clive and me he can save Belle Zenumin if he bring her to Illyria as his wife. They be married, leastways according to the law of the scrub. But they marry in hate for Illyria. When he bring her here, love stick in they craws. They do not find what they be looking for."

"What were they looking for?"

"Not love. Not peace. Things. Things which stay things. Treasure. The princess's treasure. They turn on Illyria and go back to the scrub. Tron born." She began to pace the length of the kitchen, her shadow bent and broken by the ceiling. "They bad things in the scrub—not everywhere, but in the Dark Clearings. Jimmy sicken with a wasting sickness. He not bad enough to make a Zenumin. He die."

"Ron told me how he—how he died."

"Jimmy dead long before his body be killed." Honoria's eyes were dry. It was I who felt the hot sting of tears. "Finish your posset, Miss Stella. Go to bed." Underneath the sternness of her words there was understanding and compassion.

I took my candle and went upstairs. I knew that because of me she would not sleep this night. I thought that she would spend the night in prayer.

I did not know how to pray, and I would sleep.

Up in my room the kitten was waiting for me, and when I relaxed into a smile of pleasure, I realized how tight and tense were the muscles of my body. I went to my balcony. There was a distant flash of thunder. Perhaps the far-away storm was responsible for some of the electricity in the air, and for the fact that peace did not come. A few drops of rain spattered on the beach, on the wooden rail of my balcony. The rain began to fall more heavily; the thunder was closer, but this was not a violent storm like the one my first night in Illyria. It was moving quickly, would soon be past.

But other things would not blow by so easily. I wanted, quite irrationally, to know who Ron's father was, and how he had come to Illyria. No more questions, Stella. But why not? My father brought me up to ask questions. No. Not this kind of question.

I got into bed, taking one of Mado's journals under the mosquito netting with me. An insect clung to the cloth, waving fierce horns at me. I shook the netting and he gave a wild flap of his wings and flew towards the lamp. Another insect whirred in from the window and took his place. I gave up any idea of reading—perhaps I had learned enough for one day—blew out my light, and plunged into sleep.

I slept and I dreamed.

I was wandering along a stony, shale-roughened cliff, bare, vegetationless. As I neared the sharp edge a wind came roaring down from the mountains, pushing, pushing me towards the final end of rock. I peered down, and the valley was so far beneath me that it was no more than a sea of darkness. The wind increased in force, pushing me towards the abyss. I could not press through the gale across the rock to safety. I was going to be blasted over the edge by the cold and angry elements.

I tried to scream, and no scream would come.

Then my wrist was grabbed; I was pulled back, through the fierceness of wind, back across the shale to a flowering field; and there I fell into the fragrance of grass and flowers, my legs weak with terror and relief.

Ron was holding me, not Ron the angry, the austere; but Ron gentle, tender, loving.

What had started as nightmare ended as joy. All fear fled. I slipped into a spring-filled, zephyr-caressed meadow of sleep . . .

I woke up during the night and got out of bed to go down the passage to the bathroom. As I started to cross the threshold I stumbled over something and almost fell. I could see nothing, and for a terrible moment I felt a surge of panic like the beginning of the dream. Then I bent down and touched Finbarr's fur as he rose, with rheumatic difficulty, to his feet, and nuzzled into my outstretched hand, giving me a warm gentle lick of his long tongue.

"Finny!" I whispered. "What are you doing here?"

He followed me down the hall, then back to the bedroom, and lay down once more across the threshold. I felt as if he were guarding me.

FOUR

1

In the morning Aunt Olivia could not get out of bed. She wanted to see Ron, and Ron only, despite Aunt Irene's loud disapproval, and Uncle Hoadley's gentler suggestion that Clive drive him into Jefferson and return with the doctor.

"No, Hoadley, I can't stand your doctor. He's a boa constrictor without the pleasant disposition. So you'll just have to take the train into Jefferson."

"Dear Auntie, whether I take the train or the carriage to Jefferson has nothing to do with it. I want you to have proper medical attention."

"Ronnie's proper medical attention. You know that as well as I do. You saw to it."

Aunt Des pulled me away from the argument, starting to talk quickly and rather loudly, as though she did not want me to hear. "The train makes two trips a day, Stella, it's really very convenient. It goes into Jefferson in the morning, and comes back in the afternoon, in time for dinner. When the children were little—Terry and Ronnie, that is, because of course there was no train when we first came to Illyria—the big event of the day was to meet the afternoon train. They got so excited! One of their special treats was to be allowed to take two pins, ordinary sewing pins, lay them on the rail, and after the train had come by, the pins would be flattened into a cross, and they'd put them with their treasure. I still have one of the little pin crosses that Terry gave me—I keep it in my sewing box."

Uncle Hoadley came out of Aunt Olivia's room.

"Well?" Aunt Des asked.

"Your sister can be exceedingly stubborn. I'm taking the train into Jefferson—not that that has anything to do with it. Stella, she asks you to come in, please."

Aunt Olivia was like a small bird, huddled in pain and fever in the great four-poster bed. She insisted that I be the one to stay with her while Ron examined her and gave her a needle against the pain. "If you want me to be good, then I will be," she said to Ron and me, "but *you* have to want me to be brave, or it isn't worth it. Nobody can be good and brave in a vacuum. We have to be good *for* somebody. And don't tell me I have to be good for God, or for Jesus, or any of that stuff. I believe in Darwin this morning."

Ron looked at me across the bed and smiled. It was a good smile, merry, and full of love for the old lady. His voice was gentler than I'd ever heard it before. "When I was a little boy I used to try to be good for you, Miss Olivia, because you asked me to. But all I ask you now is that you try to let me help you, even if I have to hurt you." Ron the doctor, calm, absolutely sure, was totally different from Ron the acerb and uncertain young man I walked with on the beach.

"The baby—" I said. "Did the little boy find you last night?" He nodded. "Was everything all right?"

"The baby's fine."

"The mother—"

"She'd lost too much blood by the time I got there. The Zenumin midwife bungled."

"Like the twins' mother—"

"Miss Olivia," Ron said briskly, "you'll do what I say, won't you? That's the kind of good I want you to be, just to do what I tell you. This will hurt, now. Hold Mrs. Renier's hand tight. Yell if you want to. Go on. There. Almost over. Sorry to have to hurt you this way. Easy, easy. Done now, and I'll give you something to cut the pain. Relax, now, Miss Olivia, stop fighting the pain, it just makes it worse." His dark hands against the fragile body were tender, loving. Healing hands.

"If I don't fight the pain I'll weep," Aunt Olivia said.

"Go right ahead, Miss Olivia, if it will help."

"When you were little—" her words were a series of small, painful gasps—"and you and Terry played together, and we were all happy and loving, you called me *Aunt* Livia. You and Terry. Both of you. That's how I like it."

"Not any more, Miss Olivia."

"Why not?"

He smiled. "Honoria and Clive wouldn't approve." Then, "I'll stay with you for a piece, Miss Olivia, till you get sleepy. And, thank you for your help, Mrs. Renier."

I was dismissed.

* * *

In the late afternoon we all had tea in Aunt Olivia's room. Aunt Irene complained about the tea and the heat, and asked Honoria to fix her a bath before bedtime.

"Irene," Aunt Mary Desborough reproved, "you oughtn't to make Honoria lug those heavy hot-water cans upstairs when you can just as easily go for a swim."

"I want a hot bath, Auntie. I don't ask for one very often."

"You were just going on about how hot you are," Aunt Olivia said.

"Auntie, sometimes a hot bath is more important than the weather."

"Are you that dirty?"

"Auntie!"

"She probably is," Aunt Olivia said to Aunt Des and me. "Who knows where she was off to all day? For which, as now in fire I am to work them to their good, So will I melt into a bath to wash them in my blood."

"Really, Auntie," Aunt Irene protested, "that's hardly apt."

"Apt enough." The old lady pushed against her pillows and grinned. "Stella, Des, identify it."

Aunt Des tapped her foot. "One of your ghoulish, obscure modern poets, I suppose."

"It is not! It's Robert Southwell: late sixteenth century."

"Ghoulish and obscure, anyhow."

"Point for me."

"Oh, all right. But I don't think it's fair."

"Certainly it's fair. It's not my fault if you're losing your memory."

"I can hardly be expected to remember everything written by every obscure hack."

"In any case, life's not fair. You ought to realize that by now."

"Aunties, that's enough. Stella, do you happen to have a handkerchief? I seem to have mislaid mine—" Aunt Irene fumbled in her sleeves, in the pocket of her skirt—"and I don't want to ask Honoria or Clive to go upstairs."

Aunt Mary Desborough reached into her work basket and pulled out a handkerchief. "You just asked Honoria to go upstairs and fix you a bath."

Ignoring this, Aunt Irene looked at me. "Stella?"

I handed my handkerchief to her, just as Clive came in with a plate of tea cakes. Still with the plate, he turned and went out.

"Clive!" Aunt Irene called. Waited. Called again, "Clive! Now where is he and what is he doing? Clive!"

"Yes, Miss Irene?"

"Where are those cakes?"

"Right here, Miss Irene."

"And more bread and butter, too, please."

Honoria came stalking in and held out a freshly washed and ironed handkerchief. "Miss Irene."

"Oh, thank you, Honoria, but I already have one."

"Here is one of yours, Miss Irene. I will take Miss Stella's."

"I've used it."

"Yes, Miss Irene. I will wash it."

"Oh, don't bother, Honoria. You can do it later."

Honoria held out her hand. "Now, Miss Irene."

Aunt Irene tightened her lips, but put a handkerchief into Honoria's hand.

"What's this about?" Aunt Mary Desborough asked.

"Finish your tea, Miss Des," Honoria said.

The next morning after breakfast Aunt Irene cornered me. "Stella, honey, maybe you'd drive into San Feliz with me while I pick up some grits and rice for Honoria, and maybe some white bacon if there's any worth getting? We'll do a proper marketing in Jefferson tomorrow, but there's no use toting staples on the train. I do hope you're planning to come with me?"

"Yes, Aunt Irene. I'd like to."

"The ride on our funny little train may amuse you, and of course I'd like to show you some of Jefferson. Hoadley will have a carriage meet us at the station. This morning I'm just going to take Hoadley's little landau to San Feliz, and I do hate going alone."

It seemed ungracious to refuse.

We trotted along the beach. Aunt Irene, fully corseted even in the heat, impeccably dressed in a dark-green skirt and pale-green ruffled shirt, made me feel like a country cousin in my loose blue lawn dress: I cared more about keeping cool than about being fashionable in the heat. Anyhow, Aunt Irene was the colonist, and an Utteley to boot. I had already absorbed some of the great-aunts' prejudices. But I had to admit that she handled the little horse easily and well.

In San Feliz she threw the reins to one of a group of little colored boys who evidently hung around to perform this service for a few pennies, and I followed her about the dusty, musty shed near the station which served as supply store for the beach. Aunt Irene peered into barrels of various grades of hominy, rice, sugar, flour. Shafts of sunlight, heavy with flour dust, struck through the dimness. She made her purchases, chattering about the weather, Jefferson society, the Yacht Club, my arrival from England, Lord and Lady Dowler, the weather again. I bowed, smiled, and swept out of the store by Aunt Irene, followed by another of the ubiquitous little boys staggering under the weight of sacks of hominy, rice, sugar.

We had hardly pulled away, Aunt Irene clucking at the little horse and slapping the reins, when she said, "*I* know what let's do! Let's go pay a little visit to Granddam Zenumin!"

I answered quickly, too quickly. "No. I'd rather not."

"But why, honey? It will be interesting for you. You really should see what it's like back in the scrub."

"I want to write Terry."

"Of course you do, but you can do that later."

"Thank you, Aunt Irene, but it's so hot—"

"Not on the creek, honey. It's shady and cool. And Granddam Zenumin's going to be mad if you don't come back— yes, I've talked with Belle. I know what happened. The Granddam won't understand if you don't come, and it's not good to have her angry with you, Stella honey. Believe me, she has powers."

I asked, "Stronger powers than Honoria?"

"Honoria won't use her powers, and if the Granddam has a mind to, she can cause you pain and hurt."

My laugh sounded false in my ears. "I suppose she'll make a doll to represent me and stick pins in it and put a curse on me?"

"Yes, honey, she will."

I suddenly had an image of Aunt Irene sitting at my dressing table, taking a long brown hair from my comb, and of Honoria retrieving it from her. "Was that why you wanted my hair? Or why you tried to get my handkerchief yesterday? To give to the Granddam?"

"Not to hurt you. So she could see what was going to happen."

"Why did Honoria stop you if that was all?"

"I told you, honey. Honoria won't use her powers, and she's jealous of anybody else who has them."

"Why do you want to know my future, Aunt Irene?"

"It's not just *your* future, honey. It affects me, too. We don't live separately, more's the pity. You'll find that out when you've been a Renier longer. You can't ever say, 'It's my own business.' And don't you want to know where Terry is? I should think you'd care."

"Of course I care! But I don't want Granddam Zenumin making guesses and getting me upset. Belle said if I went back I wouldn't have to have my fortune told."

I had made a mistake.

"Of course not, honey! Nobody's asking you to do anything except be polite and kind to the Granddam. If you're not, she could hurt you, or someone you love. Believe me, honey. I don't want to frighten you, but believe me."

I was not frightened for myself. I was frightened for Terry. And I was frightened for our baby. If the old woman was right and I was indeed carrying my husband's child—and I thought that I was—if the old woman could know this much, could she hurt the little, unborn creature? "All right, Aunt Irene, I'll go, just to be polite. But I don't want to stay long."

My ring felt hot on my finger. The sun struck against it. The gold glinted, absorbed the intense heat.

I looked inland and realized that we had already passed Illyria. We drove in silence, looking out to sea; Aunt Irene had stopped her social chatter, and was urging the little horse along at a swift clip. We turned from the ocean towards the dunes and stopped by an old post, perhaps left from a long-gone ramp or sea wall, to which Aunt Irene tethered the horse.

"Leave your parasol, honey, it'll just get in the way. There's only a few minutes' walk, not long. Most of the way is on the creek."

We climbed a dune, the same dune I had climbed with Belle, and followed the tiny path to the dark waters.

In the shade of a large water oak, which leaned over the creek so that some of the leaves dipped into the water, was the canoe. The old woman was not in it this time; Belle was. The sunlight sifting through the trees turned her dark skin to a deep bronze lit with rose; she looked very beautiful waiting there, her eyes closed, the morning heat bringing small drops of moisture to her forehead and upper lip. I was drenched with sweat, hot and disheveled, my hair untidy from the entangling vines. Aunt Irene's face was shiny as butter, though her clothes were not in the least disarrayed. But the heat seemed only to intensify Belle's beauty.

"Belle, we're here." Aunt Irene's voice was high and excited.

Belle slowly opened her eyes. It was as though she were returning to us from far away. She greeted us courteously and helped us into the canoe. In the daylight I could see that it was a primitive one, hollowed out of a tree trunk. She took a paddle and pushed at one of the snake-like cypress roots and the canoe moved from the bank into the dark water. A white heron, startled, flew flapping across the creek. A kingfisher flashed blue.

"Know you're hot, Miss Stella, ma'am." Belle plied the oar deftly and the canoe shot ahead. White butterflies fluttered about the banks on either side, shimmering against the darkness of water and undergrowth. "But keep your hands in the canoe. Water moccasins about this morning. See that old log over yonder? What looks to be an old log?" I looked at an ordinary log, half submerged in the water. "Ain't a log."

"What is it, then?" Even as I looked, two eyelids in the log opened, then blinked closed.

Belle's laugh tinkled. "Be an alligator. Sleeping in the noonday heat. Won't bother us none unless we poke it. Then it wake up in a temper and gobble us up, quicker'n you can bat an eye."

I could no longer see where those strange eyelids had been. It looked like a log, and nothing but a log.

When we had gone several yards beyond, Belle reached up and snapped a piece of dead branch off one of the trees and threw it back at the log. The log stirred; the heavy eyelids opened, and then an enormous mouth with sharp, savage teeth opened and snapped, as though after an insect. The water stirred sluggishly under the canoe.

We skimmed forward again. Belle pointed to a flash of deep rose back in the green jungle. "That be a flamingo, Miss Stella."

The trees arched, locking branches over us. We moved through a dim green tunnel. The sunlight barely penetrated, but the heat was fierce and steady. I kept wiping my face with my handkerchief, which quickly became sodden and useless. But I was fascinated with the beauty, the exotic birds calling and flying in the dimness, the fluttering of butterflies low over the water, the Spanish moss dripping from the branches so that we had to bend our heads low in order to avoid its tickling tendrils. At the water's edge a strange grey beast snuffled, raised a blunt, mean-looking snout, and glared at us.

"That be a razorback pig, Miss Stella."

Gradually the trees lifted, grew farther apart. We could see the sky, intensely blue, shimmering with heat. "Here we be," Belle said, and guided the canoe towards the shore. "Miss Stella ma'am, I want to thank you for coming. It mean might a deal to me. I know people been saying things to you, things about Zenumins—"

"*I* haven't—" Aunt Irene started.

"I know you hasn't, Miss Irene. But others has. Others what got less right. I 'preciate your not listening, Miss Stella, ma'am. You are a true friend."

A group of little boys, half naked, came running to meet us, to pull the canoe up onto the bank, to help us out.

I stood on the river bank, batting at the insects which swarmed about us. Flies clung to the faces and torsos of the little boys, but they paid no attention. A dozen or so wooden huts, on stilts, were scattered about. Underneath these, chickens were scrabbling, and indiscriminate yellow dogs, scratching at fleas, gnawing at bones, yapping, tumbling about with little brown babies, some with damp and drooping diapers, most of them naked. Around a few of the cabins were flowers, but they were straggly and lank, like weeds. There were occasional patches of garden, though I did not recognize any of the plants. Around the attempts at cultivation the wild growth of the jungle pressed. The babies looked well fed, but perhaps their little bellies were just too protruding, their legs not quite straight. Here was a kind of poverty I had never seen before.

In the center of the clearing were stones blackened with smoke; they were evidently used as a communal fireplace and I thought that a fire out of doors, at night, would be more bearable than any kind of stove in those rickety, tinderbox cabins. Some of them had corrugated tin for roofs; the heat struck against this and shimmered angrily. From a few of the windows stove pipes stuck out. Through doors propped open to catch any stray breeze, I could see dim figures moving within; they seemed strangely shadowy and insubstantial.

I brushed at the flies.

Belle was beside me. "This is where my Tron growed up. This where my Ronnie should have growed."

Aunt Irene was on my other side. "But would you have wanted him to grow up here, Belle? Didn't you want him to have his chance?"

"Ronnie my baby. They took him away."

"But he's a doctor now. Think how much good he can do."

Belle looked down at the packed earth beneath our feet. "I want my son should love his mother."

"But he does, Belle, of course he does."

Belle took my arm and urged me to the dead fireplace in the center of the clearing. She waved imperiously and a big boy, perhaps moving into adolescence, came running out of one of the cabins, bringing with him a bucket which he up-ended for me to sit on. I looked towards Aunt Irene. Since she was older, I expected her to be seated first, but she motioned to me to sit, walked over to the fireplace, spread her hand-kerchief over one of the stones, and sat.

"I go get Granddam," Belle said.

Aunt Irene leaned towards me. "Apologize to her..."

Belle went to the nearest cabin. In the dimness of the small and shadowed porch I had not seen the rocking chair, or the old woman in it. Belle helped her down the steps. In the sunlight she looked like an untidy grey pudding bag. Her cottony white hair was partly tucked under a dirty cap, and bits of it sprang out uncontrollably. Her skin was black with a tinge of grey, quite unlike Belle's beautiful dark copper, or Ron's creamy coffee color. She came hobbling towards us, leaning heavily on Belle's arm, looking hundreds of years old. Perhaps she was.

Aunt Irene rose. So did I.

"I tell you Mrs. Renier come, Granddam, and here she is," Belle said.

The old woman peered at me out of her yellowed eyes. If she had been less hideous to look at she might have been less frightening. She could not help being old and poor and ugly. "Miss Irene make you?"

"I'm sorry if I offended you the other evening. I was very frightened once by a gypsy in England—" My prepared apology trailed off under her glare.

"I be no gypsy."

"Oh, I know, and I'm so sorry if—"

She held a grey claw towards me. "Let me see your hand."

"Please. I do want to talk to you, and make your acquain-tance, but I'd rather not have my fortune told."

The claw still beckoned to me. "I tell you nothing."

I held out my hand. She looked at it, making incompre-hensible murmurings. It was worse to have her perhaps seeing things about me, about Terry, about our baby, and not telling me, than anything she could actually say. But I didn't, wouldn't permit myself to believe that she could see what was going to happen. She could make guesses, she could invent things to tell me, and that part of me which was superstitious would believe her imaginings and be influenced by them. If someone says to you, 'You look marvelous today!' then you feel splendid, full of health and energy. But if someone says instead, 'My dear, what on earth is the matter? You're so pale, you really do look ill,' then suddenly your head starts to ache, you begin to feel that you are coming down with something. So powerful is suggestion that it can actually affect your physical being, it can change the pattern of your day. It *can* change the future. I did not want to hear anything from this old woman, either good or bad.

She released my hand with a loud cry, as though she had seen something she did not like. She spoke not to me but to Belle, drawing Aunt Irene into the periphery of her words. "I told you she bring evil."

"No, Granddam," Belle protested. "Mrs. Renier be good."

The old woman shook her head, seemed to shrink into the bundle of her clothes. "I do what I can, but the lines are powerful. We make the offering tonight: one old nag, the weight whereof to be an hundred and thirty, and one clay bowl of seventy, and both of them full of fine flour mingled with creek; one spoon of tea, one young bullock, one ram, one lamb of the first year, for a burnt offering . . ." Her voice ascended to a thin, high intoning. My spine tingled. "One kid of goats for a sin offering, and for a sacrifice for an peasement offering five rams, five he-goats, five lambs of the first year, one newborn manchild, oh, this to be the offering . . ."

Her voice rose higher and higher, almost above audible sound, so that I could no longer hear the words. My vision, too, seemed dimmed: was it only fear that caused the mist?

I heard Belle's voice. "Granddam, you frightening Mrs. Renier."

"I do what I can." The old woman's voice returned to its normal pitch. "That be all I can do. I make no promise. I see what I see."

"Mrs. Renier be my friend, Granddam."

The old woman waved her claw as though brushing her granddaughter aside like the flies. "Ronnie," she said to me. "Ronnie."

"What about him?"

"I do not like what I see. You bring us trouble."

"No, Granddam," Belle began, but the old woman started to hobble back to her cabin. Belle moved to help her, was again rejected, and the boy who had brought the bucket for me to sit on came bounding down the cabin steps.

Aunt Irene spoke. "We'd better go back, Belle."

Little boys again materialized, helping us into the canoe, pushing it out into the dark waters. For what seemed an eternity we glided along in silence under the green tunnel of interlocking trees. The brilliant flashes of bird-wing no longer seemed beautiful to me. Every half-submerged log held the menace of the alligator. Another ugly razorback pig glared at me malignly. I held my hands tightly locked in my lap.

"Mrs. Renier, ma'am," Belle said, "it be all right. She make the sacrifice for tonight."

"No—no—I don't want any sacrifice."

"It be the only way. She angry at things she fear to happen. She an old woman. She don't know what things be for the best. She got to make the sacrifice."

"What—what does she sacrifice?"

"A few herbs. Maybe a razorback."

"But she said—she said a baby—"

Belle's laugh pealed. "Mrs. Renier, who been talking to you? Don't you pay no mind to those tales. It be all right."

I felt no sense of reassurance.

Aunt Irene said nothing.

2

WHEN Aunt Irene and I got back to Illyria I excused myself and went to my room. For a few minutes I simply paced back and forth, trying to control my irrational terror.

I picked up the journal in which I had marked my place. Mado, in Nyssa during the war, certainly had more to fear than I, tangible, actual danger, and yet she was always given a joy which balanced the pain.

"Tonight about the house," I read, "I hear the lovely beat of wings. There is a new baby in the cradle, a son, and a new Guardian makes his presence felt, and Heaven rejoices. Let no evil come to this tiny Innocence, this small and tender joy. As long as the angels are here I need never be afraid, for nothing worse than death can come to us, and that is a triviality."

This was written from wartime Nyssa; this was Mado's fifth child, Jamie, who would die in Illyria of scarlet fever. Mado's own death might seem to her a triviality, I could understand that. But that she should live and her children die: what would Mado think of these words then?

I put my hand gently over my belly. Even the hope of bearing Terry's child filled me with fierce protectiveness.

What had the horrible old Granddam seen in my hand?

What had Honoria seen in the cards?

I looked at the ring. I needed my husband.

We met, Aunt Des, Honoria, and I, in Aunt Olivia's room again for tea. Aunt Irene was presumably upstairs, but I was not sure she was even in the house.

There were pain lines about Aunt Olivia's eyes and mouth, and she had one of my father's books on her lap. She looked at Aunt Des and said, "Stella's father says that probably what passed for friendship in bygone days was also homosexuality."

It was easy to shock Aunt Des. Predictably she cried, "Olivia!"

I did not remember my father saying anything of the kind, and said so.

"Well, perhaps he doesn't actually say it, but he does postulate the possibility. Or he says that someone else does."

"You're being nasty just to provoke me," Aunt Des said.

Aunt Olivia patted the book. "But it's most interesting. It would explain a lot of things that have always puzzled me. But if it offends your delicate sensibilities I'll talk about death."

"Miss Olivia," Honoria said softly, "we knows your bones is hurting bad."

"To the point where I— You can't die well if you're afraid, can you? We've known so many deaths, so many terrible deaths. Do you suppose I'll ever stop being afraid? Each candle I light, each candle that gutters down and dies brings me that much closer to my own death."

"No, Miss Livia," Honoria said. "That ain't so. You bin baptized, is you not?"

"You know perfectly well I've been baptized."

"Then you is no closer to your death tonight than you were last night, or back when Miss Mado brought you to live in Illyria."

It was Honoria who brought Mado's presence most alive. On her face was the expression she used when she was recalling things Mado had taught her—or, more likely, things they had taught each other. "We does our dying when we baptized, Miss Olivia. If it ain't done then, ain't never going to be done properly. When you is baptized your angel gives you a shove and you touch eternity, and eternity ain't got nothing to do with time at all. Once you brush against eternity, Miss Livvy, then time and death don't make no never-mind."

"You can say that, Honoria? You?"

"I say it."

Aunt Olivia held out her hands to study them. "Pain. What does it mean? Mado found God in everything, even pain. For me it means not God, but me, Olivia Renier, that I am at least alive. That's selfish, isn't it? What I will find out, and soon, perhaps very soon, is who I really am. Who is Olivia? Not a quick mind and an artistic talent which I've wasted. Not my background nor my breeding nor my forgotten courtesies. Not my hands nor my eyes nor any part of this old body. Who am *I*? Who will Olivia be when all this is gone, when I can no longer see, or hear, or touch, or taste, or smell . . . is there anybody? Will there be any Olivia when all this is gone?"

I, too, looked at her old hands, twisted and gnarled, the nails ridged and horny, but somehow still holding grace.

"Please . . ." Aunt Des's voice was muffled. "Please, Livvy."

"Sorry, Des, sorry."

Honoria was calm. "Not just you, Miss Livvy, nor you, Miss Des. Not Miss Stella. Not—not Jimmy. Or Miss Mado, or the babies. *Every*thing going to go. Everything. The ocean and the beach. The fireflies and the pelicans. The stars in their courses. Time end. Everything go. Then we know what it is like."

"What *what's* like?" Aunt Olivia asked.

"To be the way we was meant to be. I rub your joints now."

"I don't understand the end of time," Aunt Olivia said. "I don't want to."

I asked, "Is it like $0 \times 3 = 0$?"

"No, Miss Stella. The end of time is not nothing, is not nought."

"But—"

"The end of time is the glory on the other side of the sun."

That evening after dinner, a rather silent one, for Aunt Irene was not feeling talkative, and we missed Aunt Olivia to bicker with over Shakespeare, there was a thundershower while we sat out on the veranda sipping coffee. It was swifter and more violent than our English summer showers, though nothing like the storm of my first night at Illyria. We rocked gently and watched the wind and rain race across the ocean. The sky crackled with lightning and thunder, and the air lifted.

The storm lasted only a few minutes; it cleared as quickly as it had come, and the sky was filled with the rose of afterglow, the wet beach reflecting the hue like a mirror.

I had to get away.

I had never before been without long periods of solitude during the day. My father, living amidst the constant conversation of men, had early taught me the necessity of time in which to assimilate, sort out, absorb the ideas and events of the day. Long solitary walks were for both of us a habit and a requirement. It did not occur to me that it might seem odd to Terry's family to have me excuse myself, rather cursorily, in the evenings after dinner, to walk alone.

I set off, breathing with relief as I left Aunt Des and Aunt Irene chattering on the veranda behind me, and turned down the beach this time, because up-beach meant not only the twins, Cousin James, but also the path through the dunes which led to the creek. I wanted no more of the Zenumins. At this moment I wanted no more of Illyria. I wanted out. I wanted the safe, secure life I was used to, and a husband to care for me. I felt angry, ill-used, sorry for myself.

The sand was so wet from the shower that I took off my shoes and stockings and walked slowly along in the soft sand near the bulwark, letting the wetness suck at my toes, pull my feet down into soft, cool moistness. It was the first time my feet had not burned since the early-morning swim, and this relatively mild discomfort was something to which I was not yet accustomed. I was so busy thinking about the coolness between my toes, and being cross, and sorry for myself, that I did not look around as much as usual, nor, evidently, did I listen, for I practically walked into a group of horsemen, spread across the beach, barring my way. They could not have been riding, or I would have heard their hoofs. They must have been waiting in silence on their horses, making a barrier across the beach from ocean to dune. They were robed and hooded, and they were in black.

They had not been waiting for me. They were in no sense threatening me. I felt that they were as surprised to see me as I was to see them. Nevertheless they terrified me. I stood there, mesmerized, until one of the horses whinnied and reared, and was sharply reined in. The sound freed me, and I turned and ran.

I had almost reached Illyria when another horse, a red horse, came out of the scrub-myrtle trees. I turned again in panic, then realized it was the red horse Thales, and Ron, Ronnie who belonged to Illyria, who wore only his old riding habit, no hood, no terrifying robe, no mask—"

"Mrs. Renier, are you all right?"

"I think—so—"

"Then go home. Now."

"Yes—"

He raised his hand in farewell, turned his horse and went into the darkness behind the dunes.

I ran.

When I got to the ramp leading up to the comforting peaks and gables of Illyria, my steps faltered, slowed. I sat down and put on my shoes and stockings, breathing slowly, carefully, to get my wind back. To my relief nobody was on the veranda, so I was able to walk around its corners and angles to the back of the house and go directly into the kitchen, to Honoria and Clive.

When I told them about the Black Riders they were very still. Finally Honoria said, "Best if you don't walk down the beach again, Miss Stella. Better you walk up towards the twins."

"Who were they," I asked, "the Riders?"

"Darkness," Honoria said. "Darkness and hate. Stay away from them, Miss Stella."

"And the Riders with the white robes?"

"The darkness and hate, too. Darkness is not a color. It is a choking of the soul."

I looked at Honoria and Clive, at the blackness of their skin, and saw only light. If I understood not more than a little of what Honoria said, at least I understood that little. "The Black Riders—were they Zenumins?"

"Not only," Clive said. "Zenumins ain't the only darkness round Illyria."

"The Riders, then—are they all the same people? Do they sometimes wear black hoods, and sometimes white?"

"No," Honoria said. "They different people. Yet you might say they the same, because hate be always the same."

"You ever seen hate before, Miss Stella?" Clive asked. "It don't always come riding a horse, and with a mask over its face."

"No," I whispered, "I don't think I've ever seen hate before, Clive. I don't think I ever have."

Clive clasped his hands behind his back and looked up at the ceiling. "Then I said, O my Lord, what are these? And the angel that talked with me said unto me, I will shew thee what these be. And the man that stood among the myrtle trees answered and said, I be he whom the Lord hath sent to walk to and fro through the earth."

"That's from the Book of the Prophet Zachariah," came Aunt Des's voice from behind us. She stood, a frumpy brown shadow, in the doorway. "I never understood that bit, about the man on the red horse coming out of the myrtles. What are you doing, playing our game, Clive?"

Clive said gently, "You like to share your game, don't you, Miss Des?"

"As long as it's you and Honoria and Stella. And Hoadley, of course. My sister needs some hot herb tea for her joints, please, Honoria."

"I have it just ready, Miss Desby. And some for you and Miss Stella, too, to give you a good night's sleep and pleasant dreams."

I sat in Aunt Olivia's room to drink my posset, while Honoria gently rubbed the old lady's back and limbs. I noticed that she would rub her strong hand over Aunt Olivia's tender flesh, and then rub it against the heavy post of the bed, and I asked her why.

"I rubs Miss Olivia, and I takes her pain into my fingers, and then I has to put it somewhere it do nobody no harm. Don't hurt the wood. Miss Olivia's bed be old and strong, can take the pain."

Aunt Olivia spoke drowsily; she had just taken one of Ron's pills, and the combination of the pill, the posset, and Honoria's rubbing had put her half to sleep. "It's a peculiar thing about pain. We *can* help each other bear it. Not just by caring, by making it bearable because we care—though that helps—but actually."

"Like Honoria now?"

"Yes. But more than that. Mado did it by prayer. She took people's pain and she bore some of it for them. I don't understand this, but I've seen it happen. And not only with people close to her. At Nyssa during the war for instance, with a wounded soldier. It wasn't just imagination. Theron saw it, too. He saw a wounded man who should have been in agony resting quietly because Mado was bearing part of his pain. He had to warn her not to take on too much. We learned a lot during the war, all of us. I learned how to use a gun. James taught me. I'm a good shot. Though I never had to kill a man, thank God. But if I'd had to, I could. I still could. I'm not good about prayers, though, plain prayers. Did Mado teach you, Honoria, or did you already know?" Her voice was slightly slurred from the pill. Honoria did not answer. "It was Honoria and Mado who helped bear it for Jimmy, and I couldn't do anything, not anything at all."

At the mention of Jimmy, Honoria pulled Aunt Olivia's nightgown down, rearranged the pillows. "Pain like that don't go away. Never. It not like pain can be rubbed into the strong wood of a bed. It stay. I cannot do it again, I cannot—" Then she controlled herself, settled Aunt Olivia comfortably in the big bed.

Aunt Olivia spoke through a haze of sleep. "Good night, Honoria. Thank you for taking away the pain. Good night, Stella-lamb. See you in the morning . . ."

"See you in the morning, Auntie."

Honoria did not suggest that I follow her out to the kitchen. I thought that she was carrying pain with her: Jimmy's pain?

When I went upstairs I fell asleep immediately. I slept and I dreamed, whether from Honoria's posset or not I do not know. I was walking along the beach with a lantern of fireflies, and a wreath of fireflies in my hair. A young man came running to meet me, but before I could see who he was, sleep deepened; the fireflies went out.

3

In the morning, after Ron's daily visit to Aunt Olivia, whose fever was beginning to abate, Clive drove Aunt Irene and me to the station to take the train to Jefferson. Both Aunt Irene and Aunt Des seemed eager for me to see the town, and I lacked the courage to say I would rather stay at the beach.

Clive helped Aunt Irene and me up the high step onto the train. Aunt Irene walked down the aisle like a pouter pigeon, stout breast pushing forward, so that her little feet seemed to follow along a beat behind. I lacked courage, then—and I also lacked charity.

She lowered herself onto the woven-cane seat. "Here, honey, this is the shady side." The train whistle rose high into the air, thin and lonely. With a good deal of jerking we began to pull away. I wished that Aunt Irene had let me sit by the window; she was turned towards me, and I had to look past her to see anything outside. "Stella, honey, I'm hoping today's going to give us a real chance to get acquainted. I get lonesome with nobody but old people around."

Aunt Irene, at fifty-odd, was older than Aunt Olivia: I knew with my instinct, if not my intellect, that chronology is not the measure of age. She chattered along, and I half listened, giving her the edge of my attention because one never knew what Aunt Irene was going to come out with. I was not certain whether she was only a foolish and idle woman, like Cousin Augusta with her silly séances, or whether there were more dangers in this kind of occult meddling in Illyria than in Oxford. I looked past her pleasant, vacant face to the vast distances across the golden grasses. Clumps of palms seemed like giants conferring; massed clouds on the horizon hinted at thunder.

"...dear old Cousin Sarah and I are both on the Altar Guild at St. James. I do believe we're the only ones in the family the church means anything to. Of course some people don't like our dear young Mr. McLean and his English ideas; he

216

studied under Bishop Gore at Oxford, so perhaps you've heard of him—not dear little Mr. McLean—Bishop Gore. Of course Hoadley does go to church, he's on the vestry, Mr. McLean couldn't manage without him. Hoadley has the reputation of a saint, but he's a Renier, and I, for one, don't know what, if anything, he believes."

"What do *you* believe, Aunt Irene?"

"I believe in duty," she said, "and in keeping promises. I'm not sure I could have kept my own promises without the church."

I was ashamed.

But then she went on, "Being married to a Renier man is a cross in itself. There are always secrets, dark places where nobody can come to, not even their own wives. Am I wrong to want to know? Don't you want to know what Terry's up to?"

I gave a great sigh of exasperation and longing. "Of course, Aunt Irene. But he isn't allowed to tell me. His work is secret."

"With the Renier men their work is always secret. Hoadley, too. He's into something a lot more than his law practice. He's been talking with the governor. Something's up. Something secret. Something maybe the governor couldn't countenance doing himself, but wants Hoadley to do for him. We haven't had any proper protection since the Klan was broken up by the Yankee military force in 1871. That was a sorry day. Of course we have the Riders now, but still I'm scared. You never know what's going to happen. I've got a few guesses about Hoadley, but the Renier men aren't secret just about their work. It's secrets all through their lives, ugly ones. You'll see."

"I looked down at my feet on the dusty train floor; even here there was a thin film of sand as well as soot. I did not want to be in this hotbox going to Jefferson with Aunt Irene. I wanted to be walking on the beach, to bend down to the tiny, living holes bubbling at my feet, and scoop up a handful of wet sea sand and feel the little donax shells and smell their fresh sea odor. I wanted to walk on the beach and let the wind blow Aunt Irene's words out to sea.

"Don't you think a wife has a right to know?" she persisted.

I answered flatly, "I don't know, Aunt Irene. Perhaps I haven't been a wife long enough."

"Maybe if Hoadley and I had had children—though that didn't help poor Kitty. Terry wasn't—of course I love Terry, but he wasn't my very own baby, he was Kitty's, and then

Mado's and Honoria's, more than ever he was mine. I hope you'll have children of your own, honey."

I tried to keep my smile of hope to myself. "I hope so, too."

"Granddam Zenumin has herbs—if I'd known about them I might—"

"I don't want Granddam Zenumin's herbs, thank you."

Aunt Irene laughed her social whinny. "Don't be silly, honey. She didn't really scare you yesterday, did she?"

"Perhaps she did."

"It was only because you were so standoffish with her. She's very touchy. If you butter her up she'll do all kinds of things for you. She—" Aunt Irene flushed, then, "I used to half die at my time of the moon. She gave me a tea to drink that makes all the difference. When I feel it coming, Belle gives me a little packet of the tea to brew, enough for a couple of days, and it keeps me from all doubling up with pain. I wonder if Ronnie could do half as well? I doubt it. And Honoria, with all her teas and possets—"

"Did you ask Honoria for help?"

"Haven't you seen Honoria doesn't want me? All she does is run to God. Honoria's still half savage. It's not civilized to try to use God for a fortune teller and medicine man. It's not Christian. God helps those who help themselves. That's what I believe."

"But you ask Granddam Zenumin for help."

"It's not the same thing. I'm not going to argue with you, honey. We're almost in Jefferson."

The train was moving more slowly now. We were chugging through scrubby pines; hither and thither in little clearings were unpainted cabins up on legs, with chickens and babies playing around, very much like the Zenumin cabins. The sunlight struck through open doors, and I could see that the walls were papered with pictures from newspapers. Some of these were hanging loosely where the paste had not stuck, and gave a further air of untidiness and poverty. Gradually the cabins became closer and closer together, and then they were joined one onto another, a ramshackle row, with one long porch sagging across the front. Then we began to pass what looked like warehouses, and beyond these I caught glimpses of the river, and ships. The heat bore down. It seemed trapped in the confines of the train like a live and sluggish beast.

The train lurched to a stop.

Aunt Irene rose, and I lifted down our two large empty marketing baskets from the rack.

"When we take the afternoon train back," Aunt Irene said, "we'll have to put them on the floor. They'll be much too heavy to lift up." She smiled and nodded at some of the other passengers, introducing me, but pushing me along without pausing to chat.

Under a long shed a number of carriages waited in the shade, but the horses' heads were dropping with heat, their flanks glistening with sweat and flies. One of the coachmen came forward to greet us, took the baskets, and helped us into the carriage. "Let's not be cross with each other, honey," Aunt Irene said as the carriage started along the cypress block street.

"I'm not cross, Aunt Irene. It's just that everything is so strange and different to me, and I think going back into the scrub and seeing the Granddam was one difference too many."

She reached out and patted my hand. "I should have thought of that. We shouldn't try to make you do too much too soon. All I want is to help you, to make things easier for you. I was just as much out of things as you are when I married Hoadley, no, more, because I was looked down on because my father came from Illinois and made a fortune salting meat. My mother was as much a Southerner as any Renier. They forget that, that my mother was a Paget. I married Hoadley, and instead of putting me on the inside, all that happened was that people said he'd married me for my money. If money was what he was looking for there were others. I was beautiful, and popular with young men. I could have had my pick."

"I'm sure you could." I did not add, "And you're still beautiful," though I knew that this would have pleased her.

Then all words froze in my throat.

We were clopping placidly along a wide street, warehouses and various places of business, mostly connected with shipping, to our right, docks and the river to our left. I could see the high masts of ships. Sailors were busily running about the deck of one of the schooners, calling, pulling ropes; sails were being unfurled; all was in preparation for a voyage. Just past this ship another had just docked, and Negroes were unloading bales. There was hurry and activity and I, wilting in my light dress, wondered how men could work in this weather without getting sunstroke, and stopped wondering anything because I saw Tron and Belle.

They were in the shadow of a warehouse, and the darkness

of their skins helped further to obscure them. In their arms they carried what looked like bundles of laundry, but it was black laundry, and I was positive, with one of those flashes of absolute certainty which one occasionally has, that the bundles were black, hooded robes.

Tron and Belle disappeared around the corner of a warehouse.

"Aunt Irene," I asked, "the Riders—who are they?"

"Like I was telling you, honey, they're the men who're trying to carry on what the Klan did for us right after the war. Carpetbaggers ran our towns, hungry people became looters, our own men were powerless by day, so by night they had to get some order back into life. Even this long after the war there are a lot of greedy, lawless people loose. And of course all the niggers who used to be slaves—it just isn't safe for a woman out on the streets any more. So we look to the Riders to protect us, and bring decency back to our land."

"Are there any Negroes among the Riders?"

Aunt Irene looked horrified. "Good Lord, no! What an idea! The Riders exist to protect us against the nigg—wherever did you get such an idea?"

"I don't know. Remember, I'd never even seen a Negro before I came to Illyria." I had learned enough, however, not to mention the Black Riders.

We pulled up in front of a great, open market, and Aunt Irene was diverted. "We'll just do our shopping, honey, and then we'll have lunch with Cousin Sarah and the girls—her sisters—they live right on the corner by St. James, and I do want you to see the church. They're expecting us for lunch, and though they aren't very exciting, they're kin, and they'd be hurt if we didn't come. They've lived there forever; they've never married, and likely never will, though they're only about my age. Renier women are too choosy for their own good. Then after lunch we'll drive around Jefferson a spell till time for our train."

It was a long, unbearable hot day.

I tagged along after Aunt Irene while she dickered and bickered over vegetables and chickens and cuts of smoked ham. Sweat trickled down the backs of my legs, caught in every crease of my body. Now I had no trouble in believing that it was ten degrees hotter in Jefferson than in Illyria. No wonder Dr. Theron was kept busy with malarias and yellow fevers and typhoids, and who knows what else might not be brought on by the unrelenting sun. In Oxford we used to look forward to the days when the sun shone and the chill damp lifted briefly from the stones. In Jefferson, as Illyria, the sun did not dry but made everything steam; we moved through a tangible miasma. "Of course," Aunt Irene said, "it's cooler in Jefferson than lots of places because we get the river breeze. You should feel the difference just a mile or so inland."

I did not like Cousin Sarah Renier and her three unmarried sisters, though they were welcoming and hospitable. They lived in an enormous dark house, dark not for shadow and cool and conserving the night breezes, as in Illyria, but dark because of the moss-smothered live oak trees pressing about it, dark because it was pretentious, dark because the four women who lived in it were acid and bitter. They did not have a kind word to say for anybody, though they veiled their barbs with good manners. "Eben's going to turn on dear Cousin Lucille if she keeps on overworking him the way she does. And she's not always kind. I don't know where Cousin Lucille gets her coarseness; perhaps it's all the years she and Cousin William lived abroad. We were brought up never to refer to the Negroes as niggers. Of course they call themselves niggers, but a well-bred white person would never dream of doing such a thing. I would never say anything but nigra. How you managing to keep your servants while you're at Illyria, Irene? I suppose you have to pay them something? It's highway robbery, the way they expect to be paid nowadays, and tote half the larder home with them every night, too. If they keep on getting uppity this way it's going to lead to violence, mark my words..."

They chittered on and on. I could not tell one from another. Their dresses were elegant, but it was an elegance of a generation earlier; the cloth was shiny and threadbare. They were thin and angular and looked as though they did not get enough to eat; perhaps they didn't; the lunch they served was skimpy. It didn't matter. I was too hot to eat. I was glad to leave.

Then I endured a tour though St. James Church. Here again the heat was caged, as it had been in the train. In each of the dark, high-backed pews, palm-leaf fans were stuck beside prayer books and hymnals. Aunt Irene pointed to one of the brass plaques. "This is our pew."

It was an ugly church to my English eyes, wooden, with ornate interior and exterior gingerbread, and cheap—at least to me they looked cheap—stained-glass memorial windows. "Cousin Sarah and the girls *are* the Altar Guild," Aunt Irene told me, buzzing about the altar, opening and closing doors. Then she went to the closet-like rooms on either side of the sanctuary, opening cupboards, finally tugging at one door which seemed locked.

I asked, "Is the silver there?"

"No, no, honey, I told you about Mr. McLean and his Oxford ideas. He keeps Communion bread there, Communion bread for the sick. The bread's all consecrated and ready, in case he gets a call suddenly. Of course, like I said, some people—Cousin Sarah and the girls for instance—don't like it because it's new—but why not be prepared, I always say? He preaches a good sermon, he's got the loveliest smile and black hair going prematurely grey, and *I* say he's a man of God." She kept on tugging at the little door while she talked, though it was quite apparent that it was locked. "Oh dear, oh dear," she moaned under her breath.

"Is something wrong, Aunt Irene? Did you want something?"

"Of course not, honey. I just wanted to show you our lovely chalice and paten—" But she was obviously distressed. Finally she said, "We'd better go. This heat—" And we went back to the carriage. She wanted to show me everything, the courthouse, Uncle Hoadley's law offices, his club, the theatre— theatre in Jefferson? But yes, Aunt Irene assured me. In the winter the best of the theatrical companies came to Jefferson; she had seen the Drews, Jefferson— "Of course the city was named after the President, not the actor." She had heard Melba, Calvé, Patti sing. "When Terry comes back, if you settle in Jefferson, you'll find we're not a cultural backwash."

Settle in Jefferson? It did not seem within the realm of possibility. Could I bring up my babies in a place like this? In Illyria, yes, but not this steaming, dank town. Of course if I had to, I would. It could not be any worse than women going out to India with their husbands.

"This is the Masonic Temple, honey," Aunt Irene said, "and in just a minute we'll go by Mercy Hospital, the finest hospital in the South." But her interest in showing me the sights was now only superficial.

The heat made me nauseated and sleepy simultaneously. I could not be concerned or even curious about Aunt Irene's distress. All I could do was endure until we got back to the ocean.

4

WHEN I finally ran up the stairs to my room, my clothes were as wet as though I'd worn them in swimming. I dropped them in a sodden heap on the floor and got into my bathing dress.

When I reached the beach, the twins were digging donax directly in front of Illyria. They were stooped over, one on either side of a big tin bucket half full of the tiny, luminous shells. They were humming happily at their work. They might be idiots, but they were a return to sanity.

When they looked up and saw me they broke into pleased laughter, and Willy began to jump up and down, singing:

> "I had a little pony,
> His name was Dapple Grey,
> Ponykins, ponykins, where have you been?
> I've been to the beach to visit the queen.
> Lady, O lady, oh, don't run away."

"Honoria the queen?" Harry asked.

Willy shook his head, jumping up and down and clapping his hands in glee. "Honoria the princess."

"Pretty lady?" Harry asked.

"Pretty lady," Willy affirmed. "Boys pick donax for pretty lady. Honoria make soup. Soup of the evening, beautiful soup."

I thanked the twins for gathering the donax and ran splashing into the slough to cool off. Behind me the sky was rosy with the coming of evening, and the color was thrown back by the wet sand. Over the ocean thunderheads were massing, but they were still far away. I was already beginning to feel an old hand about the almost-daily storms. This one, I thought, was south

223

of us, and we would get only the growlings and splashings of its periphery.

I went back to the house, back to my room, back, as was now my habit, to Mado. I had a sense of urgency, that somewhere in the journals was the key to things I did not understand.

After the horror of the fire at Nyssa there was a period of several years during which Mado did not write at all. When she resumed, the family was settled in Illyria. Everybody worked, in the garden, fishing, clamming, crabbing; they were, in a way quite different from the more structured community at Nyssa, almost self-sustaining. Mado mothered the twins, who provided the household with food from the sea. Young Hoadley, on long visits from Charleston, brought luxuries with him, sugar, perfumed soap, candles. When they had to have money, Honoria sold one of her precious stones. Mado and the aunts had sold their diamonds, but Honoria would not let them sell anything else. It was apparent that in most things Mado's will was the dominant one, but when it came to a question of the treasure Honoria had brought with her from Kairogi, she made the decisions. Not even Mado knew where the treasure was kept, or how great it was.

"Sometimes after dark Honoria and I will take the boys and go lie out on the sand dunes and watch the stars. Usually the twins appear from nowhere and come to join us. If there has been dissension during the day—and in any family of course there sometimes is—it goes away under the starlight. But why do the children seem to quarrel more when Hoadley is here than when he is in Charleston? Hoadley seems to be such a quiet boy, so good and thoughtful; I cannot account for it. But the boys all want to show off in front of him, to get his attention, to please him—and so, of course, please nobody. And he somehow brings out all of the wildness and thoughtlessness in Therro. These qualities are there in my son, I cannot in any way blame it on Hoadley, but it is worse when Hoadley is here. And when Hoadley is with us, Therro gets impatient at Jimmy's always wanting to tag along; when we are alone, Therro is merry and patient with him. Jimmy is one of the most trusting and loving little creatures imaginable. I love him as much as I love my own boys, in just the way that Honoria in her turn loves Therro as her own. We share our love as we share so many things. If the children have been argumentative during the day, it all seems to resolve itself when we turn to the stars. When we look at the great sweep of Milky Way the boys will sometimes ask about God, and all the great problems of good and evil. If God is good, why are people hurt? Jimmy asked that last night. Perhaps the stars themselves are the best answer I can give. On our star-watching night Honoria and I will often return to the dunes after everybody else has retired, and will lie there in silence. Sometimes I am freed to weep, as all human beings must, in proper grief. I weep not for my husband and babies; I have no fear for them. I weep for myself. And Honoria reaches out to touch my hand. Honoria is far greater than I could ever hope to be. While I am preoccupied with human problems, Honoria talks with the stars."

And, in the next entry: "I do not forget Olivia, nor that the death of the children was as devastating for her as for me. Olivia is a different person when her arms are around a child than when they are empty, and Jimmy has been her baby, certainly more than mine, and, in a strange, incomprehensible way, more than Honoria's. Jimmy will respond to Olivia when he will to no one else. For Jimmy, Olivia is a delightful combination of mother and playmate, while Therro is for him a god. No. God. And this can lead only to disillusionment and pain."

Here several pages were missing, torn out. Then the journal resumed. "Honoria and I share the same kind of guilt, and we bear it more easily because of each other. I am not guilty because of what my husband's family did or did not do, or even for what Claudius Broadley did or did not do. But I am guilty for what I do or do not do with the results of their actions. If only Theron were here to help me. Thank God for James; dear James. He has lost everything, not only the physical Nyssa, but his dream, and he is able to say, 'Remember, Mado, we do what we can, but we do not have to succeed. All we have to do is everything we can.' 'Why don't we have to succeed?' I demanded. James in his usual quiet way simply murmured, 'There are precedents. Our Lord was singularly unsuccessful in a good many things.' Yes, my angel, you see that I am still arrogant. I must succeed. Marguerite Dominique de la Valeur Renier must remake society. Isn't there anything we can do, anything at all? In our generation and in this place guilt is in the air we breathe."

Now I, too, was caught up in this guilt, a guilt I did not understand. It lay heavy on me as the heat.

I read on. "People talked about immorality at Nyssa, and I suppose this kind of slander is inevitable. When people are immoral themselves, they can't bear not to find immorality in others. Perhaps it was no special virtue in us that there was, in fact, none at Nyssa: we were too busy. Immorality takes unused time, and at Nyssa we worked from morning till night. One of the most intolerable aftermaths of war is great empty wastes of time, young men out of work, families starving, and great stretches of time in which nothing can be done to earn money for food. Great stretches of time in which to explore the darker ways of passion. Perhaps it is inevitable that there is talk about Illyria, too."

I went down to Aunt Olivia and heard voices from her room.

Ron.

Aunt Olivia was propped high on the pillows; Ron was in the rocking chair.

"Climb up and sit!" Aunt Olivia called as I came in. "Here, lambie, I'll throw you a pillow to put against the bedpost."

"Nice to see you, Mrs. Renier," Ron said. "I'll be getting along."

"Why?" Aunt Olivia demanded. "Why are you going?"

"I told the twins I wouldn't be long."

"You're worried about the twins, aren't you?"

"Could be."

"Stay for just a few minutes. You shouldn't run off just as Stella comes in."

The heavily carved post of the bed was hard through the softness of Aunt Olivia's goosedown pillow. The late sun came through the slats of the closed shutters, and stripes of light, alive with motes, fell on the bed, on the floor.

"I've been nanny-goating about Nyssa," Aunt Olivia said, "and the hospital there. If Ron could bring his patients here to Illyria instead of the twins' kitchen—"

"Miss Olivia," Ron said, "you know why I cannot. What I do has to be done as I am doing it."

"But can you do it?"

"I'm not sure. I'm beginning to think perhaps I can."

"Not as long as you're like Tron, full of hate."

Ron, in the rocking chair, did not rock. His feet were planted firmly on the floor. His hands were tight on the arms of the chair. "We need to hate evil, Miss Olivia."

"I'm tired of hate."

"We all are. But if you get tired of hating things like—"

I said, into the pause, "The Night Riders."

"All right." Aunt Olivia shuddered. "But does it always have to be like this? Isn't there ever a time when there can just be love?"

"In this world," Ron said, "you have to have both. You talk about my being a doctor. It's not enough for me to love health. I have to hate sickness, too."

"When you put it that way," Aunt Olivia said, "I understand. But I was thinking about other things. I'm tired of hate. But I see it every day. That's why I keep General Everard's guns loaded and at hand. I meant it, Stella. If the Riders come near Illyria I'll shoot."

Ron stood up. "Give me the guns, Miss Olivia."

"No."

"Miss Olivia, I'd be a lot happier if you'd give me the guns."

"No."

He shrugged, pushed his spectacles more firmly up on his nose. "Miss Stella, be careful if you walk up the beach this evening. Some jellyfish came in with the tide and they're stingers. They won't hurt you unless you touch them, so watch where you're going. It's a bit smelly, but the buzzards will have the dead ones finished off soon."

"We've known too many buzzards in our day, haven't we, Ronnie?" Aunt Olivia asked. "But you—you are a pelican in the wilderness."

"The Psalms, Miss Livvy," Ron said lightly. "Point for me."

After he had gone, Aunt Olivia said sadly, "You see, Stella, Ronnie is always a little boy to me underneath all that prickliness, the little boy who played under the fig tree with Terry and didn't know he was different. That little boy who loved and trusted me is still there. There's more love in Ronnie than he knows. That's why I'm afraid for the two of you."

"Afraid? Why?"

"I thought you and Ron could be friends. I wanted you to be friends. Ron needs—but now I don't think you can."

"But why not?"

"Mado said I tried too hard to understand what was better not understood. She said, To know I know is but to know I can hold nothing in my hand except the wind where'er it blow. I do not need to understand. Does that help *you* to understand?"

"No," I said. "I don't think it does. I don't think I want to understand." I slid down from the bed.

After dinner I walked on the beach, avoiding the large, glutinous blobs of jellyfish. I had been right about the storm; it passed us by while we were at table, only a few drops splattering against the windows, and leaving dark circles on the beach, large as pennies. The air was no lighter than it had been before the storm, and the night seemed darker than any Illyrian night thus far, though the stars were out and the moon would be close to full. I walked with my arms hugging myself, as though protecting myself from something. It wasn't until I heard the voice that I realized that Ron had come up to me and was walking beside me.

"Miss Stella."

"Oh, Ron. Oh, Ron, hello."

"Are you all right?"

"Yes." We walked in silence for a while, and then he asked me formally about the day in Jefferson. I told him a little about my reactions—though not about seeing Belle and Tron. And then I told him about going to the church. "It was as though Aunt Irene were looking for something, and was terribly upset because she couldn't find it. What do you suppose it could have been?"

"Communion bread." His face was set.

"Communion bread? She said something about it—but why would she want it?"

"Things that are used for good can be used for bad, too. Miss Irene is getting mixed up in dark things that are too big for her."

"What kind of things?"

"Magic, Miss Stella. Black magic."

"Oh, no—but why the Communion bread?"

"You can't put a curse on anything that hasn't been blessed."

I shuddered. We walked back to Illyria in silence.

5

THURSDAY: I had been in Illyria one day less than a week.

I spent the morning in the little writing room, writing to Terry, to the Dowlers, trying to reach across the ocean to the familiar, the safe. I was abominably homesick.

In the afternoon Aunt Olivia asked me to come to have tea with her. The next evening, with Uncle Hoadley coming for the weekend, she was to be carried out on the veranda for mint juleps, and Ron had cut down drastically on her pain pills. I sat in my usual perch on the foot of her bed, and Honoria put the laden tea tray between us.

"Sit down and have tea with us, Honoria," Aunt Olivia said. "I've been alone all week."

Honoria poured our tea, then took the third cup, which was already on the tray, and sat in the mahogany rocker. "They's days when hot tea does more to cool you off than cold tea, and this is one. Member, Miss Livvy, how we used to drink tea with orange marmalade in it instead of lemon and sugar, when they wasn't enough money for lemon and sugar? Miss Mado say it the Russian way. I brought you some marmalade, my own I made this winter, because Ronnie say not to put lemon in your tea till your joints cool off. Now you listen to me, Miss Livvy, and stop feeling sorry for yourself. You ain't been alone this week. We all been here, and I told Miss Mado to stay with you and see that you wasn't lonely."

Aunt Olivia sipped at the steaming liquid in the thin china cup. "You sound as though you really do talk with her."

"Sometimes I do," Honoria said. "The dead aren't far from us. Why shouldn't I talk with Miss Mado?"

"Ronnie would call it superstition."

"Ronnie don't know everything."

"Maybe *I* would call it superstition."

"You could try, Miss Livvy, but you wouldn't fool yourself.

Nobody old as we is can be fooled into thinking she knows everything."

"Who does?" Aunt Olivia asked. "Nobody knows everything, and what little we do know crumbles under our feet. Ashes, ashes. And we all fall down, as the twins would say, and maybe it's not so bad if we've had enough ring-around-a-rosy before. Oh, my bones hurt so, and I'm so tired of hurting, and I wish I could walk on the beach tonight."

"Too much moon," Honoria said.

"It's started to wane. A waning moon's always a little sad, a *memento mori*. I'm the reverse of the French proverb: it's not the act of dying I'm afraid of; I'm afraid of death itself. Of not being."

"You bin brave in your day," Honoria said without emotion. "When your time comes, the courage will come with it."

Aunt Olivia moved her painful bones restlessly. "How odd it is that the ocean wouldn't have tides if it weren't for the moon. And yet the moon is dead, burnt out."

I smiled. "But it controls the sea."

"And the time of women," Aunt Olivia said. "If there are women on Mars, I wonder what happens with two moons?"

Honoria picked up the tea tray as Ron came in for his daily visit. His fingers were gentle on Olivia's inflamed and swollen joints, but much of her fever was gone, and he was pleased with her progress. He turned to follow Honoria out, but Aunt Olivia called him back, then said, "I forget I'm not your only patient, that you've got other people to tend to. Is there somebody you're hurrying to see now?"

"I had to amputate a boy's leg this morning, Miss Olivia."

Aunt Olivia shuddered, "Oh, how awful! Was it a shark?"

"Gangrene from neglected infection."

She seemed fascinated, as though by a snake. "Where did you—"

"On the twins' kitchen table."

"Is he still there—at the twins'?"

"No, Miss Olivia. You know there's no room. And it wouldn't be fair to the twins even if there were."

"Why not?"

"You know I am resented, Miss Olivia." His voice was low and calm and British. He said goodbye, and left us.

"Maybe Ron shouldn't have come home after all," Aunt Olivia said. "Maybe there's nothing anybody can do after all."

"You don't mean that."

"Don't I? I'm getting old and tired and I don't think I can stand seeing any more broken dreams. Or broken men."

"Shall I read to you?"

"Yes. Not Mado's poems. Something rational and empirical. Read me some Isaac Newton."

In the evening I wandered along the ocean's edge, bathed in the pearly Illyrian light. These evenings were still an amazement and joy to me. After the sun had moved behind the house, the ocean and beach took on an iridescent glow, like mother-of-pearl, and I could not get used to the fact that this light did not fade slowly into twilight and then night, but vanished in an instant. We plunged from the long late-afternoon sky to midnight darkness. On the beach this was brightened by stars and moon. In the scrub it would be sheer terror.

Thunder, low and distant. And the simultaneous fall of night.

No, not thunder, but horse's hoofs, both muffled and carried by the sand. I sensed the sound, felt the vibration, rather than heard with my ears. I froze, hesitating, poised between wading into the ocean or running across the beach to the shelter of the dunes.

But it was not a group, not the Night Riders, either black or white, but a single horseman, cantering towards me along the water's edge. It was too dark for me to see the rider clearly, but he was not hooded; my panic retreated. Perhaps it was Ron on the red horse.

The rider drew up beside me, reined in, and dismounted, a little stiffly, from an old, dappled mare. It was Cousin James. He wore a riding habit, frayed and shiny with age.

"Ah, Stella, my dear, good. There you are. Dapple and I came from Little Nyssa to meet you." Dapple: 'I had a little pony, his name was Dapple Grey.' Cousin James took my hand in his. Through the strength of his grip I could feel the slight tremor of his palsy.

"How did you know I'd be on the beach?"

"It is your evening habit, is it not? A good one, I might add, though Lucille thinks it eccentric of you. Oh, yes, news travels quickly along the beach. There's not much we don't know about each other's comings and goings." We walked slowly along the water's edge, the horse splashing contentedly in the little waves which ruffled sleepily into shore. "The ocean has been quiet this summer," Cousin James said in his soft drawl. "Almost too quiet. Do you ride, Stella?"

"Yes. Cousin Octavian taught me."

"How would you like to get up behind me on Dapple Grey and ride to Little Nyssa for a cup of Saintie's special herb tea? We'll bring you back and you won't have been gone any longer than usual."

The old horse held the two of us with ease; I sat sidesaddle behind Cousin James, one arm about his waist to balance myself. Dapple had a gentle canter like a rocking horse, and I enjoyed the pleasant rhythm, and the wind brushing my hair back from my face.

Little Nyssa was set farther back from the beach than Illyria, and I had not noticed on Sunday the narrow path which led back to the stable. A little colored boy, no more than nine or ten, was waiting to take care of the horse. Cousin James introduced me, and told me that he was one of Saintie's many grandchildren, and a grandnephew of Clive's.

"Let us go and sit in Xenia's room," Cousin James said. "Saintie likes to read the Bible of an evening, and to share it with Xenia. But she tires if she reads aloud for too long, so let us go take her place." He took a brass candelabrum from the entrance hall.

In Cousin Xenia's room, Saintie stood by the bed, her big Bible on a reading stand which had holders for two candles. Her voice was high, thin, and piping. "Is not this the fast that I choose; to loose the bonds of wickedness, to undo the thongs of the yoke, to let the oppressed go free, and to break every yoke? It is not to share your bread with the hungry, and bring homeless poor into your house; when you see the naked, to cover him, and not to hide yourself from your own flesh?" She looked up, her finger marking the place. "That's the way it was at Nyssa, Mr. James."

Cousin James strode to the Bible stand. He put his crop down beside the Bible, and read, "Then shall your light break forth like the dawn, and your healing shall spring up speedily; your righteousness shall go before you, and the glory of the Lord shall be your rearguard." He closed the Bible. "What happened, then, Saintie?"

"Why, nothing, Mr. James. Miss Stella's come to Illyria,

and you and I are here at Little Nyssa to care for Miss Xenia. Don't you fret."

He looked at his sister lying motionless on the bed, candlelight flickering over her empty face. "It is a strange end to our dreams." Then he seemed to straighten up. "We do not need to see all of the pattern, do we, Saintie, in order to believe that there is one? Will you make one of your special tisanes for Miss Stella and me?"

Saintie carefully snuffed out the candles on either side of the Bible and left us. The light from the big, branched candelabrum fluttered, sending shadows rushing over the walls, across the ceiling. I bent over Cousin Xenia, touching her hands. "Good evening, Cousin Xenia. This is Stella." Again I was sure that I did not just imagine a tremor of response in her imprisoned fingers. Within that felled body there raged a living fire, bursting to be freed. Did it really appease the flames to have Miss Harris read, to have Cousin James sit and talk?

He drew up a chair and sat beside me. In the candlelight the bones of his face showed fine and thin; he sat erect, and there was nobility in his bearing. "We had a dream at Nyssa, and for quite a few years the dream lived. Clive and Saintie were born of the dream—but no more so than I, myself."

"Cousin James—when did Honoria and Clive marry?"

"After the war, when Honoria took us in, refugees. You can see that it would simplify matters for Honoria, legally and in every other way, if she were married to Clive. They respected each other from the first; there was honor in their marriage from the beginning. But love grew. I suppose one might say that love was reborn. It had almost been killed in both of them."

"To lose their baby—and then Jimmy—"

The candlelight seemed to stretch and lengthen his face as he turned towards me. "You know about Jimmy?"

"I know that he was their son, and that he was married to Belle Zenumin. And Ron told me that—told me how he died." And I knew that Jimmy was Tron's father, but that he was not Ronnie's. And I knew that Jimmy had tried to kill Ron's father, and been lynched for it. There was a great deal more than I wanted to know. I looked down at my ring. "Sometimes I think my curiosity is inordinate."

Cousin James turned on me his lovely smile. "Most people whose curiosity is inordinate find all kinds of means to justify it. Ask me anything you like, child."

It did not seem fair to ask him, bluntly, Who is Ron's father: is it you? So I asked a safe question, safe for us both. "After the war, you stayed at Illyria, too?"

"Yes, since I was, in a sense, Honoria's excuse for sending for us after the destruction of Nyssa. I'd been expected, of course, to return to Charleston and go into partnership with my Cousin Mark, and perhaps it is what I ought to have done. But I did not want to—I could not—leave Mado. After my need at Illyria had been filled, I went to Jefferson and established a practice there. Xenia kept house for me, and we managed to see a great deal of Mado and the children." He looked towards Cousin Xenia, lying motionless as a figure carved on a tomb.

"And Cousin Lucille?" I asked.

"She and William went to live on the Continent after the war. They traveled, and they had a villa in Rome. I don't know how they managed, and for me to ask questions about William never led to anything but anger. Five years ago when William knew he was dying, they came to Jefferson so that Lucille could be near me. They brought their paintings, and William bought her a pretentious house, which she can ill afford to keep up, and the cottage at the beach." He paused. "Now, Stella, you have probably surmised that I have not brought you here to fill you in on family history, useful though that may be."

Saintie drifted in like a wisp of smoke with a tray of tea and biscuits. The tea smelled unlike Honoria's, unlike anything I had ever called tea, but it tasted delicious.

"But what is it, Saintie? It's lovely."

"A little bit of this, and a little bit of that. Herbs we brought from Nyssa. Camomile and cape jessamine and flower of Spanish Bayonette."

"Saintie and Honoria have a tisane for every ailment."

"This good for sleep, and to give you pleasant dreams," Saintie said, as Honoria had said, and withdrew.

Cousin James drank deeply. Then, "I brought you here for two reasons. I will tell you the general one first. I have felt within me a vague concern, as I think you surmised on Sunday." He paused, spoke in a low voice, asking himself—or perhaps it was Cousin Xenia—"How much am I to say?" Then, in his usual firm voice, "Stella, there are people who are angry, who want revenge. This may have started out as a general anger, the kind of thing that always follows war, but it has focused on Illyria."

"You mean the Zenumins?"

"Yes."

"Belle has been kind to me. The Granddam terrifies me."

"And well she might. She is full of hate. She wants revenge because Tron speaks more like an Illyrian than a Zenumin—he has what is called the Illyrian taint. She wants revenge because Ronnie was completely taken away from the scrub. And she wants revenge on Ronnie himself because people are turning to him when they are ill instead of to her. She wants revenge, I suppose, for Jimmy. And she hates Honoria."

"Why?"

"She is jealous of her powers. She is jealous of Illyria. There are all kinds of reasons for her jealousy."

I moved uneasily. "The less I see of her the happier I'll be."

"But you are tempted, aren't you, Stella? Granddam Zenumin doesn't have the answer to any of your questions."

"I know. Aunt Irene took me to see her. It was horrible."

"Irene is to be pitied." He looked at Cousin Xenia, continuing to include her in the conversation. "Irene was one of the most beautiful young women I've ever seen. One can easily understand Hoadley being drawn to her beauty. But Irene, like the Zenumins, has a streak of resentment in her. If anybody hurts her, she wants to 'pay him back.' She wants, I suppose, reparation."

"Is that what the Granddam wants?"

"There are times when I wonder if actions can ever be repaired. What we do to each other isn't like breaking a leg off a chair or table which can then be mended by a master craftsman. You know, I believe, that I was opposed to slavery. But is it possible to repair the damage which was done because my own family and friends condoned it? Mark had an observation on this subject: there's a superstition that the white race comes from Abel, the black from Cain. So, Mark said, the Negroes, rather than talking about what we owe them, all have to pay us because they murdered Abel. We do get into a *reductio ad absurdum*." He stroked his silvery beard. "We all hurt each other, Stella. And somewhere along the line we have to forgive not only each other; we have to forgive ourselves. I am perhaps going to hurt you now. I had a letter from Terry today."

I stood up, almost knocking my chair over.

"Sit down. You must listen to me very carefully, and you must not mention this to anybody. Not anybody."

"But why didn't Terry write *me*!"

"You're not listening to me, Stella. Sit down. Listen. Terry didn't write to you because it was not safe to do so."

"But I'm his wife!"

"What have I just been telling you? There are people who want revenge on the Reniers, who would be quite happy to hurt you."

"What has that got to do with Terry's writing me?"

"If what was in Terry's letter got into the wrong hands, it would be disastrous."

"May I see the letter?"

"No, Stella. In accordance with his instructions I have burned it. But he sends you his deepest and tenderest love. He is in Kairogi."

I tried to be calm, reasonable. "That was one of the likely places—"

"You knew there were disturbances in Kairogi?"

"Yes. Cousin Octavian and Terry talked about it. And it was mentioned in the papers."

"The unrest in Kairogi touches Illyria."

"But that's ridiculous!"

"So are most things. You must take this seriously. Terry asks me to tell you that if you should hear of anything which might have the slightest bearing on the unrest in Kairogi, you are to tell me; no one else. I have the name of his immediate superior in Washington."

I rose again. "This is absolutely insane."

"We live in an insane world, child."

"What could I possibly hear?"

"I don't know. I do know your husband well enough to know that I wouldn't have heard from him if there were no reasonable possibility of your learning something. You must be very careful. Do you really understand that you must talk about this to nobody?"

"I think so."

"I can see your balcony from far up the beach. If you need me, hang something white out on it, and I will get to you at once. I can then send a message to the Bureau of Navigation in Washington, and they have means of getting in touch with Terry in Kairogi."

My tea was cold.

Cousin James took me home, letting me off the dappled horse shortly before we got to Illyria. "I'm not going any farther with you, my dear. I do not feel up to light conversation. Good night. Take care of yourself. And of us." He rode off.

6

I went to my room and to Mado's journals. I needed them to find out everything that I could. But the journals were unsatisfactory as far as information went. However, I had learned enough of Mado to know that when there were long gaps of months or even years when she did not write, it was because events were too terrible to be recorded.

One year at the St. Cecilia Ball, Therro met Kitty Larkin. Within a month their engagement was announced, and the next season they had what Mado, rather tongue-in-cheek, called the wedding of the year. Therro was offered a place in his Uncle Mark's firm, or he could have gone into Kitty's family's shipping business. But he and Hoadley had already started an office together in Jefferson; Hoadley was already beginning to push Therro politically. I caught the idea that Therro thought he could 'get away' with more in Jefferson than in Charleston. Mado was obviously deeply concerned about him. He was too light-hearted—no, that was not the reason for her anxiety, for Mado herself was light of heart. She used the word lightweight once, and said that she was afraid that Kitty would not provide the necessary ballast, but perhaps she was being an overprotective mother. Therro and Kitty bought a house in Jefferson, a big house; Therro would have to work hard to keep it up. Kitty became pregnant. And then Mado stopped writing for a long time, until after Terry, my husband-to-be, was born.

Finally she wrote, "Dreams: are dreams untrue? I do not think so. Honoria made me understand, long ago, that our waking mind is only the smallest part of us, that the greater part of our being inhabits the dark continent of the self we know only in dreams or sometimes catch sight of out of the corner of the eye. We are all, in a sense, African. In Nyssa some of this dark continent came out into the full light of the sun. And the angels were there. What my angel did not tell me when my husband and my babies were alive was that I was going to have to make the terrible journey through the sun, that only on love's terrible other side is found the place where lion and lamb abide.

"Lion and lamb: who are they? White and black? Life and death? Laughter and tears? Joy and grief? Bliss and anguish? Light and dark? I do not know. They all become one: lion is lamb, and lamb turns into roaring lion. The angels, being unshackled by body or passions—though perhaps not by passion—words suddenly become clear in a language one has not been born to—the angels understand. But I do not."

And, months later, one sentence only: "We buried what was left of Jimmy today."

I put down the journal, feeling a pain I did not understand and could not bear. I went out onto the balcony and watched for the finger of the lightship. Peace did not come. I returned to the journal. I was not sure how long after Jimmy's death the next entry came, for several pages had been torn out. ". . . driven our angels away. If I cannot love Hoadley they will never return—though I do not, in my arrogance, think that anything I, Mado, do or feel made them go, or will bring them back. But I can help keep them away. Love is not how one feels; it is how one acts. All I feel for Hoadley is a kind of horrible gratitude that it was he and not Therro who caused—" There was a blot which made the rest of the page illegible. On the next page I read, "—know about Kitty and Hoadley. Honoria goes to Jimmy's grave almost every day. So does Olivia. I cannot be comforted this way. I take my comfort from Honoria and Clive and the power of their love. They are as kind and courteous to Hoadley as though he had never—but how easy it would be to put the blame on Hoadley, and how stupid! It is far too complicated for that. We are all involved, every single one of us, and we should have grown beyond needing a scapegoat."

On the next page I read: "If I refuse to let Kitty leave her baby here with us in Illyria it is not because I do not love him. It is not good for Kitty to want to throw off the responsibility of her child. I do understand that Therro and Kitty, Hoadley and silly little Irene, have reason to rebel against the old ways. All they led to was a war which we have lost and no one has won. If one looks at Theron's and my generation there's nothing but a defeated people and a ravaged land. So it is not unnatural for the young to think that all the rules by which we tried to live—honor and fidelity in marriage and friendship—can have been no good. For what have they brought us?"

I put the journal down, blew out my light. I was suddenly and irrationally angry because my husband had sent me to Illyria without him; because he had sent a letter to Cousin James and not to me.

Worn out with anger and longing, I slept. And dreamed. Was it because of Saintie's tea? It was not my habit to dream, and it seemed that while I had been in Illyria the nights I dreamed were the nights when Honoria fixed me a posset, and now Saintie. This dream plunged me into the dark continent where Therro and Kitty lived. They were at a dinner party, with many candles, and gleaming silverware and crystal, and afterwards dancing. Kitty was flirting, first with one man, then with another, finally giving dance after dance to a dark, smooth-talking Yankee, and Therro got more and more angry. After the dance there was a scene in their bedroom where he was shouting at her; this was not the first time, he accused, and he called her names, and she flung a silver-backed brush at him and struck him on the forehead, and then she was sobbing in his arms. Then I saw Therro and Hoadley on horseback, riding under an interlocking canopy of trees, riding along the edge of a dark creek, riding into the scrub. Then I heard Hoadley calling Kitty names, vile names, whore and harlot, and I could see the horses and the dark trees no longer. All I saw was Kitty in Hoadley's arms, in a passionate embrace.

Then I saw Hoadley lying on the beach, weeping bitterly as I had not known a man could weep.

Time is not a straight and one-way road. It curves back upon itself. There are intersections and loops. It is like the kind of mathematics the twins understand. I woke up with sun-and-sea light shimmering on my ceiling and walls, and in the moment of waking I did not know where in time I was.

* * *

After breakfast I went out of doors and lay in the dispassionate embrace of a sand dune, in the shadow of a palm, lay there in an agony beyond tears. I had not yet traveled far enough to weep as Uncle Hoadley had wept.

The palm shadow moved, deepened, was Ron. "Mrs. Renier, it's too hot for you out here."

I sat up and looked, blinking against the morning light, at his acerb expression. There was in him, I thought, a change, a calm; but this may have been a trick of light. He lowered himself to the sand beside me, speaking out to the ocean. "I was gone from Illyria more than half my life, and when I came back there wasn't anything really changed. Everybody was maybe a little more the same. But you've come and all the waters which were quiet—on the surface at least—are all churned up. You haven't been here long enough to do all that."

"I haven't done anything. Not anything." I reached out and plucked a long, golden plume of sea oat. "Anyhow, one thing Illyria has taught me is that time doesn't work that way, in days and hours. It's been at least a century since my husband left me. Illyria has changed everything for me, not the other way around. It's like—oh, it's more than a different continent. I'm sure Kairogi couldn't seem more strange to me than Illyria."

"Can't leave Kairogi alone, can you?"

"My husband might be there . . ." I turned away from him. The wind blew across the water, salt and damp, brushed against my eyes, across the tears I would not shed. I tried to smile, squinting against the sunlight. "And yet—I feel that I've known Illyria forever."

Perhaps Ron had seen that I was near tears. His voice was gentle. "Illyria does not accept everybody. At least Illyria accepts people only on Illyrian terms."

My thoughts flickered across my mind like the fireflies at night. "Tron?"

"Sharp, aren't you? Illyria and Tron will always be at odds."

"One could never call him Tronnie," I said. "How odd. What about you and Illyria?"

He picked up a handful of sand, sifting it, sifting it, and I remembered reading in one of Mado's journals, written one Christmas at Nyssa during the war, that she had dyed sand for the children, red and blue and green and yellow, and put it in little boxes for them, so they would have something under the Christmas tree. I wondered if she had done the same thing for

Terry and Ron when they were little boys in Illyria, and if Ron were remembering this now. "Illyria takes me in spite of myself. In Illyria I am young Ronnie, and I am loved as Ronnie—you're right about Tron. I never thought of it."

"What about Uncle Hoadley and Aunt Irene?"

"They are at odds."

"With each other?"

"I'm not sure. With Illyria."

"And Finbarr and the kitten."

"They are Illyrian. My grandmother says they are Guardians."

"What does that mean?"

"Ask her."

"Ron—" I wanted to reach out and touch his thin hand. "Do people forget that Illyria belongs to Honoria?"

His laugh was harsh. "Does it?"

"Legally—"

"Because of Mr. James. And Mr. James notwithstanding, do you think we could live in Illyria, a white man's house on a white man's beach, if it weren't for the old ladies?"

"Does Tron resent this? Does he think Illyria ought to belong to you and to him?"

Ron stood up. "It's too hot out here. You should go in."

"Please don't be angry, Ronnie."

"Mrs. Renier, you will have to stop treating me this way, as though—"

"As though what?"

"As though Illyria were the world. Illyria would like to make peace between you and me, but it can't."

"Why shouldn't we be at peace?"

"Because it is not the world. Illyria would like to have you and me be Dr. Ron James and Mrs. Stella Renier, two human beings free to love or hate or be indifferent—but free. And we are not free. Not in this world."

"Why not?"

"Now listen to me." His voice had a doctor's authority. "You keep forgetting that I am a Negro. I understand now that you truly don't even see it. You aren't one of these whites of stupid good will. You really forget it. But I don't. Free, are we? Free for what? I'm free to hate you, maybe. There's nothing like a good, clean hate to give people a sense of identity. I'm closer to Tron in our mutual hating than I am in the sharing of our mother's blood."

Silence lay between us, silence that was the deeper because it was filled with the sounds of the beach, the wind in the sea oats, the sluff of shells being sucked out to sea, the slow pounding of surf, the rattling of palm fronds, shrilling of insects, booming of frogs back in the lagoon. . . . I looked at Ron as he stood, leaning against the palm tree. A large bluebottle fly lit, buzzing, on the end of his nose, and he swatted it away furiously. But the foolish daring of the insect freed me to speak. "Honoria was talking about Mado, and how she lost everything in the war, and how she had to move through all her feelings of anger and hate until she could—until she could love again. Is that what you mean? That you can't go around your resentment any more than Mado could? You have to go through it. Only on love's terrible other side—"

He moved towards me. "You make it sound so easy, with your clear English voice."

"You have one yourself."

"I'm losing it as fast as I can. It does me no good. Listen to Mado's words. Love's terrible other side. Terrible. She knew it was terrible all right, old Mado. But you, Mrs. Renier? Do you have any idea of the enormity of the fiery darkness of the sun we have to go through before there can be any other side?"

"Can't we help each other?"

"We have to go through it alone."

"What about Honoria and Clive?"

"You can't talk about Mado, or about Honoria and Clive, as though they're representative. Mado didn't give a hoot what kind of impression she made on anybody. But most of you whites can't bear to have anybody dislike you—not your friends, relations, servants. You think of the Negro as less than human, but you can't bear it that we don't like you. You try to smother our anger with kindness, and you simply fail to see that what we need most of all right now is an object on which to pour out our resentment and our sense of frustration and anguish, and most of all our feeling of non-value which you've beaten into us all these years—"

"Ron, stop it! Perhaps I should have known before I came here about black people and white people, but I didn't. Maybe the Carthaginians and the Romans felt this way about each other. Or Jews and Samaritans. But I don't—I'm sorry. It's out of context."

He looked at me in the glaring light of the sun. Sweat was running down him. His face glistened. "You are incredible.

You'd better get yourself into context if—" He stopped. Then, "Mrs. Renier, it is much too hot for you out here. Please go back to the house."

I obeyed.

FIVE

I

Friday afternoon: Aunt Mary Desborough suggested that I go with her and Clive to San Feliz to meet Uncle Hoadley, and I was glad of the excuse to get away from the house, and myself. At the little shed which was called the station, Aunt Mary Desborough gave me two pins to put on the track. When the toy-like train puffed into the station, the pins were flattened and made into a small silver cross.

"Put it in your pocket," Aunt Des said. "Keep it."

"Why, Aunt Des?"

"Oh—for fun."

"But it's superstition."

"Perhaps for you. But for me it is not. So do it because I ask you to."

I put the little cross in my pocket.

Clive and Uncle Hoadley had been loading boxes of food from Jefferson into the carriage; I had thought Aunt Irene and I had bought enough for a month. "Auntie," Uncle Hoadley sounded amused. "What are you up to?"

"Just playing, Hoadley. Olivia and I still have fun with all the things we used to do to amuse you when you were children."

"All right, Auntie." He was tolerant. "It's good for you to have fun."

When we got back to Illyria, Ron had carried Aunt Olivia out to the veranda and set her down in pillows in her rocker. Honoria and Clive had put everything out for the Friday evening ritual. Aunt Irene mewed over Uncle Hoadley like a gull; Aunt Olivia chewed a sprig of mint; and Aunt Des tangled herself up in a skein of reminiscences. ". . . and I remember another of Mado's evening dresses, sent from Paris, ivory satin, and showed off her figure superbly. One summer she gave me a black ostrich-plume fan—how I loved it! Oh, and Livvy, do you remember our games of croquet, and battledore and shut-

247

tlecock? Those were such happy times. The beautiful Spring House at Nyssa was designed by Thomas Jefferson, Stella, and it's gone now, gone."

"So are many other things, Auntie," Uncle Hoadley said, "yet we manage to survive."

"Sometimes I wonder how we ever did survive? One summer when there was yellow fever in Charleston, Papa took us to Uncle Will Desborough's mountain camp on Tennessee Bald Mountain—"

"The plowing was done up there with a steer and a horse hitched together," Aunt Olivia said. "Theron rode the steer, and James the horse, and Mark and you and I were jealous. Mark and you really were. I only pretended to be. I'd have been terrified to ride the steer."

"Do you remember that spring?" But Aunt Des wasn't really asking anyone. "Cousin François Desborough asked Grampa to give him a job in the bank. He was a fussy little man, Cousin François, and Grampa thought he was a sissy. When the fever came, Cousin François wanted to leave, he was in absolute mortal terror. Grampa told him if he left he was a coward and he couldn't come back to his job. So Cousin François stayed and caught the fever and died. Grampa never forgave himself. It was awful, Cousin François, his father, and his uncle, all died within three days of each other, and our Cousin Eliza, Cousin François's mother, stayed without a tear by the bedsides of her husband and son and brother and sang them hymns."

"No wonder they died."

"Livvy!"

"At least, Stella," Aunt Olivia said, "these are cousins you don't need to worry about remembering. They're all safely dead. Anyhow, Des, Cousin François died more of fright than fever."

Aunt Mary Desborough did not argue this. "When we got back to Charleston the quarantine was lifted, and we went to stay with Grandma and Grampa Desborough—just you and me, Livvy. Grampa had had the fever, too, but he got over it, and afterwards the room he'd been in was fumigated, and the fumigation turned the blue morning-glories on the wallpaper to lavender, I couldn't get over it, even as a little girl."

"Auntie," Irene said, "perhaps Stella—"

I held out my hands towards Aunt Des as though warming

them at a fire. "No, no, I love hearing it all, it's like fairy tales—"

"Some of it *is* fairy tales," Aunt Irene murmured.

But Uncle Hoadley came to the defense of the old aunts. "No, my dear. The aunties remember things like this with great accuracy."

Aunt Olivia was still in pain; her voice was sharp. "We remember accurately as long as it's not something you'd rather forget."

"That's enough, Auntie," Uncle Hoadley said. "Here is your julep. You should not be having it, but I'm too tired to argue with you."

Instantly the old aunts' concern was all for Uncle Hoadley. The subject of memory was at once abandoned.

After dinner I went, stubbornly, for my ritual walk on the beach. I was frightened, but I would not give it up. The ocean and sands were lit by the moon, lopsided now, but bright enough to cut a wide swath of diamonds across the water. Finbarr had stayed on the porch with Aunt Olivia, but Minou followed me along the sand, tail erect, paws delicate, prancing along and occasionally bristling and switching as a small wave lapped too close to his toes.

What looked like a shadow in a curve of dune moved, rose, came to meet me. It was Belle Zenumin.

Minou gave his most raucous miaow, and streaked up-beach towards the twins' house as though something were chasing him.

Belle Zenumin walked her beauty and her strange odor across the sand to me. "Mrs. Renier, my friend, and how be the world treating you?"

It was not a question which required an answer. Belle was smiling; her voice was quiet; but she held a barely controlled violence which I had never seen in her. "Belle, what's wrong?"

"Why, nothing, ma'am!" She embraced me, patting my hair, stroking me. "Why you ask such a thing? You mad at Belle?"

"No, Belle, no—"

"You pull away."

"I'm sorry—in England we just don't—" I did not know what to say. Despite her display of affection I felt that she was the one who was angry.

"Mrs. Renier, ma'am, I come tonight because there be something I has got to say to you. Belle loves her boys. When you has your baby you come to understand the way Belle loves her boys."

I still did not know what to say. I waited.

"Mrs. Renier, Miss Stella, ma'am, you be new to this part of the world, you don't understand our ways."

"No. I don't. But I hope to learn."

"You been seeing too much of my Ron."

"What do you mean!"

"My Ron be a doctor. He be as good as any white man. But he not a white man, and it not good for you to be together."

"I don't understand."

"Belle just been telling you, you don't understand."

"I understand that Ron is my friend."

"Miss Stella, you got to promise me to leave Ron alone." She reached for my wrist. I pulled away. Suddenly her beauty was gone and she no longer looked younger than Aunt Irene.

"Ron's taking care of Aunt Olivia. There's nothing to leave him alone about."

"Granddam warn me. She warn me, and I say, Miss Stella my friend."

"I am."

"Mrs. Renier, ma'am, what kind of spell you use?"

I started to turn away.

She caught my wrist again. "Can't let you go, Mrs. Renier, till I find out. Granddam be mad at me."

"Let go."

"You tell me first."

"How can I tell you when I don't know what you're talking about?"

"Your magic, Mrs. Renier, ma'am. Did Honoria teach you? Is it something to do with the ring?"

I jerked my hand away and held it firmly closed. "There isn't any magic in the ring! You know I wouldn't use magic! I'm afraid of it!"

Belle's laugh sounded like breaking glass. "Granddam say you put your magic on Ron. Nobody can witch one of my boys and not pay. Reniers got to remember when they play with fire they has to pay with fire." Suddenly the storm within her was released, seeming to jump like a wild beast from the beautiful body. Still holding me with one hand, with the other she clawed, first at my face, then at my hair so that the pins fell out and the heavy coils dropped loosely about my shoulders. I gave a cry of pain and terror.

"Ashes, ashes, we all fall down!"

My cry turned to a sob of relief. Willy ran up and began pulling at Belle Zenumin's arm. She gave a sharp yank and I let out another cry as some of my hair came out.

Willy began to hit her; I think Harry bit her. I was faint with shock and terror. When she flung herself away from the twins, she turned and spat at me. Then she ran up over the dunes. I fell to my knees on the sand.

I suppose the twins carried me to their cottage, but I knew nothing clearly until I was lying on a hard, short bed, and Ron was bending over me.

"Ron—your mother—"

His voice was quiet, but it held pain. "Did she hurt you?"

"I think she pulled out half my hair."

"Can you tell me what happened?"

"I was—very frightened."

"Did she hurt you?" he asked again.

"I think she scared me more than anything."

"You're bleeding."

I reached up to touch my face. "She scratched me—"

"Yes. I'm sorry. I'm very sorry. Tell me about it."

"I don't know—it didn't make sense—it was all frightening—that I was using magic—"

"Jack be nimble, Jack be quick,
Jack jump over the candlestick."

Willy and Harry came through an open doorway, both giving a leap over an imaginary candle. Willy carried a coffee pot, Harry a tray with four mugs.

"Here comes a candle to light you to bed,
Here comes a chopper to chop off your head."

They set the coffee and the mugs on a small table. "Pretty lady all right, now. Don't be scared," Willy said.

"Scared of Zenumin. Bad." Harry looked apologetically at Ron.

"Pretty lady, welcome."

Now I was able to sit up, look around. We were in a small room with two narrow bunks—I was lying on one—both covered, like the day bed in Illyria, with rather scratchy Oriental rugs. A small table was set in front of the fireplace. A lamp hung from a nail on one of the ceiling beams. My faintness had passed. It had not come, I thought, from terror alone. I put my hands over my belly in a protective gesture.

Willy poured coffee. The familiar fragrance was comforting. There were beach grasses in a big milk can in the fireplace. It was cozy and a reminder of childhood. But this was not a dwarf's cottage in a fairy tale. It was a room in a country even more incomprehensible.

The coffee was strong, but quite hot, and nut-like in flavor. I lay propped on one elbow and sipped. Ron sat on the second bunk and stared broodingly into the dark fireplace. Willy and Harry sat on two stools and looked at me. I thought that there was something they wanted to tell me, but that their vocabularies weren't up to the task.

"Ring," Willy said. "Ring good."

"Never take off," Harry said.

"No. I never do."

Willy filled the other three mugs. "Good to eat together." Now I saw that there was a plate of some elderly-looking biscuits on the tray.

Harry beamed around the table and then over to me. "Together."

Ron got up from the bunk and went to the third stool. Willy held out his arms. "All hold hands." He reached for Ron, for Harry. As Ron started to close the circle, Harry shook his head.

"No, no. Lady, too. *All* hold hands. No fall down."

The room was small; it was easy to include me in the twins' circle of love. I held Harry's hand with my left, Ron's with my right. Willy raised his head. "Oh, God, thank you for all. Thank you for stars and ocean and wind and tides and pretty lady and docdoc and coffee together. Amen."

Ron dropped my fingers quickly. Then we all reached for our cups. The twins raised theirs to me in a wordless toast, and I lifted mine in return.

"Feel gooder now?" Harry asked.

"Yes. I'm all right. I'm sorry. Thank you, boys, for helping."

Ron took the lamp from the hook and came over to examine

me. "It's a deep scratch. Do you think we can blame it on Minou in order to avoid questions from Illyria?"

I heard Minou's familiar miaow, and he came in from the kitchen, whiskers and tail quivering. "I will say it was Minou."

"I'm going to clean the scratch. It may sting."

"That's all right."

"Minou take the blame," Willy said. "Minou don't mind."

Ron cleaned my cheek with cotton and, I suppose, alcohol. He looked at my scalp where his mother had grabbed my hair. "She did get a handful of your hair."

"Tell Honoria," Willy urged.

"Honoria know, will know, must know," Harry said.

"Yes, boys." Ron took my cup and poured me some more of the hot, strong coffee. "I will tell Honoria and Clive. But it's best if the others don't know."

The twins took their cups and the coffee pot out to the kitchen. I could hear the splashing of water from the pump.

"Your faintness—" Ron started.

Ron was a doctor and I trusted him. I told him that I was almost certain that I was pregnant. "But I'm fine, now. It was just because she frightened me—I'm so sorry, Ron, I keep forgetting that she's your mother—"

"You would do well to remember it. Perhaps it is all right for Miss Olivia to give me a child's trust. It is not all right for you."

"Why isn't it? Have you read Mado's journals?"

"Why? Miss Olivia gave them to me. I should not have read them."

"If she gave them to you, why shouldn't you?"

"They weren't written for public consumption."

"Was that why you were reluctant to read them?"

"No."

"Then why?"

He moved restlessly about the small room. The cypress timbers of the low ceiling seemed to press down on him. "I always loved Mado and the great-aunts—but only as a small boy loves. So when I went to England I got over the love. I didn't want to blunder into it again."

"But you did."

"You know I did. And I learned things I didn't want to know."

"That makes two of us. Aunt Olivia is not as much a child as she seems. Mado made that quite clear—if we couldn't figure it out for ourselves. And why shouldn't I trust you as she does? When I have my baby, I want you to deliver it."

He turned away. "I do not find that amusing."

"It's not a joke! I care enough about my child to want the best.".

He made no denials. "Let's go. We'll take it easy. Sorry I don't have Thales tonight."

The twins saw us to the door. "Tell Honoria and Clive," Willy reiterated. "Tell Honoria about the lady's hair."

I touched my scalp, which still hurt. "It's all right. I still have plenty. And it will grow back."

"Moon old tonight," Willy said. "Shadows long. Pray, pretty lady. Pray."

"Willy and Harry pray. All numbers pray. All stars pray. All grains of sand."

"All drops of water," Willy took up the chant. "All the little waves, all sandpipers and pelicans, pray." And then, "Tell Honoria."

"I will tell Honoria," Ron said.

"Oh, she brought jasper," Willy entoned, "and gold, like unto clear glass."

Harry continued, "Oh, she brought jasper, and sapphire, a chalcedony, and an emerald; oh, she brought sardonyx, sardius, chrysolite, beryl, and oh, she brought a topaz, a chrysoprase, a hyacinth, and an amethyst."

"And oh, she brought twelve pearls, and gold, pure gold, even as if it were transparent glass." Willy stopped the chant and said in a straightforward manner, "Badness after them. Do not let the Bad get them. Tell Honoria."

"I will tell Honoria," Ron promised again. "Good night, boys. You'll be all right on your own tonight?"

"Come back," Willy said.

Harry echoed. "Docdoc, come back tonight."

"Very well. I'm going to walk Mrs. Renier home, and then I'll be back. But it may be late."

"Before moonset?"

"I'll try. You'll be all right till I get back."

2

WHEN we had walked along the beach in silence until the light of the twins' house disappeared behind the dunes, I asked Ron, "What was that about, what Willy and Harry were chanting?"

"Can't you guess?"

"I'm not sure."

"You read the journals."

He was going to make me say it. It was dark; a cloud brushed across the face of the moon so that our expressions were veiled. "Honoria's treasure—the treasure she brought over from Kairogi—"

"What about it?"

"Your mother wants it."

The moon came out from behind the cloud. He bowed his head. "How badly do you think she wants it?"

My voice was as low as his. "Badly enough to hurt somebody to get it."

"Why do you think she wanted your hair—or anything that belonged to you?"

"To put Black Magic on me, I suppose— Ron, do you believe in magic?"

"No."

"Then it doesn't matter, does it? that she has my hair?"

"There are other ways of hurting people than magic."

I looked at our feet moving slowly, side by side, along the moon-washed sand. "She was always so kind. And so beautiful."

"Most clearings people have lost their teeth and their youth by the time they're thirty. Life in the scrub is not kind."

"How does she—" I started, did not finish, nor did he answer. The sand was cool under our feet. I felt the damp through the thin soles of my summer slippers and remembered the shoes I had lost my first night at Illyria. Had Belle Zenumin been after those? "But why would she want to hurt me? I've never done her any harm, and I don't know where the treasure is."

"You don't understand about resentment and revenge, do you? You've always been the people who, to my mother, are *them*."

"Who is *them*?"

"Everybody who belongs to Illyria."

"But you belong to Illyria, too."

"Do I?"

"Honoria does. And Illyria to Honoria."

"But not to me."

"You're Honoria's grandson."

"Not by blood, Mrs. Renier. It really isn't your concern, is it?"

"I'm a Renier now. I have a right to know."

He said, gently, "Perhaps you're happier not knowing."

I was finding it hard to breathe. "Ron—I'm sorry—could we stop for a minute?" I shivered under the starlight, the moon-light. I hoped that Willy and Harry were calling on the stars for prayer, on the grains of sand, on every drop of ocean. Was that, then, what prayer was about? Ron took me to the shelter of a dune to rest. A light wind moved across the stars, rustled in the palm branches, stirred with the sound of wings.

Ron said, very softly,

> "*Mica, mica parva stella,*
> *Miror quondam sis tam bella,*
> *Splendens eminus in illo,*
> *Alba velut gemma caelo.*"

Terry's words for me. *Mica, mica, parva stella.* Who had taught Terry that when he was a boy? Aunt Olivia? Then she taught it to Ron, too, and the Mother Goose rhymes to the twins. . . . The tears began to flow down my cheeks. I had not cried this way since Terry left me. I tried to choke down the sobs, not wanting Ron to know.

But he said, "Don't be frightened."

"I'm not crying out of fear!" I said. Because I trusted him completely I flung myself at him as though he had been my father, and sobbed loudly. He held me, strong and comforting.

Through my tears, I said, "Aunt Irene tried to get a strand of my hair, and a handkerchief. Why?"

"To give to my mother, I suppose."

"For magic?"

"Yes."

"Why would Aunt Irene have anything against me?"

"I don't imagine she does. But what my mother asks her for, your Aunt Irene will get."

"Why?"

"My mother could blackmail Irene and Hoadley without batting an eyelash. And would."

"On what grounds?"

"All kinds. Including my paternity."

"But Uncle Hoadley is not your father. Who is?"

"Can't you guess?" he asked again.

"I'm not sure. Can you?"

"It's no longer just a guess with me. I made my mother tell me. I had to be sure. I trampled on her magic and I twisted her wrist and I made her scream until she told me. I did that to my mother."

"Who—who was he?"

"You want to know, go ask Mado." He stood up. "They will be wondering where you are." We slid down from the shifting sand. He let me hold to him until we got to the firmness of beach. Then he shook me loose. "What good does it do me to know? You ever been digging for oysters?"

"No."

"Oysters lie low in grey, muddy clay. You know where they are because you see little bubbles, bigger than the donax blow, and sudden squirts of their juices, and then you dig down in the mud to get them. If you like oysters I suppose it's all right to go digging in the mud. Oysters happen to make me sick. I am sick, sick. Knowing who my father is makes me, Ron, Theron James, with a borrowed name, even less than I was when it was all beneath the mud. I'd be like Tron if I could. But I'm trapped by Illyria. I'm trapped by Honoria, who is my true mother, and by Mado who is my grandmother as well as Terry's. I'm trapped by those angels of hers."

"But they're gone."

"Not far. Honoria and Clive keep them close. They won't let them go far from Illyria. And when you came, they moved in closer."

"Why—when I came—how could I have anything to do with Mado's angels, with Illyria?"

The kitten appeared out of darkness, twining its sleek softness about my ankles. "We're here," Ron said.

The scratch on my face was accepted as having been made by Minou.

"He scratched my hand the other day," Aunt Irene said. "I warn you, we're going to get rid of that cat if he scratches anybody else. Stella, hon, you do seem to be taking longer and longer walks. People will talk."

"Who, Aunt Irene? There isn't anybody to see me."

"Cousin Lucille will find out. Mark my words." But she turned back to her game of backgammon. "This is the last game for tonight, Auntie. We've already stayed up too late, waiting for Stella."

"Sorry, Aunt Irene."

"We don't expect young people to be thoughtful nowadays. But at least don't forget to say good night to Aunt Olivia. She will be very hurt if you don't remember her."

"I won't forget her. And I'll say good night to you now."

But I went out to the kitchen before going in to Aunt Olivia. Ron was standing with his back to the summer-cold iron range. Honoria was bent over, her hands clasped about herself, as though someone had kicked her in the stomach. Clive's voice came out of the shadows; he had taken off his white coat, and because of his dark shirt and trousers I had not until then seen him. His voice was steel.

"Honoria, you think her magic be stronger than the Lord? You gone back to your old gods in Kairogi again? Send them back where they belong, old woman. Send them back. And pray."

"I been praying."

"Pray more."

"I is wore out. You tell the Lord, Clive. You tell him. You tell him to do something about her magic."

"You got to believe. You got to believe in the Lord."

"I seen too many bad things."

"How? How you seen them?"

"Some he showed me."

"The bad ones? He show you those?"

"Some."

"The worst bad ones? The evil ones?"

She whispered, "No."

"How you see them?"

Honoria, the tall, the strong, the stern, faltered to her knees. "Forgive me."

"It is not me you ask."

"Yes. Yes, it is. I know the Lord can forgive. I'm not sure about you."

Clive took her arms in his thin, fine hands. Honoria, still on her knees, leaned against his frailness.

I had seen Cousin James pray, and I believed him. But now for the first time I witnessed the prayer of utter desperation, of abandonment. Honoria was putting herself, and whatever it was she had seen, entirely into God's hands.

For the second time that night the tears streamed down my cheeks.

God! I cried silently. God: be! Please be.

I said good night to Aunt Olivia and went upstairs. The house was dark and quiet. A candle burned on the landing. I undressed and fell into bed, pulling down the mosquito netting. I was too tired to read.

It wasn't only the mosquito which came in through the carelessly tucked net that wakened me. It was pounding at the surf's edge, the same strange thundering I heard my first night in Illyria.

I hurried to the balcony. The horses were galloping up the beach, ridden by hooded figures in white. I stood watching after them. I stood long after they had disappeared into the night. Then, again, I heard the sound of hoofs. It was a single horse, ridden by a horseman robed in black.

I turned back to the room and lit my lamp, then went downstairs, on the off-chance that Uncle Hoadley might still be on the veranda. I had no idea what time it was, but guessed that he seldom came to bed before the small hours. I tiptoed across the front room. Through the screen door I could see the light of his cigar arc-ing back and forth as he rocked. My foot creaked on an ancient board.

Uncle Hoadley rose. "Tron?" he asked softly.

"It's Stella."

"Stella! What are you doing up at this hour?"

I said flatly, "I saw some hooded men riding on the beach."

"Don't concern yourself, child."

"But who are they!"

"It's all right, child, don't worry. It's just a group of young-sters getting together. They often do on a weekend." He rested his hand lightly on my arm; he seemed to like to touch me with his long, sensitive fingers. His hand was cool and a little moist; a glass of whiskey and water stood on the floor by him.

"Were they the Night Riders?"

"It's nothing for you to trouble yourself about. I see to it that they don't get out of hand."

"Are they all youngsters, then?"

"No, child. Those you saw tonight, probably. But many of them are mature men. We have to see that law and order are kept."

"Law? Order?"

"Yes, Stella. Law and order concern me deeply. You know that."

"What about the riders who wear black?"

I had startled him. For a moment he did not answer, but sat with his cigar halfway to his lips. "Child, you are new to our country and our ways. You would do best to remain in bed at night."

"Uncle Hoadley, it's my country now, too. I want to learn more about it."

"Then let me help you. Don't go off on tangents of your own."

"I'd be very grateful if you *would* help me."

He studied the glow of his cigar carefully for several mo-ments, as though seeking inspiration. "The aunties will be delighted to fill you in. They are, in an odd, off-balance way, highly educated. But of course that is a tradition in the South. A lady should be able to talk intelligently on any subject, though she must never flaunt her knowledge, nor presume upon it."

"Not only the great-aunts. Honoria and Clive."

The small light of the cigar paused in mid-air, then resumed. "Mado taught Honoria a great deal. And Clive was given an education at Nyssa that was unusual for a slave."

"Ronnie was sent to school in England—" I wanted, I needed to hear Uncle Hoadley's version. "Who sent him?"

"That's beside the point, Stella. Presumably someone who thought it the correct thing to do. Whether or not it was, I am not sure. Often when we think we are acting for the best it turns out to have been for the worst. I am constantly finding this out in my own life." He leaned over and stubbed out his half-smoked cigar on the veranda floor. "Sometimes I have kept a promise, simply because I, Hoadley, have made it, when it would be better to break it. This point in time in which we find ourselves is no hour for either impulse or blind loyalty, any more than it was when Mado came to this country as a young bride and could not understand why she should not upset applecarts."

It was quite clear that Uncle Hoadley was warning me: 'Do not try to be clever, Stella; do not ask questions; do not go back to the War Room or the map on the wall; there are secrets there which only Tron Zenumin and I know. Do not try to find out too much about the hooded riders, either the white or the black.' But all he actually said was, "I loved my Aunt Mado too, you know, Stella. But I am not under the illusion, as the aunties are, that her lofty idealism was a virtue, or her imaginary angels a safeguard. We live in a world of extraordinary complexity and very little light, and I have spent far too much of my life cleaning up the chaos made by the idealists to have any illusions about them."

The warning was in his voice again.

He said, "I will add one more thing. I agree with my Uncle Theron and my Cousin James that we were wrong to bring the slaves over from Africa and that we must pay for this wrong. What I am trying to do, right now, is to make this payment in a realistic way, so that perhaps your children will not suffer for the sins of their forebears. My plan may seem extreme, but when one is dealing with malignancy only extreme methods are possible. And I am not alone. I am being backed in high places. Now, good night, my dear."

I accepted my dismissal. I no longer had the slightest desire to ask questions. I did not want to know what Uncle Hoadley was going to do.

3

Iɴ the morning after breakfast I went out to the kitchen.

Ron was there, and so were the twins, come to be fed, corn bread and love. They brought in the little tame lizard and let him run about the kitchen table, climb up onto our arms and shoulders. It clung to the soft stuff of my dress with its little cool claws, and rolled its jeweled eyes at me, and the twins clapped their hands in joy. But I understood that the lizard was to be brought out of the hanging basket only by Willy; this was his great and special privilege.

Minou pranced into the kitchen, tail twitching, paws lifted high; followed by Finbarr, elderly, creaky, tail pluming; followed by Aunt Olivia, leaning heavily on her silver-handled cane.

"Miss Olivia—" Ron went to her.

"You said I could start moving about, and I knew you were all in here, and I'm tired of being left out."

"All right, then. Sit with us for a spell."

"I want a cup of coffee."

"No, Miss Olivia. Too acid. I'd rather you take tea in the morning for a while longer."

Finbarr circled the kitchen table, sniffing ecstatically. Willy surreptitiously slipped a bit of corn bread to him. Minou jumped onto the windowsill and watched us condescendingly, his sides pulsing with the bliss of his purr as he absorbed the warmth of old wood, of the slanting rays of the morning sun. The breeze lifted and ruffled his fur, the breeze which always stirred about Illyria, brooding over the face of the waters.

"Honoria," Aunt Olivia said, "do you think you have time to rub my back with witch hazel this morning?"

"We'll see."

"I love the smell of witch hazel. Only of course it shouldn't be spelled witch at all. It should be w-y-c-h, as in wych elm.
262

'Wych' means wild. So it's only wild hazel, that's all. It has nothing to do with witches. I'm glad. Ronnie, when can I go back into the water? It does ease my joints."

"Next week, Miss Livvy, if you keep on doing this well."

The old lady leaned lightly on her elbows, always slightly lemon-scented. "To feel the sharpness of the shells—oh, Ronnie, the pleasure of *feeling* is worth the small discomfort. To feel the shells and sand, to relax in the warmth, to know the sun . . . it means . . . it means . . ."

Ron's voice was gentle. "What, Miss Livvy?"

Aunt Olivia drew in her breath sharply. "You're a doctor, Ron, don't you know? Life. That I am alive."

Willy took the little lizard and laid it on the table by her hand.

She smiled at him, stroking it. "I wish I still believed the way I used to before Nyssa burned. It was all tidy: heaven and earth and hell. Now I can't tell them apart. What do you think, Stella? When I die, will there be any more me?"

In the kitchen of Illyria, here with Honoria and Clive, the twins, here with Ron, there was no place for evasion. "I don't know. My father didn't—didn't believe in the things the Church teaches. And I just took it for granted that he was right. Until he died."

"And then?"

"It didn't make sense, the idea that my father was not, that death had stopped his being. But that's as far as I've got. I think he was right about the Church, you see. We can't turn our backs on science."

Aunt Olivia giggled. "Man and monkey: now why does the Church go into a panic about things like that? Why should it make God any less God if we're descended from monkeys? Any more than it made him less God when Galileo said the world wasn't the center of the universe? It just puts *us* in our place, that's all. God's already in his. Oh, my loves, my loves, I blow hot and cold. Sometimes I'm all seientific and dust to dust and ashes to ashes and that's the end."

"Ashes, ashes . . ." Willy whispered.

"We all fall down," Harry said, and blew his nose.

Aunt Olivia returned the lizard. "If I could die like Mado . . ."

"How did she die?" I asked.

"The way she lived. She went into death the way she went into every new morning. She had a great deal of pain, but she never complained. We knew when it was very bad because she got white around the mouth. Honoria made her some kind of herb tea, and that helped, didn't it?"

"Some," Honoria said.

"Every day she got weaker, but it never stopped her laughter. The day she died she called me in and said she had one last request to make of me—" Again the little girl's giggle. "I'm not sure what I expected. Something cosmic, I suppose. But what she asked was that I find something each day to laugh at. She said, 'Cry as much as you like, Livvy. Grief is part of life, and a good part. But you must balance it with laughter.' I've tried, and mostly I've succeeded. Some days it's been hard to find anything funny. But looking at myself looking for something funny can be funny itself. Then she asked for Honoria, and they were alone for a long time. I've often wondered what they said." She looked at Honoria and smiled.

Honoria did not smile. "She asked me to make her ice cream."

"*I* heard her ask you that," Aunt Olivia said. "When the ice cream was ready she said it was the best you'd ever made. She ate a whole bowlful. Then she smiled and said that it was time, and she gave a little gasp, and she was dead."

Minou jumped down from the windowsill and pounced on an invisible enemy. Finbarr rose creakily and stood leaning against Aunt Olivia. She fondled his ears. "Thank you, my dears."

"You're all right, Miss Olivia," Ron said.

"I'm afraid of the dark. Do you know how frightened I am? Well, of course you do. I tell you, not only with my words, but with all of me. . . . To go willingly. That's important, isn't it? To give all this up freely, not holding on."

Ron said, "You're not going to die yet, Miss Livvy."

"Someone is. Someone from Illyria. One of us." Aunt Olivia accented her words with her cane. "Irene was in hysterics this morning because Belle told her someone in Illyria is going to die, and she's scared out of her wits. She's even more afraid than I am. But I doubt if it will be Irene. Irene said that when she went swimming this morning there was a dark shadow hovering over the ramp, a buzzard moving in slow, even circles, his wings almost motionless, gliding around. Waiting for death. I'm with Irene in hating buzzards."

I, too, had seen the buzzard, had stood on the beach and been caught in the shadow of its circling.

Aunt Olivia banged with her cane, and said, too brightly,

"Who can identify: If we begin with certainties we will end in doubt. But if we begin with doubts, and bear with them patiently, we may end in certainty."

None of us could.

"Bacon. *De Augmentis*. Did I begin in certainty? Is that my trouble? I don't think so. Being certain has never been one of my virtues—or vices. And it doesn't take second sight to predict death in a house full of old people. Stella, will you and Ronnie help me back to bed? I think I'm a little tired."

I felt a string pulling me, an invisible string, tugging, drawing me to the unused wing of Illyria where there was a used room, a War Room, a room used by Uncle Hoadley and Tron.

I pushed the revolving bookcase in the library. The door creaked itself around so that I could slip into the ballroom. Finbarr tried to follow me, but I pushed the bookshelves back and tiptoed softly across the sandy floor. Behind me I could hear Finbarr whining and scratching at the bookcase.

I did not listen. Would not. I was drawn through the empty rooms, upstairs and down.

Tron was at the desk in the War Room. I had known he would be. Yet I had come. I wanted to see the map. I looked across the desk, past Tron, who blocked half the map. But it was Africa. The colored pins marked Kairogi.

Tron spoke in his rather frightening parody of Uncle Hoadley. "What are you looking for, Mrs. Renier?"

I protested too loudly, "I'm not looking for anything. I'm just exploring." There was no longer any doubt that the War Room had something to do with Kairogi. I had to go to Cousin James.

I turned to leave, but Tron stopped me. "Explorers don't explore for nothing. Explore for something. You looking for what? Tell Tron."

"Terry, I suppose."

Tron was very still, as though everything in him had stopped, the blood in his veins, his heart. He had taken me literally.

"No, no, not really, not here in this room—"

"Then why you say it?"

"I just meant—I need to find out about him, his background, his home—the way I was doing the other day when I came here. He told me—"

Tron leaned across the desk. I thought he was going to grab me as his mother had done. "What he tell you?"

"Just about Illyria, and how much he loves it—"

"And?"

"That's all."

I knew that Tron knew that I was lying. "Miss Stella." He was very gentle, very courteous, very Uncle Hoadley. "I did suggest to you, didn't I, that it would be wiser for you not to come up here?"

"But why?"

"Miss Stella, why don't you trust me?"

"Why should I? Your mother pretended to be my friend, and then she hurt me."

"Now, Miss Stella." A small-bodied, long-legged spider was crawling across the big green blotter on the desk. I watched it approaching Tron, scuttling along as though in a hurry. Tron picked it up. "You just don't understand my mother. She didn't want for to hurt you. The Granddam had her all upset and angry. If you'd just been nice to her and done what she asked and not gone running off with the twins that way—that was very wrong, Mrs. Renier, ma'am, very foolish." Slowly, absently, Tron pulled one leg off the spider, then another and another, one by one, then dropped the mutilated blob of its body to the floor. "You listen to me, and to my mother, and everything be all right." A mosquito shrilled past my ear, louder than Tron. "Mrs. Renier, ma'am, you sweet and pretty and young. Don't take it amiss if little old Tron give you a warning. You don't want to get hurt, you do what Tron tell you to do." He reached up and clapped his hands against the mosquito, rubbed the blood on the blotter.

I shivered. Suddenly and at last I understood. I understood that nothing times three equals nothing. Nothing. I had seen his nothing annihilate a spider, a mosquito. I could easily see in my mind's eye this nothing taking a magnifying glass and gently roasting ants to death.

If zero is nothing, so is hate. Not the hate of passion, but the hate I felt from Tron, freezing the warmth of his politeness. This hate can destroy something.

Take three apples and multiply them by this kind of cold nothingness and they will disappear.

Willy and Harry knew that. This was why they had reacted as they did.

I ran from the room.

* * *

Out of the House, down the ramp, onto the beach, forgetting the straw hat. I had to get to Cousin James.

The sun hit me like molten brass. Even with one of the shading hats I could never make it all the way in the heat of the sun.

But I started up the beach.

I had not gone far when I came upon the twins with a bucket of crabs. They waved their arms in greeting.

I felt a shadow, a movement behind me. I turned in panic. But it was Finbarr, come to guard me.

"Go home, pretty lady," Willy said. "Too hot. Boys used to sun."

"Too hot for lady." Harry nodded.

Willy held out his cupped hands, opening them slightly, and the lizard poked its head out, weaving it inquisitively back and forth, jeweled eyes gleaming. "Go home pretty lady. Bad nothings is out."

"Bad, bad nothings." Harry wrinkled his face anxiously.

The sun was indeed battering me. I reached my forefinger towards the lizard, and Willy held him out so that I could stroke his head. I felt the strange coolness of the green-gold scales. "Boys, is Ronnie at your cottage?"

Willy shook his head. "In scrub."

I tried to think what I ought to do. They were quite right. It was too hot for me to walk to Little Nyssa. "Boys, could you get a message to Cousin James for me?" They nodded. What kind of message would they be able to carry in their short-circuited minds? If I could put it into numbers, into a mathematical formula, they would manage with no difficulty. But I didn't know how. So I made an inept and, I hoped, cryptic rhyme.

> "Stranger than a potion
> Is my news for 'cross the ocean.
> If you can come with Dapple
> I'll give you both an apple."

They repeated it several times. Then Willy gave me the lizard. "Put in basket. Boys go now."

"Stella! Stella!" Aunt Des beckoned from the veranda.

"Boys go now." They trotted off.

I returned to the house, holding the little lizard carefully. Aunt Des had one of the big straw gardening hats in her hand.

"Stella, you know you oughtn't to go bareheaded in the heat of the sun. You'll get heat prostration." She held out the hat.

"I'm coming in now, Aunt Des. I just have to put the lizard back. Then I want to write Terry."

"Come to Olivia's room, then. She's feeling lonely. We have all the writing materials in there."

But what could I say to Terry? If a map of Kairogi in Illyria were really important, he would hear of it long before a letter could get to him. Nevertheless I wrote. The great-aunts' voices plashed about my head; and through my written words, which pinned down and made real a danger I did not want to admit, came the safety of Aunt Des chattering gently about the old days and the billy goat and wagon Theron had when they were children. The billy goat ate everything he could find and teased the little girls—which little girls? The great-aunts, of course. Though I had finished my letter I was only half listening.

"Do you remember the walk in back of Grampa's house where the garden went down to Legare Street? It was made of octagonal stone blocks, white and grey. One of our games was to catch the large grasshoppers with bright black and yellow legs, harness them with thread, and then race them over the flagstones. If the grasshopper balked or dropped off a leg, that race was lost. But all we had to do was catch another one."

Aunt Olivia looked over the top of her book. "It occurs to me that that game was no better than Tron roasting ants to death."

"But Tron did it on purpose, to hurt, to kill."

"We killed the grasshoppers sometimes."

"Yes, but we didn't enjoy it, we didn't do it on purpose, we didn't even think about it."

"Does that make it any better—not thinking about it?"

There was no comfort anywhere. I left them.

All day I waited for Cousin James.

When I went up to rest, I spent more time on the balcony than on the bed. I had tied a white petticoat to the rail, but surely the twins would have reached him long before this?

I opened Mado's journals, my fingers unsteady. Mado had a passion for joy, a passion for justice, a passion for compassion, beyond anything I could yet comprehend, though I realized now that she had brought them with her to her new country only embryonically, that it was in the climate of Nyssa and Illyria that they had been nurtured and developed. Would something of the same kind happen to me? Did I even want it?

I went back to the balcony. The white petticoat hung limp, and there was no one on the beach.

4

UNCLE Hoadley remarked on my tenseness during dinner ("You seem a little on edge tonight, child. Heat bothering you?") but made no comment when I left the veranda without touching my coffee. I could sense Finbarr following me as I walked down the ramp, and then he was beside me. I put my hand on the comforting roughness of his head. I listened for the twins, but heard nothing but the usual Illyrian night noises: mosquitoes, locusts, crickets; the long, low breathing in and out of the sea; the soft swish of the little waves lacing the sand; and a splash as a predatory bird swooped into the water after a fish.

Out of the darkness the twins materialized beside me.

"Mr. James gone, gone."

"He gone. Mr. James gone."

It took me a while to understand that Cousin James had not vanished into the blue, but that he had gone into Jefferson for the day.

"Did he come back on the evening train?"

The twins could not get words out. I thought that they were trying to tell me that he would not be back this night, but would return tomorrow. They sang the rhyme about ride a cock horse to Banbury Cross but I could make no sense out of it. Willy took my hand reassuringly. "Boys told Docdoc. Docdoc tell Mr. James."

I left them and started up the beach. For my own peace of mind I had to get to Little Nyssa. If Cousin James were not there, I could find out something from Saintie.

Ahead of me up the beach was a speck, a horse and rider. Cousin James!

No. It was Ron, on Thales. As he neared me he dismounted and came walking along the edge of the water. The red horse bent down to Finbarr, and dog and horse nuzzled in greeting.

The tide was low, and the dock high out of water. Ron helped me up. "Miss Stella, the twins came to me this afternoon. What's up?"

I hesitated. "Oh, Ron, I don't know. I wanted to talk to Cousin James."

"But he's away."

I looked at the dark shadow of Ron's face and wanted to tell him everything. I trusted him without question. But Cousin James had specified that I was to tell no one at Illyria. "Ronnie—the twins are afraid about something—something about Honoria and Clive being taken away. Have they said anything to you?"

"They've tried."

"What are they afraid of?"

"I don't know. They can't put their fears into ordinary words. They sing veiled warnings and I don't understand them. Why I think I can protect my grandparents or the twins I don't know. Or you."

"You can. I know you can."

Suddenly he held up his hand in warning. "Finbarr, sit. Stay. Hold his collar, Miss Stella. Don't move. Just sit here on the dock as though nothing—" He leaped down to the sand and ducked out of sight under the dark and rotting boards of the dock.

I had not been listening to the sound of hoofs pounding towards us like the breakers. A mass of white swept past the dock. Finbarr, growling, pressed protectively against me. I clutched his collar. I turned my face from the White Riders and looked out over the ocean. The Riders came so close that I could smell the hot sweat of the horses. I closed my eyes. Held my breath. The horses swept on down the beach. They did not slow down.

I opened my eyes, turned.

One hooded horseman veered away from the swirling white mass to splash through the water and then up on the sand, close to me. He circled about the dock, but he did not stop. The horse gave a whinny, and the rider galloped him down the beach after the others.

"Ron—" I whispered. "Ronnie—"

He did not come out until the Riders were out of sight.

Then he emerged from the shadows. "Miss Stella, it is not good for us to be seen together."

"Did they see you?"

"I don't think so. Please go home now. Please take care of yourself."

"All right. And—"

"Yes?"

"Take care of yourself, too, Ronnie."

He helped me down from the dock. A wave crept in and lapped at the toes of my shoes, dampened my skirts. Ron raised his hand in farewell, then mounted Thales and rode up the beach towards the twins' house.

The veranda was empty when I got home. I heard Mozart coming from the piano in the front room. Finbarr whined and scratched at the screen door. We went into an incongruously calm scene of domestic peace. Aunt Olivia was at the piano, straining forward to see the music. Aunt Des and Aunt Irene were at their backgammon board. I did not see Uncle Hoadley. Finbarr flopped, panting heavily, beside the piano.

"Hurry up, Auntie." The dice rattled impatiently. Aunt Irene was always trying to speed up the old aunt.

I stood watching for a moment, then went out to the kitchen.

Honoria and Clive and Uncle Hoadley were sitting at the kitchen table. "Honoria," Uncle Hoadley said, "I grieve."

"Rest yourself, Mr. Hoadley."

Uncle Hoadley looked into his tea cup. If he had been Aunt Irene I would have thought he was trying to see the future in the tea leaves. "This is no time for rest. There is work to be done, reparations to be made. To you. To Jimmy."

Honoria said, "Maybe that not up to you, Mr. Hoadley."

"Why not up to me? Me, of all people? After all that happened with your boy?"

They turned to look at me, standing in the doorway, starting to back out. "Come in, my dear," Uncle Hoadley said. "What I want to say to Honoria is something you ought to hear."

Honoria drew up a chair for me, went to the dresser for a cup and saucer.

"Honoria," Uncle Hoadley said softly, "wouldn't you like to be a princess again?"

"No again, Mr. Hoadley. What I is, I is."

"Are you? In Illyria? Not the way you were in Africa."

Uncle Hoadley's voice was more Southern than I had ever heard it; his consonants were slightly blurred.

Clive spoke. "Mr. Hoadley, leave Honoria be. You not feeling well."

"Clive, all I want is to help. You know me well enough to know that." He reached across the table and with the tips of his long fingers touched Honoria's hand. "But I must have money."

Honoria's face was its most inscrutable. "Speak to Miss Irene. She give you some."

Uncle Hoadley shook his head. "No. It would be fitting if it came from you."

Clive warned, "Miss Stella—"

"It's time we stopped protecting Miss Stella. Honoria, listen to me. What I want, I want to use for you. You and Clive. Ronnie and Tron. For all your peop—"

Honoria cut in. "You and Tron got something between you. I known that for a long time. Whatever it be, I don't want no part of it."

"How do you know? You don't know my plans. I do."

"Mr. Hoadley, you and Tron don't belong to work together." Honoria withdrew her hands from the table, folded them in her lap. "No, Mr. Hoadley. I know what you after. But you not going to get it. Nor Tron, neither. He after me, too. Even if I could, I wouldn't be party to letting you do something wrong. Forget the treasure, Mr. Hoadley. Don't go looking for it. Gone. Gone long since."

"I don't believe you. When you took Ronnie from Belle—"

"They be no point in hindsight, Mr. Hoadley. Maybe we done wrong. But we done what his father ask us to do. It be time for bed, now. Finish your posset, Miss Stella."

I had not noticed when she filled my cup. The shadows seemed to crouch heavily in the kitchen, barely pushed back by the lamp on the table.

Uncle Hoadley put his hands down on the table and leaned. "It isn't right for Illyria to withdraw from the world."

"Can't get out of it, Mr. Hoadley," Honoria said.

"But you're trying to."

"No, sir," Clive said. "We wait and we pray. That be all."

"It's not enough. There isn't time to wait. You don't understand that the things which are going on in the world today are so impossible that nothing Tron or I could plan is strange or out of place. You read the Bible, Clive."

"Yes, sir."

"Then think about this: The time has come to destroy those who are destroying the earth."

"I done thought about it," Clive said.

I finished my posset. "Good night."

I followed Uncle Hoadley into the front room, bade my good nights there. Uncle Hoadley stood at the foot of the stairs, holding a candle. "Good night, child. I am extraordinarily tired." Indeed he looked it. His face was as pale as his hair, his eyes dark shadows. He looked as though he were in physical pain.

"Good night," I said again, and went upstairs.

In my room someone had lit my lamp. I thought I saw something on the floor beside my bed and went over to see what it was.

It was Willy's little lizard, and it was dead. Someone had stepped on its head.

Tron. There was no doubt in my mind that it was Tron.

I felt violently sick.

I knelt on the floor by the little creature, fighting nausea and tears. When I could move, I went to the mahogany highboy, opened one of the top drawers and took out one of my best handkerchiefs. I wrapped the lizard in it. There was a small bloodstain left on the floor. Again a wave of nausea enveloped me. I swallowed, swallowed, was finally able to move from my room, holding the lizard in its lacy shroud.

In the living room they all turned to look at me. "Someone has killed Willy's lizard. I am going out in the garden to bury it."

Aunt Olivia flung down her book and rose, wincing as she tried to move too quickly. "Stella, who—"

"Bring a candle, please."

"Child," Uncle Hoadley said. "You must be mistaken."

"I am not mistaken. Someone stepped on his head."

Aunt Des put her hand to her mouth. "No, oh no—"

Uncle Hoadley asked, "Would it not be wise to wait until morning?"

The tiny stiff body seemed extraordinarily heavy in my hand. "No."

He stood. "I will come with you."

Not responding, not waiting, I went through the dining room, through the kitchen, pausing to get one of Honoria's heavy stirring spoons to dig with. Aunt Olivia followed me with a lighted candle, limping, making a small cry of pain as she tried to keep up with me. I slowed my pace to hers, and we moved down the pink brick path in the moonlight to the fig tree. The wind shifted the leaf patterns. When I bent down to dig a small grave under the fig tree, Uncle Hoadley leaned over me. He had stopped for a small spade, and without speaking he put his foot on it and dug up a clod of earth. I knelt beside the hole and laid the lizard in it. Still without speaking, Uncle Hoadley replaced the earth and tamped it down.

I stood up. "Thank you. I'm going to bed now."

Aunt Olivia reached out and touched my skirts but did not attempt to hold me. In the light of the candle which she held, I could see that her eyes were filled with tears.

I ran up to my room. The kitten was lying in the middle of the bed in his favorite Sphinx pose. He looked at me with wide, unblinking eyes. "Minou," I whispered. "Oh, Minou."

He jumped down from the bed and left the room, tail erect and twitching. I undressed and got ready for bed. As I was pulling my nightgown over my head I heard sounds approaching my door. I froze.

It was Finbarr. He stood in the doorway, looking at me, wagging his tail comfortingly. Then he lay down across the doorsill.

I went onto the balcony and waited for the lightship. Its steady finger swept across the ocean. Darkness again. I waited. The light came again. Then, down below, I saw another moving light, smaller, more erratic. Uncle Hoadley. Uncle Hoadley pacing on the promenade.

I returned to my room. Finbarr was still stretched across the doorway. I could not possibly sleep. Underneath the mosquito net I felt stifled. I moved restlessly on my pillow. My hair was damp with heat. So I turned to the journals.

Mado wrote, "Honoria came to me today, saying, 'I know that you are grieving because you are so merry. When your laugh is most free, then you are hurting most.' I have not wanted Honoria to know that now I understand all that she has kept from me about Jimmy's death. Perhaps for the sake of our friendship it is best that she think she had protected me from this knowledge. If I die before her, I will tell her then."

I did not want to know. Or, rather, I refused to accept what I already knew. I turned back in the journal. "Therro came to me the morning before he died and said, 'Mother, I want you to know that the only good thing that has ever happened to me is that you have always loved me with open hands.' He held his hands out towards me, but instead of touching me, as he had seemed about to do, he returned his hands to himself and buried his face in them. Through his fingers I heard him say, 'The others have clutched, and I can't bear it any longer.' Then he looked at me and gave me his warmest, brightest smile, and said, 'I think I'll go for a small sail,' and went, and Kitty with him.''

I put the journal down and slid into sleep, sleep which came with the suddenness of the Illyrian night, and with a dream. I was sitting on our dock with Ron. In my lap was a small bowl of insect-repelling oil. Its fire burned brightly. I turned it in my lap, playing with it, watching the flames dance. Somebody, somewhere, a long time ago, had warned me not to play with fire, but I did not understand why. The flames were blue and gold and beautiful. A firefly flew across the ocean towards Ron, and he held out his hands to catch it. It turned into a star, and he threw it back up into the sky. The fire in the bowl licked over my fingers. The little snakes' tongues on my ring flickered out to meet it. My hands were circled with flame. Another star came down and glowed on Ron's outstretched palm. He threw it into the sea. It went out with a hiss which wakened me.

I opened my eyes. I was not sitting on a black and barnacled dock. There was no bowl of fire in my lap. The dream fizzled and went out, like the star in the ocean. And I could no longer evade the knowledge that Terry and Ron were brothers.

5

IT had not really needed a dream. I had already guessed it. But now I had to accept it.

Finbarr stirred from his place across the sill of my door, growled. I could not see him, but I knew that his hackles had risen. The growl continued, low in his throat.

I listened.

Nothing.

Then my ears caught the sound of feet ascending the stairs, softly, secretly. I pushed through the mosquito netting to light my candle. Only a faint flickering of starlight moved against ceiling and walls. I lit the candle and held it up, and saw a tall shadow, barred by Finbarr, in my doorway.

"Stella." It was a whisper, urgent, unidentifiable.

Ron—everything in me cried out. Ron. But I could not move my lips to say his name.

"Stella, what is Finbarr doing here?"

"Uncle Hoadley! I—I suppose it's cool for him across the sill. He gets the breeze . . ."

"Finbarr." Uncle Hoadley bent down. Finbarr growled. "If Finbarr is going to get vicious in his old age—"

"Finny," I said softly. "Come."

Stiffly Finbarr stalked across the room to me, leaned against the bed.

Uncle Hoadley followed him. "Child, are you all right?"

"Yes. Of course."

"I thought perhaps you needed—" He came closer to the bed, pulled up the little chair. I smelled spirits.

"I'm fine, thank you, Uncle Hoadley. I don't need anything."

"Perhaps a fuller explanation of the conversation in the kitchen?" The beam from the lightship swung across the room and touched the silver in his hair, accented the ascetic bones of his face, the hollows of his eyes. I wanted no further explanations. I didn't want to know anything at all.

"All men are pursued by demons. Ask Honoria. She knows. I shared mine with my closest friend. With Therro. Since his death I have fought the demons, but I am beginning to think that he was right: life cannot conquer them. Only death." He approached my bed and began fumbling with the mosquito netting.

"Uncle Hoadley, Therro was Ronnie's father, wasn't he?"

His hand dropped. "Who told you?"

"Nobody told me. But everything—everything points to it."

Uncle Hoadley took matches from his pocket; his hands were shaking as he slowly lit my lamp and blew out the candle. "Therro was my friend. I loved him. And I loved Kitty. Oh, God, I loved them both. I took the blame for what Therro did, because of what Kitty and I had done. I told Kitty it was I who—but she did not believe me. She had to choose between believing me and believing Belle. But I thought that everybody else—that Ron himself—"

"But why? Why would you do such a thing?"

"Sin has to be paid for. I sinned. It was reparation. And it was to save Therro and Kitty—their marriage. And to save Irene. It was far less humiliating for Irene to think I'd fathered Ron than to think that Kitty and I—" He sat down in the little chair by my bed, his hands dropping loosely between his knees. "To save—to redeem—"

"Uncle Hoadley—you're not—you're not Terry's father, are you?" I did not think I could bear it.

"I doubt it, Stella. As far as I know I have never fathered anyone. But I do not suppose anyone will ever know for certain. I do not suppose that even Kitty knew. I used to try to console myself with the thought that I might be Terry's father. But I think it unlikely. I could not. I thought I could save Jimmy; I could not do that, either."

"When Jimmy went out to kill Ron's father, was he after you or Therro?"

"Therro." Uncle Hoadley rose, walked towards the balcony, looking out through the dark. "But only I knew that. The others—even Mado—thought he was after me. It would have killed Mado to know that Therro—I tried to save Jimmy. I tried. But I did not belong to the Riders then, I looked on them with contempt; they were beneath me. I should have realized that in a war-torn country no weapon is too lowly. I belong to the Riders now. I am one of their leaders. And they have learned that there are some things I do not tolerate." He came back towards the bed. In the wavering and smoky light from my lamp his face looked ravaged. "Stella, do you know why I must have Honoria's treasure? I must have it. It is imperative."

I whispered, "Please go, Uncle Hoadley," but he did not hear.

"I could not prevent what happened to Jimmy because I did not belong to the Riders. Even now the time is coming when I will have no right to try to stop them, no matter what they want to do. There were uprisings of slaves before the war, led by freed Negroes, and we put them down. To suppress an uprising now will be more difficult, and patience is running out. If the Negroes attempt anything—and they will—I cannot be responsible for what will happen to them."

Tron killed ants with a magnifying glass. Tron pulled the

legs off an inquiring spider. Tron stepped on the head of a little lizard who had never done him any harm. What would not Tron do where he hated? And where Tron led, others would follow. I did not think that there was anything Uncle Hoadley, or anyone else, could do to stop what lay ahead.

He began to pace between the balcony and my bed. "If I am to save Honoria and Clive I must have money. You must help me get it."

"For what?"

"I took you to the yacht basin. You saw our fleet. We have almost enough now, but not quite. When we have enough, there will be a large ship waiting out at sea. Then Tron and I together will be able to free his people." He paced to the window, back to the chair. "Open your mosquito netting. I want to see you." His hands reached out to the loose netting which still half covered the bed. "Better. Better. Don't be afraid. Won't hurt you. Just want to look—" His long, fine hands groped towards me, drew back before they touched me. "We will have to make them come, Tron and I and the Riders."

"Tron's riders?"

Uncle Hoadley shook his head. "They'll be put on the ship, too. It's the only safety for them, for any of them."

"But, Uncle Hoadley—"

"Why are you so surprised, child? This is not a new idea, not my private dream. Lincoln thought of letting the freed Negroes go to Liberia, to make a nation for themselves there. But his mistake was in 'letting.' How many people, white people even, know what is best for them? Do you, child, know what is best for you?"

I put my head down on my knees. "No."

"How much less, then, the black people? Do you think Honoria would return to Kairogi of her own free will? Do you think Clive will go, just because I provide a way and 'let' him go? Do you think Ron will choose to go to Kairogi, just because it is best for him?"

"No!" I cried, raising my head. "Not Honoria and Clive and Ron, you can't mean that!"

"Of course I mean it, child. We can't pick and choose who is to go and who is to stay. We'll start with San Feliz and every Negro here. Then we'll spread out. All those we brought over from Africa, all their descendants, must be returned. It's the only hope."

"But why! Why!"

"To avoid more blood, more horror. Child, it's been proven time and time again in history that when a nation begins to tolerate the mixing of its blood, its downfall is imminent. Think of Greece and Rome. Once their line lost its purity, the disease of decay struck them with its filthy hand. Have you not read your Gibbon? Your father would understand what I am talking about."

"No, no, my father would never—"

"Therro knew. After it was too late. He knew that he had killed Kitty long before they were drowned. But Mado never knew. Nor James. Cousin James, saying prayers with Saintie over Cousin Xenia, is living in a plague town without grasping the significance of the crudely painted cross with THE LORD DELIVER US painted in streaming red letters on the door of each afflicted household. That sign is on the door of Illyria for those who have eyes to see. But Tron and I are the only ones who—"

"No, Uncle Hoadley, no—"

"Tron, with clear and calculated wisdom, had denied the pollution of his blood. Tron will be King of Kairogi. I have promised. So Tron works with me. Unlike Ron, who is one of those poor creatures who are the result of our illness, a doomed mongrel who is woefully unfit in every way to belong to the race he emulates—"

"*You* sent Ron to school in England! *You* gave him his education!"

"I promised Therro. I was wrong to keep my promise. I only hurt his bastard further."

"No, Uncle Hoadley, no—" I could only repeat, helplessly.

"For Ron, Kairogi is the only hope. They'll need doctors. As long as nobody is foolish, nobody will be hurt. All will go smoothly. If I get the money, the money for the big ship. This is the only way we can make restitution for the mad dreams of people like James with his impossible Nyssa."

"But Nyssa—"

"Was insanity. There is no place in the suffering of a real world for a Nyssa. Nyssa was a household of plague. May the Lord deliver us." He leaned towards the bed again. "Stella, you are young and you don't understand me. I want you to understand me. I feel that you, as nobody else, can understand all my pain, all my prayers." His face came closer to mine, closer. "I will give you anything, anything. No strings, no strings." His breath was heavy, horrible. "Is love with no strings as unreal as Nyssa? Am I blundering? Is it the demon again?

Do you tie strings on your love for your husband? What do you make him pay for it? What?"

I drew back in bed, pushing against the vertical brass bars of the bedstead. "I don't understand. Please go."

"You have yet to learn: nobody loves for nothing. You must learn—"

"I know it's not for nothing."

"You don't understand. But you will. Nobody gives love. There is always an asking price. Irene's is perhaps simpler than most. What is yours?"

"I don't—I don't have one—"

"You'd better learn. Fast. It is foolish to give love away. It's the dearest commodity on the market. If you can get more than the going price, get it. Oh, God. I am not myself tonight. I am, to be precise, drunk. In wine there is truth. I have always tried to give love away. But nobody wants it when it is given. It is desired only when there is a price, and the higher the price the greater the desire. Is your price too high for me? Is it?" His face came closer, dead-white like the moon.

"Finbarr!" But Finbarr was gone.

"Stella, my only little guiding light in the dark." His wet lips brushed close to mine. His hand fumbled at my nightgown.

"Mr. Hoadley."

He gave an anguished groan and drew back.

Clive stood in the doorway, Finbarr beside him. "Mr. Hoadley, you not feeling well. You having one of your bad times. Come, Mr. Hoadley. We go walk on the beach till you feel better."

Moving unsteadily, like crumbling stone, Uncle Hoadley followed Clive from the room.

Honoria came to me. Honoria held me as she had held Aunt Olivia my first night at Illyria. I cried, I babbled incoherently. "The twins were right. They want to take you away."

"Hush, Miss Stella. Hush. Hush."

"They want your treasure."

"Nobody going to get the treasure. Hush."

"Kairogi—the twins were right—" I could not pull my words together. I could not breathe in the dark terror which smothered me.

"Hush, Miss Stella. You do not have to say it."

"The cards," I gasped. "What was in the cards?"

Honoria's strong arms tightened around me. "Hush, Miss Stella. Do not ask. If you do not know, it is our only hope."

"But can they do it? Can Uncle Hoadley and Tron do it?"

I felt something wet and hot on my cheek. Honoria's tears.

"Cousin James," I cried, flinging my arms about Honoria, trying to hold her as she was holding me. "I must tell Cousin James!"

"It is God we must tell. Miss Stella, tell it to God."

"But I don't know God." My tears mingled with hers.

6

In the morning I woke with a headache, and my skin was burning hot. I tried to get up, sat on the edge of my bed, and waves of nausea rode over me. I did not have the strength to answer when I heard a knock on the door.

Honoria entered, felt my cheek with the back of her hand, left me tangled in a skein of pain, returned with cool compresses for my head. "You be all right, Miss Stella."

"What's the matter with me?"

"Things just got too much for you, too much heat, too much everything. Don't you fret. You be all right. The baby going to be all right."

How did she know about the baby? Comforted, I rolled over and slept.

Ron stood by the bed, his hand lightly against my forehead, my cheeks. "Don't worry, Miss Stella. It's just a combination of fatigue and reaction and heat."

"But last night—"

"Honoria and Clive told me. It's all right. Go to sleep now."

"Ronnie, get Cousin James. Promise me. Tell him."

"I'm not sure just what to tell him, Stella."

"Tell him what happened last night."

"What exactly did happen?"

I began to retch, and he held a basin for me wiped my

forehead, my face. "Cousin James, please, Ronnie, please—"

"I will tell him. You must try to calm yourself, Stella." He held both my hands in his. I lay back, the fit of vomiting over. He held my hands while I fell into sleep.

When I came to, the shutters were closed against the noon-day sun. Uncle Hoadley stood by the bed, looking down at me. "You have had a touch of heat prostration, child. Don't worry. It's not serious. You'll be feeling your own sweet self again in a few days."

"Last night—" I said.

"You did not quite know what you were saying. I tried to calm you, but you were delirious. Just try to forget about it."

I turned my face from him and wept.

Honoria brought me a cup of broth. I sat in the strength of her arm, sipping from the spoon which she held to my lips. "Honoria—Clive came last night when Uncle Hoadley was here—was I delirious?"

Honoria put the broth down on my bed table, enfolded me in her arms. "Perhaps some, Miss Stella. But only some. Mr. Hoadley's demon was on him last night. When he sits on the veranda drinking whiskey all evening, that be always a bad sign. And Finny come for Clive. Finny never do that without he got cause."

"But Uncle Hoadley—"

"Miss Stella, I don't know what Mr. Hoadley say last night, but I do know he ain't never learned to say 'I am sorry.' It always got to be the fault of somebody or something else. This time it easy for him. He can say it all the sun."

"Honoria, I'm frightened."

"No, Miss Stella. That be like Mr. Hoadley pushing it off onto the heat. You got to be strong and ready. And you got to get well. Lie back now and rest."

"I have to see Cousin James."

"Yes, Miss Stella. Today be Sunday; we go to Little Nyssa for Morning Prayer."

"I can't—"

"No, Miss Stella. You sick from too much sun. You and Miss Olivia stay in Illyria with Finny and Minou."

"Does—how much does Aunt Olivia know?"

Honoria stood looking down at me, a half smile on her austere features. "Nobody ever knowed how much Miss Olivia know about anything. Sometimes I think Miss Olivia herself don't know. Don't fret, Miss Stella. I take everything in my hands and give it to Mr. James to offer to God."

I closed my eyes. Whatever was in the broth Honoria had spooned me eased the pounding in my head. All I could think about was the pain, and that it was diminishing, becoming bearable. I had no room in me to think about Uncle Hoadley, or Ronnie, or Cousin James, or even Terry. I simply breathed, slowly, trying to keep the pain from jolting back.

When I opened my eyes again Cousin James was sitting beside my bed. In his rumpled white suit, his silvery mustache and beard, his gently trembling fingers, he represented a hope of sanity, of safety. "Cousin James—" Forgetting my head, I struggled off the pillows.

"Lie down, Stella. Take your time." His voice was calm, unperturbed.

But I stuttered in a feverish rush to tell him everything—Kairogi—the map—Tron—the lizard—Uncle Hoadley—Kairogi—

"Hush, Stella. Don't try to talk yet. I'm sorry I was so slow in getting to you."

"The twins—my flag—"

"Hush, my dear. I did not get back from Jefferson until early this morning. I saw your 'flag' on the balcony but I could not come to you until after Morning Prayer. Clive managed to tell me something of what happened last night."

I was burning hot and shivering simultaneously. "Did it really happen?"

"This is what we must find out. But you are not going to be able to tell me anything coherently unless you lie quietly and try to speak slowly and calmly, trying to separate dream from reality as much as possible. I should not press you while your fever is so high, but time is essential." He reached out and took my hand. I quieted.

"I suppose I really have sunstroke?"

"I think you undoubtedly have a touch of the sun. It's not surprising. We forget how violent our heat is to someone not accustomed to it."

"Was I delirious last night, then?"

"You had a very high fever."

"Cousin James, I remember things I'm sure weren't caused by fever. I didn't have fever when I sent the twins to fetch you."

"Why did you send the twins, Stella?"

I told him about the room with the map of Africa, and the little flags stuck in Kairogi. "But I didn't know what it was all about, then. All I knew was that it seemed odd to have a map of Kairogi there, and that perhaps it was something you'd think Terry should know."

"You are quite right."

"Cousin James—if it wasn't delirium—I know why the map is there."

"Try to tell me."

"Uncle Hoadley came to me—to my room—last night. I know I didn't dream that."

Cousin James asked quietly, "Had he had too much to drink?"

"Yes, but it wasn't just that—"

"Did he try—" Cousin James cleared his throat. "Did he try to kiss you?"

"Yes, I think he did. But it wasn't just that—"

"Take your time, Stella. Try to remember calmly."

"He talked about the boats in the yacht basin—and that he and Tron are going to take all the Negroes—Honoria and Clive—and everybody—and send them back to Kairogi." Cousin James was silent. "Was it—was it delirium?"

"It does sound fantastic, Stella. But I have learned not to discount the fantastic. Can you tell me anything more?"

"He said something about Lincoln and Liberia—"

"The Liberian experiment is a real one."

"So Kairogi—"

"Stella, do you think Tron has any idea of going to Africa?"

"Uncle Hoadley promised Tron he'd be King of Kairogi. I know Tron feels Illyria ought to be his. So perhaps—since Honoria was princess in Kairogi—he'd feel he's the legitimate pretender—"

"Yes, Hoadley would assume that would appeal to Tron. He's always had delusions of grandeur."

"And the boats *are* in the yacht basin." I saw them."

"There are always boats in the yacht basin."

"This many?"

He nodded thoughtfully. "This could very well be the kind of wild, misguided idealism Hoadley might get involved in."

"It didn't sound idealistic. It sounded as though he thought Honoria and Clive and Ronnie weren't people at all, as though they could be disposed of like cattle."

"Stella, I'm not sure how much of what you remember is

fact and how much is not, but no matter how much Tron would like to be king of something, I don't think it would get him to Africa. His ambitions are here."

"But he *is* working for Uncle Hoadley."

"He is perhaps using Hoadley. And this is very dangerous. I have heard rumors of Terence Ronald Zenumin's activities, and they do not involve a return to Africa. They are far more simple and primitive than that."

"What?"

"Revenge. We have had uprisings of Negroes in the South before. I know how terrible they can be. If there is a cosmic justice in these, and there is, it has nothing to do with the justice of love. And what Hoadley is trying to do has nothing to do with justice at all, though in a madly logical way he is quite right."

"Right!"

"We did do wrong when we brought slaves over from Africa, and we are left with the fruits of that wrong. The parents have eaten sour grapes and the children's teeth are set on edge."

"But sending people back to Africa—"

"If we don't, what will happen? Won't there be uprisings of angry people like Tron?"

"Yes, but—"

"These uprisings will be bloody. Innocent people will be killed."

"But, Cousin James, even if Uncle Hoadley could send the Negroes at the beach back to Africa, what about the rest of the country?"

"If this plan is real, and not the strange logic of a single madman, I don't suppose for a moment that it would stop here. I've known Hoadley all his life; he can be very persuasive. I don't imagine he is the only one involved in this. It is not impossible that this is only a small part of a wider, long-term, very carefully organized plan."

"You're talking as though it's all real."

"It well may be, Stella. I don't know for certain, but I cannot afford to write it off as a madman's dream. Or your delirium. I think this is something beyond your imagining. If we have done wrong in bringing people here from Africa, and we have, and if we are reaping the results of that sin in rebellions and uprisings and murders, then, if we do not want these disturbances to accelerate so that our children, and our children's children, will suffer from them, then we must return the black people to the continent from which we took them, and so wipe out, in that way, the evil we have done. If we do this, there will be no race problem for the next generations; they will never need to fear the Negroes."

"But, Cousin James, *you* don't think—"

"No, Stella, of course I don't. We can't wipe out past violence by more violence. We can't save ourselves, or future generations, this way. We can, perhaps, open a way for those who want it, as with Liberia, but we can't force it."

"Can you stop it? Can you stop Uncle Hoadley?"

"Not singlehanded, certainly. But I will get in touch with Washington, and hope not to be discounted as a crackpot. I hope my record will give weight to my words, despite the fact that I have nothing tangible to tell them."

"What were you doing in Jefferson yesterday?"

"Talking with Washington about Tron and the Black Riders."

"Cousin James, I want to ask you about Ronnie." I turned my face away from him.

"Ronnie is an extraordinary young man."

"He is Terry's brother, isn't he? Therro was Ronnie's father."

I was not prepared for Cousin James's astonishment. "But Hoadley—"

"Not Hoadley. Therro." I told him what Belle Zenumin had said. "And Aunt Olivia gave me Mado's journals to read. Mado never said it, but—"

"What has Olivia said?"

"She hasn't."

"It explains—" Cousin James stroked his beard. His hand trembled more than usual. "It explains a great deal. We tend to forget that Olivia knows how to be silent when she wishes to. Did Hoadley say anything to you last night?"

"I think so. I'm not sure." My head pounded.

"I have misjudged again. Hoadley has gone all these years allowing everybody to think— God forgive me. Therro was the person in the world Hoadley came closest to loving. He idealized him. This must have been a bitter blow, far worse than Therro's death."

I said nothing about Uncle Hoadley and Kitty. I did not think it was all dream and delirium, but I could not be sure. We stayed in silence, then, for a long time. I am not sure just when Cousin James left.

7

AND I am not sure exactly how much time I lost with my sunstroke, or heat prostration, or *crise des nerfs*, or whatever it was. Ronnie visited me daily, and Honoria nursed me. There was, I am sure, something in her herb teas and broths which relaxed and sedated me, probably for the sake of the baby. I felt quickening while I lay there in bed, and for a long time my entire consciousness was centered on the tiny fluttering movements in my belly.

Uncle Hoadley came to me. When? I am not sure.

"You're better now, my child, aren't you."

"Yes, thanks. My headache's almost gone. Ronnie just wants me to take it easy."

"Stella, while you were delirious you kept calling for Ron. I think it would be a good idea if you do not see him this week while I am in Jefferson."

"He is my doctor."

"I would prefer you to see someone else."

"There isn't anybody else at the beach. And Ron is an excellent doctor. You know that, because you saw to it."

"Child," he said heavily, "you are young and innocent and naïve. You do not understand—"

"What don't I understand?"

"Perhaps Irene is right. You do not understand men. Renier men."

"I understand that Ron is a Renier."

"Ron is a Negro. He does not, and never will, have the name of Renier. Do not forget this." His voice was harsh. As I started to speak he held up his hand to silence me. "There is one thing you must know about me. I want peace. We have had enough war in our time, both within and without the family. I am, basically, as much a pacifist as my Uncle Theron. But if Ron—if Ron should ever speak to you in a way in which it is not suitable for a Negro to speak to a white woman, I will have him shot."

"You needn't worry," I said coldly. "If there's any worrying to be done, I'll do it. And not about Ronnie. About the Riders, maybe."

"Stella, if Ron does something to set the Riders on him, I will not stop them."

"What have you got against Ronnie?"

"Stella, Stella, what has happened? What has he done to you? I cannot bear this wall of misunderstanding between us."

"I've had sunstroke Uncle Hoadley," I said, and turned my face to the wall.

The twins came to my room, bowing and bobbing and scraping imaginary sand off their feet onto an imaginary mat. Their rosy faces were puckered with love and concern. I sat up in bed and hugged them both, and the three of us laughed as though we had escaped from some wild danger and were hilarious with relief.

Then the laughter ended. Willy's round face drooped; his mouth turned down; tears blurred the dancing of his eyes. He held out his hand, curling it as though to hold something, raised the forefinger of his other hand and stroked, and the ghost of the little lizard was with us.

A tear rolled down Harry's cheek. "Lady give little one back to God. Lady good. Whoever hurt lizard bad. Willy and Harry angry. God angry."

Willy nodded, still stroking with one gentle finger. "Stars angry. Moon and sun. All grains of sand. All water of sea." With mercurial suddenness he clapped his hands. "Lady better now. Lady sleep. Get strong again. Get ready."

"Ready for what be to come. Must be ready. Sleep," Harry said.

Smiling and bowing, they backed out.

On Friday after Uncle Hoadley got in from Jefferson, he knocked on my door. "Stella, do you feel like coming downstairs to the table?"

"Honoria said—"

"Stella, I am asking you how you feel. Only you know the answer to that. I think it might be good for you. I think that you are well enough to, but something is holding you back. Am I right?"

I whispered, "I don't know."

"I think that you are confusing what happened in your delirium with reality. Wouldn't you like to talk about it? To tell me what you are afraid of?"

I was afraid of Uncle Hoadley. I said, "I'll get dressed and come down for dinner. Just give me fifteen minutes."

My legs were shaky, my head a little light, but there was no more pain, and my fever had been gone for some time.

There comes a time in all illness where one has to give it up, let it go, move back into life again, and this time had come for me. We sat at the table and everything seemed as usual. Everyone welcomed me; the aunts bickered over Shakespeare; there was no feeling of impending danger in the air.

"I thought Xenia recognized me last Sunday, Livvy," Aunt Des said. "But of course you can never be sure."

"James is still looking for a miracle as far as Xenia is concerned," Uncle Hoadley said. "Too bad, because the miracle is not going to happen."

Honoria, passing silver dishes, paused by Uncle Hoadley. "More spoon bread, Mr. Hoadley?"

"Honoria," Aunt Olivia asked, "what is a miracle?"

Aunt Irene said, "Honoria, I'd like some more soldier beans, please."

Aunt Olivia held up her hand. "Wait. Honoria, what's the difference between magic and a miracle? That ought to interest you, Irene."

Honoria stood, holding the silver dish in a linen napkin. "A human being can do magic. God do the miracle. Magic make the person think the power be in hisself. A miracle make him know the power belong to God." She went out to the kitchen.

"Stella," Aunt Des said, "when the light shines on your face that way, you can still see the place where Minou scratched you."

Honoria returned. "Your beans, Miss Irene."

"Thank you. Honoria, do you believe in magic?"

"I believe in miracles, Miss Irene."

"But do you believe in magic?"

"Will you have coffee after dinner, Miss Irene? or cold tea?"

"Stella," Aunt Olivia said, "do you still have the little cross you and Des made at the train station?"

"Yes."

"Do you keep it with you?"

"I think it's still in the pocket of the dress I was wearing."

"Auntie, that's superstition, a cross made out of two pins!"

"Have it your own way, Irene," Aunt Olivia said.

I reached up and touched the thin line on my cheek which marked Belle Zenumin's scratch. That, at any rate, had not been dream. And I did not know if I believed in either magic or miracle.

In the morning I put on the dress I had worn when we went to the station to meet Uncle Hoadley. I reached into the pocket, and there was the little flat cross made of two pins. I went out to the kitchen and gave it to Clive.

He was pouring coffee from the old enamel percolator into the silver pot. "What this, Miss Stella?"

"I don't understand about the cross, Clive, so it's wrong for me to keep it. It would be right for you."

"Because you give it to me, Miss Stella." He put the pot down, took the cross from my hand, and put it in his pocket.

I continued to hold my hand out towards him, my left hand with the ring which Honoria had once worn, and Mado, and Kitty, and which now encircled my finger. "I think I understand about the ring, because it is love."

"So is the cross, Miss Stella," Clive said.

After breakfast I sat in the writing room, trying to decide what I could tell Terry without worrying him. I knew that I had to find out what was delusion caused by sunstroke and what was real. At this point I was certain of nothing, except that Belle had scratched me. This meant, at least, that the Granddam was real, too, and, probably, that Aunt Irene had taken me to the Zenumin clearing. But I wasn't sure about the War Room or the map of Kairogi or anything Uncle Hoadley had said to me that terrible night, or even the conversation with Cousin James while I was still driven by fever. Oddly, I did not doubt that Ron was Terry's brother.

It suddenly occured to me that there was one way I could make a test which would help me find the fine line between fantasy and fact. If the War Room was exactly as I remembered it, then I could trust the rest of my memory, too.

I left the great-aunts, went through the library; through the ballroom, up to the War Room with the white china doorknob.

So the door to the room was there. It didn't mean that there was anything on the other side.

I paused, then threw the door open.

The room was empty, save for a large, flat-topped desk which was bare except for a curling green blotter. The walls were bare.

I stood in the doorway, my heart beating painfully.

Then my explorations of Illyria, my discovery of the War Room, had never, in fact, happened, had been conjured up by sunstroke, or brain fever. None of the horror about Kairogi was real. It was nightmare.

No. I did not accept the verdict of the empty room. I went up to the wall on which I had dreamed there was a map of Africa, with little flagged pins stuck into the section of Kairogi. There were tack holes in the wall where a map might have been, but that didn't prove anything.

The horizon between reality and illusion flickered like a heat mirage.

I went to the desk. Ran my finger across the wood, leaving a mark in the sand dust. Looked at the blotter. It had been much used. Ink marks crossed and crisscrossed each other. It was impossible to see sentences, or even words, I picked the blotter up and took it to the window. Towards the left hand corner I saw, in mirror writing...

$$\reflectbox{\textit{Kairogi}}$$

A sudden noise made me swing around in terror.

It was Minou, tail swishing, making his most demanding miaow. I picked him up and held his small, completely real body. "Minou, I wanted it to be delirium almost as much as Uncle Hoadley wanted me to think it was. I didn't want to have to believe it. And Uncle Hoadley almost—oh, Minou, if he cleaned up the War Room to make me think it was all sunstroke, then Cousin James—" I almost dropped the little cat. Uncle Hoadley would guess that I had talked to Cousin James. He would have to do something to stop Cousin James going to Jefferson and getting word to Washington—Uncle Hoadley, or Tron.

By evening I knew what I had to do—the only thing I could do. After dinner I went for my walk. Finbarr's cold muzzle pressed into my palm as he trotted along after me. He splashed in and out of the waves, coming out and shaking water and sand over me, loping ahead, and then coming back to circle around me, long tongue hanging out. I was still a little weak, but my physical strength had returned with amazing swiftness, probably because I had been well and moving freely about my room for some time before Uncle Hoadley made me come downstairs.

Ahead of me I saw a speck, a small swirl of dust, coming closer. A horse and rider. I wanted it to be Cousin James, knew it was not. In any case what I had set out to do was find Ron and tell him everything I knew and ask his help.

He drew up beside me on Thales. Dog and horse greeted each other affectionately. Ron dismounted and walked along beside me. "Feeling all right now?"

"Yes, I'm fine."

"I'd have come by to check on you more often this past week, but it did not seem wise." Then he put a warning hand on my arm. "Come." Quickly he led Thales across the beach and in behind a dune. Finbarr and I followed. We were out of sight before I could easily identify the sound of hoofs.

When they had passed I was cold with anger. "I *hate* hiding this way! It's idiotic that we should be afraid to be seen together! Ronnie, I have to talk to you." I told him, as coherently as I could, all that I knew. It sounded, as I put it together, more than a little mad, really incredible. No wonder I had doubted it, had tried to push it onto delirium.

But Ron simply listened quietly, nodding occasionally. When I had finished he said softly, "What to do . . . what to do . . ."

"You think it's real, Ron? You don't think it's just night-mare?"

"It's nightmare, all right. But it's real."

"Would Uncle Hoadley or Tron hurt Cousin James?"

"Tron wouldn't stop at anything."

"But what's he up to? Do you think he wants to be King of Kairogi?"

"No, Mr. James is right. Africa is not in my brother's plans."

"What is?"

"His Riders. And revenge. He's king of a gang of men who'll listen to anything he tells them. Only ill can come from it."

"For you?"

"For me, as long as I have anything to do with Illyria. Or with doctoring. Or with you. You'd better go back now, Stell— Miss Stella. I've got my work cut out. If I don't get to you during the day tomorrow, I'll send you a message by the twins.

8

O<small>N</small> Sunday we had Morning Prayer with Cousin James in Cousin Xenia's room, but came home for the midday meal, since it was thought it would be too much for me to have lunch at Cousin Lucille's. For that mercy I was grateful.

And then I was given a week of grace in which to regain my strength. Each evening when I went for my walk the twins came to me, talked about Docdoc, nodded happily—so I knew he was all right, nothing else horrible had happened—and trotted along the beach with me, like Finbarr or Minou. There was a sense of waiting, of an invisible vacuum waiting to be filled. I did not want it filled; I was afraid to think about what would fill it, even with the corners of my mind.

Friday came, and Uncle Hoadley would be returning to Illyria, and this false peace would, I was sure, come to an end. I woke up on Friday morning and lay in bed, unwilling to leave the enclosure of the mosquito netting, the gentleness of light flickering over walls and ceiling, the protection of the walls of my room. There had been, I remembered vaguely, a thunderstorm during the night, but I had slept through it. I wished I could sleep all day, and thus avoid whatever storms it held in store.

Uncle Hoadley surprised us all by arriving in time for lunch. He had been fortunate enough to be able to leave Jefferson immediately after breakfast and drive down with one of the Yacht Club officers. "I am planning to take my little holiday now, and stay with you ladies for ten days or a fortnight. Cousin

James has kindly consented to take my place, as he had to come up to Jefferson on business. I could never take a holiday if it were not for Cousin James."

"What about Morning Prayer on Sunday?" Aunt Des asked.

"I am quite capable of reading it here in Illyria," Uncle Hoadley said.

"But Xenia—"

"Won't know the difference," Aunt Irene murmured.

Uncle Hoadley said that he would send messages to Saintie, and to Cousin Lucille, and then looked about the table cheerfully and commented on how well I looked, "though your cheeks are still pale, child."

I tried to rest after lunch, but, despite Uncle Hoadley's unusual attitude of relaxation because of the holiday ahead of him, I found that I did not believe him. As Aunt Olivia would have remarked, I was certain that he had something up his sleeve.

In the evening after coffee I went for my walk, hoping that I would see Ron himself, rather than just getting a message from the twins, so that I could share with him my sense of unease, of foreboding.

But the twins, not Ron, came trotting across the beach towards me, carrying butterfly nets. This evening they were not laughing. Willy dropped his butterfly net on the sand and flung his arms about me. "Mr. James gone, gone."

Harry jumped up and down in distress. "Away, away."

"He's in Jefferson, boys," I said. "He's taking over for Uncle Hoadley for a week or ten days."

They shook their white heads and Willy stamped on the hard sand for emphasis. "No. No. Gone. Not of hisself."

"Tooken. Tooken away."

"Hasn't he gone to Jefferson?"

"No, no, put him in a pumpkin shell."

"Ding-dong bell, put him in a well."

"Boys, I don't understand. What are you trying to tell me?"

Harry lifted his net high and caught an imaginary butterfly.

> *"Birdie in your cage so high,*
> *Tell me why you cannot fly."*

Willy screwed up his eyes, made stuttering, strangling sounds, trying desperately to catch hold of some words.

> *"Stone walls do not a prison make,*
> *Nor iron bars a cage—"*

I gave up. "Boys, where is Ron?"

They pointed up the beach. "He coming. Tonight. Docdoc come."

I sighed with relief. "Then I'll walk along to meet him."

The twins nodded, but not happily. Willy picked up his butterfly net, and they ran in erratic circles in front of Illyria, after butterflies I could not see. I walked along by the ocean, trying to understand what it was they had been trying to tell me. That Cousin James should be in Jefferson where he could be in touch with Washington, with the Bureau of Navigation, did make sense. The twins, of course, would not understand this, would misinterpret his absence . . .

When I met Ronnie we would go to Little Nyssa and ask Saintie. She would know where Cousin James was.

I was not far from the twins' cottage when I saw horse and rider, and my heart leapt. But Finbarr, who had been walking close beside me instead of, as usual, loping around me, growled long and low in his throat, growled as he had when Uncle Hoadley came to my room.

Not Ronnie. Tron. Tron on the thin pale horse I had seen his mother leading up the beach; Tron, followed by a small group of Black Riders.

No, no, please no.

Before they reached me, Ronnie galloped out of the dunes and jumped down from Thales to stand beside me. "Stay close to me, Stella."

Tron rode past us without pause or greeting, then wheeled around and splashed through the shallow waves to rein up beside us. He leaned down and patted Thales on the rump. "Let's go."

"All right, Tron, what is this?" Ron asked.

"Don't you know? Thought I were expected."

Ron spoke slowly and quietly. "Let us say that though you are full of surprises, Tron, I am hardly surprised to see you."

"Who told you?"

Ron said nothing.

"Grandmother?" Still Ron did not answer. Tron gave his deeper version of his mother's tinkle. "I wouldn't presume to question you about you sources, brother dear." His voice and words again echoed Uncle Hoadley. "For one who's been in other climes for so long a time you doing pretty well. Potions and lotions, drinks and dreams, stars and shadows: how it happen that you pay them so much mind, little Docdoc."

"That's enough, Tron. What do you want?"

"Don't like it when I talk Illyria, do you, Docdoc. Tron can do it just like you, only Tron mostly don't choose to. Granddam wants her. Come on." Tron snapped his fingers, and the group of Black Riders moved closer. "Bring her. Let's go. Shall the little Mrs. Renier ride with me or with you?"

"Neither," I said. "It's late, and I'm going back to Illyria."

"Oh, no, you're not, little Mrs. Renier, ma'am." Tron's voice was lazy and casual now. "When either of our grandmothers wants something, Ronnie and I hops."

"And if I don't?" Ron asked.

"Think it over," Tron said. "Matter of fact, you've already thunk, ain't you? Why else're you here, like a knight in shining armor. If you don't come along with her now, you know perfectly well we'll get her another time when you not around to protect your precious Mrs. Renier. Does Docdoc ever get a call to use a magnifying glass? Try it sometime, Ronnie, try it. Surprising how much you see if you look at people through a magnifying glass. All kinds of things they think they hiding show up. Things what need to be burned away. Tron look at the whole world through a magnifying glass. Come on, now, brother, let's get going." He cracked his whip and one of the men kicked his heels into his horse and rode up to us.

Ron pushed the horse's head aside. "Get back." Then, "Come, Mrs. Renier." He helped me up onto Thales, saying, "Tron's right. If I come with you now perhaps I can protect you. Even if I could get you back to Illyria that wouldn't stop him another time." He swung himself up in front of me.

"No funny business," Tron warned. "It don't wuth it."

"Tell your men to go," Ron said, "or we stay here."

Tron laughed, but cracked his whip again, calling out commands in a guttural speech I could not understand, and the horsemen dispersed into the scrub.

I held tightly to Ron's waist. His body was strong and firm and warm. I looked for Finbarr but could not see him.

We approached the twins' cottage and the light was warm and golden from the windows, but before we reached its comfort, Tron turned from the ocean and led us up a barely visible trail across the dunes and into the jungle. The horses pushed aside bushes and vines, and we had to bend over to escape low-hanging branches. I could feel Ronnie's heart beating, quick and strong. I wondered if he could feel mine, and sense my fear. Yet, strangely, it was not panic fear, but that heightened state of awareness which comes with excitement and challenge.

Tron reined in his horse until we caught up with him; our legs touched. He flung his words at Ron. "Chosen sides?"

Ron said nothing, though I felt a stiffening in his spine.

"Going to have to, little brother. Can't have it both ways." Then, to me, "Don't fret, Mrs. Renier, ma'am. Nobody going to hurt you lessen I give them leave. Ole Massa Hoadley not the only one to have Riders at his beck and call. What Ole Massa Hoadley can do, little old Tron can do, too. Tron be more like Massa Hoadley than Ronnie here."

"You're both mad," I said. Ronnie reached back to touch me in warning.

Tron said, "You don't do what I says, my men going to get you and have their pleasure with you. That what happen to little girls what go poking their noses where they got no business. Like in the War Room."

"Except—" I said—"there isn't any War Room, is there?"

Tron's giggle was shrill. "You're so-o right, Mrs. Renier, ma'am. Ain't never was nothing there. No map of Kairogi. Only little old Tron cleaning up, like we cleans all the rooms of Illyria every summer. That what Mr. Hoadley want you to think. But you going to think what *Tron* want you to think." He pulled ahead of us again and we moved slowly through the underbrush. When we reached the creek we tethered the horses and Ronnie helped me into the waiting dugout. Tron paddled. We moved in darkness under the locked branches of cypress and water oak. An owl cried and I started, rocking the boat. Ron steadied me.

When we reached the clearing a red glow from a fire in the central fireplace stained the water. Tron beached the canoe, and the little waiting boys pulled it up onto the sand. Swarms of insects attacked us with a wild shrilling and biting. An acrid smell hit us like a cloud. "Be it ever so humble," Tron sang, "there's no place like home. This be where Ronnie and me got borned, in one of these stately mansions."

From the central hut the Granddam emerged, silhouetted in the doorway, a wooden torch in her hand. One of the boys helped her down the rickety wooden steps and she shuffled across the tamped dirt floor of the clearing. Ron kept one arm around me. "You will stand alone, missy," the old woman said.

Ronnie did not move his arm. "Tell us what you want, Granddam."

"Us, hah? Take your arm away from her." She spat at my feet.

With a tremendous effort I moved from Ronnie's protection and stepped forward. "What do you want?"

The old woman crouched down by the fire. Beyond her, in the flickering light, a group of men and women from the encircling huts watched us silently. I felt emanating from them a hostility I had never encountered before. The old Zenumin patted the ground beside her. "Sit."

I sat on the hard-packed dirt. Ron squatted beside me.

The old woman pulled a pipe out of her pocket and lit it. Firelight did not warm grey of hair or skin. Greyness clouded her yellowed eyes. A small puff of grey smoke came from the pipe, and a heavy smell. She held the pipe out to me. I shook my head.

Suddenly Belle stood there by us holding a tarnished tray on which were four bowls filled with something hot and fragrant, and yet with an undertone of something sharp, ammoniac. She placed the tray between her mother and me. The old woman handed me a bowl. There was nothing but to take it. She gave one to Ronnie, one to Tron. Taking the fourth bowl herself she held it up, as though offering a libation. "Drink."

I hesitated.

"Drink ye all of it."

I held the steaming bowl to my lips.

Ronnie, looking at me, drank slowly, deliberately.

Tron drained his bowl and set it down on the tray.

"Finish," the old woman commanded.

I obeyed. It did not taste very different from the teas Honoria and Saintie had given me. I tried to convince myself that it was only my imagination that felt a different purpose behind the brewing of it. I put my bowl down at the same time as Ronnie.

"Now, Granddam," he said, "tell Mrs. Renier what you want."

She grinned, showing her sparse, yellow teeth. "Why should I want anything? What Mrs. Renier have the Granddam need?"

"You tell us," Ron said.

"Us. Who's us, little black doctor? Or be you black any more?"

"Granddam, why did you want Mrs. Renier and me to-night?"

"You? Who said nothing about you? Told Tron to bring her. Nobody want you."

"But I am here. And I want to know what all this is about. Now."

She slapped the dirt in front of her with the wrinkled palm of her hand. It made a dull noise, like a muffled drum. "Don't need your whiteman's medicine, black boy. Granddam knows more'n any white doctor. What call you got to give white medicine to my people?"

Ron spoke quietly, dispassionately "If they come to me, Granddam, it's after they've been to you. And you've failed them."

"You ever fail them?"

"Everybody fails sometimes, Granddam. Maybe that's something I've learned that you haven't. We don't always have to succeed."

"You be sorry you laugh at my medicine."

"No, Granddam. I do not laugh. I take it very seriously indeed. Now, why don't you tell Mrs. Renier why you sent for her?"

"Tron."

"Yes, Granddam?"

"Sit."

Tron squatted across from Ron.

"Tron say Mrs. Renier got a way with her. You got a way with you, missy?"

"I don't know what you're talking about." I slapped at an insect which was buzzing at my face.

"Tron say you got a way, and Tron never say nothing without he got something behind it. Tron say you got a way with our Ronnie. And you got a way with Honoria."

"I love Honoria."

"Love—" She threw the word away, then spat on the ground as though spitting on the word. As Belle had spat on my shadow. "All right, missy, I tell you what you going to do. You want to keep what you got swimming around like a little fish inside you, you want to keep your baby, you do what I tell you. You go home, missy, and you get Honoria to give you her treasure. You don't want your baby to die in you, that what you're going to do. I give you till tomorrow starshine. Then Tron coming for you, and you bring the jewels. Everything. Bring."

My child stirred within me and fear dimmed my eyes, dulled my ears.

"You do not do what I tell you," she said, "these curses shall come upon you." She began to rock back an forth, intoning in a terrible shrill whine, "Cursed you'll be in Jefferson and cursed in San Feliz, and cursed your baby's star."

I dimly heard Ronnie's voice. "Get up. Stella, stand up."

"The dark god shall curse you and you shall have vexation and boils and emerods and pimples and perishings because of your magics and your spells and your whorings with my grand—"

Ronnie's hand was on my elbow, he pulled me to my feet. "Stella. Get up. Help me. Stand."

"The dark god will curse you with mildew and mold and sunburn and flies and buzzards—"

Somehow I was standing, moving across the compound. Somehow Ronnie managed to get me into the canoe. I think he picked me up and lifted me in. I could see nothing but the grey smoke of the old woman, hear nothing but the grey whine of her voice. "Your womb shall wither and your breasts shall shrivel—"

Ron gave a mighty shove away from the shore and the canoe moved into the dark waters. The black cursing followed us. "And it shall come to pass, that as the Lord rejoiced over you to do you good, and to multiply you, so my Lord, the Other One, will rejoice over you to destroy you—"

Ron paddled swiftly. The Granddam stood at the water's edge, intoning after us, "When you wakest up you'll wish it was night, and when you see night you'll wish for day for the fear of your heart and the terror of the things which I curse you to see . . ."

The voice faded away like dirty smoke behind us. I clung to the gunwales and was sick with terror. We moved through a timeless river of slimy fear. Then we saw a glint of moonlight, and the horses. Ron ignored Tron's pale horse and helped me onto Thales. "Put your arms around my waist, Stella. Hold onto me." I obeyed. I closed my eyes and pressed my face against his shoulder. "Stella," he said. "Mrs. Renier." Gently he loosened my frantic clutching. We were alone on the beach. I did not see the Black Riders. Only the beach in the cleansing starlight. The moon, my second Illyrian moon, had set.

"Ron—Ronnie—can she hurt my baby?"

"Not unless you let her."

"What about that stuff she gave me to drink?"

"She could give you something which would hurt. But she isn't ready to yet."

"Why not?"

"Not while she thinks you can get Honoria's treasure."

"Ronnie, what am I going to do?"

"We're going to Little Nyssa."

I told him about Cousin James, and the twins' anxious, incoherent rhymings.

"All the more reason to see Saintie."

At Little Nyssa all was dark. He knocked and knocked until he roused Saintie. Without preamble she said, "I dreamed me a dream."

"Mr. James is not in Jefferson, is he?" Ron asked.

She shook her head.

"Where is he?"

"Illyria. I dreamed him."

"Where?"

"A room empty, hidden. He tied. Bound. Tell Honoria. She know where to look. Mr. James knowed something like this going to happen. He tell me if he not home for dinner I got to send to Jefferson. He tell me who to ask for, give me a letter. They be an instrument to send messages on, like the drums in the scrub, the drums white folk can't hear."

"You got the letter to Jefferson, then?"

"I send Sonny. He get the letter to the man Mr. James say. Then I send the message my own way. Somehow or other, somebody going to know. Mr. James say, 'Saintie, if Mr. Hoadley thinks I know what he up to, he do anything to stop me.' Only Mr. Hoadley don't know Mr. James, do he? Mr. Hoadley think he got him stopped by tying him up." Then she spoke directly to Ron. "God will bless you and send you courage to do what you has to do." She turned to me. "And you, Miss Stella. Do not try to find the answer yourself to what you has to do. Wait and have faith, and you will be told what to do."

"Who will tell me?"

"The Lord will let you know when the time comes."

Thales moved slowly along the beach. His smooth, serene stride did not jolt me. To my surprise we rode past Illyria. Ron said, "I'm going around up through the dunes to the stable, and in the back way. We don't want anyone to see us."

"But they'll be expecting me back from my walk. It's terribly late and they'll be anxious again. Let me off here and I'll go on in and then meet you in the kitchen."

Ron halted Thales. "Not the kitchen. Somebody's apt to come in. Honoria's and Clive's room. What are you going to tell Mr. Hoadley?"

I dismounted. "I'll lie. Ronnie—what are we going to tell Honoria and Clive?"

"The truth."

Uncle Hoadley was, indeed, waiting for me. The aunts had gone to their rooms. Before he could say anything I plunged into apology. ". . . so I lay down on one of the dunes, the way you sometimes do, Uncle Hoadley, to watch the stars, and I fell asleep. I'm terribly sorry. It was exceedingly thoughtless of me."

He sat on the porch, his face in shadow, his hands gleaming long and pale as they lay loosely on his knees. "I'm not sure I believe you, Stella."

"Why not? I find, since my sunstroke, that I fall asleep at the slightest provocation."

He took a cigar, clipped it with the gold cigar cutter on his watch chain, lit it, slowly, deliberately. "Stella, were you with Ron?"

"What is this about Ron? Just because he's half Renier doesn't necessarily mean that he's like the rest of the Renier men."

The arc of the cigar was arrested in mid-air.

I continued coldly, without compassion. "Actually, I was with Tron."

Uncle Hoadley put his face in his hands. "Stella, if I said or did—when I was drunk, was not myself, if I said or did anything offensive to you, I beg your pardon."

I could still feel nothing towards him but fear and distaste. I did not respond.

"I carry a heavy burden. Sometimes I am not strong enough. I want to put it down, just for a few minutes."

I went to the screen door. "But I really was with Tron, Uncle Hoadley." I went in.

9

WHEN I got to Clive's and Honoria's room, Ron had already told them. Honoria was sitting on the bed, her seersucker robe pulled tightly around her. Her large feet in the felt slippers somehow looked utterly vulnerable. "There is no treasure," she said.

"But—"

"It all gone. How they think we kept and fed all them people? It all gone, long since."

"But they think—Tron, and the Granddam—"

"And others think it, too," Honoria said. "Dreams of treasure don't die easy. Mr. Hoadley, he think it. He after me again. He sick. This my home. Don't he know that? Clive's. Mine. All of us. If we have never left Africa, then—but we was brought here, and it is our home."

"Oh, Honoria, I know, I know!" I sat on the floor at her feet and pressed my face against her knees. "And the twins— I promised the twins—"

"You will keep your promise, Miss Stella," Clive said.

My mind raced like Wally's lizard running around the silverwood of the kitchen table. "But as long as they think there's a treasure—"

Honoria started to rock back and forth, slowly, rhythmically. "I got to go to the Granddam. I got to stop them. When, Lord, when? Tell me how?"

"No, Honoria, you can't do that—"

"What about your baby, Miss Stella?"

"I will not let them hurt Miss Stella, Grandmother."

"How you going to stop them? You been away too long,

303

son. You do not know them. I do. Your mother was married to my son. She spit on his shadow. She cause his death."

Clive said, "That be not why Jimmy die."

Honoria began to moan. "I do not know, I do not know how she do it. She kiss evil, and she get its power. She spread darkness, she do, no good pretending she don't." Her voice deepened again to a groan.

For Honoria to lose control this way was as shocking as Uncle Hoadley's horrible nocturnal visit to me. But I had not wanted to comfort and strengthen Uncle Hoadley. I had wanted only to drive him further into darkness.

Honoria stopped her keening movement. "Lord. Lord. Tell me."

"What do you know, Grandmother? You must tell us."

"I be an old woman. I got to pull them apart, separate them, the things the cards told me and what the Lord say."

Clive had been sitting on the straight chair, his Bible on his knees. Now he closed it, rose, went to his wife. "Honoria." His voice was flint. "Listen to me. Once was a prophet, named Elijah. A prophet of the Lord. But people round him forgot the Lord, went whoring after the little gods."

"Like the little gods of Kairogi . . ." Honoria whispered.

"Like the little gods of the scrub. When you was in Kairogi, the little gods was all you had. The only gods. You had no choice. They was before Miss Mado show you the Lord."

"Mado, Mado . . ."

"If you go back to the little gods now, then you be doing like the people round about Elijah."

"I do not go back to the little gods. The Zenumins do."

"You think the little gods of the Zenumins be stronger than the Lord?"

"Clive," Honoria groaned, "they can do evil, they already done it, you know that, we cannot let them hurt Miss Stella—"

"They do evil only when we let them, only when we turn from the Lord."

"Nothing stop Tron when the hating is on him."

"You think the Lord can't stop Tron? Listen to me, old woman. The people round Elijah knowed about the Lord. But they turn their backs on him and build altars under the palms on the high places of the dunes."

I said, "Like the Zenumins—"

Clive's voice did not falter. "And they worshipped the little gods in the dark places. They give them burnt offerings, and when the little gods snickered and told them to bring human hearts to their altars, they do that, too. They took young men and children, they took little babies, and they sacrificed them on the altars of the little gods. And Elijah got an-angered. He say to the wizards and the witches and the magicians, you think you little gods is so big, they ain't as big as the Lord. And they say, All our little gods is bigger and more powerful than you one little Lord. Oh-ho, say Elijah, you just try the Lord and see. So they fix them altars to the little gods, an Elijah fix him an altar to the Lord, and he say to the magicians and the wizards and the witches, Call on the names of your gods and I will call on the Name of the Lord, and the God that answereth by fire, let him be God. So they call on their little gods, the gods of the spitting against the shadow, and the stealing of the hank of hair, the gods of the skin under the fingernail and the little doll and the pins, saying, O hear us. They call and the from morning until noon, and their little gods don't make answer, no answer at all, so they jump on their altars which they had made. And Elijah say, Where your little gods? they off talking with each other? they gone on a trip into town? maybe they gone to sleep coz they so tired? Why don't you wake them up? And the wizards and the witches and the magicians call and call, and nothing happen. Then Elijah say, Gather round. And he say, Pour water over the altar to the Lord. So they pour on water. And he say, Pour on more water. So they pour on more water. And he say, Pour on water again the third time. And they pour it on the third time. Then Elijah call out in a voice, Hear me, O Lord, hear me, that this people may know that you are the Lord. Then the fire of the Lord fell and burn up the wood and the stone and the dust and lick up all the water they had poured, and when the people saw it they fell on their faces."

Honoria bowed over. "What you want me to do?"

"Not just you," Clive said. "I am with you, and Mr. James. All of us who were Nyssa and who are Illyria. We going to do what Elijah do. We going to call on the Lord. He take care of the little gods."

Honoria straightened up in decision. "You be right. I go."

"Grandmother," Ron said, "Saintie told us that you would know where Mr. James is."

She nodded. "In the secret room, the room Claudius Broadley see fit to make when he build him Illyria. After the war we occasion to use it because they still people we had to hide first from the soldiers, then from the Klan. Miss Mado and I thought best we keep it secret, like the treasure, but Mr. Hoadley must know 'bout it. Likely Therro found it, wasn't much Therro didn't find, and what he did he share with Mr. Hoadley."

"How did you guess Mr. James is there?"

"No guessing, son. Food missing. Not much, likely Tron bring something in from the scrub. I notice food missing, Tron shadowing in and out, Eben asking where Mr. James be. Mr. Hoadley come to the kitchen to tell me 'bout Mr. James being in Jefferson all week, talks about some highfalutin law case, and Mr. Hoadley don't discuss no law cases with me. So I make sure Mr. James be in the secret room, see to it that he get proper vittels, and leave him be."

"Leave him!" I cried.

"Safer for Mr. James, Miss Stella. If Mr. Hoadley go to take him bread or water and he be gone, then trouble come on top of it, we got not time. We got to have time. Mr. James send messages to Jefferson; we got to give Washington time. Mr. James do not discuss with me what Mr. Hoadley planning. He trust me to know it got to be stopped."

"All right, Grandmother," Ron said. "How much time have you got? Do you know? What are you going to do?"

"I got to pray, son. Can't do nothing on my own. Then tomorrow night I go to the Zenumins, to the Dark Clearing. I was forgetting my Powers. I was losing faith. I pray now. Tonight. All day tomorrow."

"Grandmother, do you have that much time?"

"Nothing going to happen before tomorrow night. The Lord done told me that while Clive be talking. Nothing I can do without I pray. My Powers do not come at beck and call. But they will come. Then I go to Zenumins. The Lord will take care of the little gods."

"Will the powers come, Grandmother? I am afraid for Illyria. For Stella."

Honoria did not answer. She went to the open window and knelt.

How could Honoria's prayers possibly prevent the Granddam from doing harm, or keep Tron from whatever dark plan he was nursing? What did it mean, this pitting of God against the gods? I knew nothing about Elijah. It was easier for me to believe in the dark gods of the Zenumins than in Clive's and Honoria's Lord.

Ronnie said, "Ste—Miss Stella, don't leave the house tomorrow. Don't go on the beach alone. I will come for you after dinner. Don't go anywhere without me. I'll be waiting at the foot of the ramp."

SIX

I

Iɴ the morning when I went out onto the beach the air had the clear and terrible emptiness which comes before a storm. I looked up and all I could see was an incredible, blinding blue. But there was an almost invisible tremor, a crackling in the sheen, warning that before evening the thunderclouds would begin to mass on the horizon. It was a relief to think of the physical storm.

Aunt Olivia and Aunt Des were in the slough, and waved in greeting. Aunt Olivia said, "Something's going on, and nobody will tell me what it is."

"Really, Olivia why do you run on so about something going on?"

"Because, daz it, something is. And it's not right that we should be kept in the dark. Stella, do you know what it is? You tell us."

"I'm not sure, Aunt Olivia. I'm not sure of anything since I had my sunstroke."

"I asked Hoadley, and he just went all lofty. Something about some case he and James have to cope with in Jefferson."

"People have great faith in James," Aunt Des said.

"So do I," Aunt Olivia said.

"Of course you do." Aunt Mary Desborough lay on her back in the too-quiet water. "Although James couldn't keep Nyssa from being destroyed, could he?"

Aunt Olivia, dog-paddling, squinted against the brilliance of the early-morning sun. "I am beginning to learn that Nyssa was not destroyed."

"Of course Nyssa was destroyed. It was burned to the ground. There was death and horror and we lost everything."

"I wonder," Aunt Olivia said softly. "I wonder."

Clive served breakfast as usual. Honoria did not appear, and I pictured her still kneeling by the window in prayer: the safety of Illyria, of my marriage, of Terry's and my baby, all hung by the thread of Honoria's prayer.

I could not settle down to anything. Uncle Hoadley had disappeared. Aunt Des took one of the straw hats and a parasol and went to the garden. I did not know where Aunt Olivia was.

Aunt Irene, like me, was restless. She ordered the horse hitched so that she could drive up the beach to Cousin Lucille, then decided it was too hot. Finally she asked me to play cribbage with her. I tried, but could not keep my mind on the cards. Nor could she. It was Aunt Irene who finally flung the cards impatiently on the table. "Stella, I can't stand it, I can't stand it another minute."

"What's the matter, Aunt Irene?" My mind was hardly on her petty problems.

"Stella, I've done things that I ought not to have done." She picked up her cards, studied them. "Funny, this is the best hand I've had in a long time, and I don't even care. Do you suppose that means anything?"

"If you want to play, Aunt Irene, let's go ahead."

"I can't. I thought—Stella, I never had anything against you, you must understand that."

I waited.

"All I wanted was to have Hoadley love me. Is that so strange? But I know Hoadley, oh yes, I have cause to know Hoadley. I realized from the first moment he laid eyes on you . . . As for me, Hoadley's never—not from the first. I was very beautiful when he married me. You do believe that, don't you?"

"Yes, Aunt Irene."

"I was the most beautiful girl Jefferson ever—and I had money. People look down on Utteley money, but that hasn't kept them from enjoying what it can buy. They say I bought Hoadley with it, but that's not true. I was beautiful. And I was good. I wanted to be a good wife to him. To give him children. But I never liked—I never could—and Hoadley—and then there was all that horror when Ron was born and I thought Hoadley—so I went to Belle—"

"But how could you possibly go to her!"

"She kept making me promises. And when she looked in the cards she told me things that were true, so I—I kept going because I wanted—"

"Wanted what?"

"I wanted to hurt Hoadley, to get even. And not only with

Hoadley. Everybody. All of them. All these years, looking down on my Utteley money and getting fat on it. Little Irene wasn't good enough for Hoadley, or the old aunts, the old fools, or Mado, too, for all her pretending. I knew what she really thought, and when Therro and Kitty—I knew what Therro was like, I saw through him right from the first."

"Aunt Irene, what are you trying to tell me?"

"Belle Zenumin wants to hurt you."

"Why, Aunt Irene? Why?"

"Because of Ron, you little fool. She saw it in the cards— Ron is witched by you."

I felt ice-cold. "Aunt Irene, that is absolute nonsense. I love Ron as a friend, and I think he's come to be fond of me."

"Stella, you don't understand. Ron's a nigger."

"How can you say that? Ron's half Renier, he—"

"Why did you come here? You're as bad as Mado. But Belle will get you. If anybody harms one of her sons, she will never forgive. I'm warning you, Stella, because I wish you no harm. You couldn't help it if Hoadley—I know that wasn't your fault. But to let Ron—that was wicked of you, wicked. Belle told me to bring her something of yours, and I tried, but Honoria stopped me."

"It's all right, Aunt Irene." My voice was as chill as my hands. "Belle managed. She was the one who scratched my cheek, not Minou. And she has some of my hair."

"Aren't you frightened?"

"Yes. I'm frightened. But not of that."

Aunt Irene stood up. "I've warned you. I've done my duty. Nobody can say I didn't warn you. My conscience is clear. If you don't know what she can do, then it's your fault, not mine. How long is it you've been with us, and you haven't had a word from Terry, not a word?"

"He'll get in touch with me as soon as he can." I left her looking virtuously at the cards scattered on the game table, and went to the writing room.

Aunt Olivia was there. She had her little rosewood desk on her knees, but she was not writing letters. She was looking at her notebook of Mado's poetry.

"Aunt Irene's been warning me," I said.

"What about?"

"Belle Zenumin."

Aunt Olivia's finger marked her place in the notebook.

"That's a switch. She's been sneaking off to Belle Zenumin for years."

"She's—oh, Aunt Olivia, does she hate everybody?"

Aunt Olivia looked at me mildly. "Didn't you know that?"

"She wants revenge." I shuddered.

"Hasn't she had it? What about Jimmy's death? And Therro's and Kitty's drowning? It was Irene who told Jimmy that Therro had been with Belle."

"But—"

"She hit on the truth without ever knowing it herself—just like Irene. She blamed Therro for leading Hoadley into the scrub. She blamed Therro for all Hoadley's excesses and perversions. When she thought Hoadley had been pleasuring himself with Belle, she wanted to revenge herself on Therro for leading Hoadley astray, and she thought she could do it through Jimmy."

I felt as I had felt when I saw the lizard with its head crushed.

"Irene," Aunt Olivia said, "is as primitive as Belle. There's not much to choose between them." She looked down at the book of poems, then back at me. "Or between any of us, if it comes to that. Am I any less to blame than Irene because I've done nothing, because I've withdrawn from life out of fear of the damage I might do if I plunged into it? And if we had been kinder to Irene from the beginning, perhaps—oh, Stella, if we are surrounded by hate and revenge, we all share the blame. For what has happened. For what is going to happen."

"What is going to happen?"

"I was hoping you might tell me something."

I wanted desperately to tell Aunt Olivia everything, as I had told Ron. Why not? Everybody underestimated Aunt Olivia. Why didn't she have a right to know?

Perhaps she did, but I did not have the right to tell her.

But I could share with her my anxiety about Ron. So I told her what Uncle Hoadley had said, and Aunt Irene, and the ugly word *nigger*. And about the White Rider circling me when Ron hid under the dock.

"The Riders are just looking for something like this to give them an excuse to—they've been restless for a long time now, they're hungry for blood. Oh, God, they'll jump at the first excuse they get to string up a black man."

"No, Aunt Olivia, you can't mean that—"

"Can't I? You don't know them."

"But Uncle Hoadley—"

"He joined them to try to stop some of the terrible things—oh, Stella, do you have any idea what a lynching is like?"

"Ron told me."

"None of the horrors you read about in history books—the ghastly tortures of the Inquisition—nothing that has been done by barbarians, by the Chinese—Stella, we were supposed to be civilized here in the South once upon a time. Can you imagine covering a man with boiling tar, and castrating him, and tearing out his eyes, and then when he's mutilated beyond recognition, when he's a screaming, bloody mass of agony, hanging him?"

"Stop it, Aunt Olivia!"

"I wish I could stop it! But I can't! No one can! Have you ever smelled burning flesh? I have! This isn't a nightmare—we won't wake up and say thank God it isn't real. If Kitty after three days in the ocean was no longer recognizable—I saw Jimmy when Mado brought him home. It happened, Stella, the Riders did this. They still do!"

"But not Ronnie—you can't mean—"

"If someone just whispers that Ronnie has even looked at you, that will be enough, the mood they're in. Where is he now?"

"The twins' cottage, I suppose. He's coming this evening—"

"He'll be all right in the daytime. They never do anything by daylight. We'll have to get him here *before* evening, that's our only hope, and keep him here."

I wanted to think she was hysterical. I wanted not to believe her. "Even if you get Ron to Illyria, how will you get him to stay?"

"I don't know. I'll have to think of something. Maybe I'd better forget my prejudices and pray for inspiration."

"Aunt Olivia, if one believes in God, how much is it all right to ask of him?"

"I don't know, lovey. Everything, I suppose."

"Yes, but what I mean is—we can't just tell him to do everything for us, can we? We can't just say 'Destroy the Zenumins,' and 'Take care of Illyria,' and sit back and leave it all to him, can we?"

"I don't know. I don't think it's that easy. Mado said that if we offer everything that happens to us to God, then he can turn it to good."

"Even something like the babies being trapped in Nyssa when it burned?"

Aunt Olivia moaned. "I don't know, Stella, I don't know." Then she said, "Oh, lambie, we all have our little gods, and we try to manipulate them—"

"The little gods of Kairogi..."

"Not only the little gods of Kairogi. Or the Dark Clearing. I have mine, only too many of them. Hoadley, as you have found out, has his. But old age is finally teaching me that it isn't what the little gods do that matters."

"I don't understand, Aunt Olivia."

"The little gods can seem to win in the darknesses they do, and because we can't stop them, we think they've won. Honoria couldn't stop Claudius Broadley. Mado couldn't save Theron, or her children. James couldn't keep fire from Nyssa, or disease from Xenia. Clive and Honoria couldn't save Jimmy."

"Then?"

"I don't have any answers for you. I'm sorry. All I know is that with Mado the angels always won. But that was no guarantee that everything was all going to be sky blue pink and cozy, or that the little gods can't cause pain and tempt us to despair. Stella, what is going to happen now?"

Aunt Olivia wanted me to tell her. I wanted her to tell me.

2

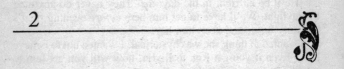

At lunch Uncle Hoadley did not appear. Clive served, and we did not see Honoria.

"There's thunder in the air," Aunt Des said. "I can smell it."

Aunt Olivia sniffed. "We haven't had a real storm for days. Just little piddling things. We're due a big one."

Aunt Irene tossed her head. "Let's hope it doesn't spoil Stella's evening walk. Stella sets so much store by her walks. Almost like she was meeting somebody."

"The way the wind's turning," Aunt Des said, "it won't come till late."

"Like Stella's first night in Illyria," Aunt Olivia said. "He makes his angels winds, and his ministers a flaming fire."

"Psalms," Aunt Mary Desborough said. "Point for me."

That day was surely dream. That it could go by and nothing happen was surely dream. That time could stand still—for it seemed that the sun did not move but hung high and molten bronze in the motionless sky—was surely dream. And hate was suspended in this timelessness.

Aunt Irene took to her room with a headache. Aunt Des rummaged around in her workbox and pulled out a little double cross, made of four pins, all welded together by the train wheels. "Look, Livvy, at this in my sewing box! I didn't know I still had it."

Aunt Olivia scowled. "Throw it away."

"Why? It must be a quarter of a century old."

"Tron and Hoadley," Aunt Olivia said. "It's a symbol."

"What are you talking about?"

"It's a symbol of what they're planning for each other. The ultimate double cross."

"Olivia, are you feverish again?"

"I wish I were."

I went out to the kitchen where Clive was washing up, his sleeves rolled up, his hands deep in soapy water. "Is Honoria all right?"

"She praying, Miss Stella."

"How can—how can God help her?"

"With love, Miss Stella. Ain't no other way." He wiped his hands, took the little cross I had given him out of his pocket and put it on the table in front of me.

"Are you on the other side, Clive?" I asked. "The way Mado said—only on love's terrible other side—is it very terrible, Clive?"

"Terror is not fear, Miss Stella. It is right and proper that we should feel terror before the power of the Lord."

"Is love terrible, Clive?"

"Yes, Miss Stella."

I went onto the back veranda. The hanging basket of sunflower seeds was empty, but the little green snake lay coiled peacefully in the geranium pot. I walked down the pink brick path to the

fig tree. The one living branch was still green and strong. Three
little figs were ripening.

I did not feel Clive's right and proper terror. I felt panic. I did
not believe that lion and lamb would ever lie down together in
Illyria.

Slowly, slowly, the sun moved. I wanted to know where
Ron was, to be sure that he would be waiting for me at the
foot of the ramp that evening. When the sun had finally moved
behind the house enough so that its rays would not beat too
fiercely on my head—I did have enough wits left not to risk
sunstroke again—I put on one of the straw hats and went to
the beach. I did not think anybody would attempt to come near
me as long as I stayed directly in front of Illyria. The twins
were wading with crab nets in the shallows just above the slough
and came running to meet me, holding out nets full of little
wriggling crabs.

"Boys, I'm so glad to see you!"

"Ron send us," Willy said. For a moment I thought that
Ron was sending them with a message that he would not be
able to come, but that was not it. "Ron say boys come to Illyria.
Boys has to wait for Docdoc here."

"Take crabs to Honoria for present. Honoria cook."

We moved across the beach to Illyria and they sang,

> "Lion of darkness, lamb of light,
> Black of day, bright of night,
> Lamb of midnight, lion of morn,
> From your death will love be born."

"Lion and lamb cry," Harry said. "Oh, sad, sad."

"Boys, what are you talking about?"

"Boys love pretty lady," Willy said.

"Boys stay in Illyria with lady. Wait for Docdoc."

"Does Ronnie want me to wait for him here?"

"No, no, boys wait."

"But what about me, Willy, Harry? What am I supposed to
do?"

But Willy and Harry gave me no answer. Time was all I
could move through, time harder to push against than the ocean
when the tide was strong. I could hardly believe it when Aunt
Irene called that Uncle Hoadley was on the veranda, and didn't
I want to join them for mint juleps?

Aunt Olivia said, "Look at that lightning."

Aunt Des said, "Please put some extra sugar in mine, Hoadley. Nobody ever seems to remember that I like things sweet. The storm's still miles away."

Aunt Olivia made a strange, strangling sound. Her silver mug clattered to the floor spilling out ice and whiskey and a sprig of mint.

"Auntie!" Uncle Hoadley sprang up.

Aunt Olivia pressed her hand to her breast, gasping, "I have a pain—oh, Hoadley, get Ron, get Ron quickly—"

Aunt Des hovered anxiously. "Livvy, what is it, what's the matter?"

Aunt Olivia sounded irritable. "I have a pain, daz it. I want Ronnie."

Aunt Irene asked, "Is it her heart? Is she having a heart attack?"

Uncle Hoadley said. "Sit down, all of you. Irene, tell Clive or Honoria to get Ron. You'll be all right, Auntie. It's nothing to worry about."

"Thank you, Hoadley—" Aunt Olivia said weakly. But as I caught her eye I was sure I saw a tiny wink.

Or almost sure.

Uncle Hoadley carried her into her room, and Aunt Des undressed her and put her into the great bed. Ron came and sent everybody away, telling us all to go to dinner.

We sat at the big, dark table, and Clive passed the silver dishes, but we did not feel like eating. I nibbled at my food until Ron came out of Aunt Olivia's room and told us that he was not sure whether it was the heart or not. There was no immediate cause for alarm, but Miss Olivia was still in considerable pain, and he would stay with her. He looked directly at me, but I could not read in his eyes what it was he was trying to tell me.

We sat on the veranda for coffee. Aunt Des said, "Why can't I go in to her? I don't want her to be afraid—"

Uncle Hoadley spoke sharply: "There's nothing to be afraid of, Auntie. Stay here until Ronnie says it's all right to go in."

I rose.

"Stella," Aunt Des said anxiously, "you aren't going for a walk, are you? Olivia might want—"

I had no intention of going for a walk, with Ron in Aunt Olivia's room instead of waiting for me at the foot of the ramp.

I was going to the kitchen. But Uncle Hoadley said, "Why shouldn't she go for a walk? Don't exaggerate things, Auntie. There's no reason Stella shouldn't go for her walk as usual. Go on, child. But make it a short walk this evening. Aunt Olivia is very likely to want to see you as soon as she feels better."

I did not want to go on the beach at all, now that the sun was behind the house. I thought that I would just go and sit on the foot of the ramp for a few minutes and then make my way to the kitchen. The light of the insect-repellent oil burned faintly against the pale blue of early evening. The stars were not yet out. I moved down the ramp, through the buzz of insects. I reached the steps to the beach and as I did so a dark shadow emerged from under the ramp, my arm was caught, a hand clamped over my mouth.

3

Iᴛ was Tron.

I had known that the day could not end without horror. I had, viscerally if not consciously, been waiting for this moment. Through the muffling hand I tried to scream for Ron. But Aunt Olivia was keeping Ronnie safe, safe from something more horrible than anything I could imagine, more horrible than anything Tron would do to me. Perhaps, as Mado said, death itself was trivial, but not the things Aunt Olivia feared would be done to Ronnie before the mercy of death.

Tron took his hand from my mouth. "If you scream I'll kill you, Mrs. Renier, ma'am." His voice was pleasant and courteous. He might have been saying, If you don't care for rice I'll bring some grits, Mrs. Renier, ma'am—

Suddenly it was all so melodramatic, so ridiculous, that I burst into a hysterical peal of laughter.

"Something funny, Mrs. Renier, ma'am?" Tron's grip on me tightened.

I tried to get myself under control. I did not want him breaking my arm, as he had roasted ants to death, or pulled the legs off the spider, or killed Willy's little lizard. "What do you want, Tron?"

"We going to the Granddam. Didn't you 'spect me to come for you, Mrs. Renier, ma'am? You going to tell her about the treasure, remember? Ain't forgotten last night, is you?"

Forgotten—"What do you need the treasure for?"

"Who knows what I'll need after tonight?" He took my wrist and pulled me along the shadow of the dunes so that it would be difficult for anyone on the veranda or on one of the balconies of Illyria to see us. "You throw our timing all off."

"How could I? I haven't done anything."

"You done enough. You come to Illyria." He jerked me up the dune.

I panted, "I told them I wasn't going to be gone long tonight. When I don't come right back they'll be anxious, Uncle Hoadley will—"

"Let him." He dragged me over the crest of dunes to the almost invisible cart tracks behind Illyria which served as road when unusually high tides made the beach impassable. There I saw the pale horse harnessed to a wagon. "Get in."

There was a pile of straw in the wagon covered with the filthy remains of an old blanket. I gagged at the stench, but I climbed in, rather than have Tron throw me in. He sat on a wooden slat nailed across the buckboards, and cracked a whip across the horse's emaciated flanks. The horse gave a wheezing groan and the wagon began to move bumpily along the rough tracks. Dunes, and glimpses of ocean through gaps in the dunes, were to the right of us, dunes and sea and vast, open sky. To our left the jungle closed in, a dark scramble of scrub oak and myrtle, tangled and twisted by the harsh salt wind. In the gathering dusk it seemed impossible that there was beauty in the scrub as well as evil, that there were egrets and flamingos, that there were young deer nibbling on the lush grasses deep within, that there were simple and gentle people who loved the children and chickens and little yellow dogs playing in the clearings; it was not all Zenumin...

We passed the twins' cottage, a chunky shadow between us and the ocean, no lights in the windows, no smoke from the chimney.

Honoria prayed to God. I still did not know how. But my spirit groped for prayer.

—Please be sitting in the kitchen in Illyria, twins, dear twins. Please be praying. You know how. Call upon the ocean and the stars and the sand. Call upon the pelicans and the gulls and the sandpipers. Call upon the donax and the little scrabbling crabs. Call upon the angels and the winds.

Lightning split the sky.

—Call upon the storm, twins, please call. Let the prayers of the stars be more powerful than the Zenumin comminations. Mado's angels, wherever you are, gather your cohorts: come.

We passed Little Nyssa.

—Cousin James, you know how to pray, please be praying. Are you safe in the secret room in Illyria? Is Saintie reading to Cousin Xenia from the big Bible between two candles? Please pray for me.

We should long since have turned into the scrub towards the Zenumin clearing. "Where are we going?" I demanded. "I thought you were taking me to the Granddam."

"We got us a little errand first," he said. "Take what you know you can get when you can get it is my motto, Mrs. Renier, ma'am."

"You really aren't working for Uncle Hoadley, are you?" I demanded.

His laugh shattered the evening air.

"Then why do you pretend to? Why?"

"Tron working for him, maybe, but not *with* him. Little old Tron learn lots from Mr. Hoadley. Like making what he call a *coup d'état*. You know what that mean? Mr. Hoadley learn Tron all about that. Best way for Tron to beat Mr. Hoadley be to know all his plans, all his great big noble plans to save the world. King of Kairogi—sound right good, don't it, King of Kairogi? But it not good enough for Tron. Mr. Hoadley's ship never going near Africa. All Mr. Hoadley's little yachts never going near that big ship. Tron going to be king, all right, but not in Kairogi."

He turned the wagon towards the tangle of vegetation which almost concealed Cousin Lucille's cottage from path, from beach. The growth was so dense about the house that I could not tell whether or not there were lights within. But there must be; it was not yet late, and Cousin Lucille never left her doors.

"What are you doing? Where are we going?"

"We going to Miss Lucille," Tom said. "Get her jewels."

"But they aren't real. They're fake."

"Now, Mrs. Renier, ma'am," Tron said softly, "I don't want none of that kind of talk."

"But it's true! She sold them all abroad! They're nothing but glass and paste."

Tron shrugged. "You'd tell me that whether it true or not. It don't make no never-mind. If I say they real, I get my money."

He jumped down from the wagon, held out his hand to me. I did not want him to touch me. I clambered down alone, shaking straw and stink from my skirts. We pushed through the overgrown ilex bushes to the door, which Tron opened with a kick. "Go in first, Mrs. Renier, ma'am. Tell her I want everything she's got."

The door opened directly into the cluttered living room, into pitch darkness. There was not a glimmer of light.

"Call her," Tron said. "Tell her who you are. Ask for light."

"Cousin Lucille, it's Stella. Terry's wife. Cousin Lucille?"

"Lights," Tron prodded, poking me with an ungentle finger.

"Cousin Lucille, where are the candles?"

Silence. Darkness. I could hear nothing but the motion of the leaves, the throbbing of the surf, the evening cacophony of insects and frogs. From the house, silence. The shutters must be closed tight, the curtains drawn. The air was stifling. No glimmer from the lightship came to relieve the absolute dark. I put my fingers instinctively up to my eyes.

"Where the hell is her man?" Tron asked. "Call him. She never lets him off."

I recalled the quiet and gentle presence of Cousin Lucille's old butler. "Eben! Eben, where are you?"

No answer.

"Mrs. Renier, ma'am," Tron warned softly, "don't try to run away now. I stop you, and you wouldn't like that, I promise, you wouldn't like it."

He let go my arm and stode across the room, falling over something. I heard him pushing aside curtains, wrenching at shutters. A flash of lightning illuminated the room briefly, but long enough to show that everything was in disorder, pictures torn from the walls, tables and chairs overturned. Tron cursed. There was the smell of sulphur as he struck a match. In its flickering light he found a candelabrum on the table between the windows. He lit the candles and held them high, moving slowly about the room.

I thought of making a dash, of trying to hide somewhere in the darkness. But Tron knew his way around in the dark. There would be no place for me to hide which would be safe from him. I stood still, just over the threshold, and followed his progress past the confusion of pictures on the floor, slashed in their ornate gold frames, past broken china and porcelain, disordered rugs, then gave a cry as the wavering candlelight illumined Cousin Lucille sitting in her big chair, staring at us.

Tron strode across the room to her. Swore again. Held the candles so that I could see not only Cousin Lucille's wide-open eyes and mouth, but wax dripping from the candles onto the blood-rimmed hole in the front of her dress. Her earrings were gone; blood dripped from her torn earlobes. There were no rings on her fingers. The neck of her dress flapped loose where her brooch had been torn off.

Tron turned away from the grey face, the vacant eyes and mouth of death. "Someone beat me to it. Come on."

"Who—"

"Half a dozen men could have done it. Or more likely her own house man."

I thought of Eben courteously wiping gravy from the place on Cousin Lucille's dress where the bullet hole was now. "Not Eben—"

"Goddam, this means—" Tron started, strode across the room and grabbed my wrist. As he pulled me across the threshold he stopped and flung the candelabrum to the floor. I managed to jerk away from him long enough to stamp out the flames. He caught me again. "Try, try, little Mrs. Renier. This a blaze can't be put out."

He hauled me back to the wagon and I climbed in, without question, without argument. We drove, on what was barely a cow path, back into the scrub. Our way was lit by the lightning, which was still too far off to be accompanied by thunder. When we got to the dark water of the creek Tron stopped the horses and made a low, uncanny owl's hoot.

It was answered. Then the shadow of Belle Zenumin stepped out from behind a cypress on the other side of the creek. She got into a dugout and paddled towards us.

Tron called, "Tonight, Mother. Give the signal. Tonight."

"Did you get—"

"Someone else got to little old Lucille first. Don't make no never-mind. Stella say they fake. We don't need them. Not now. No time. Give the signal." He raised the whip over his head and cracked it.

From all about us in the scrub came rustlings and breathings and a low moaning of excitement. Massing together around us were horsemen. Tron's Dark Riders. He stood up on the wooden seat and cracked his whip again. Torches were lit and held high over the masked figures. Horses stamped restively.

"We going to give the signal," Tron said. "Now. Tonight. Call the rest. When everybody gather, ride to the yacht basin. Burn the boats. Burn, burn! I meet you there." He jumped down into the wagon and picked me up in his thin, strong arms. He carried me roughly, as he might some slain animal. Like an animal, I was dumped in the dugout. He took the paddle from his mother, pushed away from shore. When I changed my cramped position, swaying the canoe, he said, "Don't want to swim, do you, Mrs. Renier, ma'am? 'Gators waiting." With his paddle he struck at a log. The log swam across the creek.

I huddled in the bottom of the dugout.

There was nothing but darkness and chaos and fear.

4

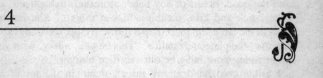

In the center of the Zenumin clearing the bonfire was blazing. I half lay, half sat on the packed earth. I think Tron carried me there; I am not sure. The Granddam hobbled towards me.

"Sit up, missy."

I managed to obey.

"All right, missy. You remember what I say last night?"

"Yes—"

"You ask Honoria 'bout the treasure?"

"Yes—I asked—"

Her voice cracked with impatience. "Tell."

"There isn't any treasure."

The back of her hand struck my cheek. "You tell the Granddam where the treasure be."

"It's gone. All of it. Long ago."

"You lie. You tell the Granddam."

"But it's gone, there isn't anything left, there isn't—"

Again the hand cracked against my cheek. I fell back on the hard sour earth into the moment of death, my own death, the death of my baby—

The old woman hit me again. "You going to tell me. You wait and see. You going to tell." She moved in an awkward, a-rhythmic dance to a tree stump on which stood a plate and goblet and held her arms out over them. With a shock I saw that she was naked, her body hideously wrinkled and grey, clay daubed on her shriveled dugs. Behind her, in the smoke and shadows at the edge of the clearing, were other naked bodies, some strangely patterned and painted, emerging from the dark mouths of the huts, and beginning to shuffle in strange and static dancing, hitting the palms of their cupped hands against their thighs so that the sound was muffled.

The Granddam, distended breasts swinging obscenely, circled her hands over plate and goblet. She squeezed her clay-daubed teats over the cup, then raised it high. "Lamia's milk, and a cock's cock," she intoned, "worms, mashed to blood, herbs and lotions, verbs and potions, hair from the head, nails from the dead, brains of boy babe, aforesaid, unbaptized, full of lies, lick and kiss, incubiss, hiss at this..." She reached down to the table and picked up a filthy, flyspecked doll, raised it up over the plate and chalice. "This be you, missy, with your baby inside. Your baby be our sacrifice tonight."

I felt a cold hand at my throat, death in the pit of my stomach. My nostrils were filled with the stench of decay; flies buzzed against my face. I was being sucked into a vast drooling mouth of evil.

From out of the shadows leapt another naked figure, stretched by his own shadow so that he seemed as tall as the smoke rising from the fire. He jumped up onto the tree stump, raising his arms high above his head. Tron. He snatched the doll from the Granddam and twirled it above him. I felt as sick and as dizzy as though I myself were being swung over his head. He thrust the doll back at the Granddam and began to shout, incomprehensible, filthy words. As he shouted he seemed to grow taller, all of him, his arms, his legs, his torso, his erect masculinity, to grow larger, larger. The figures circling the edge of the clearing began to shout, too; their hands slapped more sharply against their bare thighs.

Tron screamed, "Tonight the god will drink the man-child's blood! The god thirsts! He will drink it all!" He swung around on the stump, and on his bare rear was painted a hideous, open-mouthed face. The Granddam held the doll towards him.

I was the doll. I was being dragged towards him, towards the open, carnivorous mouth...

"Leave off!"

Through half-glazed eyes I saw Honoria stride up from the black creek's edge, followed by Clive. Honoria was dressed as I had never seen her before, in a striped, brilliant robe. Great gold earrings hung from her ears. There were bracelets on her long, powerful arms. She towered over us, formidable, taller than Tron. Firelight illuminated the stark bones of her face, the dark brilliance of her gaze. She raised her arms high.

Lightning crashed, close to the clearing, and a yelp of fear in the circle around us was crushed by the roaring of thunder.

Clive stood, a small, still figure, his Bible in his hands. His very stillness seemed to stop the dancing circle, still the thrumming of their hands. The stillness spread across the clearing, and when it was complete, Honoria spoke.

"You forget my Powers!" Her voice was deep, guttural. "Stand back, all evil ones! These curses shall come upon you and overtake you. Cursed shalt thou be in the Dark Clearing, and cursed shalt thou be in the creek. Cursed shall be the first fruit of thy body and the first fruit of thy land. Cursed shall thou be when thou come in, and cursed shalt thou be when thou goest out!" Her voice was paralyzing.

Then Tron gave a great leap. "Stop! We going to stop you! You can do nothing!"

Belle rose from behind the altar stump. She held the chalice up. "I got the skin from Mrs. Renier's cheek! It be in the cup!" Her face was distorted with hate and fear.

Honoria's voice rolled over her. "The Lord shall send upon thee cursing, vexation, and rebuke, in all that thou settest thine hand unto for to do, until thou be destroyed."

Tron poured out a defecation of blasphemies, oaths, words of hatred, obscene, perverse words which, instead of dragging me deeper into their dark depths, pushed me out, away from them, with the force of sledgehammers. Over, under, around, through them came Honoria's power:

"—until thou perish quickly; because of the wickedness of thy doings, whereby thou hast forsaken me. The Lord shall make the pestilence cleave unto thee, until he have consumed thee from off the land, whither thou goest to possess it!"

The drumming of the hands circling us had completely stopped now, was replaced by a formless moaning of fear.

"The Lord shall smite thee with a consumption, and with a fever, and with an inflammation, and with an extreme burning, and with the sword, and with blasting, and with mildew; and they shall pursue thee until thou perish."

The Granddam, gibbering, shoved the rag doll at Belle. Belle clutched it against her naked breasts. Unclothed, she was no longer beautiful. Her body was beginning to wither into the grey hideousness of the Granddam's.

"Mama!" Tron screamed. "Mama!" He danced around like a thwarted child. The face painted on his buttocks seemed to scream with him. "Mama! Get her! Kill! Kill! Mama!" This terrifying helplessness frightened me more than his acting the god.

"It be all right, baby!" Belle shrieked. "I got her hair! I strangle her with it! We kill the man-child! The god going to get his blood! He not going to thirst tonight!"

I felt something draw tight about my throat. I gagged.

Honoria's voice continued to roll over us, enormous, inexorable, rising above the approaching thunder: "The heaven that is over thy head shall be brass, and the earth that is under you shall be iron. Ye shall be plucked from off the land whither thou goest to possess it, and thy life shall hang in doubt before thee; and thou shalt fear day and night—"

The invisible cord about my throat tightened. I felt my eyeballs bulging, my tongue swelling. Tron shrieked in victorious laughter. I tried to say, 'Honoria,' and I could not.

Only her words kept the cord from its final death-strangle. "In the morning thou shalt say, Would God it were even! and at even thou shalt say, Would God it were morning! for fear of thine heart wherewith thou shalt fear, and for the sight of thine eyes which thou shalt see..."

I could not see. Dark pressed like thumbs against my protruding eyeballs.

The Granddam's voice bleated through the thunder. "She be dying! The evil one prevails!"

"Kiss!" Tron cried. "She got to kiss the mouth of the god! She got to kiss!" He danced backwards towards me.

Honoria's arms stretched higher, towards the lightning; her robes were caught in a gust of wind; they swelled out like great wings. "I call upon my Powers! I call upon the Lord! I call upon his stars, he know them all by name! I call upon the seraphim, I ride upon the cherubim! Dark, away! Hate, die! Come, Lord, come!"

Lightning pierced the clearing. The storm was upon us. But the noose still pressed about my throat. I saw through blood. Death pinched my heart.

Honoria's voice crashed with the thunder: "Die, death! Evil, begone! Knowledge which is ignorance, depart! I call upon the ocean! Cleanse and heal! I call upon the heavens: wisdom, come! Buzzards, begone! Pelicans, fly!"

As her words soared upwards and flew about us like a flock of birds, the deadly noose around my throat seemed to loosen; the paralysis lifted from my limbs, the constriction from my heart.

"I call upon the angels: hear me now! Each hair is numbered! Sparrows may not fall! I call upon the cloud: drown sin and wrong!"

The Granddam snatched the Stella-doll from Belle's hands: as she did so, I felt her fingers bruise my arms. She gave a screeching laugh. "I got the baby in her! I kill him! I kill him now!"

"I call upon my Powers—" But Honoria's voice faltered. She no longer seemed ten feet tall.

"I kill him!"

I raised my head from the dirt. Tron leapt up onto the altar-stump to receive the me-doll. He was shouting: I could not tell whether it was *kiss* or *kill*. He spun around and presented me with the naked face of hate. The Granddam thrust the doll towards his open legs.

I would not let him touch me. I cried, "Honoria!" but Honoria could not help me now. I sprang and snatched the me-doll from the Granddam's claws before she could get it to the open mouth.

I flung it into the fire.

I felt the flames.

I burned.

Lightning speared down, struck the dead tree stump, splitting it. Plate and chalice were overturned. Tron was hurled to the ground. A sudden downrush of rain hissed the bonfire; a dense cloud of smoke rose. Wind rushed through the clearing with a howling, whistling scream that drowned the Granddam's frustrated rage and terror.

I was caught up in somebody's arms, carried across the clearing to the creek.

"Ron," I cried. "Oh, Ronnie."

It was not Ron who held me. It was Cousin James.

5

CLIVE, frail and firm, pushed the paddle against the dark waters and we glided rapidly down the creek. Honoria knelt in the back of the canoe, motionless. She said, "Praised be the Lord. And the child leapt in her womb for joy," and I felt within me the delicate but completely alive and healthy stirring of my child.

It was as though my entire body had been healed and cleansed by the fire.

The storm had passed; only a few final drops of rain splattered the black surface of the water. Drops clung to the leaves, the Spanish moss; fell in soft showers as the wind stirred; it was gentle on my hair, my cheeks. The night talk of the insects began again. A turtle raised its head out of the creek water to peer at us with ancient, tolerant eyes. (Listen, child, now listen well To what the turtle may have to tell, To what the turtle may have to tell.) A frog croaked contentedly at the water's edge.

Cousin James's arms were strongly around me. He was talking, quietly, calmly. I felt an extraordinary sense of lightness, of freedom, although what he was telling me was heavy and dark in the extreme. I understood quite clearly what had been happening while I was in the Zenumin clearing. Tron's Black Riders had swept down the beach to the yacht basin, burning the twins' cottage on the way. The boats, all the boats gathered together there, the yachts and the sailing boats and the fishing vessels, were burning; the yacht basin was an inferno. The Black Riders had attacked completely by surprise, and the fires were out of control. The White Riders, taken unprepared, had rushed in a rage to gather, coming from near and far, and were converging upon Tron's men. There was going to be fighting, great and terrible fighting. At last I would understand the meaning of war; I was, myself, involved in battle. I had, in a strange and passive way, caused it, and now I had to answer for this. I had been acted upon. In the moment of throwing the Stella-doll into the fire, I had commenced to act.

At the far side of the creek Dapple and Thales waited. I rode behind Cousin James on Dapple. Honoria and Clive followed on Thales. Cousin James told me, in answer to my question, that Ron was safe in the secret room. The moment Uncle Hoadley went to join his Riders, to try to save his doomed fleet, Honoria had released Cousin James. Aunt Olivia, miraculously recovered from her 'attack,' had hidden Ron and the twins in the secret room. For the moment, at any rate, they were all right.

We emerged onto the beach just below the writhing mass of flame which was all that was left of the twins' cottage. The roof had already fallen in. The doorway was outlined in brilliant serpents of fire. Down below us to the south the sky was pulsing, murkey red, with occasional shooting thrusts of fire. "The yacht basin," Cousin James said.

I did not dare think about Illyria. I smelled flames, heard them as the wind avidly licked them. A strange hot dust swirled about us, burned our faces.

Behind us came the pounding of a horse, and a single Black Rider raced past us down the beach. There was no question in my mind that it was Tron, flying to join his men: indeed with his long black robe blowing wildly behind him he seemed to be some strange, half-human bat.

Dapple's rocking canter accelerated to a gallop. I held more tightly to Cousin James. Just before we reached the great curve of dune which held and shielded Illyria and hid it now from our view, Cousin James reined in. Clive and Honoria drew up beside us. Cousin James told them, "I think it would be wise if you cut through the dunes now and approach the stables from behind Illyria. Wait for us there."

Clive turned Thales westward. Cousin James waited until they were out of sight then slapped Dapple and we continued down the beach. Ahead of us Illyria appeared, still riding safely on its sea of dune.

And then we were swept into battle.

Horsemen, in a great shouting wave of intermingled white and black, rolled up the beach towards us. Flames streamed from their torches, wilder and more brilliant than the fire which still burned in the yacht basin. Several Riders, their robes alight, galloped their screaming horses into the sea, leaping off their mounts into the water.

Cousin James spurred Dapple towards the dunes, but as we reached the soft sand which impeded him, the wave of Riders broke about us. I felt heat from the torches, from the steaming flanks of the excited animals. I held more closely to Cousin James's slight form. Then I was snatched from him, from Dapple, was flung across the horse of a shouting Rider, my eyes covered, blinded, by the billowing white of his robe.

My screams were added to the shouts of the men, the whinnying of the beasts. I did not know what had happened to Cousin James and Dapple. I could smell the stench of fear and hate, the acid sweat of my captor. He held me pinioned across his knees. One of my groping hands clutched at the rough mane of the horse. I could feel that we were being slowed not as much by the crush of riders as by the deepening sand; then I heard the sound of hoofs on wood.

The Rider jerked me up, pulling my face free of his robes, and sat me in front of him. We were at the head of the White Riders who massed beside us. The Black Riders were pounding by us, back up the beach, torches blazing, men and horses screaming in a high, terrible wail. Some of the White Riders galloped after them, adding their shouting and shooting to the din, but the black figures plunged westward over the dunes towards the hidden sanctuary of the scrub.

Near my captor and me, riderless horses reared, neighing in confusion. At the ocean's edge a White and a Black Rider wrestled, and the White Rider went down into the water under the battery of powerful fists. Then I heard a shot, and the black figure crumpled into the water. My captor jerked his horse's head and we started clattering up the ramp to Illyria. I tried to find my voice. "Let me down—Uncle Hoadley—"

The Rider clamped me more firmly to him. "Mr. Hoadley can't stop us." We moved up the ramp, other Riders pressing behind us, and he said, "This no time for law and order excepting *our* law and order. Nigger bastards burn our boats, rape our women, Mr. Hoadley won't stop us now, he push us on."

He gave a shout as horses pushed by us, almost shoving us off the crumbling edge of the ramp.

The first Rider was Tron, his black robes almost burned off him. Only the bat wings remained. He stood in his stirrups, and the ghastly painted face seemed to laugh back at us as he raised one arm, holding a flaming brand. A White Rider shoved violently against him shouting triumphantly to see Tron and the pale horse plunge off the edge of the ramp onto the lethal Spanish Bayonettes. The beast gave a scream, louder than Tron could possibly cry.

The White Rider, hooting with terrible laughter, let us by. We pushed on up the ramp. We had reached the steps before I saw that Aunt Olivia and Aunt Mary Desborough were sitting in their rocking chairs, waiting. They had seen war before. They had seen death. When our mount stopped at the steps they rose, as though greeting a group of slightly unruly children, and came towards us, Aunt Olivia leaning heavily on her cane.

Aunt Mary Desborough spoke, looking more than ever like a ruffled brown owl. "Your behavior is inexcusable. Leave us. At once."

"Now, Miss Des." The Rider who held me, one hand firmly over my mouth, sounded apologetic as though he were, indeed, no more than a naughty boy. "Now, Miss Des," he repeated, "we don't want to inconvenience you."

"Go," Aunt Mary Desborough said. "Go at once." Only then did she seem to see that I was held by the Rider, still half covered by the flowing folds of his white robe. "Stella—"

"Put her down!" Aunt Olivia cried furiously. I thought she would raise her cane and attack the Rider, but she did not. She stood very still by Aunt Des.

"Go away," Aunt Des repeated. For a moment she swayed, reached for the porch rail for support, but stood firm.

The Rider's hold on me tightened, but his voice was courteous, almost gentle. "Don't be afeared, Miss Des. We ain't going to hurt you. You just give us the nigger and we'll leave."

"I don't know what you're talking about. My sister and I—"

"The bastard Zenumin nigger, Miss Des. That clear?"

Aunt Olivia's voice came strong. "Tron Zenumin is with his men. He is not here. And even if he were, we wouldn't—"

The Rider cut across her words. "Not him. He screaming in the Spanish Bayonettes. Let him die there. We after the other one. The brother."

Again Aunt Olivia's voice was clear and cold. "You will

have to be more specific. I don't know who you're talking about."

"The nigger calls himself a doctor, the nigger what come back to San Feliz poking into white men's business."

Aunt Des said, "Please leave us. Our Cousin James—our nephew, Mr. Hoadley—" Her old voice trembled.

"Mr. Hoadley and Mr. James down on the beach, Miss Des. Our men holding them. Nobody going to stop us now. Come on, we know the nigger's in the house. We aim to have him. He been seen with Mr. Terry's bride. We ain't putting up with that."

Aunt Olivia said, "My sister and I will not tolerate this kind of talk. You know Mr. Hoadley would never permit this rudeness. Please leave Illyria at once." The old-fashioned phrases seemed totally out of place in this night of obscenity and violence. The great-aunts were small and ineffectual in their valiance against the evil pressing towards them.

The horse under me stamped nervously, the hoofbeat sounding hollow against the boards of the ramp. There was an impatient rumbling from the Riders behind us. There were shouts and cries of men and horses from the barrier of Spanish Bayonettes on either side of the ramp. Torchlight threw flickering shadows over the veranda, over the old ladies.

"Miss Des, Miss Livvy, we wish you no harm, but you let us by or we burn Illyria."

Aunt Olivia said scornfully, "If you want to search the house quietly and peaceably, you may. But you won't find him."

"No, Miss Livvy? Mr. Hoadley done told us about the secret room. Now you just let us in, and we get the nigger, and nobody else going to get hurt."

Aunt Olivia stepped towards us with difficulty; she leaned heavily on her cane and one hand was lost in the folds of her skirt. "I don't think you'll burn Illyria," she said levelly. "Miss Irene is inside, and neither my sister nor I will leave. The twins are inside, too. I don't think you want to be responsible for murdering innocent people. White people."

The Rider kicked his heels into the horse's sweating flanks and came directly up the steps and onto the porch. His laugh was ingratiating. "We get you and Miss Des and Miss Irene out, Miss Livvy, and we don't give a hooting damn about them spooky idiots."

Two of the Riders behind us jumped down from their horses.

The old planks of the ramp creaked and groaned under the shifting, crowding beasts.

"See, Miss Livvy, they ain't going to wait much longer. We just looking to have us a nice little necktie party." He snapped his fingers and the two men who had dismounted pushed by the old great-aunts and into the house.

Aunt Des screamed.

"You won't lynch Ron," Aunt Olivia cried. "I won't permit it. I'll stop you."

"Just how you going to stop us, Miss Livvy?"

I tried to speak through the Rider's hand, which was still clamped about my mouth. "My husband—" My words were smothered in his sweaty palm.

"Your husband would lynch the nigger with us, Miss Stella."

I jerked my head and managed to bite his hand. He pulled it away and hit me across the mouth. I tasted blood.

Then I saw Ron.

The two white-robed men dragged him out the screen door, forcing him to his knees. He struggled to stand.

There was a roar from the white-robed men. Through my mind flashed everything Ron and Aunt Olivia had told me about lynching. I knew what the Riders would do to him. I fought wildly, mindlessly, to escape the arms which crushed me, to stop them, anything, anything to stop them. The black tongue of a whip flicked viciously against me.

I heard Aunt Des scream, "No! Livvy, no!"

Aunt Olivia held a gun.

The Rider drew me up in front of him so that I shielded him. Ron broke away from the men, struggled to his feet.

There were cries of "Lynch him!" from the men.

Aunt Olivia shot Ron. She shot him through the heart.

6

THE Negro uprising at San Feliz is nothing but a small footnote to history. Some men were killed, both black and white. Tron might better have been one of them, for he was no longer a man; the Spanish Bayonettes had quite literally torn him apart. True, he had already spawned so many that his seed stood in no danger of ceasing to be, but in his world he was worse than dead; he had been multiplied by O: annihilated. Aunt Des nursed him until he was able to be returned to his mother and the Granddam, and Belle came for him with nothing but contempt in her eyes. Tron would never again be king of anything, not even the Dark Clearing.

Most of his men had disappeared into the scrub; I had seen enough of the scrub to know that it is not difficult for a man to lose himself in its depths. Uncle Hoadley, with the death of his dream, moved like a dead man. He was, perhaps, more impotent than Tron, and more dead than Ronnie. With the help of Cousin James he did manage to rouse himself enough so that the inquest was no more than a formality, and the coroner did not even question Aunt Olivia; the verdict was death by accident.

This was not enough for the White Riders, and a group of them went into the scrub, still hungering after a lynching, but all that happened was that one of them was bitten by a moccasin. The snake, it was said, appeared out of nowhere; it was witchcraft.

The man died. He might have lived if they could have taken him to Ron. But Ronnie was dead.

Nobody else went back into the scrub. Neither did Tron come out.

I went to the beach, careless of the morning sun, and curled up on the hot sand of a dune, nursing my dry-eyed pain. Honoria came after me.

"Come in, Miss Stella."

I shook my head, but she held a firm hand out to me.

"Come." She pulled me to my feet. "Miss Stella, do you realize what Miss Olivia done? She kill herself when she save Ronnie."

"Saved!"

"You ain't seen a lynching, Miss Stella. Pray you never will. Miss Olivia kill herself much more than ever she kill Ronnie. She love him that much, enough to do that, and that be a lot of love. Miss Olivia mortal scared of death, and now she never walk without it by her side. Ronnie her baby, like Jimmy. For your baby you can do things you couldn't never do for yourself. That be true of you, too, Miss Stella. You can't go getting too much sun again. Come in the house now. We all grieving for Ronnie. You got some grieving to do, too. I don't forget that. But Miss Olivia—she the one who took the pain this time. We got a grief we can bear, Miss Stella, because Miss Olivia loved."

We walked back to Illyria. I asked, "Honoria—what was it that you saw in the cards?"

She stopped. The high sun threw her shadow, small and dark, against the sand. Her voice was guttural, Kairogian. "What happen was not what I see in the cards. You and Miss Olivia make it be different, when you throw the doll into the fire, when Miss Olivia take her gun and—" She bowed her head. "It were not what I see in the cards. I see Ron lynched, and my prayers not strong enough to carry any of his pain. I see what happen to Jimmy happen all over again, and nothing to help Ronnie bear it. I see Illyria burn and the baby dead and bloodshed everywhere. You make it not to happen."

I held my hand protectively over my belly. "But, Honoria, the baby might still—and they might come back, the Riders—"

Honoria raised her head, tall and strong. "No, Miss Stella. The baby be all right. God tell me. Not the cards; the Lord. And it be over. The Lord has Ronnie. It be over. For this time. Come, Miss Stella. Miss Olivia be waiting for you. She need you."

I went with Honoria back into Illyria.

The summer days and nights moved slowly across the beach. We resumed the pattern of life at Illyria, though we were not the same people we had been before that night. Aunt Irene was strangely gentle with Uncle Hoadley, stroking his thin hand, trying to find little ways to please him. Now that his power had crumbled she seemed, at last, able to love him. Aunt Olivia's strength continued to sustain her, though I think we were all fearful that it might leave her at any moment, so Cousin James spent a great deal of time with us. Once she remarked to me that it was ironic that she, who had talked so much to Ronnie about dying and her fear of death, should be the one still to be alive.

Aunt Mary Desborough worked a great deal in the garden, a floppy straw hat shading her white head. It worried her that she and Aunt Olivia no longer played Shakespeare.

Only the twins, who were living with us at Illyria, talked to me about Ronnie. My belly swelled with the life within it. Cousin James told me that he had been informed by Washington that Terry was on his way home.

I do not know when the angel began to move closer to Illyria, but Honoria and Clive, going quietly and steadily about their duties, kept listening.

I walked, one evening after coffee on the veranda, slowly up the beach. I walked past the charred remains of the twins' little cottage, the cottage where Ronnie's surgery had been. Then I turned and walked the long way home.

Coming towards me was a man, a man who walked like Terry: Ron.

But it could not be Ron.

I began to run.

The man began to run.

Terry.

I was in his arms.

Around and over Illyria the wind blew, moving through the palms, shaking them like angel's wings, angels in a great and mighty rush, returning to Illyria.

SEVEN

THEY sat on the porch of Illyria, the old woman and her grandson; she, rocking gently in the old wooden rocker; he, sitting on the steps with his head against her knees. If a drowning man can relive a lifetime in a few seconds, she thought, it was hardly surprising that she had fallen so swiftly into the deep waters of those first weeks in Illyria. She felt exhausted and yet relaxed for the first time in many days. She gave a little shiver, then yawned and laughed.

"Theron, my dear, tell you all that happened at Illyria? Not tonight—I'm too tired. You can drive me back to Jefferson now, if you like, and keep the family happy. We'll sit the hurricane out there. I don't need to stay in Illyria now. I know what has to be done."

"What, Grandmother?"

"Sometimes, when you make your journey through the sun, many things are burned before you come out on the other side. We have to let things go."

"Illyria—"

"I think so. Perhaps it's only by letting it go entirely that we can keep it. What will be done with the property if we sell it?"

"I hear they'd like to put a bowling alley here, or a skating rink."

She let out a long, low sigh.

He said, "I suppose you're right, Grandmother. But are you really sure?"

"Aren't you?"

"I admit that I have sometimes thought of Illyria as a place where I could bring Margaret and the children if things get too bad in Jefferson."

"You think if there's rioting and bloodshed in Jefferson it won't reach San Feliz?"

"Yes, of course, Grandmother, it will. It's childish of me to look on Illyria as a place of safety."

She rose, stiffly. "All right, Theron. Let us go. The storm is coming."

"And the angels, Grandmother?"

She laughed. "Yes. I admit that I worried for a moment there about the angels. Illyria's angels: I don't have to tell them where they're needed. I think they go with people rather than places. You'll need them. We're probably even further from the place where lion and lamb abide, at this moment in time, than we were sixty years ago."

He helped her down the steps, down the ramp to where the old Rolls-Royce waited; helped her in.

Then, without looking back, they drove along the hard-packed sand at the ocean's edge. A pelican, brooding on a broken and barnacled piling, rose, stretched clumsily, then soared in an arc across the stormy ocean and winged across the sky.

EPIPHANY

MORE INSPIRATIONAL PAPERBACKS FROM BALLANTINE BOOKS BB

A revelation inducing
new insight or inspiration…
addressing issues that confront us
individually and collectively…

EPIPHANY

17   TA-63